"Always Orchid is a heartwarming tale of love and resilience that reminds us of the power of forgiveness, the strength of the human spirit, and the unbreakable bond that can withstand any obstacle."

—Sgt. Noah Galloway, Purple Heart decorated veteran, author of *Living with No Excuses*

"Always Orchid explores the power of love and perseverance in the face of trauma and discrimination. A heart-warming story with compassionate connections. Readers won't be disappointed."

—Rachel Barenbaum, author of *Atomic Anna*

"A powerful, emotional story, *Always Orchid* follows the welcome reunion of lovers Phoenix and Orchid only to have the demons of his injuries and the ghosts of her past drive them apart again. Carol Van Den Hende's artistic gaze is unflinching in the depiction of Phoenix's recovery and Orchid's ongoing PTSD. Propulsive and richly detailed, this third book in the *Goodbye, Orchid* series is an absorbing read. Absolutely gripping!"

—Jeannée Sacken, award-winning author of *Behind the Lens* and *Double Exposure*

"Phoenix and Orchid's journey explores what it means to be a whole person, in body and in heart. It questions what it means to be fulfilled, whether alone or with another. Theirs is not an easy story, but Carol Van Den Hende tells it with kindness and care."

—Jeffrey Dale Lofton, award-winning author of *Red Clay Suzie*

From New York to Beijing, Carol Van Den Hende's *Always Orchid*, crosses countries and cultures, taking the reader on a journey exploring sacrifice, resilience, and acceptance. From the first sentence we are asked, "Have you ever been in the middle of a moment, an instant that's suspended between what was and what is about to be?" From this question, to the middle, and clear to the end of this compelling story, *Always Orchid* stirs emotion and self-reflection.

—Robert Gwaltney, award winning author of *The Cicada Tree*

Always Orchid

by Carol Van Den Hende

ISBN 978-1-958223-00-0 (Jacketed Case Laminate)
ISBN 978-1-958223-04-8 (Perfect Bound)
ISBN 978-1-958223-05-5 (Ebook)

Published by

Azine Press™

STORIES FOR GOOD™

CAROL VAN DEN HENDE

Always Orchid

a novel

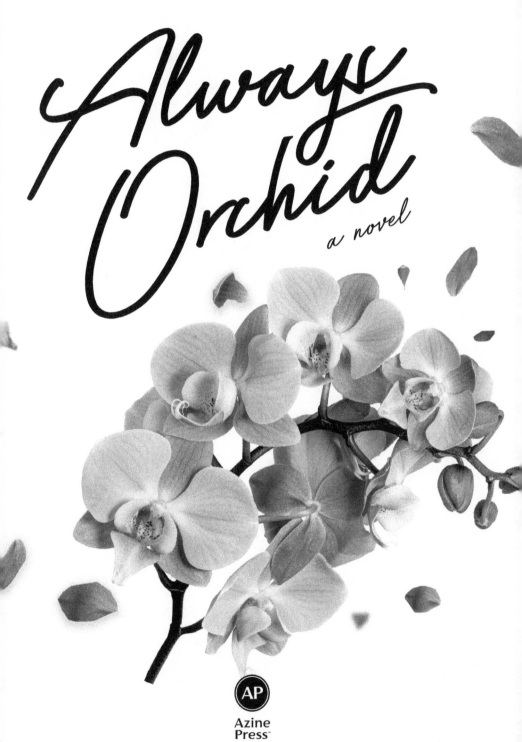

AP

Azine
Press™

Always Orchid is dedicated to Richard,

who sparked my empathy for disability inclusion by

listening with all his being and communicating

with all his heart

"The orchid grows where others cannot, enduring the hardships of hunger and thirst. Even with all the difficulty of its life, the orchid graces the world with beautiful colour and rare fragrance."

—Confucius

"We need, in love, to practice only this: letting each other go. For holding on comes easily; we do not need to learn it."

**—Rainer Maria Rilke *Requiem For a Friend*,
translated by Stephen Mitchell**

PROLOGUE

Roy

Hope is a finite resource for the homeless. Each handout and act of petty theft had whittled away Roy's dignity. Averted eyes and wrinkled noses had snubbed him, deemed him less than human. As for roots, his mother's death had eviscerated his last reserve, and so today wasn't goodbye. Today, he would join Momma.

Today, he hoped, would be a reunion.

His brain whirred with enough bourbon to execute his plan. Giant metal wheels clacked through distant subway tunnels. The next train would be his. He tipped a paper-wrapped fifth of Old Crow to his cracked lips. Not a drop left.

Never mind, never more.

Roy hadn't always been homeless. After high school, Roy had enlisted as a corporal, his first step towards independence. He had smoothed his Army-issue uniform and snuck into the bathroom to admire his reflection. Military khakis camouflaged his scrawny build. His shave was so close his pale cheeks gleamed. This proud memory made him wince when he spotted a good-looking man in a crisp, white shirt and smart pants bounding down the subway stairs.

The man, handsome and well-disposed, pushed through the turnstile, turned in Roy's direction, and ran a hand through his dark hair. His confident stride said that somewhere, this guy's opinion mattered. He drew closer, clearing a little of Roy's foggy ruminations.

Attention, soldier!

Roy's head pounded. It wasn't the liquor, not completely. It wasn't lack of sleep or lice or the layers of filth his body tolerated. It was his memories; relentless humiliations hammered his brain. What reason was there to push on? When was his last kindness? His last kiss?

He'd slid too easily from military veteran to unsheltered. His slide's momentum was inexorable. Its motion unstoppable, this fall that had unceremoniously transported him from upstanding citizen to invisible.

I once mattered. I used to matter.

Roy's head dipped towards the empty cup in front of him. There, his favorite possession, a silk orchid from his mother's kitchen vase, which she'd said would bring him luck, seemed to pulse in his hand like the blisters beneath his threadbare shoes.

Roy lifted his chin as the guy neared. His expensive clothes spoke of boardrooms and penthouses, places where Roy hadn't ever been, and if he were being honest, could barely imagine. The commuter's open, honest expression carried no sense of worry.

Instinctively, Roy's estimation was this guy wouldn't give him coins but bills. With his mother's flower still seeming to vibrate in his hand the ghost of his younger self cackled with derision. *Begging? Really, Roy?* His mother said she'd chosen a moniker that meant "king," hoping to lift him out of the poverty of their lives.

A name wasn't enough, and he was no king. Not even a prince. Even a court jester would scorn Roy's slovenly state.

The man smiled. Against the soot-stained walls, in the dingy heat hole that was the NYC subway, his teeth shone white.

Momentarily, this foreign sight of someone smiling at him startled Roy from his self-loathing. The guy paused in front of the three-square feet of oil-spotted cardboard where Roy sat. "Hey, I'm Phoenix. You want something to eat?" he asked, his diction clear and warm.

His demeanor was kind as he nodded at Roy's grimy paper cup and shoved a hand into his pants' pocket.

Roy blinked. His vision suddenly cleared. God, he'd fallen so far. He saw himself as he must appear. Filthy. Dirty. His fists balled with regret and self-hatred.

The man's charity was demeaning. Undeserved, unearned, pitying. Hot fury swelled inside his chest. The prince and the pauper. His mom had assumed that he'd be okay. Just study, just do well in school. She had been wrong, and now she was gone.

Roy abhorred Phoenix's charity. The gentleman's compassionate tone reminded Roy that he'd sunk lower than the filthy concrete below his haunches. The man's eyes widened in encouragement, as he slipped a folded bill into Roy's cup.

No. No handouts. Not today, he wanted to say but his disused voice came out a croak. Roy no longer needed money. After today, he wouldn't need anything. Emptiness beckoned. An end to his agony. His mom had been proud when he'd enlisted in the armed forces. Now, his latest accomplishment was scoring a fifth of bourbon.

Phoenix had already turned to leave. He meandered towards the tracks, distracted by a white square of paper that had tumbled out with the money. He walked away, unfolding a note.

Roy lumbered to his feet. His fingertips buzzed. He gripped the silk flower. The wilted satin inspired an idea. He'd pay for the man's donation. Roy wasn't a beggar. This was a fair transaction between two equals. The idea was ludicrous, but at least Roy's most treasured possession wouldn't be on him when he jumped, and the last thing he would do on Earth would be … a gift. Maybe the flower would make it to the light. Maybe that was enough.

A train sounded in the distance, its low rumble both eerie and comforting. Roy stumbled towards the track's edge where Phoenix stood reading the note, a smile playing across his lips. Roy extended the flower in his outstretched hand. In the light of the tunnel, the frayed flower's pink petals paled more to a lavender gray, frayed and worn, but still pretty.

The whirring wheels grew louder.

Phoenix, ear buds in his ears, was too far away to notice Roy's attempt to deliver the orchid. Roy had failed at a simple act of an exchange. Just like he'd failed at every hope his mother had ever held for him. He shoved the scrap into his pocket. He pinched the top of his thigh in frustration.

The approaching train all but roared in response.

The judge who had sent Roy to jail floated in his mind's eye. Everything fell apart after that prison sentence. Roy was canned from his minimum-wage job, which caused him to miss rent, and downward spiral into the bottle, the street, and ultimately to lose his self-respect. Fury burst through Roy's fingertips and toes until he stumbled onto his threadbare shoes. He had nada. No one. He hadn't eaten anything since the day before. *Failure.*

The train would erase him. A blot no more. Disintegrated. This was the way to go, drunk. He hungered for relief. The rails beckoned. He hurled himself forward.

A train entered the station. His chance. Each track chanted a song of nothingness. Emptiness was better than this pain.

Why the hell not?

Wind whirled from the screaming train.

God, the pain would be good.

He shoved the flower's silk into his pocket.

Roy. My name is Roy.

He teetered headlong toward the platform's edge.

There would be air. Impact. Then heaven or hell. It didn't matter.

Momma.

He leapt into the darkness.

The sensation was different than he'd expected.

He was yanked back. His shirt collar choked his Adam's apple. Weightless for a fraction of a second, he had no sense of direction. He was falling, though he wasn't clear which way was up or down. Before his scream emerged, the ground walloped his back. His head bounced.

Dazed, his vision cleared to take in a darkened ceiling. His shoulder ached, his breath knocked out of him. No slamming impact of a train. No dimming consciousness. No bleeding out.

The train squealed like an animal howling. Its effort to halt filled the station with an unbearable noise. Bellows.

He lumbered to his knees. The scene on the tracks imprinted onto Roy's mind like a flash photo from a horror flick, and over the edge, Roy's well-heeled protector tried to scrabble upright. His leg was caught under a railroad tie. He yanked to free himself until his eyes widened as the train flew to flatten him.

A scream coiled and then leapt from Roy's throat, as he witnessed Phoenix gain a moment's purchase, stumble then fall.

Roy collapsed to stretch out a useless handhold too late. The hoary mass blurred past until nothing else was visible but windows and a silver flash, blowing him back from the brink.

The cars shuddered to a stop.

Roy slunk to the bumpy edge and peered down the narrow track. It took a moment to make sense of what he saw. Shining bright against the dirty brown ground, a white sleeve trembled in the breeze, its edges shorn and dipped with burgundy. Protruding from the cuff, a man's riven hand lay curled as if reaching for the outstretched grasp of a lover.

Roy gagged. Bile warmed his throat, not unsimilar to the fist swig of cheap scotch.

It should've been him.

A conductor sprinted from the locomotive towards the fallen Phoenix. Oh, the irony. For Phoenix—the man who'd respectfully introduced himself to Roy—there would be no rising from this pyre.

Clearly, it was his fault. Roy would be arrested. Jail was worse than a halfway house.

Roy tripped backwards, forsook the paltry sum in his cup, and then bolted for the street.

CHAPTER 1

CONVIVIAL REVIVAL

Orchid

NINE MONTHS LATER, NEW YORK CITY

Have you ever been in the middle of a moment, an instant that's suspended between what was and what is about to be?

At the age of twenty-eight, Orchid Paige thought that her parents might be proud to witness her life from their vantage point in heaven. She loved her friends, had built a career, and secured a temporary work assignment in her mom's ancestral country.

This past year, she'd almost given up hope for one last fragment of happiness, after she'd fallen for Phoenix Walker—advertising wunderkind, athlete, entrepreneur—and he'd abandoned her. She hadn't known at the time that he'd left to shield her from his life-changing accident.

Tonight, they'd attended his ex-girlfriend Tish's wedding. She'd agreed to accompany him as an opportunity to say farewell before she moved overseas. Then, the truth of the evening unfurled into an unexpected twist. Phoenix's words had promised the missing piece to her joy. "Tell me we can try again. Long distance, or I'll find business in China."

Her chest had expanded with possibility, and a kiss that was soft, urgent, and not quite enough to compensate for their lost months. He was gorgeous, from the intensity of his cobalt blue irises to the scruff of yesterday's beard. To ensure she'd never make him feel less than, she didn't focus on the rounded end of his forearm visible below his cuffed-up sleeve.

She returned to the present moment as dancing throngs parted. Her feet tapped along to the pace of the DJ's pounding bassline.

Their round table and Phoenix's twin Caleb came into view. Even from afar, she could see the bride's sorority sister Gail, draped over Caleb's massive shoulder, yapping into his ear. Caleb eyed Phoenix and Orchid's approach and began to push his chair back. He gestured towards an invisible watch on his tattooed wrist, indicating to them that it was time to depart.

Phoenix leaned closer to Orchid and murmured. "Are you ready?"

She squeezed Phoenix's palm. "If we don't go, I might do something terrible to Gail." After Gail had asked about his injuries, she'd declared "I could've never survived that," making his life sound impossibly dire. Phoenix's frown had sparked Orchid's protectiveness.

He chuckled. "I'll help."

Protecting him was the least she could do. After the losses he'd sustained to save a man's life, it seemed unjust for Gail to hurt his feelings with unthinking words.

Caleb stood and joined them before they reached the table. "Bye," he said to Gail, and stalked a step ahead of them.

"Tell Tish we said mazel tov," Phoenix called to Gail, who gave a crestfallen expression as she waved goodbye.

The threesome's pace accelerated towards the exit.

Outside, the April air cleared some of her tequila fog.

Her reservations had yet to fully form.

They were perfect. As long as he would follow through on his commitments.

They were perfect. As long as she didn't allow herself to be triggered by the injuries that he had tried to hide from the wedding photographer's lens.

Along the quiet street where their car was parked, an inky black sky opened over their heads. Like a sign, a star flickered, faint and far.

Orchid ducked to deposit herself into the limo. Emotion blurred her view. Phoenix's palm protectively cupped her head, the back of his hand taking the brunt of her mad dash into the car.

The silky fabric of her tartan dress slid across the leather bench. "Ouch," she said, even though nothing hurt. Not her noggin, not her ego, not her tequila-fueled fingertips. She marveled at the zillion possibilities that spun before them.

She abandoned the wedding favors onto the carpet cushioning her high-heeled feet.

Phoenix slid beside her, and his brother Caleb on the far side. The door shut.

"You, okay?" Phoenix murmured. He mussed the spot along her hairline. The automobile glided forward.

She nodded. *Okay?* She was besotted. Besotted with Phoenix's eyebrows knitted with concern, his wave of hair that flowed against the grain of his thick tresses, his clean scent, the shape of his mouth compressed with care.

"Yeah. Sorry for my clumsiness," she said. Orchid brought his palm to her lips. He'd have a bruise tomorrow. His one precious hand would pay for his chivalry. The dark sky out the window inspired a thought. "Have you ever wondered about parallel universes? Like one where we didn't have to go through all this drama?"

Humor played at the corners of his mouth. "You mean there's a universe where I gave the suicidal guy a grand and he skipped out of the subway station happy?" he asked.

Caleb stretched his meaty neck, "Some physicists think our concept of time will be disproved. That it doesn't just move in one direction."

"Time travel? If I could go back, I'd undo a few things," Phoenix said.

She pondered all the things that could've avoided the pain of last year.

"You could undo hiding your accident from me. You could have not rebuffed me at Easter." She leaned towards him, and threaded fingers with his. His long digits had swiveled a spigot shut in a dark downtown club where they had met a year ago. They had tapped texts and emails to her during months of working on his non-profit project.

His eyebrow raised. "If I could go back, I'd tell you how I felt before you left for China."

"Me too. And now you get to come with me to China."

A frown downturned his mouth then disappeared. She wanted to take his words as a promise. *I'll find business in China.* Yet, she began to wonder about the risk in trusting him.

Hers had always been a life of striving. Good fortune? *Never, Orchid.* She could only count on herself. Trusting someone else meant ceding her autonomy.

Phoenix read the shift in her expression. "You with me, Kai Lan?" The endearment brought her back to the warmth of his arm against hers. A year ago, he'd bestowed the moniker on her the night they'd collided in a men's room, a reference to the children's TV show "Ni Hao Kai Lan."

She nodded. And started compiling the promises she'd need.

She wasn't about to give up her promotion and dream of a new life in China.

Not for anything.

CHAPTER 2

FORGIVEN

Phoenix

Birthing a new life takes nine months.

For Phoenix Walker, building one spanned that exact duration. In the three-quarters of a year since his train accident, despair had almost ended his time on earth. Then with the help of his mom, brother, friends, business partner, and therapists, he had clawed his way back. Or in his case, limped.

Now with one tuxedo-clad arm around the woman he'd almost given up because of his accident, Phoenix's heart thudded deep in his chest, calisthenics for another round in the ring.

In the back of their limo, Orchid tilted her head against his shoulder, rewarding him with her rose-scent mingled with bridal cake sweetness.

His twin brother Caleb squished his mass away from Phoenix, allowing a few inches of privacy between them. One tattooed paw capped his forehead, shielding his view of the newly minted couple.

"I don't need to stay at your place tonight. If you guys want time together, I can crash somewhere else," Caleb said.

Phoenix considered the evening ahead, the possibility of Orchid at his apartment. The last time they'd spent time there, their relationship was purely professional. They'd pored over advertising briefs and shared a meal. That was before his accident.

The thought of Orchid amidst the apartment's accessibility features gave him pause. His desires fractured in two. He'd wanted nothing more for the last year. Still, he wasn't ready for this. When he'd witnessed her care for him, and she'd confessed Tish's wedding evening was to say goodbye, he'd finally confided his feelings. Yet now, when he pictured her getting ready for bed, shedding her tartan dress, one of his t-shirts sliding over a bare shoulder, his body surged with desire while his brain stuttered on the next moments. Sure, she could handle him dapper in a tuxedo. How could he strip down to his briefs, sit on the edge of his mattress to remove his prosthesis and liner, and climb into bed with a woman he loved, when his injuries were a permanent marker of trauma, the exact thing that had triggered her PTSD?

"Or you can come to my place," she offered in the space of his hesitation.

He didn't have the wheelchair he used at home, clean stump socks or his skin balm. Worse, he didn't want to foist any of these foreign objects on her. Not this early. Yes, he'd wanted to be honest with her. There must be some way to ease her into his reality.

"Um, not to kill our spontaneity but I don't really have what I need for a 'sleepover.'"

She laughed at his air quotes and teen expression.

He pulled her closer and pressed lips against her temple. "How about we get a good night's sleep and then do something tomorrow? What are your plans? I'll do anything you want."

"Lalalala," Caleb hummed to himself with both hands over his ears.

She leaned over Phoenix and tapped Caleb's thigh with the back of one hand. "Shush. It's not what you think."

Phoenix leaned closer towards her fragrance. "No?" he mumbled to himself.

Caleb squinted at Orchid. "The problem is, I've seen tattoos of that," his brother, the tattoo shop owner, said.

"Tattoos of dance class?" she laughed.

It was Phoenix's turn to startle. "Dance class? That's what you want to do?"

"Yes, I'm scheduled for a ten o'clock. You should come with me."

"That's not really my thing." He pictured his mechanical ankle in the midst of limber Manhattan women.

She studied him, her boozy giddiness dimming as she seemed to intuit his dilemma. "How about brunch instead? Then we can shop. I don't know about you, but I'm eying new luggage for China."

He'd promised her anything. He wanted to deliver. He owed her that.

"I'm in."

"Great. Caleb, would you like to join us?" Orchid turned to his brother.

"No way. I don't even want to be in the car with you lovers right now," he declared, looking away from their embrace.

She shook with laughter in Phoenix's arms. "I know a good vegan place," she said.

"Nutritional yeast it is," he said, referencing the eggplant dish she'd brought to his office when they were working together, his introduction to vegan fare. Beautiful, smart Orchid. Her forgiveness was more than he deserved. His avoidance of her after his accident had cut her deep. He'd seen the hesitation on her face at the wedding. He hoped to never hurt her again.

At her building, Phoenix climbed out of the car to walk her to her doorman.

"Gold bullion for your thoughts," Phoenix said, pulling her warmth closer along the darkened sidewalk.

"There's so much to say. Are you for real or is this a dream? How are we going to make up for lost time? What made you change your mind?"

They arrived at her building entrance. The overhead light shined a halo onto her hair.

"You'll have to take my word that I am for real. I hope we'll have a very long time together to earn your trust. And I didn't *change* my mind. I finally realized what's been true all along."

She measured his earnestness.

His candor ameliorated some of the lines worrying her forehead.

"Caleb's waiting for you. I'll text you the address." Her hug was soft. She slipped out of his arms and into her building.

The generosity of her forgiveness blanketed him.

He joined Caleb in the back of the limo. His brother glanced over, his looming silence seeming to judge Phoenix's carelessness. Phoenix had been honest with Orchid while they'd been protected from the external world at the wedding. The car sped towards his apartment. Phoenix raked fingers through his hair, the problem harder than the computational finance classes he'd whizzed through in grad school. He refused to be a burden on Orchid.

"You guys a thing now, huh?" his brother asked.

"Looks that way."

"And you already have cold feet."

Phoenix huffed a laugh towards the darkened window. His brother had known him longest of all. Even longer than their parents since they'd shared a womb. His mom loved childhood stories of their ability to communicate intuitively. "Twin speak," she called it.

Along the sidewalk, he watched a couple sprinting down the block, cavorting and laughing. With him, Orchid would spend her time forever in search of ramps and accessible parking. "It's not that. It's complicated. We never really talked. We've got some stuff to work out."

"Like the stuff about dad making you find her?"

Phoenix eyed his brother. "No, that part's history. She made me promise to never bring up dad's request to do her a good deed. I tore up his letter. As far as she's concerned, we met at the club."

Caleb drummed his thick thigh with meaty fingers. "You ever wonder why dad picked her out of thousands of cases that came through his court?"

"I don't know. I'm biased, but I do think there's something unforgettable about her."

"Well, we can't ask him now," his brother said, looking out the window as if lost in thought about their dad who'd died a year and a half ago. The car snaked through traffic across town. Phoenix wondered what other secrets their father had kept.

Six months after his dad's death, Phoenix was shocked to receive an envelope from their family lawyer. The letter had been addressed to him.

With complete discretion, and without revealing the source of the request, could you please find and bestow a good deed on one of my long-ago cases? Judge John Walker's note had explained that Orchid Paige had come through his court as a child.

At first, Phoenix had debated whether to follow through on the unexpected request. Then, he'd decided to help Orchid and leave. But her strength and kindness and intellect overtook his logic until he had to admit that he'd fallen for her. Hard.

Before he could tell her how he felt, she overheard him telling Caleb the dilemma that their dad had asked him to find her. The truth was, after he'd fulfilled the promise to his dad, he didn't know how to say goodbye. Loving her meant protecting her. He just hoped he wouldn't have to protect her from himself.

"I should've invited Sascha to the wedding," Caleb mused aloud about his ex-girlfriend.

"Sascha's awesome. What's going on with you two?"

"Nothing, that's the problem."

"Want me to talk to her?"

"She's not going to be persuaded by some ad copy."

"That's funny. We should write you a campaign. Curmudgeonly Caleb, his bark is as bad as his bite."

"That's awful. I should feed you to a roomful of Gails."

"Gail has no tact," Phoenix recalled.

Gail, the woman who sat beside him at the wedding reception had asked about his accident and then declared "I could've never survived that." Her rude words implied that his life wasn't worth living.

He'd surmised that he discomfited others from their furtive glances. Gail wasn't the first to state what people really thought. He'd suffered their sucked breaths when they noticed his missing hand.

He had been about to slip into a dark place when Orchid had rescued him. Her embrace had comforted him, and her sharp words were a shield to deflect Gail's cruelty. "Some people are just stronger than others," she'd said to Gail. The inferred compliment lifted him above the black abyss.

Last month, Caleb tried to get his brother back together with Orchid by inviting her to a family weekend at their beach house. That night, sleep eluded Phoenix, as phantom pains scorched his missing leg. She'd come to find him, fetched his pain meds, and massaged the scars along the rounded end of his calf.

What Orchid hadn't said was how this affected her. If passersby gaped at him, what would be the impact on her every time she was with him? To love her, he needed to protect her. Somehow, he should devise ways to lessen the blow. Maybe wear his artificial arm to hide his loss. Then he recalled the prosthesis with a rounded hook at the end like a device from the hardware store. *Bad idea, bad idea, bad idea.*

The car turned onto his street. The brothers headed up to his apartment.

Phoenix wanted their relationship to work. But the risk was real. They might go all the way to China only to learn that the hazards of his everyday life were enough to drive her away. He'd had to learn how to adapt the way he did things. Everyday tasks took longer. He didn't want to picture her expression seeing him wheel around his apartment without his prosthetic leg.

Inside his bedroom, Phoenix missed the shape of her. His mattress could've held the two of them tonight. He perched on his wheelchair to pop off his prosthesis, remove his sock, and peel away his liner. Air cooled the sweat on his residual limb. He pictured her sprawled on his sheets observing him. Did she have any idea what she'd just signed up for?

No matter what, he'd vowed not to hurt her again.

CHAPTER 3

TRUST FALL

Orchid

Orchid strutted through her apartment building lobby. Newly possible futures rippled before her. She boarded the elevator, disbelieving her turn of fortune. She sensed that Phoenix needed reassurance. He'd hidden his arm from the camera lens. He'd balked at the idea of attending dance class.

Her heart swelled at the memory of Phoenix's promise, as if the muscle had its own set of lungs, its own pair of barbells. She'd forgiven him for trying to protect her in the aftermath of his accident.

The hope she hadn't even hoped. Her humorous, generous agency founder would accompany her on her international assignment.

As long as she could trust him. And herself.

Yes, her reaction to trauma and medical triggers had diminished. It had to be enough.

She stormed off the elevator into her apartment. The door thudded shut. A long-time habit, she deadbolted her door before kicking off her shoes.

What the hell had just happened? Her kitchen looked just as she'd left it, but it felt like it was from a different lifetime. B.P., Before Phoenix, she'd sipped a cranberry cocktail and armored her whole being for farewell. A.P., After Phoenix, he'd kissed her and confessed his love. The cage protecting her had no defenses against his blue gaze. Their relationship had undulated from care to pain, to love again. She'd not even hoped. So, she wasn't prepared for a beginning, much less an offer to go to China.

Fear gripped her chest.

This was the man who'd told her he had nothing for her.

Hope tried to claw its way into her internal debate.

He'd also told her he loved her.

Phoenix had been through a hell she didn't fully comprehend. This was the same person who'd supported her through every PTSD episode she'd sprung on him, who had wanted nothing more than to protect her, who'd helped her strive for success and had respected their boundary when she'd enforced a purely professional relationship. Now, she needed to make sure he was never the source of her triggers, because her unfiltered reactions might make him question his own worth. She'd rather leave him than hurt him.

She laid on her sofa and tapped her phone. "You up?"

Her best friend, Mandy, didn't text back, she called. Mandy loved a good gab. "You're in luck, Matty thinks midnight is a perfectly acceptable time to eat. What's up?" She employed a hushed whisper that bordered on comical.

"Oh my god, the wedding."

"Don't worry, hon, weddings always sucked when I was single."

"No, it's not that."

"Don't tell me that jerk did something to you. I've told you before, I'm not above punching that pretty face." Her whisper took on an angry tone.

Orchid laughed, which was just what she needed. "He told me he loves me."

"No freakin' way."

"Yes, freakin' way. He told me he'd go to China or we could date long distance."

"Wow," she breathed. In the ensuing silence, Orchid imagined Mandy wrinkling her nose. "I don't see how long distance could work," she finally said.

"You're right. Like twelve-hour time difference zoom calls?"

"There're direct flights," Mandy said.

"I get to come home once or twice a year. I'm going to have to convince him to move."

"And how are you feeling?"

"Honestly? I've never been happier and more scared, all at once. He is sensitive about his injuries, and I can't imagine how much it'd hurt him if he ever thought he triggered me."

"Do you feel like you can trust Phoenix?"

"Trust? Not my strong suit." She picked lint off the tartan-patterned dress she'd picked out to say goodbye in. How ironic.

"I guess you'll hafta go with your gut. Now, the other guy in our lives just fell asleep. Let me go put him down."

"Hugs to Matty."

"Bye."

Trust. She'd trusted that her parents would keep her safe. Then she'd witnessed the car crash that killed them when she was just twelve years old.

Trust. She'd trusted that little girls would enjoy the fairytale endings depicted in her childhood books. Happily-ever-after had evaded her.

Trust couldn't be counted on. A blind pursuit for lemmings leaping off a cliff.

She'd do as she always had. She'd be as trustworthy as she could be. When it came to others, though, she'd always prepare a Plan B. In this case, Plan B for Beijing.

CHAPTER 4

EXIT EXHILARATION

Phoenix

A new life awaited Phoenix. He woke with a reminder that everything had changed the night before. His internal promises drummed like a mantra. *Never hurt her, never burden her.*

Inside his local flower shop, petals burst in hues of fuchsia, sienna, and sunshine, clustered in bunches as if for safety. Lucky that his Upper East Side florist was open on a Sunday morning. The owner propped the refrigerated door with her back, pulling out colorful bouquet after colorful bouquet. She extended orange dahlias. "These are cheerful," she said.

Phoenix shook his head. "Yeah, but still not quite right."

"Red roses … always classic."

"Too cliché. Looks like I'm trying too hard."

"Are these make-up flowers? Go out with me? I love you?"

He chuckled. "All of the above."

"Then here's the perfect thing. Orchids are wild and complex. They look fragile, but people don't realize they're hardy. They grow in the tropics on trees, after all." She held out a potted plant with thick green leaves. The purple flowers were hued like a swimmer's hands who'd swum for too long in cold waters.

"No. Definitely not orchids." His tone emerged sharper than intended.

"Okay then."

"Sorry. Her name is Orchid, so she hates getting them. I want to get this right. I don't want to screw up." Again.

Magenta flowers, the same shade as Orchid's lips, caught his attention. Her favorite. "Let's go with peonies." When he leaned forward to point, she cast a sideways glance at the asymmetry of his left arm.

"She fights dirty." He grinned and made a chopping motion over the empty spot below his cuffed up left sleeve.

She grimaced. Most people's reaction to what was missing. "I hope you're joking. Okay, let me wrap these up. This time of year, they're from China."

China. A reminder of the one of the thorns in the labyrinth that was their relationship. Orchid's job was moving to Beijing. Heady emotions had fogged his logic last night, and the promise came spilling out. *Long-distance, or I'll find business in China.* Perhaps that was a foolhardy commitment.

He didn't want to hold her back here in New York.

The sales lady slid a blank card across the counter and accepted his credit card. She swiped payment while he wrote a card. "Anywhere in the world for you."

Traveling downtown in a car service, the tissue-paper ensconced flowers on his lap, he tapped a text. "Good morning! I'm on my way."

For months, he'd erected barriers to her care. She wouldn't be able to deal. He'd traumatize her. Strong smart Orchid busted each one. "The stupid thing is I fell in love with you, and I can't stop," she'd said.

Phoenix's phone chimed as he emerged from the car.

"I got us a table xoxo," she'd responded. Those pixels representing her kisses and hugs were generous.

He slipped his phone into his pants pocket and pulled open the door to the café. The place smelled like coffee and fresh baked muffins. Before the hostess arrived, his vision adjusted to the soft yellow light. He spotted Orchid. Her pale face brightened as he made his way to the white marble table in the back corner. She was as stunning as the beauty ads her company produced. Luminescent skin. Her dark eyes crinkled with joy. Thick hair cascaded past her shoulders.

It was more than her physical beauty. Her expression was that of a desert wanderer who'd just discovered a waterfall. *No, I'm the lucky one.*

Her face broke into a smile as she scooched out of the black leather booth. A rainbow-ribboned minidress skimmed her hourglass frame. *I don't deserve her.* Phoenix quickened the last few paces, then tossed the flowers onto the table, unable to wait another second. She opened her arms for him. He accepted her embrace, burying his nose into the rose scent of her hair. "I never want to let you go," he said.

"Then don't," she replied, her tone playful, but with an edge that belied her seriousness.

Arm or no arm, leg or no leg, they were in perfect symmetry.

He pressed his lips against the smooth silk of her cheek and let go, pulling back so he could see all of her. She gulped a breath, appearing to shake off whatever emotion had just gripped them both. Hopefully, her seeing what was left of him wasn't too jarring.

"You showed up," she said.

This well-earned distrust would take some time to dissipate. Time he'd committed to her, even if he hadn't said it in so many words.

"Of course, nowhere else I'd rather be."

She slipped into their booth. He joined her.

"You're dressed so colorfully. I barely recognize you," he said.

"I woke so happy. I can hardly believe we're together."

"It's a dream. Or a nightmare."

"Don't tell me that we're actually in a simulation, like that Jake Gyllenhaal movie *Sourcecode*. All the little clues that this isn't real. Like you not running away from me."

He felt his shoulders wince with guilt. "Sorry."

"Too soon to joke about this?"

"Depends on if you've forgiven me."

"Never. Your abandonment will be my guilt trip, my winning trick, forever."

"Forever ... I've missed you," he said.

"Since last night?" she asked and kissed him back. She tilted her head to look at him. Her dark eyes glistened, in contrast to her pale skin.

"These are for you," he said, lifting the flowers he'd abandoned on the table.

"You're sure you're not saving them for Liv or Tish?"

His eyes rolled at her jab over his admin and ex-girlfriend. "Pul-leeze, there's plenty where those came from. I stole them from the window washer around the corner."

"In that case, thank you." She pressed her nose against the posies. "You always remember my favorite."

"I'm late because I stopped at the florist's. She tried to sell me orchids."

"Ha, that would've been the end. These are beautiful."

With her contrast of dark hair, and graceful movements, she was more stunning than the blooms. She laid the bouquet back onto the table, and he held her slender hand. "How was dance class?" he asked.

"Fun. I danced off the wedding cake. Speaking of which." She lifted a wedding favor from the seat beside her. "I somehow ended up with two of them."

"Thanks," he said.

"T-n-T sounds like dynamite." She read the bride and groom's initials stamped into the white box.

"Would you want ours to be O-P or P-O?" The question tumbled from his mind into the open. Their reunion was measured in hours. He could already imagine their wedding, her wreathed in last night's full-length dress, their vows skirting the fact that he'd left her without explaining why.

"OP is the start of opulence or opportunity," she said, and captured his hand in hers.

"PO stands for pissed off," he noted.

She laughed as her thumb lingered across his palm, tracing tingles of anticipation. Then he glimpsed the emotion he'd feared. Her eyes darted to the spot where the train had crushed skin and bone. She swallowed and retrieved her hand. His throat tightened. He'd become a human detector for disgust.

He lowered his left arm so it was hidden beneath the surface of the table. A well-practiced move, but not one he'd had to employ with someone who mattered this much.

"Now, tell me everything. This China assignment is like a dream, right? What are you going to be doing? When do you go?" he asked. He was impressed with her.

"I'm lucky, I really am. I feel like my mom's looking over me, because this all started when I wanted to make her dream come true. I go whenever the work visa comes through. And the first year is a trial. If I'm not happy or they're not, I can come back to New York at the end of the year. We'll come to a mutual decision, whether to extend to a full three to five years, or to return home."

"You should be flattered. An international assignment is a huge deal."

"I'm half hoping the role will move to Singapore. I'm so conflicted about China politically."

"You'll have a layer of protection working for a Western company. Plus, you're not going for political reasons."

"Nope. Professional and personal ones. Like feeling closer to my mom."

"I wish I could've met your parents," he said.

"The surprising thing was, when I went to China, my friends said they wouldn't even consider me Chinese!"

"Because your dad's not Chinese?"

She laughed and flipped back a lock of hair. "No, they say that they can tell from blocks away because of the way I dress and carry myself. But enough about me. Tell me what you want. Are you up for an adventure in Beijing, or was that the tequila talking last night?"

His mouth opened, as he sought words to convey his care. And his fear. She made a move sound fun. But how would it be to live together? He pictured her scrambling off their shared bed as he doffed his prosthesis.

"I don't know what I'd do in Asia, for one," he said, naming a different concern.

She swished the water in her glass and watched the resulting tornado. "I've thought of that, too. Any ideas? Because just so you know, I'm not staying in New York."

He had tried to imagine his life without the anchor of work, or the city. Worse was the thought of life without the woman who meant more to him than any other. "Did you know I always wanted more time to write?"

Her hand stilled and she grinned. "Really? You write more than ad copy?"

"I almost did a journalism minor in college. I thought writing could change the world. I advocated for the underprivileged. I wrote a whole series on the lack of affordable housing."

She startled. "Is that why ..."

"Why I help people on the street? Offer to buy them something to eat?"

"That guy you saved ..."

"Yeah, I didn't have time to tell him about my thesis on society's responsibility to the unhoused before he—"

Before he tried to jump in front of the train that hit me instead.

His attempt at lifting Orchid's serious expression stumbled over the memory. She placed her hand on his, her face scrunched in sympathy.

A buxom waitress, golden hair piled up high, sidled over to their table. Tracing her trim figure were black jeans and a black, lowcut t-shirt. Her gaze swept over Phoenix's wavy hair that could never be tamed. Recognition skittered across her expression.

"Oh, hi there. It's been a while."

Her voice and angled features jostled something forgotten. An evening out with his brother's ex-girlfriend Sascha. Escaping his suicide watch at the rehab center. Cool night air awakening his sense of life outside of physical therapy. A lively music venue. Her name staggered into his memory. "Ana?"

"Right. From Rockwood Music Hall."

"Ah, yes, with Sascha." The image was clear. Drinks. Snacking on nuts. Rediscovering that living might be preferable to the alternative.

"Yeah, I'm working two jobs. To supplement my life as a bookstagrammer."

"Bookstagrammer? Are you an influencer?" Phoenix asked.

Her crooked teeth shone. "Trying. I'm seeking authors to work with. If you know of any."

Orchid's neck swiveled from Phoenix to Ana and back.

"Phoenix was just talking about writing. I'm Orchid." The love-of-his-life stuck out her hand.

"Orchid, this is Ana. We met last year. Ana, this is Orchid, my—" What was she? Maybe girlfriend but they hadn't even discussed that. Definitely not lover since they had yet to be intimate. Actually, she was his world. The thought helped cement his conviction.

"Queen," Orchid said and shook her hand.

Phoenix looked at her with new admiration.

"I'll give you guys some time with the menus." Ana backed away. He knew Orchid's look. That was the same condemnation Orchid had given his ex-girlfriend Tish at the fashion show. And his executive assistant Liv when she thought they were dating.

Orchid arched an eyebrow at him.

"You vixen," he said.

"Queen Vixen to you."

"Would it help to tell you I've only met her once before?"

"Must've made some impression."

"I've not thought of her since then." She'd always be inextricably linked with the days after his suicide attempt.

"Why should I be surprised? When I stupidly fell for a guy who looks like a Hemsworth," she said, talking as much to herself as to him. "You probably have women falling over themselves for you all the time."

With the obviousness of what was missing, he disbelieved she could think this. "There's only one queen for me," he said.

"You sure? You met Rina and Ana, just in the last six months."

"Rina who?" Phoenix joked about the Canadian woman he'd dated for a short period after his accident. He got up out of his seat and joined Orchid in the L-shaped bench. She scooted over for him and accepted the comfort of his arm around her shoulders. He breathed easier when she returned his embrace. "This is not the way I want to start the day. Today is for us. Ana will bring us food, and then she'll be dead to me."

She checked his expression. "No need to kill anyone off."

"Well, there go our plans. What do you have in mind today?"

"Um, shopping for luggage?"

Phoenix felt his lips twitch. "You sure know how to have fun."

"My assignment starts next month. I can take three seventy-pound suitcases, and that's supposed to last me until my steamer shipment shows up."

"On the literal slow boat to China."

"Exactly." She sipped around the chunks of ice in her water. "Won't you need luggage too?"

Phoenix shrugged. "Probably not. But tell me everything. What are you most excited about?"

Her demeanor brightened. She straightened. "I have my own team this time. Plus, now I know the market better. It's a longer period, so I want to travel. I didn't get to tour around much last time, so I want to explore."

He recalled the cool places in Beijing that he figured would appeal to her sense of panache. "They have miles of bags at the Pearl Market. Have you eaten at the Grand Hyatt restaurant? And the Opposite House has the best DJs on Saturday nights."

She bounced on the vinyl seat. "What about you? This can't just be about me. Are you up for this?"

Phoenix hadn't flown since his accident. He pictured navigating security. "You know, I haven't traveled since we went to France."

"I loved that trip," she beamed. It was unfair to hold her to an offer to accompany her to China when she didn't comprehend the ramifications.

"I don't really travel light anymore," he started to explain, thinking of his bevy of equipment. Ana returned, brew pot in hand. "Coffee?"

"Espresso for him," Orchid called out.

"Macchiato for her," Phoenix rejoined, naming the beverage she'd ordered the first time they'd met at Starbucks more than a year ago.

"Good memory. But just coffee would be great." Orchid's smile eased Ana's confused expression.

"Blue Sapphire martini. Dirty," Ana blurted out.

Phoenix rotated his head to stare at their server. "You remember my drink order from one night in September?"

Ana blinked like she'd surprised herself. "You ordered two. Extra olives. Pretzels and peanuts too. You were with that punk girl."

"Sascha." He recalled the night with vivid clarity. The night air that had awakened his senses. The streetlights blurred as they sped along city roads. The keyboardist and his mate on stage, their ethereal playing lifting his mood.

Ana glanced at his lap. "You're doing better?"

"Yeah." His temporary prothesis had been replaced with a high tech one. His wheelchair was only needed at night. His cane abandoned. To think he'd almost ended his existence. Today, he was glad to be alive.

"Miss?" Someone from another table waved at their shared waitress. They'd been chatting too long. Other customers needed to order.

"What's your favorite dish here?" Phoenix asked Orchid.

"The quesadillas are good. I like the French toast. Depends on what you're in the mood for."

He was in the mood to lift Orchid's mood. Her expression had wrinkled with consternation during the interlude with Ana. "You want to do both and share?"

"Sure, okay," Orchid said.

Ana nodded at their order, filled both mugs and sashayed off to wait on a faraway table.

"She remembers you from seven months ago?" Orchid asked, her voice rising.

"Apparently. You know how waitresses have great memories for orders."

She counted on her fingers. "Ana, Rina. And who's Sascha?"

"Caleb's ex."

She sipped her coffee. "Black like my heart," she said, lifting the mug in a mock toast.

"Is that a warning?" Phoenix teased. "If you need payback, just take me down to a subway station." The imagery was surprisingly painful. Airborne over rusted tracks. Phoenix gulped the scalding brew to give his eyes a different reason to water.

She placed a hand on his thigh. "Oh, honey. I wish I'd been there for you."

"I'm glad you weren't. Now, tell me about our luggage shopping."

As she rattled off her online research, his mind replayed their history.

It'd been sixteen months since she'd first charmed him, at the Pyramid Club men's room. Her wish to honor her mom tugged at him, even without the extra layer of his dad's request. Then, he discovered that she needed creative experience just when he was short a strategic planner. His dad would be pleased he'd given her a chance with the pro bono work. The first time they'd met to discuss the work, she'd been clear about their professional boundaries. After all, her boss was a former client of his.

Except his feelings for her wouldn't stay in a neat professional box. He started falling for her at the triathlon, in Paris, even at the Effies. The night before she'd left for her overseas assignment, a celebratory meal had included champagne and feelings as effervescent as the bubbly. Back at her place, she'd closed the short distance between them on her sofa. He'd leaned closer. Their soft kiss exploded every cell in him. Mitochondria vibrated faster; nuclei multiplied. He'd left on feet that felt like they were floating. But fate tsked his naive optimism.

The next day, after saying goodbye at the airport, he saved a life, and his own would never be the same again.

Before long, Ana returned with simple but hearty fare on oversized farmhouse plates.

"Who gets what?"

"We're splitting. Just put everything in the middle," Phoenix directed, then he caught his choice of words. "Not splitting. Sharing, we're sharing." He caressed her knee under the table. One side of her mouth turned up.

Ana left, and Orchid offered him a wedge of the grilled tortilla. "The vegan cheese is really good here."

Phoenix pulled out the triangle and tried a bite. Easier than fighting to cut the French toast with a fork. "What do they make it out of, if there's no dairy?"

"This one's made with cashews."

"Who knew you could milk cashews."

"Very funny." She pulled at imaginary teats.

They were still laughing when Ana came by with a pot of coffee to top off their ceramic mugs. Their appetites returned with their good moods. The quesadillas were half gone.

"Oat milk, please," Orchid requested.

When Ana had left, Phoenix mimed a milking motion. "Oats are even harder to milk than cashews," he solemnly declared.

"Promise me you'll never stop making me laugh."

"Promise me you'll never stop finding me funny."

Orchid attacked the French toast with her fork and knife, slicing the golden-brown triangles into neat squares until she'd dispatched all four pieces. *Was she a mind reader?*

"Can we even get any of this stuff in China?" she mused aloud, as she poured caramelized syrup over half the portion.

"Jenny Lou's imports stuff from Europe, the US, and Australia," Phoenix named one of the grocery chains favored by expats.

Orchid took a bite and nudged the plate towards him.

"Thank you." He forked a piece and swirled it in sauce.

For the second time that morning, Phoenix set down his flatware to loop an arm around Orchid's shoulders. He paused. The previous evening, Orchid had buttered his roll without him asking for it. Now, she cut the toasted bread without fanfare. His throat swelled with a new insight. She'd intuited these thoughtful gestures. Moreover, she hadn't fussed over doing them. Orchid had preserved his ego, unlike those strangers who rushed to open a door when he was loaded with packages, then cast looks of pity.

"You are amazing, you know that?" he asked.

Orchid laid down her cutlery and encircled his torso. "You're easy to impress. All I did was find this place on Yelp." She sighed and nestled her cheek against his chest.

"It's not the food I'm impressed with." He pressed lips to the top of her head.

Her hair shimmered with a little shake of her head. "Not even twenty-four hours ago, I was picking out a dress to say goodbye in."

"God, I suck."

"You do. I truly love-hate you."

"What can I do to make it right?"

Orchid extracted herself to look at him. He missed her warmth. "You could start by not adding more women to your cadre."

"Today was just a weird coincidence."

"It's not just that. It's just, you know, the important people in my life don't seem to stick around. So, I'm kind of always waiting for the other shoe to drop."

"Would it help to know that, technically, I could get away with only one shoe?"

Her pained expression looked like he'd just gut-punched her.

He tried again. "That sucks. Sorry to be on that list of people. You're going to have to tell me, what can I do to make it right."

"There's just one thing."

He watched Ana cross the room to another table. "What's that?" Though he already knew. He'd committed to her that they'd have a fair shot. His business had learned how to run without him. A clean slate would give him time to write, to seek new entrepreneurial ventures, and even consider training for a triathlon. His physical therapist Nadine had promised that he could return to the sport he loved.

"Suitcase shopping today isn't just for me, okay?" she said. He couldn't say no to the hopefulness in her expression.

He hugged her. "We're shopping for you. I already have enough luggage for China. When should we start packing?"

She hugged him back and reached up to touch her lips to his. So soft. He'd made his commitment. They really were good together.

CHAPTER 5

DOING THE RIGHT THING

Phoenix

"Hey, man." Phoenix grinned as Dex, his creative director and business partner, wandered into his spacious office at counterAgency. A fresh Monday. Time for Phoenix to straighten out his life. Strive to, anyway. In bed last night, he'd churned through his life choices. Leaving counterAgency would be the easy part. Then, he'd need to find purpose in his new life.

"Brah." Dex slumped into the chair facing Phoenix's desk, his bowtie quivering as the chair bounced under his weight.

"You need coffee or something? Help yourself." Phoenix waved at the Nespresso machine on the side banquette.

"How come you're so awake? I'm exhausted. The missus gave me a honey-do list longer than my arm this weekend." His beard drooped more than normal.

"Are you warning me off women? So, you know, I patched things up with Orchid."

"What?" Dex slapped a meaty palm onto the table.

"Yeah, what a turnaround, right?"

"What happened?"

"I took her to Tish's wedding and told her she was right."

"*I* was right. I called it between you two. Don't forget that."

"Yup. You're always right. That's why I'm going to let you run the agency."

"What the hell are you talking about?"

"I'm leaving. Orchid's moving to China. For at least a year. She wants me to go with her."

"Wait what? What's happening in China? You're making my head hurt. I'm going to take that coffee after all." Dex lumbered over to the side table and rifled through the basket of flavored pods to pop a dark roast into the machine. He looked out the floor to ceiling window towards the adjacent high-rise buildings.

"Maybe it's a stupid idea. But after everything I put her through, it's the right thing to do. Or at least try." Never a truer sentiment.

"You're not making sense, man. Start from the start. How'd you guys get from Tish's wedding to China?"

"It's a long story. Make me one of those too, man." The rich scent of coffee piqued his desire for caffeine.

"You're getting Darjeeling. Since you've gone bonkers anyway."

"I hate Darjeeling. We need to promote Liv so she stops screwing with my caffeine. I actually want to talk with you about making her chief of staff."

"Fine. Promote Liv. Here's a pod called Cosi. Like you and Orchid. Happy?" Dex shoved the brown capsule into its cocoon and slammed the lid shut.

"Wait, are you mad?"

"You've always said I'm off my rocker but yeah, I'm mad. Because, well, hell." His voice cracked before he could finish. The big guy angled away and bent his head. "We almost lost you, and just got you back—"

Phoenix tripped over the recycling bin to get to his friend. The empty pail clattered to the ground. Liv's efficiency left no space for garbage, only recycling.

Phoenix stumbled a little then righted himself. Dex turned towards the commotion and swiped under his eyes.

"What the—" Phoenix reached his buddy.

"Guess I'm going to miss you." Dex forced a smile.

"Shut it. There're planes. There're zoom calls. You know it."

His assistant Liv bolted into the room, her energy ballooning beyond the size of her petite frame. Her attention darted from the overturned waste receptacle to Dex's downturned face, then she stormed over to her boss.

She assessed him from the top of his disheveled hair to the bottom of his metal prosthesis. "What happened? Are you okay?"

"I'm fine. Dex has gone sentimental. His punishment is one year of Darjeeling."

"I happen to like Darjeeling."

"Oh, that's who you're buying it for."

"Seriously, what's going on?" Liv glared behind her cat-eyeglasses from CEO to creative director.

"Boss guy's moving to China," Dex said.

"Wait. What? Why are we going to China?" Liv took a step back.

"You're not going. Just me."

"Not just you. Orchid too," Dex corrected.

"Well, yes that's the reason—"

Liv, who never interrupted her CEO, turned red. "Don't. What? I—"

Phoenix tried to quell her explosion. "Before you get too excited, remember I explained that Orchid didn't know about my accident? That I broke things off with her, not the other way around?"

"So, you say."

"Listen, I have a proposal, and this is as good a time as any. Liv, you've earned a promotion. You've learned the business side of the agency. I think you'd be an excellent Chief of Staff. Give it some thought."

Her mouth fell open. She peered over her glasses.

"Hell, yea!" Dex boomed. "Congratulations, Liv!"

"You two are going to be great. The office will be more than fine. Let me draw up some more of what I was thinking, and let's meet later this week to hammer out the details. I'll be on a leave of absence, but I'll still be available for virtual meetings and consultations. I'll even come back to the States a few times during the year. Sound good?" Phoenix bent to tip up the spilled can and took his seat. "Liv, can you find time for the three of us on Wednesday?"

She nodded and pushed the bridge of her glasses back in place. "Thank you, Mr. Walker."

"Thank you, Mr. Walker? Sounds like a yes to me."

Liv straightened her shoulders and left through the glass door.

Dex ambled towards the exit, then paused. "You sure about this? Isn't it kinda fast? Were you drunk?"

"There was tequila involved, but that wasn't it. I've changed. It's corny, but I've never been happier."

"Never been happier? Did she blow you?"

"Don't be crass. We didn't do anything, except talk. I think she's the one."

"You think? You're moving to another continent for 'you think'?"

"Okay, I know. We love each other. You'll get an invite when we plan the wedding, I promise. Is that better?"

"Exactly how long have you guys been …"

Phoenix glanced at his phone. "Technically, a day and a half. And we had a few rocky moments in that time."

"This sounds like a worse idea than taking that termite account. What's your fallback plan?"

"What is this, Monday morning coffee or an Interpol interrogation?"

"Fine, I'm outta here. But we're not done with this topic. Your brand of drama is getting wilder by the week."

As Dex shuffled out, Phoenix raised his head. "Just for the record, I'm going to miss you too."

Dex paused, tipped an invisible hat towards his buddy, and left.

Well, that hadn't gone as planned. Might as well get his next call over with. He plugged in his earbuds and chose his mother's name from his contacts list. Dallas was one hour earlier. She should be up by now.

"You, okay?" Veronica's surprised tone reminded him that he'd been an inattentive son.

"I'm good, Mom. How are you?"

He listened to updates on her interior design clients.

"Why are you calling?" she asked.

"Good news," he said, eyeing the photo of him with Orchid down at the shore, before the accident. They'd been so innocent then, with no idea what was yet to come.

"Oh, yeah?"

"You remember Orchid?"

"Well, of course. Have you apologized to her?"

"I invited her to Tish's wedding." He sipped his cooling beverage, chuckling at Dex's sense of irony. *Cosi, ha.*

"Interesting tactic. How was your ex-girlfriend's wedding?"

"Good, better than good because, yeah, I more than apologized."

"How are you feeling about her?"

He leaned back in his seat. "Mom, she's amazing. When I'm with her, I feel giddy. We laugh. She's not afraid to tell me when she thinks something is BS. I told her I love her."

She let out a whoop. "Congratulations."

"Really? I thought you'd be against the idea."

"As I recall, I suggested you give her a chance."

"Yeah, except I've been afraid to commit, and she had no idea where she stood."

"I wrote an article on the perfect make-up dinner. Let me send you a link right now."

"Thanks, mom. You're brilliant."

"Always."

"I'm glad to have your blessing. She wants me to go to Beijing with her."

"Just remember that vacations can be a tough time for new couples. Figuring out how to travel together."

"It's not a vacation. Do you remember she mentioned she's heading there on assignment with Lauder?"

"What does that mean?"

"It's an expat assignment."

"You're moving?" Her tone inched upwards.

"She has a one-year commitment. She can extend longer if she wants." He kept the "up to five years" part quiet.

"Let me clarify. You went to a wedding with this woman. And now you want to go halfway around the world."

"Essentially." He held his breath.

"You're giving me whiplash. What about the agency?"

"My company's going to be fine. We have a strong bench. Honestly, I was out for months and no one missed a beat."

"You've always undervalued yourself. What about practical matters? Have you found a prosthetist there? An accessible apartment?"

"Not everything is about my leg. Beijing must have prosthetists." She sighed.

"Oh yeah, while I'm away, you might want to check in on Caleb too. He is not in a good place."

She hopped onto the diversion. "Why do you say that?"

"He's having a rough time with Sascha. She's been dating."

Veronica sighed. "A parent's job is never done. You'll see when you have kids."

Phoenix paused. "I'm not sure I will."

"Why not? You've always been good with kids. You tutored up until what, college?"

He peered down at his chair. Some days, it wasn't so easy just looking after himself. "We'll see, Mom."

"Well, I think I'm overdue for a visit. I'm not taking no for an answer." She made a kissing sound and hung up.

His mom was a Walker through and through. She was strong enough to grow accustomed to the change.

Alone with his thoughts, Phoenix flipped over his phone to send his promised text.

A message to Orchid. "Good morning!"

Just seeing her name squeezed his chest. He felt himself grinning like an idiot, picturing her sleek dark hair against some power outfit trimmed in vegan leather.

He put the phone down. She was probably in meetings, and he needed to sketch out his transition plans.

His phone buzzed.

"Sorry, I can't talk right now," was her response.

Meetings, as he suspected.

"Come over for dinner this week, okay?" He texted.

"Friday." She snuck in a quick response.

He could barely wait until the end of the week. She was now his life. *Promises made, promises kept.*

CHAPTER 6

FAMILIAL FRAGILITY

Orchid

Orchid wasn't adept at goodbyes. The assignment was giving her practice.

As she prepared to leave New York behind, coworkers streamed through her office to wish her well.

Her friend Violet stopped to see her as the afternoon sun began to wane.

"Are you working late tonight?" her friend asked, tucking the lavender hair that matched her name behind one ear.

"There's so much to do," Orchid moaned.

"Well, we're going to miss you!"

"You, too," Orchid said, and laughed when Violet wrinkled her nose at the papers on her desk before leaving with a wave. Phoenix's bouquet, on her desk, would keep her company.

Orchid leaned back in her office chair. She knew who she needed to contact. She owed a call to her mom's sister, Aunt Lily. She didn't call often, so she anticipated her aunt's harsh judgements through the phone line.

"Aiya, where've you been?" She used the Chinese saying that expressed dismay. Her voice held the familiar ring of disapproval, one that took Orchid back to school days.

"I'm still in New York. How are you, Ayi?" She used the Chinese word for aunt, a term used for blood relatives, friends of the family, even household help. The word connoted both respect and affection.

"Still the same. You should come visit before the weather gets too hot in Florida."

"That's really nice, but I have some news."

"Oh yeah?"

"Mom would be so proud. I've accepted the job in China. I should've called sooner." She cupped one of the peony heads that had begun to droop.

Her tongue clicked. "Congratulations."

"So, I'm not going to make it to Florida, but you're welcome to visit us in Beijing."

"Us?"

Orchid could feel her cheeks widen in joy. "My boyfriend is coming with me."

"Boyfriend? That does sound like good news. What does he do?"

Here was the ultimate Asian test. "He's an entrepreneur—"

She didn't get to finish. "Oh no don't tell me he doesn't have a job. Is he working on one of those tech startups with nothing but equity to feed you with?"

Orchid felt a little humor bubble at her aunt's rising ire. "First of all, I don't need anyone to feed me. I have a great job."

"I know. So don't tell me he's freeloading off you. Who's paying for him to go to China?"

"Ayi, he's paying for his own ticket, and my company's paying for housing and our driver, so there's no freeloading."

Her aunt huffed.

Orchid continued before her aunt could fire more questions. "He's very successful. He started his own ad agency. He's a founder. A CEO."

Phoenix's Chief Executive Officer title mollified her aunt. Orchid wasn't about to mention that he was on a leave of absence. "Very good. Is he nice to you?"

Orchid decided to simplify her response. No need to add ammunition to her aunt's newly calmed suspicions. "He's very thoughtful. Maybe you can come to Beijing over the summer. My company gives me extra tickets. My treat."

"Thank you. I'd like to visit the Summer Palace."

"It's a deal. I can't wait for you to meet my boyfriend."

"He'll have to pass the Ayi test. Bye."

Orchid chuckled and hung up.

CHAPTER 7

GOODBYE, NEW YORK

Phoenix

Rain sluiced against the windows of Phoenix's office, washing soot from buildings, and mud from car tires. He wanted everything he'd set into motion. A new beginning.

He listened to his business partner's download as he studied the family photo on his desk. Caleb. Mom. Of everyone, Dad was the one he wondered about, and yet couldn't ask.

"Liv's a spitfire," Dex exclaimed, leaning back until the Herman Miller guest chair stuttered in protest.

Phoenix turned away from the framed picture and towards his friend and business partner. "Always has been."

"Yeah, but she's stepped it up to a new level. God, she's full of ideas."

"Didn't I say you'd be fine?"

"Who says that's fine? I feel like I have a new boss. She's tougher than you."

Phoenix chuckled.

"Actually, maybe I gotta apologize. For getting worked up the other day. I'm happy for you."

"Man, don't let that sappiness show up in your ad concepts." He sipped his morning espresso.

"Actually, Fiona made me say that. She made it pretty clear I was being a jerk of a friend."

"You're kidding? You're the one who kept everything running while I was in the hospital." Phoenix viewed the water streaming down the exterior glass. Some part of his ego wanted to be needed, but he was also proud to have built a strong team who was more than capable of running their New York office.

"You would've done the same." Dex stood and stretched. His belly bulged against his unfashionable sweater vest stretched over a mismatched tee.

The rain shower spattered against the window, like a fresh start.

Phoenix wanted to do his part. "Alright, so let's discuss responsibilities."

Dex sank back into the seat, which promptly groaned. "Shut it about responsibilities. Just kick back and relax. You deserve it, after all we went through to start up this agency."

"Listen, I've been thinking. You've been more than generous to agree to keep my salary and benefits whole."

"No biggie. You're serving on the Board. Who knows, maybe I'll join you someday."

Phoenix snorted a puff of air. "So, I'm thinking, the Board calls are scheduled for mornings New York time."

"Which will be evening for you."

"Perfect. And I'll network in China."

Dex brightened and stood. "Good. No one can network like you."

Phoenix glanced at his buzzing phone. "Liv needs me for a transition call."

"Good luck with our boss." Dex lumbered out of the office. "Bye, bud."

Phoenix looked around at the spare office, not a paper out of place. Liv kept everything operating at maximum efficiency. Dex ably led their creative teams. His planners were fully staffed, and succession plans were in place for a new chief strategy officer. Phoenix closed his laptop with a satisfying thud. There was no self-pity. Just a fact. Everyone was replaceable. He'd do his part to support the agency from afar. Because now Phoenix's new life bloomed within a wild orchid, at least he hoped it would.

That afternoon, Phoenix's phone lit with a call. He glanced at the caller id. Not the name he'd hoped to see. Instead, a shocker.

"Rina?" he answered, picturing her actuarial uniform, a boxy gray suit and sensible heels.

"Long lost," his ex-girlfriend said with a wry tone.

"How are you?" he asked.

"I just landed the assignment of a lifetime," she said. "How are you?"

"Coincidentally, I'm going on assignment too, to Beijing."

"When? Ironically, I'm coming to New York."

"It sounds like things are going well for you then. I'm leaving next month. How about you?"

"Next month too. What will you do with your apartment?"

Just like Rina to get right to her point. "No particular plans. Guess it'll be empty 'til I'm back in six months or so."

"Wait a sec. You guys don't have an office in Beijing, do you? What, are you expanding?"

"Anything's possible. But no. It's not my assignment." He paused. They'd been apart longer than they'd been together.

"Not your assignment?" she asked.

He forged ahead. "I'm back with Orchid. She's going on assignment to China."

The ripping of the proverbial band-aid was practically audible. "What the—Orchid? Back?" she sputtered.

She sounded like she still cared. He waded into the truth gently. "Yes, it's fairly new. But I think she's always been the one."

A hiss of air sounded through his earpiece.

He felt for her. After all, Rina was the first one to help him realize that women could still see him as a desirable partner. "Let's get coffee while you're in town. If I'm still here," he said.

"Better yet. Let me stay at your place. While you're away."

He paused. What a surreal thought, to imagine Rina kicking back watching hockey on his flat screen TV.

"I don't know."

"Why not? You just said you're not going to be there. Not to play the guilt card, but my per diem sucks. I can cover your maintenance fee. Water your plants. Bring in your mail."

"Tempting."

"I've been on the phone with realtors. With my budget, I'll probably end up sleeping on a fire escape with rats for roommates."

"Oh, the pity card?"

"Is it working?"

"Maybe. Let me check with Orchid."

Rina groaned. "Bye, Walker."

He ended the call and slid his phone onto his desk. *Orchid.* Of course, her opinion mattered. His chest filled with warmth. He pictured a flight with his dark-haired beauty. *Together.*

CHAPTER 8

THE LOST BOY

Roy

R oy knew he needed to get off the streets. Otherwise, chances were high he'd expire after sun fall by his own hand or someone else's. Against the dying light, Roy shifted from one aching foot to the other.

Rages, desires, and guilt ping ponged through the emptiness inside his body. Alcohol and loneliness had almost chucked him under a train. A stranger had taken his place, his kind eyes and princely posture now rotting underground.

In the long line outside the temporary housing shelter, Roy pictured him in heaven, telling Roy's mother what her only son had done. The image of her mouth rounded in horror unearthed a moan, deep and guttural. His lids shut. His palms cupped his ears. The motion didn't halt his self-rebuke.

A voice beside him, sounding like gravel on gravel, piped up. "Ya alright, pal?"

Roy peered over to find a distinguished man, whose collared shirt was worn yet presentable and whose snowy beard was a stark contrast to his dark skin.

"I'm a terrible person," Roy said.

"Aren't we all?"

Roy had eschewed the rote and rules of shelters for too long. Today, he'd complete the intake process for temporary housing. He'd produce his government-issued ID with a trembling paw, feeling as if the laminated surface were smeared with Golden Boy's blood. The man said his name was Phoenix. Yet there was no way for him to rise from ashes.

Now, this gentleman's calm reaction to Roy's confession lessened a little of his pain.

As the line moved, this fellow client fell in step beside Roy. "First time here?"

"To this one, yeah."

"There's worse."

Once inside, everyone was required to take a scalding shower. His skin pink and shining, Roy accepted the clean secondhand clothes. He trimmed his beard. Clumps of hair littered the sink's ceramic surface. The mirror reflected a different person than the one who'd arrived. Roy was closer to the kid who'd enlisted in the military after high school. His oversized nose was even more prominent without the overflowing facial hair.

Roy, my name is Roy.

Roy fingered the silk orchid inside the clean pocket of his new pants as he lined up for the cafeteria-style dinner. The hubbub and tang of stew reminded him of his military canteen.

After Roy filled his plate, his snow-haired acquaintance gestured for Roy to join an elongated table near the center of the dining area.

The remaining open spot, between his new friend and a ruddy-complexioned padre sporting a minister's collar.

"You have to meet Father Lyndon," his newfound pal said.

The pastor folded his hands and turned to Roy. "How are you, son?"

The day's events weighed like a yoke in Roy's memory. He wanted to share the burden, the shriek of the train, Phoenix's dismembered hand, the fear that had erupted from him, and then, how he'd bolted from the station, his tatty shoes flapping against concrete.

"I'm a terrible person," Roy said. He vise-gripped his own thigh, a self-devised punishment.

The minister steepled his fingers. "Sometimes that's not for us to judge," he said.

He turned to others at the table. "How was the unemployment office?" he asked a heavyset fellow, who was overflowing the chair, buttons straining against his flannel fabric.

"The papers say companies can't find no workers. Well, I'm right here." He jabbed a fat thumb as his barrel chest.

Father Lyndon tapped his fingers against each other in agreement. "You made it to the doctor's today?" he asked a scrawny guy, who was nervously mincing his food into pellet-sized pieces.

"Yeah," he said, scratching the back of his neck. "It's real hard finding places that take Medicaid. Not like when I used to have my company's health insurance."

Here, he was among people who'd suffered hardship. Roy chimed in, the warm meal reminding him of days when he took interest in the news. "I read that 40 percent of Americans are just one paycheck away from disaster."

The pastor drummed the table beside his empty plate. "Half the stories I hear are about one turn of hard luck. Like losing a job." Their overweight tablemate nodded and stabbed a gravy-coated potato chunk.

"One fall. One illness," the thin fellow said.

"Sometimes a family member dies, and there goes your sofa to sleep on. Poof. It's no crime to be unhoused. It can happen to anyone." Father Lyndon's tone soothed Roy.

"My mom got sick," Roy said. "I left the military to take care of her. When she died, I kind of lost it. Then, when I had no more money, I tried to get a job. Places didn't seem to think my background fit what they needed."

Father Lyndon's shoulders lowered in sympathy. "Military skills are transferable. Companies just need to see how you learned discipline and problem-solving. You could go to the unemployment office, see if they could help with your resume."

The white-haired gentleman beside him bobbed his chin in agreement.

That evening, Roy started at the bottom of the shelter's ranks, sleeping on the floor. If he was patient, he'd graduate to his own bed. He wouldn't even mind the top bunk that was deemed less desirable by those who didn't want to climb the spindly ladder.

After lights out at ten p.m., and once the shelter residents quieted, the man named Phoenix haunted the space where Roy's thin blankets spread over institutional tile. The full round of his blue irises were visible in surprise, then panic, as he scrambled for a foothold on the tracks. The elegant gentleman scrambled up, then slipped down as if pushed by the force of the oncoming train. The screaming horn. The train's squeals. He'd disappeared under the silver blur, only his outstretched fingers left.

I killed a man. Maybe Roy could do something to make the stranger's sacrifice count. He fell into an uneasy slumber asleep with Phoenix's dismembered apparition hovering above him.

In the morning, at seven a.m., Roy stepped outside with the other shelter occupants. A woman clamored for their attention. She flapped flyers in the faces of passersby. Her shrill voice startled most others away. They shook their heads or ignored her.

Roy intended to go to the unemployment office. It wasn't open yet. This blond woman was dressed in a flower-print dress.

He slowed to view her papers. "Have you seen this boy?" she asked with urgency.

The "boy" appeared to be a freckled teenager, attired in a baseball cap and t-shirt. He hadn't yet grown into his oversized ears.

"I don't think so. Is he your son?" Roy asked, noting the boy's name and date of disappearance on the notice labeled "LOST."

His willingness to interact seemed to calm her.

"Yes, he's sixteen. He said he was staying with friends, but we found a note that he'd run away. I've tried a few shelters. I'm afraid he might be sleeping on the streets."

Roy paused. He could walk away, like his shelter mates had. Yet, he'd promised himself that he'd try harder, to make the stranger's death mean something.

"If you want, I could help you look. I know places people hang out on the streets. I could ask around, check with some people I know," Roy offered.

Her eyes glistened with gratitude. "Oh, please. Thank you. His dad and I would be so grateful. We love him and want him home safe."

She handed him several copies of the poster. "My number's right here. Call anytime if you find anything or have any questions. What's your name?"

"Roy. My name is Roy."

When she repeated his moniker, he felt his level of humanity rise. Then, she astonished him further. "What hours do you usually work here, Roy?"

His mouth fell ajar. He composed himself. "I'm usually here seven p.m. until seven a.m. Those are the shelter hours."

"Oh, well, thank you for your good work. Bless you. Now, I need to go to my next stop."

"Good luck," he said, and watched her scurry away.

He pictured himself as she must've perceived him, a clean-shaven man smelling of morning coffee. She didn't dub him a "client" of the shelter. She presumed Roy to be a productive, upstanding employee.

Clutching the photos of the missing boy, Roy hurried to the places in the city a runaway teen might be. He strove to live up to her misplaced hopes and assumptions. A pittance towards reparations for Phoenix's death. The man in the subway looked like he'd been going somewhere. Someone cared for him. Someone was grieving while Roy was still alive.

CHAPTER 9

BEYOND BEAUTY

Orchid

Orchid headed out her apartment building door to see Phoenix. The black tar of the streets of New York shimmered. Maybe that was because she knew she'd soon be saying goodbye to the city. Sunday church bells chimed in the distance, marking a wedding in progress. Construction crews jackhammered the pavement, their ratatat demolition a fitting accompaniment to the pounding of her heart. Even the rotten egg smell wafting from the open grates in the sidewalk didn't bother her.

Orchid arrived at Phoenix's apartment with the memory of every previous visit. She'd first come as a mentee, seeking help on a brief. Now, look where they were.

Phoenix opened the door, hair wet, fresh from a shower.

"What are you dressed as today?" he asked.

When she glanced down at her whimsical suspender outfit, he leaned close and kissed her.

"How are you, hungry bird?" His endearment warmed her, while a playful glance at the box in her hand poked at her baked goods addiction.

She slipped off her Keds and followed his broad back into the sunny apartment. A packing box sat on the ground beside his bookshelf. The pictures were gone, as well as most of his bound volumes.

"Coffee? Tea?" he asked over his shoulder. He was clothed simply, his muscular physique covered in a t-shirt and track pants that skimmed the tops of clean skater shoes.

"Sure, do you have Darjeeling?" She placed a bakery box on his counter.

He laughed. "Not here. Though just this morning, I was complaining that Liv stocks Darjeeling at the office. Apparently, you two do have something in common."

She thought of their misunderstanding that had landed her in the emergency room after counterAgency's five-year anniversary party. Enough time had passed that the irony tickled her. The scars from her stitches were no longer visible. "Well, if she's not planning to push me into a glass case, then maybe I'll have tea with her."

He ran a hand through his hair, inadvertently shaping the locks into even more appealing waves. "You two might actually like each other. And definitely no glass cases. For your sake, I hope you don't have to go to a hospital anytime soon."

"How about for the birth of our firstborn?" She felt her eyebrow lift with humor.

"Fine, I'll accept exceptions after a nine-month moratorium," he quipped.

Her mood soared at his good humor. They were packing to move to China. He'd declared his love. Life was looking up.

"Never mind tea. I'll have whatever you're having then."

As he turned to rummage around his fridge, she was struck with a new observation. Sometime during the last year, his kitchen had been remodeled to be accessible. Now she saw that the sink was lowered, with an open space beneath. A wall oven gleamed at waist height. He shut the refrigerator, a new model with a freezer drawer down below. Before she could fully process what the changes meant, he faced a round bottle with green liquid towards her. "You sure you want whatever I'm having?"

Orchid nodded, still dumbfounded that she hadn't noticed the renovations last time. Her brain intuited what they meant. The appliances were installed for someone seated.

He tucked the drink into the crook of his left elbow and twisted with his right hand. The glass spun against his smooth muscle and skin, and he sighed. Before she could offer to help, he gripped harder, and the metal cap emitted a satisfying pop.

Phoenix placed the bottle down and pulled a tumbler from the shelf above, then another. He'd poured and nudged a glass towards her. "Cheers," he said.

Orchid was overcome with emotion. Phoenix had always been so capable that she'd missed what his injuries might mean to his day-to-day life. Orchid gulped from her cup to quell a feeling that bordered on pity. The thick liquid smelled like seaweed and tasted like hay. She swallowed, then exerted willpower not to spit it out. She abandoned the cup on the counter.

"Oh god, what is this?"

He sipped his beverage. "Green smoothie. Wheat grass and stuff."

"Gross, it's almost bad enough to make me give up vegetarianism." She inched the white cardboard box she'd brought towards him. "Bakery goods to offset your health craze?" she tried.

"Temptress," he said with a laugh, and then nodded towards his living room.

She followed him, leaving her drink behind.

Phoenix placed his smoothie onto a side table and started packing titles from the shelf into the open box. "I wanted to talk to you about my place. While we're away."

He was doing all this for her. "We. I love the sound of that," she said.

"I love the sound of that too. How are your trip plans coming?" he asked.

"My vaccines are all done. But my work visa still hasn't come through."

He selected another handful of books and stacked them into the storage box. "Cool. More time in the city," he said.

"I'm completely stressed out." Orchid took a sip from Phoenix's glass then made a face.

"It doesn't get better with time," he said tranquilly. "So, what's the hold up with your paperwork?"

"Probably trade wars." She sprawled onto his sofa, which was enormous compared to her dollhouse furniture. "China and the US being at odds is not helping my work authorization come through."

"You still have two weeks, right?"

"Yes. The movers come at the end of next week. But what if I can't go?"

"Can you start your assignment remotely?"

"I've actually started reading some of the onboarding materials."

"And I get to have you in New York longer."

Orchid blushed with pleasure. Then she stated the real quandary. "Except my lease is up at the end of the month."

She absorbed his near-empty bookshelves, his sound system, the door to his bedroom, the opening leading to his marble guest bath, the accessible kitchen and eating area that could swallow her whole apartment. She imagined his calculations. "So, you don't have anywhere to stay?" he asked.

"Nope. I mean, I guess I could get a hotel, or Airbnb. I haven't asked Mandy."

"I actually wanted to talk to you about my apartment. I'm thinking about subletting it while we're away."

"You should," she said without hesitation.

"To an old friend," he continued. "You might remember."

She cut him off and blurted out her true feelings. "It's yours to do whatever you want as long as you realize that I'm totally angling to crash here."

He laughed and pulled another book from the shelf. "I want you to stay here, of course."

She reached around him, nearly toppling them both into the bookcase. "As long as I can stay, I don't care who you sublet to."

What did he want to tell her? Who cared? Because all that mattered was that she'd be moving in soon.

CHAPTER 10

COHABITATION HABIT

Phoenix

The next week, Orchid's stuff was packed up and divvied into one of three places. The movers had boxed up the majority of it to be ocean freighted to Beijing. Orchid saved her sentimental but non-pragmatic items for Mandy's basement storage unit. The rest was packed in suitcases for the temporary move to Phoenix's place. His driver waited outside of Orchid's building while Phoenix went up.

Orchid answered the door in wide-legged jeans, a crop top and platform sneakers.

Phoenix took in the sight of her ponytailed hair and groaned. "My neighbors are going to think you're a Girl Scout."

Orchid glanced down, then cracked up. "How much do you think I could get for a box of Tagalongs?" she asked.

He stepped closer and swept a finger under her chin. "Tag along? Please."

She closed the inches between them and hugged him like she'd never let go. How close they had come to not knowing this moment.

Orchid eased her hold and looked up at him. "Come with me to say goodbye to this place."

She clasped his hand and toured him around each spot. "This kitchen is the first place I tried chickpea water instead of egg whites."

"Vegan power," he jested.

She led him to the empty room in the back. "When I moved here, I finally got to have a pink bedroom." They moved to the blank space where the divan had left foot marks. "I'll miss this the most. I spent all my time here, reading or eating or working."

Phoenix leaned down and touched lips to the corner of her mouth. "I remember something else here."

She tilted her face up and returned his kiss. Honey and roses suffused his senses.

"We shouldn't keep our driver waiting too much longer. You ready?" he asked.

"*Our* driver. I like the sound of that." Orchid guided him to the front door where three rolling bags hulked. As she looked around one last time, the white walls marred with nail holes and scrapes seemed like an analogy for his own shortcomings. It hit him, he could only manage one suitcase at a time, which would leave her with the bulk of her belongings.

"Let me bring this one down and I'll come back to help you with the other two," he said, and let go of her palm to handle the largest suitcase.

She snapped to life, strapped a knapsack onto her back and slung her pocketbook across her body. "Let's just go together."

He compressed his lips as she rotated the deadbolt and maneuvered the other two bags out into the hallway.

She held the door with her back to allow him to follow. It closed with a clunk of finality. They walked down the corridor, where she pressed the button for the lift.

"Goodbyes are hard for me, even though it's just a place," she admitted, huffing as she wrestled the seventy-pound beasts over the stubborn lip. In the mirrored elevator car, he managed the call panel with an elbow.

"What is it?"

His closed lids shut out the world for a moment, then he looked at her. "It's not you."

"If it's not me, then it's you?" She tried for a joking tone.

His voice emerged low and gravelly. He'd promised her honesty. "It is me. Is this what you want? A guy who can't even help with your stuff?"

Her scrunched brow cleared. She released her suitcase handles to hug him. "Oh Phoenix, is this what's wrong? I didn't even think of it. That would've never crossed my mind. Because you did help."

He tilted his face towards Orchid, her earnestness reframing his contribution. "Yeah?"

"Of course, silly, how could I have gotten downstairs by myself? Can you imagine the uber surcharge with all these bags?"

He grinned, her enthusiasm buoying his mood.

"What do you want to do tonight, for your first night?" he asked. The thought of the surprises he'd planned cleared his remaining sliver of self-reproach.

"Hint. It's not Girl Scout duty."

"Queen Vixen," he murmured.

At his apartment building, they reversed the process with the luggage. His doorman pushed one of the pieces towards the elevator bank with them.

"This is Orchid. She's going to be staying here, so you'll be seeing her," Phoenix introduced.

"Nice to meet you," he tipped his head at her, and she replied with a grin and a wave.

"What are your favorite cookies? I love to bake," she asked the doorman.

While they wheeled through the lobby, the two of them chatted about baked goods, his daughter's nut allergies, and they'd exchanged more details about his family than Phoenix had ever heard him share before. Service people everywhere loved her.

Before the elevator doors shut, his neighbor Mrs. V skirted around the doorman and boarded the lift with them, baggage and all.

Phoenix nodded hello to her and the dog in her arms. Her stare traveled down his cuffed sleeve.

"Mrs. V, this is Orchid. Orchid, this is Mrs. V, a building board member, and her dog Elton," Phoenix said, his tone emerging with a cool edge.

The puppy allowed her to fake wave his paw, a motion to which the pooch seemed well-accustomed.

She eyed their three hot pink suitcases, then pursed her lips. "Are you moving in? We have a no Airbnb policy, you know."

Orchid opened her mouth to protest.

"She's staying as my guest," Phoenix stated, to shut down her judging tone.

Mrs. V brightened with surprise. "Well, you lucky fellow. Who knew, after all …" Her voice trailed off. He knew what she meant. His stomach churned with indignation.

Orchid spoke up, her tone sweet. "Actually, I'm the lucky one. I pinch myself. I can't believe my luck."

The doors slid open on their floor. Mrs. V ejected first, stumbling a little over the lip. "Yes, Phoenix always was a handsome fellow," she said and waved Elton's paw goodbye.

Orchid's eyes narrowed. "The nerve of people."

Phoenix's mood lifted a little, seeing her worked up. He pulled the largest case to his apartment and let them in.

Orchid followed him into the apartment and then stopped in the entryway. A banner strung over the empty bookcases. "Welcome Home, Orchid."

She looked like a lost yodeler, covered in bags and straps, simply staring. Then she abandoned her luggage and bolted towards another discovery. Phoenix dragged each suitcase into the apartment and let the door shut.

"My sofa!" she yelled. The white settee with one swooped arm added a feminine softness in contrast to the clean lines of his modern furniture. It was set up under the window, so that she could read in its natural light.

Orchid shed her pocketbook, knapsack, and shoes and plopped onto its velvet surface. She looked up at him. "I thought you had all my furniture donated."

"Yup, everything went to Goodwill. And one piece was donated to my apartment. Actually, *our* apartment."

Her eyes filled, and she patted the soft surface for him to join her.

"I have another surprise, so I'll be right back."

Phoenix returned with two slender stems in his right hand, and a chilled bottle under his left elbow.

Orchid took the glasses and placed them on his coffee table.

Phoenix watched understanding dawn on her face as he tucked the bottle under one arm to release the satisfying fizzing sound. If she looked this wrecked over screwcap champagne, his myriad daily adaptations were going to gut her.

They'd enjoyed meals and visits these last weeks. This would be their first opportunity to share a bed. He shuddered with more fear than anticipation, as he filled the flutes then handed her one.

"Tagalong, Orchid," he toasted.

She clinked his crystal and sipped the golden liquid.

"What would you like to do for dinner?"

"Did you buy all the ingredients I suggested?"

"My fridge is groaning from overtime as we speak," he said.

"Then let's go teach you how to cook!"

He looked down at himself. Inviting her here was bound to upend his life. He sucked down the rest of his bubbly.

"You're not the only one with surprises." She unzipped the largest suitcase to reveal a jumble of lace and leather.

"Those are a little small for me," he said.

"Spoil sport," she said, unable to keep a straight face.

Orchid pulled out a giftwrapped package and coaxed him to the sink, where she laid the package on the counter for him.

"I couldn't cook before the accident, so this isn't going to help matters." He shrugged.

"Open your present," she commanded.

With one hand, he ripped the paper from the misshapen object. Inside were implements similar to ones he'd used during rehab last fall. "What, did my occupational therapist get to you?" he grumbled.

It was impossible, but because they hadn't really discussed his injuries, he'd fooled himself into thinking they were almost invisible to Orchid. She'd never commented on his arm explicitly. These gifts were a window into her view. She saw what was missing. Of course, she did.

Orchid ignored his sarcasm. "This'll be fun." She bent to wash the adaptive cutting board and specially curved one-handed knife in the lowered sink and placed them in front of him.

"Mexican? Italian? What are you in the mood for?" she asked.

"You pick. I'll go get our drinks," he said.

By the time he carried each glass and then the bottle, three single-handed circuits in total, she'd littered the counter with vegetables, and placed peppers and onions on the new board. She danced over and tiptoed up to kiss his cheek.

"Who needs dinner?" she play-growled, nibbled at his lip, then winked. "Those just need to be sliced," she said. She sauteed something that smelled surprisingly rich.

He washed up and stood before the contraption. The onion was pierced onto three prongs. The pepper was wedged up against the corner walls. The paring knife worked for cleaving the onion into rings.

Old-school Bjork, from her days performing with the Sugarcubes, wailed from his speakers. "I hope you don't mind my playlist," she called over snarling vocals.

"Perfect if we're opening an underground 90s club." He looked over at her unique outfit and knocked back more of the bubbly. This could be their new life: sipping pre-dinner drinks, cooking together.

"Toss the veggies into the pan," she instructed.

She seasoned the vegetables while he stirred them.

They ate and cleaned dishes together. Orchid made him feel more at home in his own home. By himself, he never cooked. With her, the apartment was filled with obscure songs and the scent of sage.

After dinner, she joined him on the sofa and leaned her head against his shoulder. He paused typing his email on his Mac. She'd brought him a steaming cup of tea.

"I have early meetings. Would you like to go to bed soon?"

Orchid had freed her ponytail. Her slender figure leaned closer. His desire grew, and with it, fear.

"I have work to do. You go ahead to bed. I cleared out a whole dresser and the entire front closet here if you want to unpack," he said.

"I was kind of hoping for that massive walk-in," she joked.

"If you don't mind, just stick to out here. I should've told you. You can have the bathroom out here to yourself too."

"Oh," she said.

"I just thought it'd make it easier, to get ready and everything."

"Okay, sure. Did you want me to sleep out here? I shouldn't have assumed." Now, her expression deflated.

"No-no, unless of course if you want to. Go enjoy the big bed. I'll join you later." He kissed her, then got lost in her soft lips, fingers threaded through her hair.

Orchid extracted herself and moved some lacy things into the little bureau he'd pointed out. He glanced over his laptop screen as she filled his closet with long flowy dresses and satin skirts. She carted an oversized case of beauty products into the marble bathroom. He chuckled to himself. Maybe having their own closets and bathrooms was practical anyway, even if the primary reason was to delay witnessing her expression over his accessible bathroom and the wheelchair tucked in his closet.

An electric toothbrush hummed. Water splashed. He tried a sip of her brew. This Darjeeling wasn't too bad. Orchid emerged clean faced. Her lack of make-up wasn't what he noticed first. She was clothed in a silk camisole and boy shorts.

"Are those your pajamas?" He nearly spewed his tea.

"Yes, and don't look at me without makeup," she said, one hand over her eyes.

"Don't look at you? I'm a little too distracted by your getup to not look."

"Well then, you should come to bed. Screw work. Or screw ... something," she flirted, and twirled a lock of hair.

Phoenix flung his computer to the ground. He jumped up and took her in his arms. She laughed as he dipped her. He kissed her jawline, down her neck to the soft flesh below her collarbone. Her pulse quickened as he fingered her slender wrist. Orchid was delicate. She was strong. A paradox.

"I'm looking, and I like," he growled.

"Me too." Her touch roamed his back and edged down towards his waistline.

His imagination followed the path of her actions. Below his briefs, his thigh ended in a metal pole. She'd only seen his prosthesis once, during Easter weekend down the shore.

Phoenix righted Orchid and let her go. "Good night," he said. He wanted her. Having her here, fresh-faced, and ready for bed, made his desire surge. And his fear of rejection flare.

She held out a hand, beseeching him. "God, what's so important about your work? Are you writing a peace treaty?"

His teeth ground in frustration. He plucked his abandoned laptop from the ground.

Disappointed, she cast her eyes towards the overhead banner. "Good night," she said, emitting the words tinged with sadness towards the printed ones that had welcomed her.

Then he was alone.

When all had grown quiet, Phoenix turned off the floor lamp and stole into the bedroom. By the light from the window, he took in the image of her dark hair against his pillow, long lashes against her rounded cheeks, her soft breathing. Their first night together.

By then, his fear had subsided. She'd taken him by surprise was all. Of course, he'd thought about making love to Orchid. If their kisses were any indication, sex was going to be explosive. It wasn't just about physical pleasure. He wanted to make her happy in every way. Every day. For the first time, he thought of forever. Days rolling ahead of them, pleasant mornings over coffee, evenings debating news headlines. Tonight, he would shower, curl up to her warm back, and if she woke, maybe her bedtime offer would still stand.

He used the toilet and brushed his teeth. Then, seated on the closed lid, he plucked off his prosthesis and layers of socks until the air cooled the damp end of his leg. Orchid's sudden presence somehow breached the wall that separated them. He leaned over the counter to rinse the interior of his liner and pictured a ghostly Orchid, pale in her camisole, grimace over his nighttime routine.

Could he imagine divulging to Orchid that he avoided morning showers because the heat would cause his residual limb to swell, and he'd have a hard time fitting into his prosthesis? He doubted it.

He shed his clothes, hopped into the shower, and settled into the plastic bench with rubber feet. Naked, under the stream of water, Orchid's mirage leaned against the tile to await him. He soaped up and rinsed, the long-handled brush he used to extend his one-handed reach was unable to scrub away his feeling of vulnerability.

Good thing, with its hospital-grade grab bars, he'd kept her out of his bathroom.

Typically, he'd use his wheelchair at home. Tonight, his residual limb throbbed from the extra hours squeezed inside his prosthesis.

After he dried off from the shower, he strapped on a hands-free crutch, an ingenious device he could kneel on for support, and hobbled to bed. His prosthesis, clean socks, and liner were tucked under one arm, ready for the morning.

In the bedroom, he sat at the edge of the bed. His desire surged. He unstrapped his crutch and slipped under the cool sheets on his side of the bed.

She loved him. She'd said so. She'd invited him to bed. She wanted to sleep with him. He rolled towards her warmth and wrapped his arm around her shoulders, slung his thigh over hers.

Her breathing deepened. They were good together. This could work.

As he relaxed, the blunt end of his calf slipped between hers. She didn't wake, but her body jerked. This was the woman who'd nearly suffered a panic attack at the image of soldiers with injuries less severe than his, who couldn't view a cut on her foot, who was haunted by the image of her father's crushed body.

This Girl Scout might be the death of him.

CHAPTER 11

EVERY KISS YOU TAKE

Orchid

O rchid studied the contours of Phoenix's broad expanse
of chest rising and falling beneath the sheets. Pink sunshine peeked around the edges of his window shade.
His room was outfitted in white with blocks of cerulean, as if his
blue irises were embedded in every throw pillow and armchair.
She slipped out to the bathroom attached to the main living
area. Her intention was to brush her teeth and then return to
wake him with kisses along one strong shoulder. By the time
she'd re-entered the bedroom, the bed was empty. Running water pattered in his bathroom. Maybe she could surprise him. She
wandered over. One hand palmed the crystal knob, weighing
whether to disturb his privacy. The droplets drummed. *He loves*
you. He loves you not.

Too risky. She backed away and showered in the guest bath that
he'd indicated was hers.

No matter his welcome signs, she'd forever be a guest here. The
feeling transported her to a time when she'd no longer had family,
and only survived through the charity of others. Her antidote to
self-pity was to take charge. She donned sleek pants, stiletto heeled

boots, and an oversized blazer layered with thick ropes of gold. Today, she embodied Chanel meets Jay-Z.

Phoenix stalled when he spotted Orchid in their living room.

"You're gorgeous," he blurted.

She eyed his slack-jawed appreciation from beneath a spiked bun atop her head.

"You're not so bad yourself," she replied.

Together, they exited the building and walked towards his driver. She joined him in the back seat and tossed her gym bag onto the car floor. "I'm heading to dance class after work, so you don't have to wait for me," she said.

"I've always wanted to try that gym. Maybe I can buy a guest pass and meet you there after your class."

"That'd be really nice," she said, and clasped his hand in hers.

Hers was the first stop. She unbuckled and leaned towards Phoenix. He cupped her chin and swept a thumb along her jawline. "See you tonight," he said.

Orchid pressed her lips to the corner of his mouth. He hadn't shaved. He was a deity in human form, masculinity manifested.

"Bye, boo," she said, and slipped out with her bags before she was tempted to disrobe and spend forever in the backseat of the sedan with him.

That evening, Orchid threw her feelings into her Latin dance class. She stomped and twirled, every turn seeming to represent the enigma of her relationship with Phoenix. No one else had ever been this thoughtful towards her while also abandoning her. Now they were together.

Her friend Violet moved in time to the beat beside her, her lavender hair bopping to the music.

At the end of the hour-long session, Orchid turned to ask Violet about a rumor she'd heard about their old work nemesis Princeton. Violet didn't give her a chance to speak.

"Oh my god, it's that hot agency guy we met last year!" she scream-whispered into her ear. Her friend stared over Orchid's shoulder.

Orchid glanced over and played along. "No. You mean Phoenix Walker?"

"He is such a hottie," her friend breathed.

"Yeah, I've been meaning to tell you something," she said, suddenly swept up in memories over the months she'd longed for Phoenix and was crushed by his silence. Maybe that's why she hadn't divulged the relationship to Violet at the office. Her chest swelled with joy. Now, he was hers.

He strode towards them, his easy stride a distraction from the asymmetry of his left arm tucked inside a rolled-up sleeve.

"Ack, he's heading this way!" Violet yelped.

"Watch me seduce him," Orchid said, suddenly tickled by an idea.

"No way," Violet breathed.

Orchid turned to see Phoenix approaching. His muscles stretched against a workout jacket. His long legs were clothed in track pants. Wet hair dripped into his eyes, reminding her of their first trip to the shore house. Her diaphragm expanded with pride as his face brightened. He dropped his bag next to hers. She took a step towards him and tiptoed up into his arms. "Hey, boo," she said, her endearment cut short by his lips on hers. He smelled freshly showered, like the scent of soap and spice. She lost herself in his arms, and almost forgot where she was.

Violet's cry broke her reverie. "Holy freakin' cow!"

Orchid turned to see her friend training her phone on them.

"Phoenix, do you remember Violet? Violet, this is Phoenix," she said.

He loosened their embrace to stick out his hand. "Hey," he said.

Blubbering nonsense, Violet fell apart in front of them. "Oh. Hi. Yes, I know. We met, like last year. You? I remember. Um, yeah."

Orchid held onto his hand and didn't let go.

"Is the car here?" Orchid asked, to save Phoenix.

"Probably. Nice to see you," Phoenix said.

He extracted his grasp, then snagged both their bags. Violet's eyes bulged. Phoenix swung them towards the exit, gym bags slung over one shoulder.

"Bye, Violet," Orchid called.

In the car, Orchid nearly collapsed in the back seat with laughter.

"Is she normally able to speak?" Phoenix asked, as he belted them both in.

"Did you see the way she looked?" Orchid delighted at the memory.

"Has she never seen two people kiss?" he asked, somewhat confused.

"Clearly, she has never seen a god kiss a mere mortal," Orchid explained.

"You're more like a goddess than a god," he corrected.

"No, I'm the mere mortal, obviously," Orchid said, laughing.

He looked down at himself. "I'm not sure about that."

Orchid instantly sobered up. She understood in that moment, with magnified clarity, that Phoenix had not healed from his accident. His bones and muscles were sealed behind taut skin. However, his fractured self-image scattered across a carnival mirror.

After dinner, Orchid emerged damp from the shower, a towel wrapped around her torso, to find Phoenix typing on his laptop.

"Hey, no more work," she said, and took his palm in hers. His gaze traveled up. As it swept over her bare clavicle, his jaw unhinged. She closed his laptop and abandoned it on the sofa.

"C'mere," she said. He let her lead him to the bedroom, dimly lit by one bedside lamp.

Against the depth of his insecurity, she was a neophyte with nothing but her ingenuity to sway him. *Why the hell not?* She was a copywriter, a marketer, an innovator.

Orchid pointed at a blemish on her forearm. "You see this? That's from scratching chicken pox when I was supposed to use Calamine." She slid his athletic jacket over his shoulders to reveal his white tee. The slick fabric tumbled to the ground.

She turned her left palm over to show the pale marks across her fingers. "This? This was when a boy stepped on my hand in grade school to show he liked me." Phoenix raised his arms to allow Orchid to lift his t-shirt over his head and toss it onto his dresser.

She turned one leg to reveal a jagged line up one calf. "Aggressive shaving incident when I was a teen," she laughed.

Phoenix blocked her motion when she reached for his waistband. "This is not the same," he growled.

She looked up into azure irises that had darkened with pain. "It's not anywhere near the same," she agreed.

Orchid nuzzled his shoulder then rained kisses over its broad expanse, down his muscular bicep, below the elbow to the spot where his forearm ended.

As she neared the spot where the train had forever changed him, a tremor exposed his fear.

She met his eyes, silently asking him to believe her. The accident hadn't rendered him anything less than whole. The question was, could she convince him?

Her voice emerged husky, one word for every kiss she impressed into the tender skin at the end of his arm. "Phoenix. John. Walker. I. Love. Everything. About. You."

He stood frozen, staring unseeing at the pale wood floor. The furrow between his eyebrows deepened as she caressed the blunt end of his forearm.

Fear gripped her. She'd been all wrong. Misjudged what to say and do. She'd squandered the trust they had built. He would shut down and never let her in again. What now?

Then he wrapped his arms around her and rested his cheek against her hair. She squeezed him close as he released a quiet shudder.

For some time, they stayed like that, the beating of his heart against her ear.

"Thank you, Orchid Kai Lan." He pulled back so he could see her.

She waited for some monumental pronouncement.

Then, he said, "I'm going to brush my teeth."

She filled with a sense of accomplishment. Not everything had to be difficult. Intimacy could wait. Their care ran deeper than a physical connection. Instead, he'd absorbed something more valuable: her unconditional acceptance. Orchid pranced towards her sink, for once unencumbered by any worry at all.

CHAPTER 12

PHOTOGRAPHIC EVIDENCE

Orchid

Saturday arrived.

Orchid woke before Phoenix. The thrill of her good fortune hit her all over again. Phoenix had orchestrated his flight to match hers. Today, they'd attend a goodbye party with his family. This Easter, his Aunt Betsy had served her watercress soup in a vegetable base and Uncle George had advised her on her career choice. That was after his intimidating mother had accused her of hurting her son.

Phoenix stirred. She studied his peaceful features in repose, a faint furrow between his eyebrows, one arm flung overhead.

"Hi, handsome." She leaned over for a kiss.

He opened his eyes and rolled towards her. "Every day. Forever," he reminded her.

"Not if your family kills me tonight."

"You're going to be fine. Do you want to come with me for my hair cut and errands?" he offered.

She ruffled his mussed hair. She preferred his disheveled look to a barber-neatened corporate Phoenix.

"That's okay. I'll just fret here on my own. Plus, it's raining."

He kissed her cheek, then pushed up to a sitting position. He perched on the edge of the bed with his back turned to her.

She propped onto an elbow to take in his beauty, still shrouded with enigma. Their relationship could last a day, or eternity. He leaned over his left leg and began the one-handed process of rolling a silicone liner over his calf and knee. Some days, as he dressed in a killer outfit for work, she forgot about his accident. Then, an everyday activity would jar her back to reality. He didn't complain about his sacrifice for saving a life. Sadly, it seemed bottled up for him to bear alone.

Now, his grasp crossed over to roll a clean sock over his liner. She must be able to ease some burden for this magnanimous lion heart.

"I'm antsy for the party. Give me something to do. You want me to help with packing while you're out?"

He paused his struggle with the bunched fabric to glance at her. Would she ever be able to look at him and not be reminded of what he'd lost? "There's some stuff in my drawers that can go in a suitcase. But most of the rest, I'll need to go through myself. Thanks, though. How about you? You need anything from the store?"

"No thanks."

Phoenix finished stretching the elastic, inserted his leg into his prosthesis and stood his full six feet. Gorgeous, even though some days, he didn't seem to realize it. He moved with grace to his bathroom and shut the door. She heard the click of the handle and knew after these days together, the lock was a barrier against her entry. She sensed there were parts within him that weren't yet healed. His generosity when they'd first met had begun her own healing journey from PTSD. Could she help him do the same?

By the time Phoenix left, they'd eaten and cleaned up their breakfast dishes.

Rain spattered against their apartment windows. The outside world held an unknown future. Orchid looked around the space that had transformed into home, a place of solace and love. The thought of leaving left her oddly melancholy. Adventure awaited them. Yet, their everyday routine, commuting to work, the gym, and home, had become a comfort.

She stood on a chair and removed the banner that had first welcomed her. He had generously included her in everything. *Welcome home. To our apartment. Our driver.* Yet she sensed that he had walled off a part of him that he'd never willingly share.

Orchid wandered into the bedroom and neatened their mussed comforter.

His suitcase lay open, half filled with workout gear and work slacks. She opened his drawers and added stacks of t-shirts and shorts to the piles. His armoire had already been emptied. She sat on the edge of the bed, nothing left to do except ruminate about tonight's get-together. Hair and nail appointments had been completed the day before. Her outfit choices were down to two.

She stared at the six-paneled door leading to the en suite bathroom. It's just a restroom. He'd never said not to go in there. She'd been meaning to ask if he had rubbing alcohol to clean her earring posts. Surely, he wouldn't mind. *Make yourself at home,* he'd said.

Nope. He didn't deserve for her to betray his trust. The locked door every morning signaled a private space. She'd respect whatever secret he held.

Instead, she meandered over to the closet that she'd remembered for its spaciousness and lined shelves. The knob turned easily. Trepidation caused her to pause. *Your closet and bathroom are out here,* he'd said that first day. Those words had reminded her of being a burden after her parents had died. Distractedly, she yanked open the handle.

The closet yawned wider than the narrow space that had been her childhood bedroom. A window at the far side shone gray with rain. Her last time here, she'd been awed by the neat shelves, suits arranged by hue, and rows of shoes. Those still lined this space. Now, a new item shouted from center stage.

A red leather and gleaming chrome wheelchair squatted against the window. Through her research on combat-wounded veterans, she knew of the ingenuity of manual chairs, power chairs, and all types of customizations. This medical equipment didn't seem like something he relied upon.

The oversized wheels and permanently seated position didn't square with the handsome, capable entrepreneur who owned her heart. She imagined it was left over from his hospital days. Did he use his chair? She tried to picture the top of his head not even reaching her chest height, half a leg hanging over the edge of the seat, wheeling forward with one hand. The image contradicted her daily experience with him.

Orchid shook her head. This was wrong. She'd crept into his private space. She shouldn't even mention it to Phoenix. As she turned to leave, a slender volume on a shelf caught her eye. The front cover featured what appeared to be medical staff in blue scrubs. Without pausing to ponder the consequences, she reached out and flipped open the little book.

The first page showed Phoenix hunched in a wheelchair, the ends of his leg and arm swollen with bandages. *Oh god.* Images from after his accident. The missing parts of his history he'd never shared with her. At one point, his chair *had* been a part of his life. Of course, it had. He didn't just look in pain, his flat disposition looked dead inside. His despair, evident even in a photo, frightened her.

She leafed further, eager to move past the sadness she could feel burbling up. There must be happier moments captured. In another photo, Dex and Fiona smiled for the camera, seemingly oblivious to a miserable Phoenix, scrunched in his chair, jawline overgrown with facial hair.

There he was with Liv and Tish. The tension in his posture hurt her chest. Was he in physical pain? His injuries were jarring, and his tortured expression more so.

Mixed between were pictures of smiling staff, and the old Phoenix she knew, joshing with them. Of all of them, one physical therapy photo tightened her throat the most. A stunningly handsome Phoenix heaved himself up onto parallel bars, only one hand and an elbow to steady his uneven gait, a bulky flesh-colored prosthesis propping one side. Sweat formed on his forehead. His mouth twisted behind its bravado.

Feelings swirled, then sank like lead. It was worse than she'd thought. This was what he'd protected her from. *Maybe he was right to do so?*

She'd been furious that he hid his accident from her. Deeper than she'd ever felt, she could relate to why he would do so. Her perspective shifted.

It didn't necessarily mean that he didn't trust her.

Maybe he didn't trust himself to be good enough for her.

But of course, he was. She needed to find a way to show him.

Staff had scribbled well wishes on the last pages. Orchid glanced at the inscriptions, hoping the upbeat sentiments would lift her mood. "Hope you don't mind we took photos to remind you how far you've come!" a woman named Nadine wrote "I never saw someone work so hard. Keep up the good work!"

A confident block print read "In case the carrier pigeons are out, reach out anytime 988lifeline.org." What medical workers have their own website? Was it standard procedure for them to give it to discharged patients?

Orchid hadn't previously tried to imagine the immediate aftermath of the accident. Which hospital had they taken him to? Was he alone when he woke? She'd begrudged the impact on her. What about *him*? Tears tightened behind her eyes.

This little album was her one link to this trauma in Phoenix's life. Just in case, she tapped her phone and entered a new contact listed under "Carrier Pigeon."

Then on a whim, she pasted the URL 988lifeline.org into her browser bar. Two-hundred and ninety-two thousand results were returned in 0.34 seconds.

Oh. No. No, no, no. God. Please. NO.

Google screamed in oversized font: SUICIDE AND CRISIS LIFELINE.

The deadbolt clicked open. She heard Phoenix deposit his keys onto the semicircle table at the front door. No time to process what finding this meant. Orchid closed the book.

What *did* it mean? He was *that* close, you idiot. You almost lost him, and not just him abandoning you but—

"You think I'm strong but that accident messed with my head. I don't know if I can make it through another loss."

Orchid wiped her eyes and slipped out to see him.

Each step jarred her brain. Never her, never her, never her. She refused to add to Phoenix's burden. Ever.

He stood in the entryway juggling his phone and a bag tucked under one elbow, looking gorgeous in the chambray blue shirt that complemented his eyes. She saw his difficulty while he fumbled with his packages. His eyelashes lifted and followed her sight line down his left sleeve. Realizing the focus of her scrutiny, his mouth downturned almost imperceptibly, in a hairline frown. She'd seen that expression before. He'd detected her assessment and judged himself lacking. Score, minus one. *How many of these judgments did he endure a day? How many by her inadvertent doing?* He was misjudging the way she saw him. Words seemed inadequate to correct this misperception.

Orchid joined Phoenix and flung her arms around him. "You're here!"

He struggled to hold onto his purchases and began laughing. "This is some reception. Do I need to go out more often?"

"Missed you," she said, her words muffled by her lips pressed against his cotton shirt.

"I am heading out every two hours just for this."

"Okay," she promised. She relieved him of his bags and pulled him into their apartment.

"No peeking," he said.

She deposited his purchases on his sofa and studied his haircut. A few silver hairs shone through, yet the shorn sides made him look boyish.

"You approve?" he asked.

"Always," she said.

"I'm going to go shower. We're leaving in what, an hour?"

"Really? I need to get ready too. We could shower together."

He regarded her, desire battling some other emotion.

"Just to save water, you know," she said, trying to muffle the rejection she could feel coming.

"Not today," he said.

She let go of his hand and watched him disappear into their bedroom. *Let's take our time*, he'd said. Want tightened deep in her belly. For no one but this man.

After bathing, Orchid donned an iridescent minidress and boots, girding herself for the lion's den.

Phoenix ambled out to the living room, rocking a blue velvet jacket over a crisp white shirt and dark slacks. He took one look at her loose locks and punk-edged outfit and stopped in his tracks.

"I just fell in love with you all over again," he said.

She took his proffered hand. "Me too," she said.

His aunt and uncle's building whispered wealth. Orchid's heels sunk into the plush carpet. An elevator attendant chose their floor and swung closed the old-fashioned wrought-iron door for them.

"Should I have worn pearls?" she asked in the lift.

"You hate pearls," he reminded her. He noticed every detail of her tastes.

Uncle George answered the door himself. The staff must be busy in the kitchen.

"There's the international couple," he shouted.

Orchid held out her hand in greeting. He took it and pulled her into an embrace. "Thanks for making our boy happy," he said. Then he slapped Phoenix on the back. "Come join the kids in the parlor," he invited them.

George led them to a room bedecked in dark wood and rich fabrics. Harry and Stew waved from their seats around an intense game of chess. A pretty redhead jumped up when they entered. "Thank gawd you're here!" she declared.

"Lucy, how are you?" Orchid greeted Harry's girlfriend whom she'd befriended at the family's shore house.

"Better now. I knew these guys would be no fun until you arrived," she said.

The petite spitfire turned to Phoenix, hands on hips. "I hope you thanked your lucky stars for her. I hope you apologized like a thousand times. Twice over."

"I'm working on it," he said, and pulled Orchid closer to his side. At the front door, he'd encircled his arm around her waist. She recognized the tactic from Tish's wedding. For anyone facing them straight on, his loss wouldn't be evident. *Oh Phoenix, even with family?*

Aunt Betsy toddled into the room bearing a platter. "Hello, dears!" she cried and placed the canapes onto a side table.

She took Orchid's hand in both of her own. "We're so happy for you two, dear."

Phoenix leaned down to kiss her cheek. She pulled back and looked him up and down. "It's been too long. You shouldn't be such a stranger!"

"Well, there you are," came a proper voice from behind them.

Orchid rotated towards the doorway with trepidation. His mother's words from the shore house rang in her mind. *"If you hurt him, I will find you wherever you are and I ... will ... kill ... you ... with ... my ... own ... hands."* It had only been a handful of weeks since he'd rejected her at his family's Easter weekend. What did his mother make of their relationship? Maybe she wasn't expecting this reversal of fortune to last.

Betsy turned towards her sister. "Aren't they cute together?"

"Cute," Veronica answered without conviction.

"Hi, Mom," he said, and leaned down to kiss her cheek.

"How are you?" she asked and scanned him from top to bottom.

"I'm great, Mom. Never been happier, really. You remember Orchid, right?"

"Couldn't forget." Veronica swiveled away from her son to extend a hand towards his girlfriend.

The chill from her skin, as if she'd just emerged from an over air-conditioned space, traveled up Orchid's arm. "Are you cold, Mrs. Walker?" she gasped.

"Most people find me quite warm," she said.

Orchid tried to clarify but she'd already turned away to ask Phoenix another question.

Her track record with Veronica wasn't looking good.

George emerged, toting tumblers of ice and a pale golden liquid. "Chivas, or would you like something else?" he offered.

Orchid didn't often drink scotch but tonight, she was willing to settle for anything. "Thank you," she said, accepting the glass and sucking down half the liquor in one gulp.

Betsy left and returned with another platter. She offered it to Veronica, then Orchid. "All vegetarian," she said proudly.

"Oh, that's thoughtful," Orchid said.

"Phoenix told us that's what he wanted."

She looked up at the pleasure on his face. "Thank you," she said.

"We're trying to eat more plant-based anyway. It's better for the environment. Have a seat," Betsy offered.

She and Phoenix shared, quite appropriately, a love seat. Betsy grilled them about where they'd be living, what they were excited about, and practiced her limited Chinese.

"*Ni hao ma*," she said, attempting a school-taught phrase for "how are you?" that Chinese citizens barely used.

While Betsy charmed, Veronica was unsettlingly quiet.

At one point, during noisy conversations crossing over each other, Orchid leaned towards Phoenix. "Your mom might like some time with you alone," she said. He nodded.

She stood and stretched. "Betsy, I'd love to freshen up."

Phoenix's aunt showed her to a powder room down the hall. There, Orchid reapplied her lip gloss with a wand from her evening clutch. When she rejoined the group, Caleb had arrived. He towered over the chess game, which had amplified in intensity. Phoenix and Veronica shared the sofa, amiably chatting. His mom spotted Orchid's approach and let go of Phoenix's arm, intending to give her seat back.

"You stay," Orchid insisted.

Orchid walked over to the trio by the window. "Who's winning?" she asked.

"I am. I've taken more pieces," Stew said.

"Quality over quantity. I have your queen," Harry rebutted.

Orchid laughed at the brotherly competition. She turned towards Phoenix's taciturn twin, as he slurped from a can of beer. "How are you?" she asked.

He shrugged. "So-so. You?"

"Same," she said.

He turned to her. "How come? You got your guy. You're going to China."

This was the brother who had helped them reunite when no one else had even trusted her intentions. She aimed for honesty. "Now that we've spent all this time together these last few weeks, I'm realizing how much the accident has impacted almost everything in his life."

"News flash?"

"Not just physically."

"I warned you he's not the easiest person to live with."

Orchid bit her lip, weighing how much to divulge. She turned to him again. "Can I ask you something?"

Again, the enigmatic shrug.

"I haven't told Phoenix, but I found a photo album of his. From after his accident."

Recognition flickered across Caleb's eyes. "Yeah, from the nurses, right?"

"And his therapists."

"That was a rough time. He didn't want the album. I'd be surprised if he ever even looked at it. They said something about it being good for him to see how quickly he'd gotten better."

"It was upsetting to see."

He rolled his eyes. "It was worse in person." Anguish darkened his face. Caleb glanced over at his mom and brother on the sofa.

"There's more."

Caleb chugged some of his brew.

She decided to trust him. Who else could she ask? "The nurses and everyone had signed his book."

"Yeah?" he asked and wiped his mouth with the back of one hand.

The truth came out in a whispered hush. "One of them gave him the phone number for a suicide hotline."

Caleb froze, his complexion darkening, which confirmed her worst fears.

"What happened, Caleb? Please."

"You gotta understand. It was a bad time. Real bad," he said. "If he spirals, thinks he's not worthy, that's when he hits rock bottom. After he gave you up, he seemed to think he had nothing to live for.

He lost hope. He locked himself in the bathroom and tried to ..."
Caleb's voice faded. He made a slicing motion across his arm.

"Oh no," she said, her eyes filling.

Losing her had made him give up hope. Her responsibility. No wonder Veronica wasn't a fan of hers.

"What do I do, Caleb? I saw him once with phantom pain. I was afraid to leave his side. What do I do if he goes to a dark place when we're in China?"

"I took him to Walter Reed Medical Center. To meet soldiers who were blown up worse than him but dealin' with it."

"Did that work?"

Caleb nodded. "This guy Aaron lost three limbs in Iraq. They went rock climbing."

"Rock climbing!"

"I know. That dude Aaron's more buff than all of us put together."

"You're a good brother."

"But really Sascha saved him."

"Your ex?"

He nodded. "She snuck him out of rehab. Showed there was still life."

"Where'd they go?"

"A club. For live music. You know Rockwood Music Hall?"

Ding, ding, ding. Alarms sounded. "Where he met Ana?"

"Who's Ana?"

"His waitress?"

"I don't know about that. Sascha makes everything fun. She got him to laugh. He ate for the first time in a day."

"Is Sascha punk?" Orchid asked, remembering Ana's conversation with Phoenix from the diner.

A smile spread over Caleb's face over some memory. "That's one way to put it. She's gotta pretty out-there style." He eyed her vegan leather. "You guys might hit it off."

Orchid listened as he described Sascha. According to him, his ex-girlfriend was sexy, and compassionate, with a wicked sense of humor. Orchid recognized that look. He was in love with her. As she listened to Caleb, a realization ballooned that she'd be Phoenix's sole lifeline in a distant country. Surely, she could be as enterprising as Sascha if it came to saving Phoenix.

CHAPTER 13

I NEED A HERO

Roy

EIGHT MONTHS AGO

Roy threw himself into the hunt for the runaway teen. The search filled his days with a sense of purpose. Every week, he scoured one of the five boroughs, questioning those he knew in the unhoused community. He showed the boy's photo to umpteen strangers, but each was a dead end.

Weeks dragged into what felt like a hopeless forever, and probably even longer for the boy's parents, until one day, a longtime pal up in Harlem pinched the worn paper towards her nose. "Yah. I seen him."

Roy bounced onto his toes.

"Real newbie," his friend said, and gestured towards the afternoon sun. "Yah know the Third Avenue bridge?"

Roy thanked her and hurried towards the direction she'd indicated.

There he spotted a youngster looking around. He approached him carefully, not to spook him. His clothes were stiff with dirt and his hair greasy, but the freckles across his nose and the ears that stuck out, marked him as the lost boy.

He didn't go directly towards the boy but rather sidled over. He leaned against the dirty stone surface of the bridge and fingered the cloth flower in his pocket. Inside his pocket, he also discovered miniature chocolates he'd scored the day before. He opened one and took a bite. Once he figured the sweet scent had reached the boy, he extended a second brown-wrapped bar towards him. "They handed out extra candies at the shelter. You look like you could use one," he said.

Like a skittish stray, the boy stared at the offering before accepting it.

"You know your mom's looking for you?" Roy asked, keeping his tone casual.

The boy was startled. His muscles tensed in what Roy assumed was a fight-or-flight response. Roy studied the exhaust soot that marked the underpass, acting disinterested.

"It doesn't have to be like this, you know. Begging. Eating scraps." Ironic, to be touting the opposite of what Roy had spent years doing. He remembered the boy's mother's frantic expression, and it bolstered his intentions.

"Did she send you?" the boy asked, his voice tremulous.

He showed the teen the flyer. "Only someone who loves you would make this, would come to the city, and ask people to find you."

The kid's eyes filled, making him look even younger than his teen years. He rubbed his nose to hide his emotion. "Okay, but someone stole my phone."

Of course, they did.

"Do you want to call her?" Roy offered.

The scrawny kid nodded. Roy swaggered over to a group of men. He explained their dilemma, borrowed a mobile device, dialed the number from the flyer, and handed it to the boy.

"Hey, mom."

Roy could hear the mom's shrill voice filled with joy. "Oh my god, where are you?"

The boy said something then handed the phone to Roy. Roy explained where they were and directed her to meet at a nearby diner. Roy returned the phone and walked with the boy to the restaurant. Inside, the two sank into a booth and ordered coffee, probably the boy's first cup ever. In less than an hour, Roy recognized the woman he'd met at the shelter. She strode beside a man, tall and balding.

Roy encouraged the boy to accompany him to the door. Before they could reach it, his mom had flung it open and rushed inside.

"Are you okay?" she asked, both arms around her son.

"Mmhmm," the boy mumbled as his arms found his way around his mother and his dad encircled his family until the three tottered like a bear act in a big top circus.

"I'm sorry. I was so scared. And then I lost my phone," the kid said, sounding younger than his years.

"It's alright. It's okay now," his mom said.

The father pulled back then nodded at Roy. "You did good." He reached into his pocket and retrieved a checkbook. "Can I donate to your shelter? Or do you want me to mail it in?"

"Uh. Oh. That's nice. Sure."

He scribbled a sum onto the paper and tore along the perforation with a flourish. "We can't thank you enough."

Roy watched them head to the booth where the boy's coffee had grown cold, arms around each other, laughing and crying. The numerals on the rectangular check contained more zeroes than he'd ever seen.

He left with a lightness in his chest. Roy had no one. No mom, no dad, no son. No one in the world would light with that amount of joy upon seeing *him*, yet his selfless act had brought a family together.

CHAPTER 14

THIRTY GRADE

Orchid

"A few more days in the US. Anything you want to do?" Phoenix asked. She watched him deftly dice zucchini, prongs holding the gourd while he rocked the knife through its green flesh. It reminded Orchid of her parents making vegetable omelets, working side-by-side in the kitchen. She smiled, realizing they'd recreated that intimate moment right here in his apartment.

"You're getting good with that board."

"Thanks."

"Weirdly, I feel like visiting my childhood house," she said.

He placed the rocker knife on the cutting board to look at her. "Not weird at all. Big moves can make anyone nostalgic. You want to go together? We can drive out this weekend."

She relinquished her spatula and folded her arms around his waist. "Together sounds perfect."

He returned her embrace and kissed her cheek. "Then, together it is."

Two days later, they crossed the George Washington Bridge into New Jersey. They sped along Route 80 Westbound, old-school Love & Rockets blaring on Phoenix's car speakers. He knew her musical taste, taste that had been shaped by her millennial parents. She could still hold onto this part of them.

As they entered the town in Hudson County that had been nicknamed Monster Hills, Orchid studied the brick and clapboard houses. "They're smaller than I remember," she said.

"When was the last time you came back?"

"Not since I was a kid."

"Really? I'm honored to be the one to go with you."

"No one else I'd rather go with," she said lightly.

He turned to glance at her, fingers releasing and then regripping the steering wheel. He'd explained that his car didn't need any special adaptations; since his losses were on his left side, he could drive any automatic transmission vehicle.

"Slow down. Turn here," she said, pointing.

They nosed into the entrance of the steep driveway and stopped. The car grill pointed down, aimed for a grove of ancient trees.

"Let's walk from here," she said, and emerged from the passenger door, her mind superimposing the scene with sepia-hued memories of the past. Legs pumping on her swing set, bouncing a ball on the porch, running into the woods with shame after a particularly bad haircut. Her sneakers skidded along the angled blacktop, the pebbles reminding her of the present moment. She held onto the car as she circled to Phoenix's side.

"This place is full of ghosts," she said.

He offered his left elbow for support and helped her further down the slope. "Is it?"

"They repainted the place."

Phoenix shielded his eyes with his hand, eying the thick coppice of trees ahead. "It's really a big drop."

"It's steeper than I remember," she said.

As they drew closer, the big oak at the bottom of the hairpin turn looked like it had taken a punch to its gut. Her vision clouded as she took in the scabbed-over scars. She wished she'd brought a bouquet of peonies to mark the spot. They stopped a few feet in front of the trunk. "This is the place. Where they ... crashed. Where I found them. Where the ambulance came." She sucked air deep into her lungs, counting each beat like the soldier from their ads, Tammy, had taught her. *One two three four.*

His arm encircled her. "You, okay?"

"It's good that you're here. Because ..." The air wasn't working. She was twelve again. *The smell of gas. Her father slumped.* "Because it was me. They came home for me. I didn't ..."

He rotated before her and enveloped her in both arms. Her cheek nesting against his chest blocked her view. "Shh," he said, his voice comforting, his scent bringing her back bit by bit.

She exhaled one two three four. He leaned back a few inches to look into her eyes.

"It's not your fault. Check out the angle of the driveway. Do you think a handful of salt would've made a difference in a snowstorm?"

The blacktop under their feet crumbled. They could barely keep upright on a dry day on foot. "Doesn't seem like it, does it?"

"It wouldn't take a scientist to see that a speeding car on an icy day would have no chance."

Gravel slipped beneath their footing. *The car's brakes keened and wailed. Then...an exploding crunch. Impact reverberated through the trees.* "As a kid, I didn't appreciate what it'd be like to drive down this." She glared down the narrow roadway twisting through wood thickets, leading to a small house far below their current elevation. Toxicology reports found alcohol and THC in her dad's bloodstream; her parents weren't wearing seat belts.

"Do you want to knock and see if anyone's home?"

A long-forgotten smell reached her. She gagged as oil and gas and brake fluid stung her nose. "That's okay. I think I've seen what I wanted to see."

Tree branches rustled in the wind, murmuring sympathy.

She turned to climb back up to the car. Phoenix helped her into the passenger seat and shut her door before taking his spot in the driver's side.

"Is there anywhere else you want to go?"

His clean scent and the scruff of his beard brought her back to the present. *It's sad but try not to have the accident cloud every memory of your parents,* her dad's brother had advised. Wise.

She leaned over and kissed him. "I want to show you where we used to get ice cream," she said.

He grinned. "Deal."

CHAPTER 15

I DON'T NEED A HERO

Phoenix

C owardice, pure cowardice.

Phoenix had waited until the day of their flight to spring it on Orchid.

They sat on her little settee, the most feminine thing in his whole apartment, awaiting their car service.

Everything he'd need for the next six months was packed in two suitcases at the door. Her three dwarfed his.

"There's one more thing I'm bringing. Let me grab it." He tried to sound casual as he entered their bedroom. Inside his walk-in, he paused at the sight of his wheelchair. During the weeks that she'd stayed at the apartment, he'd abandoned his habit of removing his prosthesis and using the chair at home. As a result, his residual limb had been extra sore, but he assumed there'd be a temporary adjustment period.

She'd respected his privacy. He gave her credit for picking up on his unspoken boundaries. She hadn't pressed the issue of not using his bathroom or closet. She'd even been patient with his deflection of her advances. God knew he wanted to give in to her seductive curves. "People used to wait until marriage," he argued. "Bring on the wedding," she'd replied.

Now, he pushed the beast out to the living room, breath shallow with anxiety. Could the sight of this send her into a flashback? These past weeks, he'd been impressed with her seeming equanimity. She'd rarely flinched at his injuries or when he donned his prosthesis. Before his accident, he'd seen her panic over the image of blood, and injured soldiers.

He edged into her view, pushing the hulking mass out into the open. She stared at him over her phone. Her mouth fell open. *Uh-oh.*

Phoenix launched into his distraction tactic. "I bought a little something for us. I found these the day of my haircut." He lifted a trio of nylon strips off the red seat.

"Oh yeah?" She stood to join him. No screams yet.

He led them to their suitcases. "They're luggage straps, to piggyback the bags together."

He offered her a pair, then attached one to his. He demonstrated, spinning his attached cases with one hand.

"That's brilliant," she exclaimed, and busied herself buckling her matching pieces together.

Orchid pushed her two hundred pounds of clothing and beauty supplies with glee. Now came the hard part.

He sauntered over to the abandoned chair. "I figured I'd bring this, just in case."

She paused twirling her bags. He braced himself for screams past the level that even dogs could hear. He never wanted to be the trigger for that. His throat thickened, waiting for her fear.

"Red like a race car," she said. She returned to rotating her bags, shoving them this way and that.

He wheeled the empty chair over to the entryway. Orchid kept impressing him. Maybe this could work.

"Look, I can even take that with my bags!" She pushed the handle of the chair while dragging her bags behind her. He didn't think he'd ever see this sight, her exuberance while handling his mobility equipment.

An insight struck him. Trepidation over her reaction didn't reflect some weakness in Orchid. His fear was rooted in his own ambivalence.

His chair didn't always arouse shame. During the early period in rehab, it'd been his only means of mobility. At home, he was grateful for the chair's ease and convenience. Only once he'd begun wheeling out in public, he detected the subtle judgments. An averted gaze. Seated, his view landed waist-high, below the level conducive to conversations. He didn't feel as obvious with his cane. And now, he didn't even need that.

Their phones buzzed, announcing the arrival of their car.

Orchid plunked a kiss on his cheek. "Our adventure begins."

Her mood buoyed him. "So, it does."

They breezed down the corridor with their bags. The blemishes on the walls no longer felt like an analogy to his shortcomings. They were simply maintenance work, which management needed to take care of, along with a list of the building's needs.

While waiting for the lift, Orchid threw her arms around him. This time, the knapsack strapped over her shoulders didn't feel like his failure.

Mrs. V and Elton approached and stepped onto the elevator with them. "Good morning," she said. She waved the dog's miniature paw.

"Hello," Phoenix said.

"You're leaving today?"

Phoenix nodded.

"When is Rina Dubrovnik moving in?"

Phoenix remembered too late that he'd never finished the discussion with Orchid about Rina's sublet arrangements. "Um, I think next week."

"The board thinks she looks like a fine professional."

"Thank you for supporting her application."

Orchid's mouth dropped open, then her glare swiveled to lob grenades at him. She appeared to be materializing brass knuckles in her imagination and scheming when to pummel him. *Uh-oh.*

They'd gotten busy with travel arrangements and the goodbye party. He'd forgotten to bring it up again.

The elevator doors slid open.

"Maybe you can suggest the board consider installing a ramp out front. To make the building ADA-compliant," Orchid said. She was thoughtful, looking out for him.

"Um, maybe I will," Mrs. V replied. Her view scanned down his body.

She stepped off with a wave of Elton's paw.

The doorman helped wheel Orchid's luggage to the waiting car. He slapped Phoenix on the back and high-fived Orchid goodbye. These last weeks, she'd wormed her way into the building staff's good graces. Sometimes when they headed out, they treated her like royalty.

"Oh man, I'm gonna miss you guys," the doorman said out on the sidewalk where they'd gathered.

Phoenix handed him an envelope containing a generous tip. "Please be good to the person who'll be staying at my place. She's a friend. You'll like her," he said, though that prediction stretched the truth. With Rina's direct manner, she liked to joke that the odds of people liking her were 50/50.

"Take care of yourself," he told his doorman. He'd miss this place. He'd miss New York.

Phoenix joined Orchid in the back seat of the sedan. The car pulled into traffic, and the privacy glass closed.

"I wasn't trying to keep a secret from you," he said.

Orchid turned towards him, agitated. "Before I jump to any rash conclusions, is Rina Dubrovnik your ex-girlfriend Rina? The Rina who you dated last fall when you said you couldn't be with anyone? The one who was 'just who you needed' at the time?"

"Yeah, she is. And I did mean to tell you."

She rubbed an eye. "I remember. I told you to sublet to whoever you wanted."

"I planned to check with you, and then we got so busy with the party and packing, it slipped my mind. She's back in New York for a short-term thing. She needed a place. I was trying to get rid of my place. It was good timing. It doesn't mean anything."

Orchid puffed her cheeks and blew a noisy breath. "The weird thing is, even if that's true, I feel like asking you not to come."

Phoenix swiveled towards her, anxiety thumping inside his chest. Out the front window, he could see that they were heading towards the tunnel into New Jersey. "Talk to me, Orchid. You said we should keep lines of communication open."

"The thing is, I don't think I can go back to your place without thinking about her sleeping in our bed. Sitting on the little sofa where we first kissed."

He felt his lips compress. "Truthfully, I didn't think of that."

"It's not just about Rina. Although this sucks big time. It's just I wonder what else you've forgotten to tell me. It took a lot for me to forgive you and try to trust again. I thought I could trust us to go to China together and start our lives together. I know we haven't talked about stuff like marriage, but for me, this is a big commitment. Are we ready for this? Moving overseas together? Maybe you shouldn't come on this flight."

He sucked a deep breath. He respected her, loved her. "Really? Nothing's ever felt righter to me in my life."

She regarded him, her eyes saddened with pain-wrung wisdom. "I believe you, or at least, I want to believe you. You've hidden so much from me and continue to hide things from me. Even while we've been living together. So why don't we start with honesty? Like, why haven't we made love? Why did you lock me out of your bathroom? What else haven't you told me?"

They were in New Jersey, less than a dozen miles to work this out before they'd arrive to Newark Airport.

Where should he start? The wheelchair that he'd shunned while she lived with him. His adaptations.

He started with the simple truth right before them.

"I'm not gonna lie, it's not going to be easy to be with me. Like, I haven't flown since the accident. I don't really know what I'm doing," he said.

She frowned.

"I read about it. I can go through security with my prosthesis, they just have to wand me. I called the airline, and they can take my chair, but they're famous for really high damage rates, which sucks for people who rely on them for mobility."

The sadness in her eyes deepened.

"If my residual limb swells, I'll have to take off my leg during the flight. Then I might need a chair to get off the plane. Or hop. Or crawl. And worst, I have no idea how mortifying all of that will be. For me. For you. I figured it'll be a 50/50 chance you won't want to deal with the hassle."

Her eyes widened, as she took in the most honest picture he'd ever stated aloud.

Now that he'd started, his momentum built. Some desire wanted to rip away her naivete and expose the ugly truth. "Do you know that I'm considered severely disabled? It's a government definition. The military even pays insurance based on level of injury. My hand is like a 60 percent disability and my leg is a 40 percent disability. Does that mean I'm 100 percent disabled? Is this the honesty you want?"

A tear trickled onto Orchid's shiny backpack. He watched it slide over the rounded edge and plummet to its demise. Orchid's salt and liquid and DNA. He already missed her. So, this was how he'd lose her. He thought he'd have more time before some aspect of his reality would frighten her away. Never did he think their happy bubble would last a mere fourteen days. *Goodbye, Orchid.*

The spigot on his candor flowed wide open now. He'd be heading home by himself in this very car, so he may as well unload everything.

"Did you know that Beijing is one of the least accessible cities in the world? That in China, some people consider disability a punishment for sins from a prior life? Karma. So, they discriminate against people with disabilities. I could be treated like a pariah there. You think it's bad the way people look at me here. Mrs. V being shocked that a woman might even want me. Gail wondering how I could live with myself like this." He swept a hand over his lap, indicating the pieces left of him.

Orchid interrupted with a hand on his arm. "Stop it. China's not perfect. I looked into it. And honestly, maybe I'm the one being selfish. Because I wanted you to come anyway."

He couldn't stop now. She wanted the truth, she wanted to know what he'd been hiding from her. "You've never been with me to a show or event. Have you ever tried to clap one-handed? I pitched a new account after the accident. The client didn't listen to a word I said, they were too distracted by the way I looked. That's when I knew I wasn't adding anything to the agency. I'm a liability. Is that honest enough?"

Orchid opened her mouth and nothing came out. He couldn't pause his momentum anyway.

"That's the tip of the honesty iceberg. This is what I've been hiding from you, trying to look the same as before the accident. That's why we haven't made love, not because I don't want to. Not very appealing, I know. There's more where that came from. I probably should've been honest sooner. So, you knew what you were signing up for. I really am selfish. I totally get it. You are under no obligation. I still wish you the best, Orchid. Go have that amazing life you deserve. I'll always love the time we had."

They sped along Route 78.

Furiously, Orchid dug through her bag. She pulled out a wad of tissues and blew loudly. "I'm stronger than you think. You don't have to pretend for me."

"I was never trying to hurt you."

Their car swept up the airport terminal ramp towards the business class counters.

Phoenix slid open the glass partition. The driver glanced at him from the rearview mirror, his expression a silent apology.

Orchid peered into her makeup mirror. "You turned me into a mess," she said.

That damned grief on her face. He wanted to hold her, and figured he had no right. "You're still beautiful."

"Now you're blind on top of everything else."

Her humor dissolved a sliver of his distress. Resilient Orchid could survive anything. Time to say goodbye. "Curbside check-in," Phoenix directed.

They slid to a stop in front of the valet service. Phoenix circled to the trunk to point out her three fuchsia suitcases to the porter.

He stopped the guy before he could pull out Phoenix's own luggage. Instead, Phoenix palmed him a few generous bills.

"Wait. Your stuff needs to come too," Orchid said. She stepped off the curb towards him, her eyes red.

Phoenix frowned into the trunk. His wheelchair lay on top of his bags, an emblem of everything he no longer was, a warning of a forever future.

He'd just articulated half the reasons he wasn't right for Orchid.

"Maybe you should go on your own, Orchid. We can talk later. Think this through. Honestly, now that you made me say all this stuff out loud, it seems pretty dismal."

"Come with me. We can talk on the plane. We can talk in China. We'll figure it out together. You can come back anytime you want. You were planning on coming back at the end of July anyway, so give us these few months. I didn't know, Phoenix. I didn't know any of that. You always seemed perfectly fine. I'm sorry."

Orchid tugged her tunic over her leggings. He recognized that outfit, the same one she'd donned for her trip to China ten months ago.

He was bleak.

She was beautiful.

Stay?

Go.

"You gotta move. The cops circle here all the time," the valet said.

Her attempts to accept his reality had been valiant.

"You're twenty-eight. You want another half-century of this?" Phoenix asked her. He wasn't reverting to reverse psychology. He wasn't trying to be dramatic. It had taken all his energy to get through the last ten months since his duel with a train. His burden, not hers.

She tiptoed up to press lips to his cheek.

With her soft touch, his defenses eviscerated. For the first time that day, his own tears threatened. She helped him fight off sentimentality with humor, "I can't vouch for fifty years, but let's at least make it through the next fifty hours and see what China has in store for us." Then she pointed out his luggage and pulled a bill from her pocket for the porter.

CHAPTER 16

LONELY IS THE NIGHT

Orchid

Orchid's anger over Rina had been overshadowed by the honesty of what Phoenix had shared. What their honest conversation had unearthed was more seismic than any ex-girlfriend.

His confessions left her emotions as raw as if she'd just skidded bare legged across summer concrete. His monologue was meant as a warning. "You don't want this," he was trying to say. That same misbelief that had led him to hide his injuries from her last year.

He waved her ahead of him through the airport security line. She waited with her bags and observed him standing, his uneven reach outstretched as personnel manually patted down his torso and legs. Next, the agent swabbed his prosthesis and tested it for chemicals.

During these additional steps, he ignored nearby onlookers. She intuited that the airport protocol had cost his self-estimation more than just extra minutes from his day. On the other side of the metal detectors, he straightened and looked down at her, a question in his eyes.

"Will a thorough flogging help?" he asked.

"That might be enjoyable." She play-swatted at his round rump, encased in soft khakis, and then tiptoed up for a kiss.

Orchid slung her backpack over one shoulder. Together, they navigated the terminal. At their gate, they took adjoining seats.

"Here's a shortcut. How about I give Rina the boot?"

Just him asking the question loosened any remnants of self-righteous anger. "If you'd asked my opinion in advance, I probably wouldn't have supported her staying. To be honest, though, it's your place. It's up to you."

An announcer came over the loudspeaker. "For our flight to Beijing Capital Airport, we're boarding passengers with disabilities, travelers with children under the age of two, and anyone needing extra time for boarding."

An airline staff member helped a gray-haired woman in a wheelchair maneuver towards the gate entry point.

Phoenix glanced over at Orchid. "I don't mind waiting in line. But if you want, here's one perk of being with me."

His meaning took a moment to dawn on her. *Phoenix* qualified as a passenger with a disability. "Nah, if you're okay, let's let others who need it board early," she said.

When first class passengers were summoned, they stood together to enter the jetway. Orchid caught him glancing at her.

Once on the plane, the sight of their luxurious business class seats reminded Orchid of their Paris trip. He'd generously given her his spot in the front of the plane.

"This time, you don't have to sit in coach," she said, referencing the center seat he'd taken in her place on their flight to France.

Today, he let her pick the window seat.

After takeoff, their stewardess offered them warm nuts and champagne.

"Cheers," Orchid said, lifting her glass.

"Jeers, did you say?" His flute clinked hers.

"Tell me about Rina," she said.

He put down his glass and ran a hand through his newly shorn hair. "She's nothing like you. Not a creative bone in her body. She's an actuary. Very pragmatic. Loves hockey. You know she's Canadian, right?"

"No, I didn't. What else?" she asked, wondering what Rina lacked that ended their relationship.

"She's career-focused and smart. So, I guess that's like you. She doesn't care about the demand side of the business at all."

"I hate myself for asking, but what does she look like?" Orchid pictured the waif-like angel she'd imagined when Phoenix had called her just the person he needed after his accident.

He pulled out his phone and scrolled back to last year. "Here."

A plump, unsmiling woman with a dirty-blond bob in business attire stood beside Phoenix with a cane. "You like serious types?" Orchid asked.

"She's not always serious. What about you? Your exes?"

"Funny that we haven't talked much about this. I've dated lots." Orchid pictured the broken souls who'd hurt her on their way to their own rock bottom, and the nice guys who couldn't get past her façade to diminish her defenses.

"I'm not surprised. Anyone who meets you would want to get to know you," he said straight up, without flattery.

"Not true but thanks. I scare off the preppy, strait-laced guys. My taste tends to be self-destructive. Juvie. Cutters. Addicts. The ones that need saving."

"You're with the wrong Walker." He nudged her empty glass with his.

"Actually, that was the old me. Now I'll take anyone with bubbly."

He handed her his flute and she emptied it.

The stewardess returned to take their meal orders. "I have a vegetarian meal for you, Ms. Paige."

After she left, Phoenix leaned closer to Orchid. "Nutritional yeast," he whispered in a conspiratorial hush, referencing their inside joke from the first time she'd introduced him to vegan fare.

She couldn't help it. The champagne had loosened her inhibitions. She laughed. Pure and simple. He was her Adonis. Her funny man.

"I can't believe we're going to be in China in less than twelve hours. So, what now? We should talk through stuff, right?"

Phoenix looked up towards the airplane air vents, then over at Orchid. He was the most beautiful man she knew. He took her hand and asked, "Yes. Let's start with this. You asked me to never introduce you as just my friend. What would you like to be called, my queen?"

She'd thought about this before. "I'm your girlfriend. I'm your partner."

"Then I'm your boyfriend," he agreed.

Her mouth widened in humor. This bastion of masculinity was no boy. And he was way more than a friend. The limitations of the English language.

She felt a devilish grin form. "In China, you're my trailing spouse."

He groaned at the phrase that referred to the non-working person in the relationship. The stereotype was an expat wife who spent her days splurging on spa services, shopping, and lunches.

"Actually, I think a queen deserves a king," he said, straightening.

His humor crumbled any last vestige of resentment. She laughed and wrapped both arms around him.

"Ah, the royal route is working, that's good," he said lightly. Then, he leaned closer to return her hug.

Their flight landed through the smog of the city previously known as Peking. The airport code still bore the letters PEK.

As their plane taxied, Phoenix leaned down to affix his prosthesis. He grimaced as it settled in place.

"Phoenix, you know you don't have to do that for me, right? If you need a wheelchair, use a chair, okay?"

His look of gratitude told her she'd intuited his dilemma.

He limped off the flight with an arm around her shoulders. They traversed customs, baggage claim, and tugged their bags into the noisy terminal.

A little carousel of goods caught Orchid's attention. "What would you pick out for me here, if you could?" she asked.

He frowned. "This is clearly a test I can't pass. It's a trick. No matter what I say, you're going to stomp off, right?"

She laughed. "Yeah, you're probably screwed."

He perused the jade carvings, emerald-hued earrings, and greeting cards. Then he brightened. He presented her with a cellophane-encased stack of playing cards. "I challenge thee to a game of Egyptian Ratscrew!"

Déjà vu. Last summer, she'd imagined this exact scenario. He'd remembered her childish lapse at his family's shore house.

She threw her arms around him with a reference to the movie, Matrix. "You are the one, Neo!"

Phoenix pulled out a little of their Chinese currency.

He asked for a price from the vendor, who responded with numbers typed onto a calculator.

Phoenix exclaimed in mock surprise over the expense, starting the expected dance of bartering.

They settled on a number that was ridiculously cheap by American standards but left the vendor gleeful.

Phoenix handed her the cards showcasing dancing kittens.

"Thank you," she said.

"*Bu keqi*," he said, practicing *you're welcome* in Chinese.

They pivoted their bags towards the horde of drivers sporting signs.

Orchid spotted her name and, like a schoolgirl, imagined their initials carved together and encircled by a Cupid. OP + PW, k-i-s-s-i-n-g.

She caught the driver's eye, and he spread his lips, revealing brown teeth. He asked her identity, using her Chinese name.

She assented and then introduced Phoenix using a Mandarin-sounding version of his last name.

The driver grabbed two of her strapped-together suitcases and began darting between travelers and baggage towards the exit.

Phoenix gestured towards her remaining luggage. "Here let me take that."

He bent over her heavy bag and slung it onto his chair. The three of them emerged into a parking structure. The driver led them to a black SUV and hefted their belongings into the trunk.

Orchid joined Phoenix in the backseat.

The driver offered them bottles of water.

Phoenix shook his head.

"No thanks," she said in Chinese. She didn't want to take wasteful one-time use plastic.

"We have our own driver," she whispered as the car pulled out of the parking garage and headed towards the highway.

They snaked into the city, towards Chaoyang where she had selected housing that would be near one of the largest urban parks. Once they reached the inner circle of Beijing proper, the scale of everything made Manhattan seem quaint. The sidewalks were filled with dark heads bobbing. She searched for a face like mom's, round-cheeked and heart-shaped.

His speech in the car ride to Newark Airport had exposed her to some of his challenges, and pain. To her, he was simply the most amazing man she'd ever met. This man had launched his own ad agency. He wrote award-winning campaigns. Dined with high-profile clients. Generated hundreds of millions of dollars of value. And he was only thirty-two. No labels could do justice to the complexity of his intellect, creativity, and experiences.

She hoped that the apartment she'd picked would suit his needs. She realized belatedly that she'd never asked him. Maybe she'd been as selfish as he had. They both needed to learn how to be a couple.

The car stopped at a tall apartment building.

"If you don't like our place, we can find another one," she promised, and squeezed his hand.

He was here for her. It was more than she could've imagined last year.

At the same time, he'd nearly betrayed her trust. They were on trickier footing than she'd feared a year ago.

"Setting low expectations. Good tactic." He grinned up at the high-rise building.

Phoenix and Orchid went inside to produce passports in return for keys while the driver retrieved their luggage.

Phoenix limped to the elevator with Orchid, in contrast to his normally graceful gait.

"You, okay?" she checked with him during the elevator's ascent.

"I'm hangin' in there. You?"

She slipped her arms around him and pressed her cheek against his chest. His heartbeat in her ear, strong and steady. Her bruised ego was healing. "I'm exhausted. I need a real bed. Most of all, I'm happy you're here."

He returned the embrace. "Xin," he called her, using the Chinese word for heart.

The lift deposited them on a floor that smelled like cooking food.

She turned the key in the lock, hoping the photos she'd used to choose their new apartment had been accurate.

Inside, she realized the website hadn't done the place justice. A sunny kitchen opened to a small eating area, sprawling living space and a corridor leading to their bedroom.

"Do you notice anything about the floor plan?" she asked, indicating the space furnished in tasteful cream and gray hues.

"Almost like our place back home," he murmured, his gaze sweeping the blond wood floors and minimalist Danish-style built-ins, then landing on her. Home. He'd been generous to extend his home to her. She didn't take that label lightly. She knew what it was like to live without one to call her own.

The porter had left their bags in the foyer. Orchid shucked her shoes and towed her things towards the bedroom.

Phoenix followed with his luggage.

Their suite was larger than the one in New York. She showed him the adjacent guest room. "Perfect for when my aunt visits," she said.

"I want to meet your family," he said.

Inside their bedroom, beside their queen-sized bed, they unzipped suitcases, pulling out essentials.

"I'm going to shower before hopping into bed. Want to join me?" she asked.

"If anyone's hopping, it'll be me," he said.

She groaned. "Is this your campaign to make me feel sorry for you?"

"I never want anyone to feel sorry for me. This is my campaign to win you with humor."

She tiptoed up to kiss his cheek. "I'm yours."

He kissed her back. "Good, but that's not going to stop the bad jokes."

She led him by the hand to their bathroom.

At the threshold, he halted.

"You did this? For me?" he asked. He swiveled to take in the roll-in shower, waterproof seat, grab rails, and lowered sink.

She stared up to study his wide-eyed reaction. "If it's not right, we can still change stuff."

"This is what I tried to hide from you. In New York," he said.

"Oh Phoenix, there's no need to hide. Lucky me, now I can sit to shave my legs," she said, finding the upside to their accessible bathroom.

He leaned down to envelop her and released a breath he seemed to have been holding for a long time. "You're too good to me. What would you like while we're here, my queen? If you could have anything?"

She nestled into the safety of his arms and thought. "We're going to have fun together. Do things. Everything we missed when you were too stubborn to tell me the truth last year. You should come with me to dance class. Explore the city."

"Fun is good. Except I'm not sold on dance class."

She tiptoed up from her stockinged feet and kissed along one scruffy jaw. "You said anything."

"Okay. Anything," he breathed in one ear, and threaded fingers through her hair to return her tenderness.

They woke at midnight, discombobulated by the time difference. Noon at home.

"Let's go explore," Orchid suggested.

Phoenix pulled her into his arms. "I can't believe we're here."

Then he good-naturedly got dressed and accompanied her into the warm night air.

Among the streets threaded with people, they were just another couple. Phoenix was right. She couldn't believe they were there either. Not just a new physical locale. Rather, to have a relationship with no drama. China was their clean slate.

They crossed from their slick urban setting into the cobbled hutong, the centuries-old traditional neighborhood. T-shirted old men sat on their stoops watching the foreign passersby watching them. She didn't know how many of their stares were for being a mixed-race couple.

Phoenix leaned on her to steady his gait over the uneven stones paving the road.

"How's your leg?" she asked.

"I'm limping to get out of dance class," he said.

"You'll need a doctor's note, minimum."

"Okay, *xiao jie*," he whispered naughtily into her ear, one arm slung over her shoulders.

"If anyone hears you," she play-threatened over the phrase that literally translated to "little miss" but over time had come to connote a wanton woman.

They exited onto a brightly lit avenue closed off for pedestrians.

"Oh, a night market!" Orchid exclaimed.

"Peng you, lai lai!" Crafty vendors called them "friend" hoping to snare wealthy Americans into spending money. They walked faster.

"Is this where you want to have dinner?" Phoenix teased as they passed stalls serving deep-fried scorpions, crickets, and seahorses.

Orchid's stomach lurched. "If I weren't already vegetarian, this would be enough to sway me."

"Me too. Maybe it's bad timing to ask, do you want to eat somewhere?"

"I'm not hungry, you?"

"I'm fine too, hungry bird."

"Then let's head home," Orchid said, her mouth savoring the word that evoked images of a shared space and a shared life.

The next few days, they slept at times which were at odds with the country's clock. They made themselves go outside for circadian-altering sunshine, staggering out into the daylight in search of food. They discovered little eateries where bowls of noodles were obscenely cheap.

They bought fruits, produce, and tofu at grocery stands. At home, Orchid unpacked Phoenix's adaptive cutting board. The two of them relished their habit of cooking together.

The kitchen was smaller than Phoenix's New York space but featured the lowered sink and bottom-drawer freezer she'd noted at his place. As he leaned down to scoop ice into a tumbler, Orchid puzzled how he never appeared to need those accommodations at home.

On Sunday night, after a week of acclimation, Orchid pulled a long face after dinner. "I'm bummed I have to leave you and go to work tomorrow."

"Someone's gotta earn an honest living," he joshed.

"I've just paid off my student loans, and now I need to support your dumpling habit," she ribbed him back.

"Oh, that's nothing. I also have expensive taste in booze." He stood to fetch a bag from their kitchen counter. Phoenix offered the item to Orchid.

She pulled out a bottle of clear liquid. "*Baijiu.*" She wrinkled her nose at the Chinese liquor that translated literally to "white alcohol" and was often consumed during business events. "Do you actually like this stuff?" she asked.

Phoenix pulled out their playing cards from his shirt pocket and placed them on the table. "Nope, but I need every advantage to beat you at Egyptian Ratscrew."

She laughed with delight and twisted off the lid. "The Chinese custom is if I drink, you drink." She poured a thumb high portion into each of their empty water tumblers.

"*Ganbei,*" he said, toasting her. She lifted her glass to his call for a "dry glass" and tossed back the Chinese fire water. He followed suit.

"This stuff is viler than I remember." She made a face.

"Perfect. Loser takes a shot," he declared, and grasped the cellophane with one hand.

Orchid knew from prior experience that he wouldn't appreciate her offer of help. He resorted to using his teeth to pry the edge of the package loose.

She busied herself pouring another round for them.

"Lush," he said with a mischievous smile.

She sipped the tart-smelling liquid. "This is stuff for the desperate."

"Truly awful," he agreed with a grin.

"Maybe it'll be your lucky night," she teased.

She hadn't given up even though she was pretty sure he'd continue to forestall her advances. Perseverance would wear him down.

"Ha."

He discarded the clear wrap and pulled the deck out with a flourish. "Watch this."

Orchid leaned in.

Phoenix split the deck one-handed, half the cards between his thumb and forefinger, the other portion between his ring finger and pinky. He deftly fanned the two together onto the table.

"You're ingenious," she said.

"I learned it on YouTube. One-handed shuffling."

The baijiu made her brain fly high. He lifted his cobalt eyes to hers, and an electric desire shimmied down her abdomen. Her skin remembered the feel of his full lips and the unshaven scruff along his chin and jawline. She leaned over the table, marveling how his expression softened until her lids shut out her blurry view, and their mouths met. The cards slipped and scattered. She imagined them airborne, each errant jack tumbling over aces until the sevens and queens danced like fools.

"You know what, screw Egyptian rats," she breathed. She stood to take them elsewhere, never mind games or dishes. In her booze and love-induced haze, she straightened right into the hanging table lamp. Its metal hat gonged.

"Ouch." She rubbed the bump on her head. That wasn't her smoothest move.

Phoenix chuckled. Yet he rose and enveloped her in his arms. He kissed her hair.

"You smell amazing," she said.

"Really? I was thinking I smell like grain alcohol you'd score from the streets of the Bowery."

Orchid tilted her chin. She fingered the V-neck of his shirt and slipped the first button out of its opening. His relaxed pose tensed in her arms. Yet he didn't stop her progress. She spoke low, as if comforting a feral cat, while unfastening one button after another. "The Bowery?" Down his muscular chest. "Your caliber is more boardroom." Revealing the taut muscles of his abdomen. "Though I'd rather see you in the bedroom." She untucked his shirt tail. His sharp intake of air accompanied a quick grasp at her hand. She captured his fingers, ignoring the fact that he was trying to stop her. Fibers of her intuition sensed unnecessary fear. She stretched up. Her lips butterflied kisses along his jaw. "Phoenix Walker, I. Love. You."

His free arm roamed her back. Her kisses grew hungry.

"I more than love you. I adore you. I lust you," he promised.

She pulled him towards the bedroom, not breaking their contact. Would he allow this? She hadn't seen his full naked glory. He still locked the bathroom door for privacy.

God, she was gorgeous and wild. Everyone else in his life fell away compared to this beauty. Her mouth on his neck said she wanted him. How could she be sure when he hadn't allowed her to see his fully flawed self? His nightmare from his days in the hospital had faded, but he hadn't forgotten Orchid's look of repulsion buried in his subconscious.

Next to their bed, she let go of his hand to free her shirt over her head and step out of her skirt. She flung back their sheets.

"You're so beautiful." He fingered the soft flesh below her lacy bra and leaned down to taste her lips.

"You're not too bad yourself." She stripped off his button-down and let it fall to the floor. That morning, he'd carefully cuffed his sleeves so he could use his residual limb, while leaving his loss discreetly covered. Now she'd denuded him of his protection.

"Are you sure?" Even to him, his tone wasn't joking.

Orchid feathered a finger down his chest, past his navel, and dropped to his belt buckle. "More than sure," she said, and loosened his pants.

He stepped out of the pooled fabric, his need growing more intense than his fear. She didn't cringe or flee at the sight of his prosthesis. Yet.

Her expanded pupils heated him with desire. He held her close, their mouths unable to get enough of each other. *Honey. Roses.* With one hand, he grasped the back of her bra, and miraculously, the tug loosened the clasp. She flung the extraneous garment aside. The feel of her bare skin against his chest almost undid him.

"Where have you been all my life?" she whispered with humor.

He laced one finger into the slip of fabric around her hips, and the panties slid to the ground. She freed him of his briefs. He groaned, restraining himself. Then he caught sight of his wheelchair in the corner, the mirrored closet doors beside it reflecting two bodies entwined. Beautiful, slender Orchid being pawed by a lopsided embrace. His stomach hitched. He cast a wild look towards the bathroom. Excuses. Where?

"I'm going to—"

She must've seen his stricken expression. One palm gave his chest a little push. "You are a stunning man, Phoenix John."

His legs backed into the bed, and he let his knees buckle onto the mattress, taking her with him.

They rolled onto the white expanse. This wasn't his first time since the accident, but this time was fraught with risk. Orchid mattered more than anyone. The woman who couldn't handle photos of combat-wounded veterans when they'd first met. "I was worried I might have to wait three years," she laughed.

"You still might," he warned her. *Don't you see what I see?* He wanted to interrogate her about the sight he'd witnessed in the mirror.

She pressed against him, her hips circling a delicious motion. Her mouth lavished kisses down his bicep to his forearm, murmuring between each tenderness. "You tell me what you like, or don't like okay?"

"I like," he groaned.

Orchid touched her lips to the smooth end of his arm. "You are a hero, Phoenix."

"I'm not," but his protestations didn't matter, even to him.

He paid homage to the plump edges of her breasts, lips roamed her bare skin. The sensation of her so close, when he'd been aching for all of her, was more than he could take.

Orchid reached into the side table drawer, pulled out a small square, and ripped it open. It was his last chance to stop her. He was too far gone. His grasp tremored with anticipation. How was he going to roll the condom one-handed?

"Can I do the honors?" she asked, checking his expression.

"All yours," he murmured, and swirled a distracting path along her inner thigh.

She straddled him. She was warm, a perfect space for him.

Their bodies found motion, entwined, thrashing.

Unable to take the delicious frustration anymore, he flipped them so that he was on top. Her calf brushed against his prosthesis. He paused for her visceral reaction. Instead, she pulled him in with a throaty cry. Bucking, pushing, she arched her back.

Feeling her tighten, lose control, cry out, he joined her, thrusting until her bones unhinged and she lay in a jellied heap, panting. His mind exploded. Conscious thought vanished.

"You're a goddess," he said, breathing hard, lying on her, heavy and warm.

She entwined her arms around him, then her legs, and sighed.

"I'm so happy," she admitted. "And all I can think is, when can we do this again?"

Something inside his chest loosened.

CHAPTER 17

GREAT WALLOP

Phoenix

China was an opportunity. To see if they could build a life together. To explore business. And for self-discovery. In college psychology classes, Phoenix had read about self-actualization, Maslow's theory that once people acquire the basics of safety and belonging, they might strive to be the best person they could be. The last year had been an acceleration of that journey. What he'd lost in mobility he'd gained in empathy.

Phoenix cooked breakfast for Orchid's first day at the office. His occupational therapist would be proud. He chopped onions and mushrooms on the adaptive board that Orchid had prioritized in one of her seventy-pound suitcases. He whisked eggs, holding the bowl in place in the crook of his left elbow. The redolent aroma of simmering vegetables reminded him of their evenings spent cooking together. After years of living in his apartment, it hadn't felt as much like home as those weeks when Orchid had shared the space with him.

Last night had broken another perceived barrier. He was ready to bust them all. The world looked completely different than it had just last year from a hospital bed.

Orchid emerged barefoot from their bedroom in a silk blouse and swingy skirt that skimmed the smooth skin of her naked thighs.

Phoenix turned off the stove and strode over to take her into his arms. She was more redolent than the meal simmering. "The eggs are hot, and you are hotter." He leaned down to kiss her soft lips.

"Ditto," she whispered between breaths.

The oven timer dinged in a higher range than his New York appliance, a tinny interruption to their embrace.

"Come eat." He beckoned her to the bar stool beside the kitchen island and slid cheese omelets onto plates already dressed with fruit salad.

"Since when did you become Martha Stewart?" she asked, sampling a bite.

"I'd prefer to think of myself as a protégé to Chef Orchid." He slipped into the seat beside her and tasted the eggs.

"Well, if this is her handiwork, she's hired." She nodded with approval.

He put down his fork to touch his fingertips to his lips. "She's the best. Chef's kiss."

She laughed at the compliment and hugged one arm behind him. "What are you doing today?" she asked.

"I'm going to work out. Lunch with an old colleague. I'll unpack then check out the neighborhood."

"I can send the driver back for you if you want." She forked a piece of dragon fruit onto her tongue, a little of its fuchsia skin visible against the white flesh.

"Nah, I'm good. I can get everywhere on foot, singular." His lifted fingers forming a single set of air quotes produced a groan from Orchid.

"Stop it. No more jokes at your expense."

"Only at yours?"

"Not that either."

"What do you want to do this weekend?" he asked her.

She swallowed, and an impish grin passed over her face. "I signed up for dance class."

"Did I really promise?" he asked, pretending not to know the answer.

"You did. What do *you* want to do?"

"We should tour around. I'll do some research and let you know what I find."

Her phone buzzed. Time to end their little cocoon. She rose, and he accompanied her to the door.

"You be good." She slipped on her red-bottomed high heels, picked up her hardcore laptop case studded with grommets, and kissed him. He missed her already.

"Always. You, knock 'em dead," he said.

Then she was gone, and time stretched before him.

In New York, they'd both navigated the city with ease. Here in China, this was Orchid's gig. Her corporate apartment. Her assignment. Her company driver.

In Zhong Guo, the middle country, he was in danger of being nothing. A trailing spouse, though he was no spouse. Agency founder, though he'd relinquished his agency responsibilities. Who was he? Phoenix Walker with the hampered walk. Phoenix Walker brother, son, *boyfriend*.

He'd committed to her. Her condition was China.

Phoenix pictured his business card. In his imagination, the white card stamped P.W. tumbled and tumbled, a simple slip with nothing else printed on its blank surface.

He shook his head over the image. This was one of the fastest growing regions of the world. Surely, he could turn this into an opportunity. Liv had contacted his network and organized meetings with one of his old colleagues.

First, he'd check out the nearby park. It was one of the largest in Beijing, and its proximity was a key reason that Orchid said she'd chosen this set of condominiums. He donned his running blade, a high-tech carbon curve that gave him freedom.

He tread carefully out his building and towards the running trails at Chaoyang Gongyuan. His running prosthesis tugged on his residual limb, pulling his left side with extra weight. His blade was fitted with a heel that made walking short distances possible, but the longer prosthetic length meant he needed to watch for twigs or broken pavement that could interrupt his gait. As he neared the park, he could see elders exercising the peaceful, slow-motion postures of tai chi.

Other white-haired parkgoers sat on park benches. One tossed a handful of breadcrumbs towards a quarrel of sparrows and raised his head at Phoenix's approach. A half-dozen spectators turned in unison. This time last year, he'd been training for summer triathlons. Now, he was a cause for gawking. He hoped some of it was due to being a foreigner. He accelerated his stride and broke into a run. At least when he ran, the open-mouthed stares were a blur. The wind on his face cleared his mind. Passing flowering trees, he explored his possibilities in this country. Where could he make an impact?

He pounded kilometer after kilometer, pondering solutions. Work. Play. Love. Legacy. The pro bono work was satisfying. Tammy, the star of their first PTSD ads, truly made a difference for that community. Maybe he could too.

The exertion felt like progress. The sweat a cleansing. Despite the soreness in his limb, he jogged back to their apartment building, wanting to prolong the clarity that movement produced. At home, Phoenix discarded his wet workout gear in a pile in the bathroom. He sat on the plastic seat that Orchid had thoughtfully procured. What if she hadn't had that forethought?

He rested on the non-slip surface and released the socket to remove his running leg. It was an impressive feat of engineering and design. He knew he was lucky. Not every person who wanted them could afford athletic prostheses, which most insurance policies didn't consider medically necessary.

Next, he stripped off socks and his silicone sleeve. Air cooled his residual limb.

Phoenix finished and reversed his way out of the shower. His hop over the threshold was not one he was ready to foist onto Orchid. He strapped his hands-free crutch to his left knee and hobbled out to the bedroom. Once he'd donned his prosthesis and clothes, he felt more like himself. Here was his mission. His own experience had shown how much more could be done to help people with disabilities.

The lunch place where he was meeting his friend was a few blocks away. This colleague had done exactly what Phoenix had been thinking he could undertake in China. Kit had moved to Asia and was collaborating with venture capital partners to form a new enterprise.

Inside, the restaurant was cool and dark. The hostess led him into the dining room and waved towards a table in the far corner. They hadn't seen each other in years.

Ah, Kit's short trim hair looked the same. He stood to greet him. "Long time no see!"

Phoenix reached his buddy and leaned in for a hug when the guy froze. Based on his widening stare, Phoenix realized there'd be no way for his friend to have known some crucial information.

"Oh my god, what happened?" burst out of him.

Phoenix chuckled at Kit's shocked expression as his friend sank into his seat.

"Sorry, man, I mean how are you? Or obviously not so gr—" Kit tried again.

Phoenix pulled out a chair and joined him. "I'm good. How are you?"

"Um, I guess I'm okay. Damn, I am so sorry." He pawed at an eye as if to clear up his vision.

Phoenix paused, absorbing the impact of his rolled-up sleeve on Kit.

"Thanks. Honestly, it's not as bad as your expression seems to think." Phoenix fingered the menu, pondering his responsibility as an ambassador to a community he hadn't applied for.

Kit swung his jaw shut. "You hungry?"

"Sure. I just came from working out, so lunch sounds good."

"Working out, nice." Kit's nod seemed to indicate a new sense of possibility.

Phoenix picked up his menu and studied the unintelligible pictograms.

"There's English on the other side," Kit said.

Phoenix flipped over the menu. "The good thing with Chinese food is that everything's already cut up. No need for a knife." The lines on Kit's face deepened with understanding, then he picked up his phone.

"Let me know what you want to order. I'll put it into the app," Kit said.

"Spicy dofu. My girlfriend's vegetarian and she's rubbed off on me," Phoenix said.

Kit typed the tofu dish into his phone and put it down. His mouth widened. "Girlfriend, well, good for you, good for you."

Phoenix assessed his tone. It didn't carry the patronizing sneer that Mrs. V's did. Yet Kit didn't even know half of it. "You'd like her, she's a whip-smart marketer for Estee Lauder. We're here on her assignment."

"I'd expect nothing less."

"I'll introduce you."

"How's your agency doing?" Kit asked.

"It's good. We're getting some recognition for the work with combat-wounded vets."

"I don't think I've seen that."

"Check out the case study on our website. How about you?"

"I'm starting to work with Chinese national brands. The insights will blow your mind. You have to put aside every assumption you might make in the West."

"How did you find your Chinese business partner? It seems like the only way to start a new business here."

"It mostly comes down to networking. Let me know what you're looking to do, and I will introduce you to a few people. I was really pumped when I heard you were coming. There's others in the industry who see it as a threat, but I think we could partner on something."

A server came out with several platters. She placed them in the center of the table with two bowls of rice.

Kit thanked the waitress, and she bowed in return. He'd always been a charmer.

They dug in, spooning savory scoops from the shared dishes as was the custom in China. The flavors and spices were more subtle than the high-sweet, salty, or spicy notes in Americanized Chinese food back home. Many Chinese secure the bowl with one hand and shovel rice down their gullet with their other. Although Westerners typically considered this behavior gauche, the Chinese believed that eating with gusto pays a compliment to the chef.

Phoenix pivoted their conversation from business talk.

"How's your family doing? I remember your wife telling me that the kids are becoming quite the musician and artists. None of that killer business instinct from their dad," Phoenix laughed, recalling the plump woman who loved telling stories of her children's antics.

Kit shook his head. "She left." He ladled tofu onto Phoenix's plate, then his own.

"Left?"

"She couldn't take China anymore. The pollution, the politics. She took the kids. I have visiting rights when I'm stateside."

"Aww that stinks. Now I'm the one who's sorry."

"I could've gone too, I guess. But Asia is where it's at, am I right? So, tell me, what kinda business are you thinking about in Beijing?"

Phoenix hadn't fleshed out any specifics. "You know, the older I get, the more I want to make a difference."

"You've become a bleeding heart?"

Phoenix ignored his interjection, and continued, forming the idea as he talked. "I keep thinking there must be a way to help people with disabilities. Lobby for accessibility. Get people the basic medical equipment they need. In China, we could start with awareness, overcome prejudices."

"Overcome prejudices?" Kit's skepticism was evident in the way he wrung his napkin with both hands. *Two hands.* His friend tossed the tortured fabric onto the table, where the cloth surrendered face down in the orange sauce.

"Some of it is rooted in Buddhist and Confucius beliefs, you know."

"You mean the idea of karma?"

"Yeah, you do something bad in your past and get payback in your current lifetime."

"Not sure how you're going to overcome beliefs steeped in thousands of years of tradition."

"Well, first of all, disability isn't inherently something bad. It's been an adjustment for me, a different experience, but not necessarily bad. People can change. For one, we could educate them on how prevalent it is. Globally, almost one in six people has a disability. If you make it to old age, there's an 80 percent chance you'll acquire some type of disability." He'd always admired the wounded warriors whom he'd met through his advertising campaigns. Then after his own accident, his respect trebled. Every day required a heretofore untapped strength. Not just physical aptitude to navigate stairs and a world that assumed four capable limbs, but also the mental fortitude to slough off the sideways glances and assumptions of weakness.

"Gotta hand it to you. Hearing you talk about it is changing *me*."

"One down, a billion more to go." Phoenix's lip twitched with humor.

Kit leaned back. "If I can ask, whatever *did* happen to you?"

Phoenix followed his buddy's glance at his arm.

"Would you believe I saved a guy from jumping in front of a train and took the fall myself?" The blur of headlights as he slammed into the tracks flashed before him.

"Holy hell. What?" Kit grew wide-eyed.

"Or I could tell you about the shark attack."

Kit chuckled. "You're a freaking inspiration."

"Nah. You setting up a business in China is an inspiration. My agency winning awards at Cannes. That's an inspiration. Otherwise, I'm living the best I can, like all of us."

Kit nodded. His eyes cast towards the smoke-stained ceiling. Phoenix knew his buddy's contemplative expression meant Kit was cooking up a new idea. Phoenix's chest filled with a new sense of potential. His experience could help broaden others' perceptions; he had a new mission to share his hard-won empathy.

His run and Orchid's love filled him with power. He wasn't diminished. He waved to the waitress, making the universal sign for the bill.

"Oh, I paid already, my treat. You need to download WeChat," Kit said. He showed a green icon on his phone.

"Thanks," Phoenix said.

They walked out into the sunshine together. Phoenix recalled the optimism he'd experienced on his way into the restaurant. Which was renewed by a sense of mission. Somewhere in this world, he'd make a difference in disability rights.

Orchid stayed late at the office that night and didn't return until past eight.

"I'm so sorry!" she called, as she floated into the apartment and lit up everything in her path. She tossed her punk-worthy bag onto the ground and flew into Phoenix's arms. "I missed you, and here I am late on day one."

He laughed, buoyed by her joy. "Your punishment is having to eat my cooking."

"I don't mind. Your eggs were the best thing I had today."

"I doubt that," he scoffed. Yet he led her to the table with pride.

She washed her hands while he plated their meals.

Orchid padded from the bedroom barefoot. He looked up from pouring them wine. "God you're gorgeous," he breathed.

"You're looking pretty great too. If I wasn't so hungry, I'd suggest skipping the meal." She hugged him from behind.

He put the bottle down and rotated to return the embrace.

"Mmm yummy." She pressed her lips against his neck.

"I missed you. Tell me about your day."

They sat and clinked glasses.

"It was great to see my team, but it's the cultural expectations that are tough to navigate," she explained.

"China's hierarchical, and the US is egalitarian. Culturally, they're polar opposites."

"Gender bias isn't helping me. Or US-China trade tensions. My nemesis from last year has it out for me again."

"Wang Ming?" he asked.

Orchid nodded. "He says one thing one-on-one then turns one-eighty when we get into meetings. I don't know if it'll be different this year."

"You can't assume he has the same ethics we take for granted."

"That's why IP law gets no traction here," she said, referencing the issues with intellectual property protection.

"You're going to need to hammer out agreements with the guy behind closed doors, and then publicly state them on the offense in those meetings. We can role play if you want," he said.

"Thanks, I'd like that. What about your day?"

"I ran for a solid hour at Chaoyang. You were smart to get us so close to the park. Tomorrow, I'll check out the pool here."

"You're going to get fit and fatten me up on delicious food. It's not fair," she grumbled.

"Delicious food?" he asked, fishing for a compliment.

"Oh no, I don't mean your meal," she laughed, and then stole a bite off his plate.

"Speaking of food, how was lunch?" She speared more food from his plate. He nudged his dinner towards her. *Hungry bird.*

He sighed and nodded towards his arm. "Guess this took him by surprise."

She swallowed her food. "Are you okay?"

"It actually gave me an idea. Whether there are ways to introduce more inclusivity in advertising here."

"The thing with Asian beauty is that it's traditionally fallen into one narrow band. Pale skin, big eyes, double eyelids. For the right brand, there's an opportunity to diversify into more looks, more body types, different abilities."

He straightened with admiration. "You are going to change the world."

"We," she corrected him. "We are going to change the world."

"Can you believe we did it? We're in China."

They were good for each other, a pair forged from the same elements of charity and hardship. "Now, tell me, what would you like to do to celebrate our first weeks here? We should plan some fun."

Orchid thought aloud, her long lashes blinking with each path of her ideas. "There's shopping, the Olympic Bird's Nest, and there's always those deep-fried scorpions at the night food stall, the thought of which makes me feel sick."

"You know, the Great Wall is considered an engineering feat."

"I remember my mom speaking of it with awe." Nostalgia wet her eyes. Something powerful made him want to grant her every wish.

"Let's do it. Before the weather turns hot," he said.

She chewed and swallowed. Her gaze flitted down towards his lap. "Are you okay to hike? I think it might be strenuous."

Still touchy from Kit's lunchtime reaction, his ego rose to dismiss her concern. "I'm fine. I ran Chaoyang Park today. I'm training for a tri. I can handle a walk."

Mollified, she finished her last bite and tossed her napkin onto the table. "Then I'm in."

"I know how else we can train," he murmured, and unable to delay any longer, he rose and took her with him. The dishes could wait.

On Saturday morning, Phoenix grumbled as they stepped into the dance studio, "Is there any way to get out of this?"

"I bet you'll love it," she countered.

She wiggled in the silver gleam of her form-fitting pants. Her off-the-shoulder top exposed a hint of midriff. She was adorable.

"Look who's a morning person," he paused her dance step to bestow a soft kiss. He lost himself in the feel of her skin against his. She slipped a hand under his tee. After a moment, she pulled back to take in his scruffy grin.

"You're a good sport. Let's go get a good place," she suggested.

"Is there such a thing?" he asked. He accompanied her into the room lit blue. Three disco balls twirled from the ceiling.

Orchid took a spot in the middle row. Phoenix joined in the spot between her and the right wall. A dozen other women filled the spots around them.

"I'm the only guy here," he said.

"I know. I'm going to have to fight off the hordes," she responded.

A pumping bassline echoed off the walls.

"Just follow the instructor," she said.

A slim woman with a headset warmed them up with a v-step, swinging her arms, and kicking up her heels in time to the music.

Orchid's reflection emanated sweet and sexy all at once. Phoenix mimicked the instructor's moves. The music liberated his limbs. He managed not to trip over his artificial foot as they crisscross stepped to the left. Halfway through, he could feel sweat drip into his socket.

They ended in a downward dog position, everyone else on palms and heels. He modified to a plank on his elbows.

The hour left him surprisingly invigorated. Blood pulsed to his fingertips.

After the final stretch, Orchid bounced up. Her cheeks rounded with hopefulness.

"You were great. You should sign up!" she said.

He rose and planted a kiss on the corner of her mouth to lessen the sting of denying her. A little salt mingled with her rose scent.

"This is your gig, Kai Lan. It suits you perfectly. Every time you leave for gym class, I'll be daydreaming about you in silver spandex."

A passing dancer must've overheard their conversation. She swung her ponytail over one fuchsia-clad shoulder and leaned conspiratorially towards Orchid. *"Xiansheng hao shuai."*

Phoenix felt his scalp tingle with embarrassment as his brain translated the Mandarin. *"Your husband is very handsome."*

Orchid laid a hand on the woman's arm and gave a sharp shake of her head. "Bu—" she denied.

His upper lip warmed with a new source of shame.

Then the woman he loved smiled up at him and revealed the twist. "He's not my husband," she said in Chinese.

"Not yet," the other dancer predicted, and glided out of the exercise room.

"And you're definitely *shuai*," Orchid said, emphasizing the word *handsome*. The sound of the last vowel fell away between the tang and softness of their lips.

The next day, Orchid's driver chauffeured them to Mutianyu, the Great Wall entrance north of Beijing. No sense going to the overcrowded site closer to the city center. The cityscape fell away to reveal olive-hued shrubbery against a gray sky.

In the back of the car, Phoenix reached for Orchid's hand.

"Have you ever been to the Opposite House?" he asked.

Her eyebrow arched a question mark. "Opposite House? Is that a place for people who hate each other? People who are like oil and water? The opposite poles of magnets?"

Humor burst from his diaphragm through his nostrils. He pulled her into a hug, the seat belt straining across his chest. "Where'd you get that idea? It's a five-star hotel."

She turned and took in his expression. "In that case, tell me about this dancing."

"They have a cool club in the basement. The DJs used to be pretty decent on Saturdays."

"Tonight?" Her ebony lined lids rounded in surprise.

"If you're up for it."

"Always." She took advantage of their proximity and pecked his cheek.

The car slowed and pulled into a parking spot at the bottom of an incline. They disembarked and waved goodbye to Shifu.

Orchid accepted his outstretched elbow and tucked close by his side. Together, they climbed the hill towards the Great Wall entrance. He inhaled, filling his chest with the clear countryside air. Optimism swelled.

The pedestrian walkway up to the cable cars was lined with vendor stalls of tchotchkes. *"Peng* you!" Shopkeepers called them "friend," hoping to sell them goods. They sauntered by, lost in their couple bubble.

"I'm so excited. What kind of place am I dressing for? What kind of people go to the Opposite House?" she asked.

Phoenix described the oversized wooden doors, the modern furniture that looked more like art pieces than seating, and the darkened dance floor with an understated vibe.

Everything and anything seemed possible between them. *International travel, dancing, tourist sites, and next, he'd find meaningful work in China and train for a triathlon.* Or a paratriathlon made accessible for those with disabilities.

Together, they boarded the aerial car and soon, the ground fell away beneath their feet as they were lifted high. Orchid stifled a squeal.

"Don't like heights?" he guessed.

She buried her face in his shirt. "Oh, no I'm perfectly fine. This is my excuse for hyperventilating."

He kissed the hair hiding her face and laughed.

Soon enough, they were deposited at the opening to the Great Wall. They walked along the undulating stones. Wind ruffled their hair. The sky blew blue to the edges of the horizon.

Along with Chinese families, tourists, and hikers, they picked their way over the uneven path, which staggered up and down into roofed turrets and lookout points. The vista unfolded in patches of shrubs, trees, and dimpled mountain cliffs. Like a slithering Loch Ness, China's famous wall snaked over the mountain ridge, steepling and plummeting with the wild terrain.

"My mom always said this was a beautiful place," Orchid said, as they paused to admire the expansive views.

"Thirteen thousand miles of hand-hewn rock, built before modern-day machinery. Still standing after almost three thousand years. The ingenuity of using a physical structure for protection. The coordination of all that labor. I think she was right."

"Have you been studying Wikipedia to impress me?" she asked.

He hugged her closer. "Only if it's working."

"What'll impress me is if your Opposite House DJ plays EDM."

"Electronic dance music? I seem to remember you liking postpunk industrial."

Her feet skipped a little jig. "Now you're talking."

"You hungry? Want to grab a bite before our night out?"

"Cool, let's turn back and toboggan," she suggested, referencing the gravity-powered metal slide that brought adventurous riders down to the parking lot level. They'd already hiked for several hours. He didn't want to admit to her that his leg was growing sore. Discomfort had become a daily companion since vanity convinced him to abandon his wheelchair. Heading home to rest before a club night was a good idea.

He nodded and looked in her eyes. "I can't wait to get you back to our place." She tiptoed up, capturing his meaning. Her lips were soft, first against his neck, then along his jaw. A shiver ran up his torso until suddenly, he couldn't get enough of Orchid. He leaned to meet her mouth. Her kiss exploded. She smelled of roses and honey.

Children's voices punctured their locket of privacy, reminding them that physical intimacy would be a cultural anomaly here. Phoenix and Orchid released their embrace, and eyed the hazardous descent. A pair of visitors were traversing towards them, kids in tow.

"I must be out of shape." Orchid rubbed her thigh.

"I have an exercise in mind," he whispered.

As they paused, faces in the wind, a young man wearing a hoodie and baggy sweatpants neared, black hair sticking out from under a baseball cap. "Hey are you guys American?" he called with a friendly smile.

Phoenix nodded. "Yeah. New Yorkers. How about you?" The guy's dark stripes of eyebrows, deep grooves of dimples suited his tanned complexion.

"Well, how about that. You know Rockaway Beach?" he asked, his syllables drawn out with a lazy drawl. He paused before the couple.

"Yeah, on Long Island," Orchid said.

"It feels good to speak English. I look Asian but I don't know Mandarin." He turned from Orchid to Phoenix.

He had to raise his nasal voice above the shrieks of two children bounding from one side of the path to the other, chasing each other up the slippery stones. A set of parents trailed them, huffing up the incline behind their rambunctious grade-schoolers.

"I'm Billy." The guy stuck out his hand. Before Phoenix could return the gesture, a small figure zagged right towards them, shrieking with her brother closing in on her.

"Watch it!" Phoenix called out.

Too late. The children's bodies struck and separated the threesome with surprising force. Little kid limbs entangled with Phoenix's. They all went down.

Phoenix landed hard on one side. His knee bounced against the unforgiving stone.

He caught his breath, then struggled to sit up and check on everyone.

"Aiya," the parents scolded, catching up. The kids sprung up with a giggle. They seemed unhurt as they bounded away.

Orchid leaned onto an elbow, dazed.

"You, okay?" he asked her.

She looked up into his eyes. "Yeah, I think so. You?"

The Chinese parents shouted apologies and ran off after their unruly pair.

"Hey!" Orchid cried but they were gone. Off to ruin someone else's day.

Phoenix sat up and looked over at their new acquaintance. Billy was crouched over his shin. Phoenix's own leg was pulsing with discomfort. He hoped he wouldn't have to remove his prosthesis and hop all the way to the wall's exit.

"Oh man. My leg." Billy pulled up his left pants leg and Phoenix could feel his eyes widen. From underneath his sock emerged the familiar sight of silver metal. As the hem lifted, a rounded ball joint gave way to a titanium pole.

"I need to make an adjustment but don't have any tools," Billy said.

"You have some in the car, right?" Orchid asked Phoenix. Leave it to his brilliant, empathetic girlfriend to both take this new development in stride and also know where he stored his torque wrenches.

Phoenix grabbed the fabric of his jeans to reveal his own prosthesis. "I do. You want to wait here while I get them?" he asked.

Billy chuckled. "I have to admit, I came over because I noticed we were both amputees, but I didn't know we had more in common than meets the eye. Let me see if I can get up." He braced himself against a nearby section of the wall and hoisted himself to a standing position.

"Holy mother," he said when he tested some weight on his prosthesis. "I did something bad to my leg."

Phoenix rose just as Orchid scrambled to her feet and steadied his wobble. "I can run down for you. Or hobble, as the case might be," he said, feeling his residual limb swelling inside his socket. "I'm Phoenix by the way, and this is Orchid."

She nodded a greeting towards Billy, her forehead wrinkled with concern.

Billy took a limping step, then another. "It's at least a half hour down and another half hour back up. I don't want to kill your whole day. I think I can make it."

"Lean on me," Phoenix offered, positioning himself on the guy's right side, taking the place where a left leg amputee would normally place his cane.

Billy placed an arm over Phoenix's shoulder. Phoenix slowed his pace to match the smaller man's stride and wrapped an arm around his waist.

Orchid trailed the men and pulled out her phone. "I'll tell Shifu to bring the car closer," she said.

They made their way down the slope, the unending waves of scrub brush around them were oblivious to their human plight.

"Those kids had no manners," she said, slipping the phone back into her pocket.

"If we were in the States, that'd be a lawsuit, for sure," Phoenix said.

"I probably didn't fall right. My therapist taught me to drop and roll but I wasn't thinking about that," Billy said.

"I didn't really enjoy the fall either." Phoenix ignored the throbbing below his knee.

"Can I give you guys a hand?" she asked and closed in on Billy's left side. He slung an arm over her shoulder, easing Billy's weight on Phoenix's shoulder.

"You know what would be a great innovation? Great Wall touring drones that would double as ambulances." He grinned at the two of them.

"You are the most creative person," she said.

They could spot the line to the cable car in the distance.

"Do you guys do something creative for work?" Billy asked, his dark hair bobbing with his limping gait.

"Kind of, I'm in marketing. Phoenix is the really creative one," Orchid said.

"Orchid's being humble. She's leading a new product launch here. I used to make ads. How about you?" How weird that sounded, *used to*.

"I used to teach surfing. But then I had an accident." He nodded his chin downwards. "And before you ask, no, it wasn't a shark attack."

The three of them laughed.

Their pace slowed as they neared the cable station. They waited in line for the next descending cable car.

Inside the enclosed cab, Billy sat between them. "Thanks, you guys did right by me."

"Do you need a ride?" Orchid asked. They glided quietly over the treelined hill, their progress seeming laughably fast compared to their slow progress on foot.

"I can call a rideshare," he said, pulling out his phone.

"No need. We have a car. Do you want to go to a medical clinic?"

Billy palpated his pants leg. "I think I'll just go back to the hotel and rest. See how I'm doing tomorrow. Thanks though."

"I'll tell the driver that we're here," Orchid said, her thumbs flying over the screen as the cable car came to a stop.

Shifu's eyes widened at the sight of the three of them approaching the car.

Phoenix and Orchid helped Billy to the front seat, where he pulled his legs in and sighed. "Thanks."

"Where are you staying?" Orchid asked after they'd settled into the back seat.

"Crowne Plaza, Lido," he said, naming a hotel in the northern area of Beijing.

"Oh, that's only fifteen minutes from us," she said.

Their driver nodded in understanding.

Now that he was seated, Phoenix's knee pulsed with agony.

As the car snaked down the hill, Orchid leaned towards Billy. "Do you want to stop at a store for anything?" she asked.

"I think I just need a stiff drink tonight," he said.

"Come by. We have *baijiu*," she offered. The car merged onto the main road.

"Oh man! *Baijiu*. My dad's Chinese and kept a bottle of that in the fridge. He was the one to buy moon cakes for Autumn Festival."

"Moon cakes. Those always seemed weird to me as a kid but now the thought of them makes me nostalgic. Kinda like zongzi."

Billy joined in her reminiscing. "Oh, those are wrapped in bamboo leaves, right?"

"Yeah, they look bizarre but they're delicious."

"I can't get enough jiaozi or baozi while I'm here," he declared.

As Phoenix listened to the new friends compare notes about Chinese dumplings and steamed buns, he pondered when they'd be able to try Orchid's childhood food traditions. The car slowed through city traffic.

"You'll have to come over," she said to Billy.

"Thanks, but you guys have done enough."

"You have someone waiting at the hotel for you?" she guessed.

He shook his head. "My girlfriend and I were planning to move here to teach English. This was going to be our cultural immersion. Because she's Chinese, and so's my dad. But after I ..." he paused and took a deep breath. "After I got hurt, her parents didn't want her to be with someone with a disability. They said she'd have a hard life."

"Man, that sucks," Phoenix interjected.

He turned to look at them. "I was mad at her parents. I was madder at her. She didn't fight them. She came to the hospital to tell me goodbye. So, I promised myself the moment I was mobile enough, I'd come to China, even if it was on my own."

"In the hospital? That's cruel." Phoenix recalled his own vulnerability in those early days after the train had changed his life.

"I saw you guys looking happy. I wanted to meet you, to prove to myself that not every woman is going to run the other way."

Orchid peered at Billy. "You know that love is love, right? I don't think of Phoenix as someone with a disability. He's just Phoenix to me."

Her words were meant to comfort Billy. They flooded Phoenix with warmth.

"You're a bigger person than she was," Billy replied.

The car pulled into the Crowne Plaza. "Do you want me to go in with you?" she offered.

Billy pushed open the door and got to his feet. "I can make it," he said.

"Tell me your number, so we can check to see how you're doing tomorrow," Orchid said.

He recited ten digits, and she typed them into her phone.

"Thanks. Bye." He waved to them and closed the door.

Shifu directed their car south towards their apartment complex.

"Love is love?" Phoenix asked, taking her hand.

"I was trying to help him. Was that too corny?" she asked.

"It was just what he needed. And you didn't just help him. You helped me," he said.

She leaned against him, her cheek resting on his chest. "In that case, corny was worth it."

He paused, afraid to break the news to her. "I'm sorry but we might need to save the Opposite House for another night."

"Of course, Phoenix. Whatever you need." she said.

"I didn't want to make a fuss, but I busted something too," he said. Then he popped off his prosthesis. There was immediate relief. Followed by a sinking feeling that this wasn't something he could just shake off.

The driver sped to their apartment building.

"How 'bout I run up for your chair?"

Phoenix's lips parted in surprise. "Thanks."

Orchid issued a flurry of commands to the driver, and then ran inside. Her Mandarin impressed him. She sprinted, with his prosthesis tucked under her arm like a football. A comical sight which gave him a moment's reprieve from the aches in his body. Knee. Throb. Shoulder. Ache. Elbow. Twinge. He was a mess.

"*Ni keyi ma*?" The driver asked if he was okay.

Phoenix wavered his hand, the universal sign for so-so. He'd barely qualified for the scratch and dent bin before today's tumble. Next stop, junkyard.

Before he'd left the US, his mom had asked about prosthetists in Beijing. He'd waved off her concern as motherly worry. With his tools, he could make the myriad minor adjustments to his prosthetic leg himself. Now, he missed his team of professionals in New York.

Orchid returned wheeling his chair. The sporty red had bolstered him when he'd selected it. Now, it bore the hue of warning, the tincture of blood. *It's an amputee chair, weighted so it won't tip back. This one's a one-handed model,* his nurse at the hospital had told him, introducing him to his new life.

Orchid bounded back like the epitome of youth in yoga pants and hiking boots, her ponytail trussed high into a crown.

"All the king's horses, all the king's men couldn't put Phoenix together again."

"Oh, Phoenix. I didn't know Humpty Dumpty sat on the *Great* Wall."

The driver looked at them like they'd lost their minds, Orchid leaning on his chair cackling, Phoenix doubled over his truncated leg.

Here came the hard part. For weeks while they shared his apartment in New York, he'd concealed his chair from Orchid. She'd never seen him in it. He'd kept it hidden in his closet until the day they left for the airport. Now, he used one hand to engage the brake. Phoenix mustered dignity to exit one-legged from the car, and pivot into the red leather seat.

"Shall I drive this chariot?" Orchid offered.

"No, thanks. You're thoughtful for asking, you know that?"

"*Bu ke qi*," she acknowledged the compliment by saying 'you're welcome.'

They bade the driver goodbye and wheeled through their building's foyer. The scale seemed grander from his waist-high view.

While riding the elevator to their floor, Phoenix looked up at Orchid. "How are you feeling?"

"I might have a bruise or so. It's nothing, really. Let's worry about you."

"Let's not worry at all," he said.

She leaned down and kissed him. Her hair held the scent of fresh air.

"We're going to name today The Great Wallop."

He hugged her back, cheek to cheek. Her arms encircled his shoulders.

"Love you, Walker," she murmured. She pressed lips to his cheek. He raised an arm to hug her back, no matter how much it hurt.

They exited the lift and entered their apartment. Much had changed in the twelve hours since they'd left that morning. They'd made love three times in the twenty-four hours before then. Now, he was no longer upright. Phoenix settled in their living room to inspect the damage.

"I'll find some ice," she offered.

"I'll take mine in a glass with *baijiu*," he suggested with a wink.

"Exactly," she agreed, and then returned with a freezer pack for his knee, and two tumblers for their evening in.

No Opposite House. Quite the opposite.

In the morning, Phoenix woke to find his knee swollen, and his back stiff. No worse than the many sports injuries he'd suffered in school days, he told himself. There was no way to fit his distended joint into a prosthesis though.

He wheeled out to find Orchid seated with her laptop propped on their dining table. It was well past the time she'd normally leave to avoid the worst of morning traffic.

"Still here?" he asked, raking a hand through his uncombed mane.

Orchid peered over her computer screen to halt his motion with her striking features. This morning, her irises shone purple in the slanted sunshine. Dressed in peacock blue chiffon, she appeared the epitome of the beauty industry. "You've given me the perfect excuse to play hooky." Orchid rose to intersect his path. She leaned down and enveloped him in a cornucopia of scents, her floral shampoo, and perfumed tea on her lips.

He returned her hug. "Yes, the Great Wallop. Lucky me."

"That's the perfect name. Oh, I have something for you." She straightened, breezed into the kitchen, and returned with a plate and ice pack.

"Brekkie?" she offered and settled the meal onto the tabletop.

He wasn't hungry. He joined her anyway. She'd dotted mini pancakes with banana slices.

"I don't deserve you."

"Definitely not. How are you feeling?" Orchid asked. She molded the pliable gel pack around his swollen knee.

"Not as bad as being run over by a train."

Her wrinkled nose disapproved of his flippancy.

"Sorry, stupid joke. I'm fine. How about you?" he asked.

She settled in her seat across from him. "I've told my office that I'll be remote for a day or so."

"I don't need a babysitter."

Orchid leaned close and ran a finger along the scruff of his cheek. "Babysitting's not what I had in mind."

After two days, Phoenix convinced Orchid to return to work. In her absence, Phoenix journaled, tapping memories into a fresh document on his laptop. The words hurt less written in the third person. "Phoenix never believed today was goodbye," he told no one in particular. The images flowed to his fingertips.

"... the beggar stumbled right for the open track.

"Without thinking, Phoenix dropped his phone and bounded forward. He grabbed the guy's coat to pull him away from the blurred train speeding towards them. The man jerked back. His bearded mouth screamed with fury. For a moment, they swung with wild centrifugal force. Suddenly, the guy yanked himself free. Phoenix tripped backwards. His feet scrambled to find purchase. Until there was just air over the edge of the platform.

"With a split-second to grasp at nothing, Phoenix crashed through the empty space to thud onto the

*track. He could feel the train's screech judder. The
sickening crush of steel slicing bone.*

*"What had become of the man from the subway sta-
tion? He'd swung from passive to suicidal in minutes.
Was his life better now? Or had he finished the job
Phoenix had interrupted?"*

He stopped his musings. Fiction. It'd be easier to pretend the
story was fiction.

Over the days at home, Phoenix penned thousands of words,
typing one-handed and using dictation software. He pieced together
events from his brother's accounts. He called his mother.

"There you are. How are you?" she asked.

"I'm good. Well, not my leg, but otherwise okay. Orchid's doing
well at work."

"Leg? What's wrong with your leg?"

Leave it to Veronica to hone in on the detail he didn't want to
emphasize. "I fell at the Great Wall. Some kids ran into us. Now, I'm
home resting."

"You have decent doctors there?"

"The orthopedist I found seems good. I'm going for an appointment next week. But listen, I have some questions for you. About
my accident."

"Are you sure, Phoenix?"

The emotion in her voice got him. "Please don't get maudlin on
me," he requested.

"I'm proud of you. I really am. You're in a good place if you want
to talk about it."

"You don't really know Orchid, but I have to say, she's been a big
part of this, helping me feel okay about the accident."

"Isn't that ironic? After you'd spent all that time trying to hide
it from her?"

Phoenix took a deep breath. "You know what, that's the real story. Losing an arm and a leg is just the start. But me thinking Orchid wouldn't stick around, and then finding the opposite, that's the real deal."

"Don't forget your mom," she said.

"Of course not," he laughed. "Now fill me in on the stuff I missed. Tell me how you found out. How you came to the hospital. Caleb and Sascha. Aunt Betsy coming by."

Veronica hesitated. Phoenix heard her expel air. "Oh, honey. The two of you were our life's pride. Then, it was like I didn't know how much I loved you until the hospital called."

They talked. She asked as many questions as he did. Their conversation lit the darkness of those chapters with the pale hue of hope.

CHAPTER 18

RARE REDEMPTION

Roy

For the first time in a long while, Roy felt worth something. He rubbed his thigh at the shelter dinner table, full of glee as he recounted the story of the runaway kid's reunion. After the meal, the minister slipped Roy a green bill. "You should keep some of the reward money."

Roy nodded, unable to find the right words of gratitude.

The next week, the runaway's mother returned to the shelter. She looked puzzled as she intercepted him at the shelter door.

"Oh, hello," Roy greeted her.

She brightened. "I've been trying to reach you. My son has an idea to help other teens. He wants to tell his story to our community paper. The reporter wants to interview you."

Roy couldn't identify any downsides, and so she jotted the reporter's phone number onto the back of a receipt. Helping one family had changed the course of Roy's fortune. The shelter staff regarded his relinquished check like a bonus. Father Lyndon congratulated him publicly. Roy applied for a free government cell phone, easily qualifying under the poverty guidelines. The next week, he called a New Jersey news outlet.

The reporter loved Roy's military background and selfless act. The article heralded him a hero, and after the story ran, Roy started reading the cases listed with the National Center for Missing and Exploited Children.

Roy savored the idea of reuniting families. He honed his sleuthing skills and learned to use the center's resources for online research. His cell phone gave him a treasured link to the world. Prospective employers could now reach him directly, without him having to check emails from one of the shelter's public computers.

Each skill was a step towards independence, a nod not only to Phoenix's memory but his bravery. Too bad that the handsome man had to give his life for Roy's new chance.

CHAPTER 19

HUTONG HUMDINGER

Orchid

Orchid would never tell Phoenix. Not after he'd moved around the world for her.

There was no upside to divulging her struggles at her job. *How had she sunk so low?*

When she'd visited China the year before, she'd been able to assess the business issues and recommend winning strategies within six short weeks. It was the effectiveness of those recommendations that landed her this full-time offer.

Yet here she was, more than a month and a half into her assignment, and her first leadership team presentation had not inspired resounding support.

The unit's chief marketing officer threw Orchid off kilter when he questioned her understanding of Chinese customs.

"How do you plan to convince men beauty routines aren't just for women?" he'd asked from the head of the boardroom conference table.

She'd flubbed her way through an answer that relied too heavily on insights from American consumers. The thirty-minute meeting hadn't been a disaster, but she also hadn't secured any strong endorsements. The outcome seemed nothing like her success a year ago, even though she'd employed similar approaches to her work. She'd embedded into the retail market, met with customers, and ingratiated herself with her team and agencies.

Honestly, the dynamics of this role weren't the same as last year's. For one, the players had changed. The sponsor who'd recruited her to come to China had accepted a new assignment back in his home country. It was challenging to discern who to trust. In their New York office, Violet had been her confidante. Together, they'd translated subtle clues and made sense of the shifting political winds. Here, her coworker Wang Ming's oily face smoothed into a pacifying smirk whenever he saw her. She sensed he was sabotaging her credibility behind her back.

During cultural training, her teacher had discussed the difference between Eastern hierarchical standards and Western egalitarian perspectives. The class felt like an intriguing set of theories. Now in real-life, the clash of values created workday follies. In truth, the stress had materialized into terrifying dreams. She'd woken in sweaty nightclothes. Once, she'd even walked in her sleep, only rousing to consciousness after she'd nearly tripped over Phoenix.

Billy had updated her on his visa process and had invited the couple to join him for a drink that evening. She had texted Phoenix to see if he wanted to go out.

"I'm not really feeling up to it," he responded.

She wasn't surprised. He'd been reticent to leave the apartment since his leg was still hurting after the fall at the Great Wall. Given her foul mood from work, she'd better go blow off some steam before arriving home. The car dropped her off at the alleyway that Billy had described in a message to her, and then Shifu left to find parking. Their driver was incredibly patient, sometimes waiting for hours until she was ready for him again. As the sun set, the air cooled, calming her senses from the day fraught with friction.

She pulled the twist tie from her ponytail, letting her hair fall around her shoulders.

"It looks pretty that way." She turned to find Billy.

"Would you believe my hair used to be blue?"

His lips parted. "I believe it," he said.

"Phoenix isn't able to join us. He sends his apologies," she said, then asked. "How are you doing?" He led them over cobblestones through the old Beijing neighborhood known as the hutong. At night, the narrow streets were barely lit. Her platform heel slipped over a rounded stone, and she caught herself with a jolt. He offered an elbow for stability.

"Bureaucracy is maddening here." As he filled her in on navigating his visa applications, they twisted through narrow alleys. She imagined Phoenix's chair bumping over the slippery stones.

"Modernista. We're here," he said and pointed at a yellow awning.

Inside, a low jazz melody hummed through the cozy place with black and white checked floors, a semi-circle stage with red curtains, and a lit bar. They sat at a little round table and ordered drinks and tapas.

"How'd you find this place?" she asked.

"I have a list. You know there used to be a hidden bar behind a hot dog stand?" he asked.

The waitress returned with their cocktails. They thanked her and clinked glasses. The first sip flowed sweet and cold.

"The place isn't very accessible," she said.

"That was one of the things I was worried about coming to Beijing."

"Phoenix still can't wear his prosthesis," she informed him.

"I hope it wasn't because he helped me get down from the Great Wall," he said.

"I don't know."

"I've only had one time that I haven't been able to wear my prosthesis. It's tough because it feels like going backwards," he said.

She nodded. "Phoenix is trying to make the best of it. He's using his time to write."

The waitress returned with a platter of bruschetta, croquettes, cheeses and silverware.

Billy dipped a breaded ball into the aioli sauce. "So, how was your day?"

Orchid sighed.

"Not good?" he guessed.

Orchid shook her head. "Not good."

Billy ate while Orchid described the early questions that tripped her up. Her insecurities spooled out. When she finished speaking, she felt spent, but also relieved to share her worries.

Orchid took a deep breath and tasted her food. The savory flavor zinged her tongue while the soft dough soothed her palate. After the first bite, she realized how hungry she'd been. She chewed the vegetarian fare and swallowed as she listened to Billy's questions trying to help her figure out what went wrong.

"It's like I lost the magic I had when I was here last year," she said.

"They must have a reason to want you here. It can't be cheap, to pay for an expat."

She metered out a splash of olive oil onto her plate. "You're right. They value my insights. The way I wanted to change things up," she said.

"Cool. So, if you could change up anything, what would it be?"

A laundry list popped into her mind. "I'd change disability inclusion. I'd make accessibility a priority. I'd change people's perceptions to accept disability as a set of experiences like anything else. One that can be positive, or challenging, or just human."

Billy swallowed. "That's a nirvana that would mean my girlfriend's parents wouldn't have felt the need to protect her from me."

She lifted her gaze from the cooling croquettes. "I'm sorry that happened to you. You know Phoenix tried to hide what happened to him from me, because he thought I'd run too."

"You're a saint not to have run."

"I'm no saint. I'm a flawed person who's lucky to have met Phoenix."

The music grew more insistent. Suddenly an answer to her work woes flooded her brain.

A voice echoed over the speakers, "Join us on the dance floor for swing lessons!"

Her foot began tapping to the jazzy beat as she polished off the last piece of bread.

"Want to dance?" he shouted over the music.

She wanted to, but Phoenix awaited her at home. She rose and tucked some money under her tumbler. "Thanks for dinner. I better go. But you stay. Have fun!"

As she left, she saw Billy join the gathering crowd on the dance floor. She hurried out to the street and texted Shifu to meet her. Inside the car, she'd jot down her new ideas. The combination of her cocktail and impassioned speech had just filled her with the most creative new product line ever, one that would position her company as a leader, all while making strides in inclusion.

CHAPTER 20

QIPAO DREAMS

Phoenix

China was a conundrum with its stodgy, old-world beliefs comingling with contemporary pursuits. Stone temples towered over speeding vehicles. Superstitions loomed large beside balding men sporting shirts emblazoned with trendy logos.

Phoenix and Orchid, as a couple, were their own paradox. Mostly, they were more alike than not, despite the contrast of divergent upbringings. Their values, their humor, and their compatibility trumped any superficial differences.

Orchid had maintained her composure after Phoenix returned from his orthopedist's appointment with a prescription for physical therapy.

"Want me to go with you?" she'd asked

He appreciated the offer but went during the day while she was at work. A few weeks in, he was glad not to have her there. Rehab sucked. Not because Phoenix didn't want to do the work. He wasn't seeing progress.

"It still hurts?" the physical therapist asked him. The guy was competent but didn't have the insight into Phoenix that his US therapist, Nadine, would have.

They were standing at parallel bars, similar to those Phoenix had first faced nine months ago. He remembered his frustration at only being able to grasp one side and balance on an elbow on the other side. Today was no better. Worse even. Last year, physical therapy had given him hope. Nadine and her goals. Now, his abilities seemed to have regressed to the early stages immediately after his accident.

Phoenix tried another step, and another. "The pain is a seven out of ten." He caught a glimpse of his limping gait in the mirror.

The guy raised one tattooed arm and tugged at his ear, a sign things weren't going well. "You could come more often if you want, or you could see what the doctor thinks."

"Yeah, okay, I'll do that."

"Keep doing your exercises. You don't want to lose muscle mass."

Phoenix headed to the locker room to change, then wheeled out to the car. *Lose muscle mass*? Yeah, he didn't want that. He'd lost enough already.

The driver sped to the restaurant to meet Kit.

He had invited Kit out to escape being stuck in his head. And stuck in the apartment. When he'd called, Phoenix had warned, "My treat. It's only fair to let you know I'm in a chair, so I'll need an accessible place."

Beat.

"How about you pick the spot this time?" Kit replied.

Phoenix zipped through the automatic doors towards the restaurant called China Palace. The website claimed the place was accessible, the nearest restaurant to tout this distinction.

He held up his forefinger and middle finger to let the hostess know there'd be two guests.

Her lower jaw unhinged. Let her stare. He was mobile, adept at maneuvering his wheelchair with one hand.

She led him into the dining area, away from the main foot traffic.

A dark-haired waitress in a traditional *qipao* dress approached with a teapot. Her pretty smile widened as he looked up.

She offered tea.

"Yes, please," he answered in Chinese.

Her skin blushed pale pink up the rounded collar of her neckline as she poured. She backed away from the table with a slight bow at the waist.

Being by himself didn't usually bother him. However, Chinese lunch patrons didn't seem to have the social etiquette to which he was accustomed. Rather than keeping their curiosity subtle, one older couple openly gaped, staring at Phoenix as they chewed their food. Staring wasn't considered rude in China. He didn't have the energy to engage in discourse about inclusivity, so he ignored them and lifted the tea to his mouth.

Kit strode over, decked out in a smart suit, his blond hair neat. His old colleague rounded the table to shake Phoenix's hand, and then froze with his palm midair.

Damn. His friend had pictured meeting a one-handed Phoenix in a wheelchair, not missing more limbs.

"I told you about the chair," Phoenix started.

"Oh my god, what the what happened to you?"

"I fell. At the Great Wall. A few weeks ago."

Kit sank into his seat. "What the hell. Are you suing them?"

"No."

"I'll get you a lawyer. It's tough here. They don't value individual rights like we're used to. But you're a foreigner. There's bound to be something. Oh my god."

Phoenix understood his misassumption. He wanted to laugh. He wanted to cry.

"This was from the train accident," Phoenix explained.

Kit nodded, finally understanding.

"You are a hero, man."

Phoenix cut him off from this unproductive line of thinking. "I'm not. Accidents happen, and now I'm trying my best. Which is all any of us can do."

Kit's eyebrows knitted together. "You really had me thinking after our last lunch. Now I'm on overdrive here."

Phoenix aimed his phone at the black and white code on their table. "Speaking of lunch, what would you like?"

"I've heard the tofu is good here," Kit grinned a nod to their last meal.

"Sounds good." Phoenix tapped a few more entrees into his WeChat app and showed his screen to his friend. "Anything else?"

Kit picked an eggplant dish, and then leaned back. "You were right last time, you know."

"It happens occasionally. What was it this time?"

"About disability awareness. There's a long way to go here."

"Damned superstitions. I've been thinking. The power of media has been used for good again and again. How could we leverage that here?"

"For one, my agency could take on more pro bono projects. You should come work with us on it. Be an advisor. Hell, be the talent."

Phoenix was discomfited by the stares of fellow lunch-goers. The idea of being in the public eye was even less appealing. "My girlfriend has the same foolhardy idea," he said.

"She's whip-smart, you said so yourself. You'd be like a celebrity. A good-looking guy like you. The media would throw themselves all over it. Turn you into a heartthrob."

"Kit, you're delusional. You yourself have nearly lost your cool every time you've seen me. You think a Chinese audience is going to find me a heartthrob? Or heartburn?" He aimed for sarcasm to tug his friend off this fruitless path.

"It'll totally work. You see, we're trying to change perceptions, right? Humanize the experience? So, let's flip the narrative. Nothing wrong with grandmas in wheelchairs, but we'll show them a handsome foreigner bench pressing jeeps or something." He gestured towards Phoenix's biceps bulging under his short-sleeved shirt.

"I think you've lost your mind."

"No, you were totally onto something last time. You were right to put me in my place. I've been an idiot. I'll prove it to you right now. Look at the girls here checking you out."

Phoenix glanced down, his mouth twisting over the memory of the older couple. "Believe me, that's not why they're looking."

Their dark-haired waitress arrived with a server tray. She set several bowls and dishes onto their table.

"Everything fine?" she asked in Chinese. Her blush fanned farther along her neckline.

"Miss, do you think he's handsome?" Kit asked her, one eyebrow raised as he enunciated the question in Mandarin.

"Don't harass our waitress." Phoenix wanted to smack his friend.

She took in Phoenix's blue eyes from under long lashes. "Yes. Definitely, yes." Her blush traveled to her cheeks. She backed away and fled.

"See?" Kit asked Phoenix, tapping his chopsticks for emphasis.

"That proves nothing. You put her on the spot. What else is she going to say?"

"It's not just what she said. Exhibit one is that she said it twice. Exhibit two was the expression on her face. If that wasn't the look of a crush, I don't know what was," Kit answered.

Phoenix served his friend cubes of spicy tofu, and then dished some for himself. He was glad the chopsticks weren't the disposable type he'd struggle to split apart one-handed.

"The question is, what actually overcomes discrimination? Think about all the automatic judgments we make every day," Phoenix pondered aloud.

"It's the only way to make it through a day. If we had to dispose of all our assumptions, we'd just be babbling idiots in the corner trying to fight our way out of a paper bag."

"Like you, last time."

"Ouch."

"Though to be fair, I should've given you a heads up."

Kit stirred rice into his spicy sauce and they discussed their agencies between mouthfuls.

As they finished eating, Kit used his chopsticks to indicate the gaping couple. "What's up with that table over there?"

Phoenix waved an arm over his lap to indicate the whole of him. "That's the China stare."

"We're Westerners. We're going to get stares."

"You're getting stares for being a blond executive. I'm getting stares because people can't figure me out. How I get around. Where half of me went. I'm a medical miracle." Phoenix gestured for their check.

The waitress came over with a shy smile to offer Phoenix a folded paper with both hands.

Phoenix took the square with a bow of his head. She'd clearly understand why he couldn't comply with the polite Chinese expectation to accept items with two hands.

She backed away. Kit stood, looking puzzled. "Didn't you pay via the app?"

"Maybe this is a receipt." Phoenix opened the folded note and flattened it onto the table.

Kit looked over his shoulder and burst with glee. "She gave you her number."

Phoenix wheeled back from the table as if her contact info were sparking flames.

"Don't leave that. You'll hurt her feelings," Kit said.

Phoenix looked up at his friend, and then around the restaurant. Their waitress was not in sight. "She's not even here to see," he said.

"But she'll find it when she cleans up. Or worse, her coworkers will. She'll never live it down. You can't do that to the poor girl."

"Woman, she's a woman."

"There you go. You're already fighting for her honor."

"You take it. You're the one who gave her the wrong idea about me."

"If she sees me take it, that's even worse. Like we're horse trading." Kit whistled and sauntered towards the exit.

Phoenix sighed and placed the handwritten note inside his pocket. He rolled after his friend and out into the sunshine.

"Start thinking about our campaign," Kit called with a wave.

"We'll see." Phoenix spotted his driver and wheeled over to the waiting car.

CHAPTER 21

HAIRLINE FRACTURE

Phoenix

"You don't have to come with me, you know," Phoenix said, as they rolled out to the car.

"I'm not missing it," Orchid replied.

She held his hand as the driver sped them to a western-friendly clinic accustomed to treating expats. At the hospital parking lot, in the accessible space with the extra width, Orchid helped set up Phoenix's wheelchair. The gray-green building saluted the blue sky.

Phoenix transferred, feeling his mouth downturn as the motion bumped his leg. She kissed a soft corner of his lips.

Orchid toted his prosthetic accoutrements and followed him into the facility.

Inside the waiting area, wheelchairs abounded. For once, Phoenix fit right in.

A no-nonsense receptionist checked them in. She raised an eyebrow when Phoenix shared his surname.

"I know, the irony," Phoenix said.

They were shown into a clean, white room. An unlit x-ray view box hung on the wall. Orchid deposited Phoenix's things onto the paper-covered exam table.

"What are you missing at work today?" Phoenix asked.

She ran down her calendar at Lauder. "New product test findings. Monthly sales results. Politics," she laughed.

"I'm glad I gave you an excuse."

Phoenix wheeled over and wrapped his arms around her hips. "I love you."

She leaned down to return his embrace and nibble the tender spot along his neck.

"Never mind lunch after this," Phoenix growled.

Orchid was laughing when the doctor entered. She let go to take a seat.

"How are you feeling?" the doctor greeted them.

"Better if I can get out of this thing," Phoenix waved at his chair.

"Is your leg getting any better?" she asked as she washed her hands.

"If not being able to stand is better. It's been almost two months."

"Things take time," she said, and manipulated Phoenix's knee from his seated position.

"It feels like it'll be never."

She listened to his lack of progress and palpated his injury site. "Does this hurt?"

"The swelling is gone. The physical therapist has me working on flexibility. But my leg can't bear any weight. And there's more phantom pain." Phoenix shot a guilty look at Orchid.

"Phantom pain? You didn't tell me," Orchid accused.

"How often?" the doctor asked.

"A few times a week, sometimes every day."

Orchid frowned. She'd only witnessed his phantom limb sensation once, when they were down the shore at his aunt and uncle's house for Easter. She'd fetched his pain meds and massaged away the sharp stabbing sensations until he'd fallen asleep.

"Sometimes, there's less phantom pain when you're wearing the prosthesis. You want to try it here and show me?" The doctor directed the question at Phoenix.

"Okay," he said. He snagged the silicone liner that Orchid had deposited onto the examination table and began rolling it up his leg one-handed.

He yanked on a sock. His residual limb had grown slender during the months in his chair, so he pulled on a second one. "There's been some atrophy," he said.

The doctor noted something on his chart.

Phoenix settled his knee into its socket.

"The Great Wallop's not going to keep us down … not for long," Orchid said.

He held the exam table's edge and tried a step. The doctor stayed close to his side. She looked tiny beside his six-foot height.

Phoenix grimaced.

"Sometimes, it takes a bit to get used to again. You'll have to work your way back up to the hours you're used to."

Phoenix's expression dipped.

"I'm not giving up." He limped two steps, then his knee buckled. The doctor steadied one elbow.

"Do you own a cane?" the doctor asked.

"Yes, it's in the car," he said.

"You do?" Orchid's surprise slipped out.

"Your bags were filled with beauty supplies, mine with medical devices," he quipped.

"Let's get an x-ray. The nurse will take care of you. I'll be back once they develop the films."

After the examination, a nurse wheeled Phoenix to radiology for x-rays and then back to the patient room with Orchid.

She left them to await test results.

"I'm joining Caleb on his no-kid campaign," she commented lightly.

"Those brats," he said.

The doctor entered and clipped a black and white image onto a lighted wall panel. "It looks like yours was a traumatic amputation?"

Easy with the jarring language, he silently pleaded.

"Yeah, the train was pretty traumatic." Phoenix glanced at Orchid. Between the medical terminology and his broken state, he wouldn't blame her for bolting. Her face was paler than normal, as she stared at the surreal x-ray of a leg ending a few inches below a knee. Where the eerie glow of white bone ended, skin and muscle pulsed gray around the angled tip of his shin.

The image unsettled him. He'd expected his severed bone to stop in a blunt stub. Instead, ghostly white branches curled like claws from the distal end of his tibia.

"The good news is no breaks or fractures."

"Okay. Is there bad news?"

"Have you ever been diagnosed with heterotopic ossification?"

"That doesn't sound good but no. What is it?"

The doctor traced her finger along the twisted growths on the film.

"It's bone overgrowth. Right into the soft tissue. It's more common with traumatic amputation. It happens more often with combat-wounded veterans. They're still trying to figure out why. Researchers hypothesize that it has to do with stem cells, or macrophages, trying to heal the amputation site."

"So, it's not supposed to look like that?" Orchid asked, her stare unblinking. Her mouth downturned at the corners.

"No," the doctor answered Orchid, then faced Phoenix. "If it's the bone spurs, then your prosthesis would've been uncomfortable before the fall."

"My leg has been hurting for a while. Even in New York. I thought it was because I was wearing my prosthesis so much longer. I stopped using my chair at home," he said.

"When was that?"

"A few months ago."

"Did you stop because I had moved in?" Orchid gasped, putting together pieces of his puzzle, understanding dawning on her face, followed by a rush of guilt.

Phoenix glanced at her and nodded. "Yes, but it's not your fault," he said. Phoenix turned to the doctor. "What do we do about it?" he asked.

"Sometimes it doesn't bother patients, so we don't do anything. Other times, you might need an adjustment. Then, there are cases where the patient requires excision surgery, to remove the bony spikes." The doctor traced the blunt end of his leg on the film with one finger.

"Excision surgery?" Orchid echoed the doctor's words.

The doctor looked at her and demonstrated on Phoenix's leg to answer her question. "Yeah, it's where we cut the muscle flap, clamp off the vessels, and shave off the excess growth." Her finger traced a circular line around the rounded bottom of Phoenix's leg, then mimed a sawing motion.

They needed to operate on his leg again. His knee jerked with the thought of scalpels slicing his flesh, hardware sawing his bone.

"Could this keep happening? More growth and more surgeries, and after a while ..." Phoenix began asking the doctor. Then he noticed Orchid and halted. She looked frozen. He saw her suck in a breath. Her eyes glistened.

Phoenix rolled over towards her and put a hand on her arm. She took his hand and looked straight at the doctor. "How soon do you think he needs the surgery? Are there any risks?"

"Technically, it could result in a higher amputation but that's unlikely. He has good length in his residual limb, so I'm not that worried about losing his knee. Unless there's infection. There's always risk with any surgery. Like anesthesia risk," the doctor responded.

She spoke so casually about Phoenix's body parts. *Higher amputation. Residual Limb. Infection.* She tossed off "losing a knee," as light as if mentioning a dime dropping out of a hole in his pocket. Orchid's questions safeguarded him while he himself was sinking into worry.

"I should probably see my surgeon in the US," he said.

The doctor nodded. "Good idea. Is there anything else I can do for you?"

"No, thanks," he said.

Orchid squeezed his palm, her hand soft in his callused one. "A plan forward, a diagnosis, that's progress."

He listened to the ping of machines in the next room. Ball peens clanged a mechanical dirge.

"We'll get you the best care," she promised.

They followed the doctor out to the lobby. The full impact of surgery had yet to sink in, for either of them.

CHAPTER 22

DOCTOR'S ORDERS

Orchid

O rchid read Phoenix's suffering in the curve of his back as
they passed the receptionist's desk, out through the automatic doors, towards their awaiting car.

"Do you still want to head out for lunch?" she asked.

"I'm up for it. How about you? You've been looking forward to
showing me the restaurant you'd found," he said.

"Let's go, it'll be fun," she said, and allowed her fingertips to
alight along his left forearm, a way to stay connected as they rolled
over the pavement.

Shifu opened the doors for them. With a one-legged pivot,
Phoenix transferred into the back of the car.

Orchid pulled up the center of the chair to fold it like an accor-
dion and handed over the heavy object to their driver. She joined
Phoenix in the backseat while the driver secured the chair in the
trunk. Physically, Phoenix looked more like himself with his prosthesis on.

"To the restaurant," Orchid told the driver in Chinese as the car
pulled out of the parking lot and headed towards the highway.

"Maybe there'll be booze," Phoenix wished aloud.

"I could use a nip of *baijiu*," she added.

At the mention of the famous Chinese liquor, the driver lifted a hand, toasting the couple.

"Are you better?" the driver asked Phoenix in Chinese.

"*Hai keyi*," Phoenix answered that he was okay.

The driver shifted his eyes from the rear-view mirror to the road ahead of them.

"You're a trooper to come today," Phoenix said.

"I wouldn't miss it."

Phoenix snorted. "Like the hospital is your favorite place."

"Maybe not. But you're my favorite person."

He leaned closer to take her hand, his one source of mobility in her palm. Inhale. His pads had grown callused from months in the chair. She thought of buying him a glove, the fingerless type that would leave his dexterity intact. "You're an angel."

This beautiful man with expressive eyes, and kindness to the stars and back. He was a giant to her. A hero. Her love.

"How are you feeling?" she asked.

"It's better to know what's going on. How are you taking it?" he asked.

"I'm worried about you. What are you thinking about doing?"

"I'm sorry to do this to you, but I think I'm going to have to head back home, to my regular surgeon."

She nodded and imagined Phoenix's recovery, limping with a cane in hand. With his sole grip occupied, how would he even open a door? She'd never heard him complain about the difficulties in his everyday life.

His sad pained leg had no idea it was in danger of being bisected. It jutted out on the padded protrusion they called a stump board. Who the hell named these things, as if what Phoenix was going through wasn't hard enough. Words mattered and became part of people's inner monologue. Instead, maybe they could call it his cloud cushion, his chair could be his throne, his crutch a power stick.

She'd known so little about his rehab after his accident. Only the bits she could glean from Caleb, and the photo album she'd seen. She squeezed his shoulder, her silent promise to support whatever he needed. Today, their lunch could bring them some cheer, relief from medical concerns.

With today's news, she knew what she'd do. The doctor had provided a diagnosis, she'd learn everything she could about revision surgery and how to prevent orthopedic issues.

The car pulled in front of the gleaming windows of a hotel.

Their driver approached with Phoenix's chair and opened both doors. As Orchid circled around the back of the car, she spotted a black cane on the trunk's carpeted surface. She grabbed it, in case some unexpected step hampered his chair.

When she joined him on the pavement, he looked up at the tacky sign imprinted "China Palace."

"This is where you wanted to go?" he asked, not hiding his skepticism.

"Yeah, you mentioned liking it for lunch. So, I figured it must be accessible."

Phoenix concentrated on maneuvering through the automatic doors. Together, they traversed the polished floors of the lobby.

This was truly one of the few places in their vicinity that could accommodate wheelchairs. Other places had claimed accessibility yet when she visited, she'd find a wooden stoop or stairs barring the entrance and no ramp. The government had passed barrier-free regulations but the inconsistent implementation meant more blockades rather than fewer.

"I have a funny story about this place," he said.

"Oh yeah? You can tell me over drinks," Orchid said. She held onto hope that maybe a light-hearted lunch could salvage the day.

"*Liang wei?*" the hostess asked if they were a party of two. Orchid gave her name, and they were led to a table tucked in the far corner with a chair already removed, as Orchid had requested. She sighed with relief that they wouldn't subject him to extraneous fuss.

Orchid leaned the cane next to Phoenix's chair, and they opened their apps to order. "My friend Star had a shrimp dish the other night that looked good. You should branch out."

"Vegetarianism has grown on me," he said.

A pretty waitress in a high-necked qipao joined them at their table.

"Would you like tea?" The woman blushed as she bent her head, dark ponytail swishing over one shoulder as she used the proper pronoun for "you" to offer them a hot beverage.

"Do you have *baijiu*?" Orchid asked for Chinese fire water.

The young server's eyes raked over Phoenix. She blushed, nodded, and left.

"So, my story," Phoenix began, but Orchid spoke at the same time.

She leaned forward to distract Phoenix from brooding over the disappointing doctor's visit. "How many Interpol spies do you think are here?" she whispered in a conspiratorial hush, scanning the late afternoon crowd.

Phoenix was game. "More pressing is how much data the Party is gathering as we speak. Did you know that in the eighties, if you went to a state dinner, they'd end the meal with individualized desserts under aluminum covers? When you'd lift the cover, your favorite dessert would be underneath."

"What?" Orchid was surprised at this quirky tidbit.

"You might think that this was a welcoming gesture. You'd be wrong. It was the government's way to say they know everything about you, down to whether you like whipped cream, and how you take your coffee."

"If they bring you a double espresso at the end of this meal, I'm going to freak out."

The waitress returned with freshly rouged cheeks and lips. She placed two stemmed shot glasses on the table and filled them from a decanter.

"*Ganbei!*" Orchid toasted Phoenix with the Chinese phrase that literally translated to "dry glass," meaning they should drink the whole shot. They swallowed the stuff that smelled like pure alcohol. The clear liquid burned on the way down.

"Mother, this stuff stings," she laughed. Then, warmth spread, coating some of Orchid's grief from the day that hadn't gone as she'd hoped. Orchid gestured for more.

"I better tell you that story about this place," he said.

The waitress refilled their glasses while studying Phoenix from beneath dark lashes. Blush traveled far above her collar to flush her neck and cheeks red.

A waiter arrived with a server platter full of dishes. The busboy unceremoniously deposited their meal onto their table. The waitress escaped.

Then the unperturbed guy departed, and Orchid turned to Phoenix. "She knows you."

"As I was saying, I wanted to tell you something funny about this place."

"She has a thing for you."

Phoenix chuckled. "It's a ridiculous story."

He ladled tofu and vegetables onto her plate.

"So, you remember I ate here with my friend Kit?" Phoenix asked.

"Well, yeah."

"He was trying to prove I could be the face of a campaign to raise awareness for people with disabilities."

"What does this have to do with *qipao* girl?"

"He asked if she thought I was handsome, to prove a point to me. And she misunderstood the question. So, she gave me her number."

Orchid's confusion turned to humor. "You're collecting waitstaff admirers all over the world. Ana, and now her."

Phoenix exhaled at her softening expression. "Please, don't be upset. I'll let you win at Egyptian Ratscrew."

Orchid chuckled. "That game is pure luck."

He spooned more food onto both their plates.

"I read that the dofu is really spicy here," she said, and tried a bite.

"The eggplant is good here too," he said.

"What's this about you being the face of a campaign?"

"I got Kit all fired up about disability awareness. He thinks I should be the talent."

"You have my vote. And the waitress seems to be Team Phoenix too."

His grin was her reward. He shook his head. "You are too much."

She leaned close. She couldn't wait to curl up in bed with him that night. "Not too much for you."

CHAPTER 23

REVISIONIST SCALPEL

Orchid

Back at home, Phoenix sequestered himself in the bedroom to write while she caught up with work. He was still tapping away at his keyboard when she began to prepare dinner. She missed him at her side, chopping greens.

Orchid slaughtered turnips with a butcher's knife that had come with the furnished apartment, fuming over the fate of everything. Unfair. Not fair that he'd have to undergo surgery again. She decapitated the green shoots, skewered the thin skin, and gutted their tender flesh.

Water boiled, waiting to torture their quartered bodies.

She used Phoenix's adaptive cutting board that was still out from the veggie omelet he'd pan-fried for her that morning.

After she placed their meal into the oven, Orchid slipped into the bedroom. She could hear a steady rat-a-tat against the keyboard in the spare bedroom that doubled as an office. An idea formed. She changed her outfit and knocked on the guest room door. "Dinner!" she called.

A few minutes later, Phoenix rolled out to join her at their round table, set with steaming dishes.

His gaze swept over her high-necked qipao. Then he doubled over his chair with laughter.

"If you can't beat 'em, join 'em," Orchid said, and swept a hand down over the embroidered pattern of her dress.

Phoenix wheeled over to the open spot at the table.

"How's your writing going?" she asked him, and spooned food onto both their plates.

"It's hard to believe I have so much to say," he said. He speared a bite of vegetables into his mouth.

"You said you've written hundreds of pages already?"

"Yeah. And now that I talked with Mom, I want to get everyone's viewpoints."

"Even mine?" Orchid asked.

"Especially yours. After I'm farther along, you can read it."

Orchid's fork stilled. His journey, in his words. "I'd love to."

"When I go home, I'd like to get input from my family."

"Of course. That makes sense."

"It's just that you're in it too."

"I trust you. Share it with Caleb. Give it to his girlfriend. Whatever you want. Whatever will help."

He raised his wine glass. "To *our* story."

Orchid clinked his glass with hers and pictured their day. Phoenix represented the greatest acceptance she'd ever known, more even than the care of her parents, because he'd *chosen* to love her. The unconditionality of its nature healed her in ways no one else had. She'd support him no matter what he needed.

"Tell me what's on your mind," she said, and popped a bite into her mouth.

"I left a message for my doctor and looked into flights," he said. Straightforward, no drama. They were both growing.

"Mm hmm. Do you want me to come to New York with you?"

He abandoned his fork and placed a hand over hers.

"That's really generous. Your assignment is an opportunity of a lifetime. Your work is here. I get that. I understand."

"How long will you be gone?"

"I don't know. If there's surgery, there's a recovery period. Rehab. And no guarantees," he said.

"I'm really sorry you have to go through this."

And she was. A year ago, she was falling for him and fighting it. Then, he'd fallen and since then, he'd been fighting battles that most people had never endured. Sorry couldn't capture the feeling of injustice that ached under her diaphragm.

It wasn't the first time that catastrophes had befallen the people she'd loved.

After dinner, she fell into a fitful sleep. She was wakened by a rough slap against her shoulder. A figure clamped a paw over her cry. His face gaped open with angled daggers for teeth, glistening in the moonlight. He twisted her head to take in the apparitions of people who'd suffered because of her. Dad, Mom, Phoenix, and other shadowy plaintiffs ballooned into view and pressed against her. Each muttered incantation. "Selfish, selfish, selfish" "Undeserving, unde-serving, undeserving." Phoenix reared up, cheeks wet with suffering. *Oh Phoenix, what's wrong?* "Cruel, cru-el, Cruella," he reproached.

Orchid pushed them all away. She catapulted out of bed. Her stomach roiled. Before Orchid could reach the bathroom, Mandy sprang from her closet, her face full of fury "Monster!" she accused and thrust an object into her face.

Baby Matty floated before her, frozen like a wax mummy. Orchid shrieked. Mandy appeared, screeching with outrage. Her soft ma-ternal fingers lengthened into javelins pointed towards the ground. Matty lay still at Orchid's feet. Blood pooled, spreading from his limbless torso.

It was Orchid's turn to scream. Her hands were murder. She yielded the butcher's knife, dispatching tender turnips into bloody stumps.

Bile churned. The weapon flew from her grip. She bolted for the toilet. Just as she reached the bathroom, the door swung open. Shadowed by the entryway, a figure crouched in a wheelchair. Empty pants legs swung from the lip of the chair. The ghost of her father. Castigating her. The attacker materialized the butcher's knife from nothing and heaved it towards her exposed jugular.

"No!" Her legs tangled, and she plummeted overboard, weightless, midair. Her voice escalated, piercing her ear drums until she was gasping for oxygen. Then she hit water. Sinking deeper than the Mariana trench. Sea creatures with more legs than octopi slithered snake limbs down her throat until she was choking, and crying, and vomiting.

CHAPTER 24

FOR POSTERITY

Phoenix

P hoenix's leg throbbed. He wondered whether to get out of bed and risk waking Orchid. Early morning dawn peeked through the window. Since the fall at the Great Wall, everything he did would need to be weighed against what he was physically capable of. What he'd previously taken for granted now seemed rare, precious, and unattainable. He tried not to sink into the dark spaces that beckoned in the gray stretch before morning. *Incapable. Half.*

He shook his head against despair.

Gingerly, he sat up and tested a little motion. His knee complained. He kept it crouched at an angle as he inched over the mattress towards his chair. Up on one foot, then down again into the seat. A pile of dirty clothes impeded his wheeled progress. In the bathroom, he swallowed two anti-inflammatory pills. Too bad they didn't have such an easy fix for inflamed emotions. There was an ad idea in there somewhere.

When Phoenix swung the door open, a figure careened towards him. His reptile brain spiked for a split-second before his rational mind recognized the stumbling shadow as his girlfriend.

Spotting him, she staggered back. Eyes wide, one arm warded off his approach. "Nooo!" her scream ratcheted up several unnerving octaves. She tripped on the bedside table. Something crashed to the ground. Phoenix launched himself out of his chair and wrapped himself around her just as her legs tangled. He broke her fall onto their bedroom floor. His mind blanked with pain.

It took a moment to recover his bearings. She writhed in his arms, wild with tears, tearing at her clothes. "Orchid, shhh, I'm right here."

He'd witnessed her panic before when she'd been confronted by photos of injured soldiers. He himself now triggered those depths of repulsion. Pitched on their wooden floor, desperately grappling with her writhing, was not part of the doctor's physical therapy regimen.

"It's okay, shhh."

He propped up to a sitting position, comforting her.

Orchid's wave crested, then terraced down, bit by bit.

She quieted, then whimpered in his arms. "There you go, there you are." Phoenix smoothed her hair out of her eyes and pressed lips to her forehead. Her slender form trembled with vulnerability.

His words came from some long-ago parental memory. How his mother had comforted him when he'd scraped an elbow. "It's okay, sweetheart. You're okay." His knee pulsed an angry beat; it was not ready for these gymnastics.

Orchid's darting eyes settled on his wheelchair. She shrank back.

The sleek design and racing wheels represented a top-of-the-line model, a necessity for his mobility. Yet in this moment, he saw the hulking red alien as she saw it. Foreign. Other.

When she quieted, Phoenix guided her into their soft bed, and covered her. During the time that she slumbered away her nightmare, Phoenix held her tight. Now, sun motes floated towards their comforter, and over their shared dresser, her four drawers to his two.

He pondered his family back home. Caleb and Sascha had their share of drama. Yet, they co-owned a business and worked together on a regular basis. Their issues centered on a difference of life goals. Issues they could discuss. He hoped they would. He wondered how he could help his brother the way Caleb had helped him.

Orchid's issues were visceral, not something they could solve through conversation. At night, her polite artifice of daytime behavior stripped away to her actual base instincts. The immutable facts of his life frightened her.

She stirred and drew a deep inhale. He kissed her hair, his one anchor in this foreign land. Her eyelids opened, took him in, and shut again.

"You up, hungry bird?"

"How come you're so chipper?" she grumbled.

"Because you've been asleep like umpteen hours and I'm happy to finally have company. How are you feeling?" he asked.

Her eyes opened. "Oh," she said.

"Did you have a bad dream?"

She nodded and hung her head.

Phoenix nuzzled her cheek. "Sorry, sweetie. Want to tell me?"

She sat up and pointed at his bedside table. "Is that water?"

He righted himself and handed her the glass. "*Baijiu*," he joked.

"Booze? Okay then, Egyptian Ratscrew afterwards."

He laughed.

She drank hungrily and looked down at her bare fingers. "That was a terrible night. Everyone was haunting me. My dead parents. Mandy. Then I drowned in an ocean."

"What? That's screwed up."

"I felt so guilty, everyone was blaming me."

He pressed lips to her hair and asked, "What can I do?"

"Nothing. It's just. Do you ever think I'm bad luck? Do you ever wonder ... if I'd taken a later flight? Or not asked you to come with me to the airport .... You wouldn't have been at that station at that time."

Phoenix drew her closer, his sensitive girlfriend. "My accident isn't your fault."

"But don't you wonder? Ever?"

He grew wistful, trying his damnedest not to believe that she was wishing for the person he was. "I used to wonder if there was something *I* could've done differently. I think that was the bargaining stage of my grief. In some ways, that day wasn't all bad. I couldn't stop thinking about you."

"Me?"

He nodded. "When I was waiting for the train, I was listening to your playlist. Missing you already."

She held him so tightly that it distracted him from the ache in his knee.

"Don't feel guilty. Even if I could, I wouldn't change a thing."

She hiccupped a breath and stared up at him. "You wouldn't?"

"I've imagined it. If I'd let the guy go. I would've witnessed his death. And done nothing about it. That would haunt me more than this." He waved down towards the sheet dipping halfway down his calf.

"You're a hero. My aunt is going to love you," she predicted.

"Let's hope," he said. "I'm nervous to meet her."

"Good. That means you care what my family thinks. Plus, that'll be good motivation for us to clean up."

"I'm in," he said.

Orchid ticked her list off each finger. "Before she arrives this weekend, we still have to grocery shop, do the laundry and sort through the mail."

"Do you want me to wear my arm for her?" He'd been considering how the woman who had raised her would assess his injuries.

She pulled back an inch, like the question had startled her.

"Um, you don't have to do anything special—"

Cutting her off, he answered, "I'll try it on. It's been a while since I've worn it."

"Only if you want to."

"If the place is going to be that clean, we should invite some people over," he said, on a roll with ideas now.

She perked up and hopped out of bed. "Ooh, good idea. It'll take the scrutiny off us." She began to fold the clean laundry.

"You've mentioned your friend Star from work," he said, and transferred to his chair to come help. She had thoughtfully saved the shorts and dish towels for him. Symmetrical items with minimal edges were easier to fold one-handed.

"Yeah, Star would love to meet you. And how about Billy?"

"You mean Billy from the Great Wall?" he asked, thrown by the name he hadn't thought of in a while.

"Yeah, he texted that he's still in Beijing."

"Sounds like fun," he said.

By Saturday afternoon, their apartment was buffed and stocked with snacks. Shifu had messaged that he was on his way back from Capital Airport with Ayi.

Music hummed in the background as Orchid plated hors d'oeuvres and Phoenix garnished the vegetarian charcuterie board.

Their buzzer sounded. Orchid admired Phoenix's strong shoulders flexing beneath his blue button-down as he wheeled to their front door. He looked sharply dressed in charcoal gray pants. He'd used his arm prosthesis this week. The flesh-colored hand appeared natural peeking out from under his sleeve. Wheeling with two arms increased his speed.

"Come on in," Phoenix said, shaking hands with Billy from his seated position.

"Oh, is that a lightweight chair?" Billy asked, following Phoenix into the apartment. He waved hello to Orchid. His straight Asian hair was slicked back, offsetting the youthfulness of his string-tie hoodie. The duo meandered to the refrigerator where Orchid heard the clink of bottles and chatter about mobility equipment.

The doorbell rang. Timely bunch.

Orchid went to open the door. Star stood in the doorframe and thrust out a potted flower.

"Orchids," she said, accepting the gift.

"*Lan hua* are good luck in Chinese," Star said, using the Chinese name for orchids.

"Thanks, Star," Orchid nodded, realizing that here in China, her unusual name didn't feel like a burden. In a country where orchids signaled good fortune, she didn't mind receiving them as a gift. She waved her friend inside.

They joined the men in the dining area by the food. Star shook their hands with a slight bow and handed a gift bag to Phoenix.

"Thank you." He pulled out a flat box with Chinese characters on it. "Origami," he said.

Orchid pointed at the picture of a mythical flying creature made of gold paper, its majestic wings sweeping below the bird's crowned head. Its tail spiraled, longer than its torso, each spike made of a multitude of perfect folds. "Is that a phoenix?" she asked.

Star nodded. "In Chinese culture, a phoenix is a gift from heaven to the empress. It brings prosperity and peace," she told them.

Orchid's phone lit with a message; her aunt was on her way up. "Excuse me," she said.

"I never knew that. Does your name have a celestial meaning?" he asked.

"In Chinese, my name *xing xing* mean star star, twins," Star explained.

"I have a twin brother," Phoenix offered.

Orchid hurried to slip on her shoes and go down to help her aunt with her suitcases. She could hear the trio behind her laughing. It had been a good idea to create a celebratory atmosphere. When she opened the door, Aunt Lily was already heading towards her, their driver toting her baggage. Ayi spotted Orchid and raised a hand in greeting.

They met at the threshold for a hug. "Hi, Ayi."

Her petite frame felt frailer than the last time they'd seen each other, like a hard hug could crack a rib.

"Aiya," her aunt declared using the universal Chinese phrase that equated to a mild uh-oh, or oh my. She pulled back so she could study Orchid at arm's length. "You're too thin."

Of course, their time together would begin with a critique. There really was nothing like family.

"You look nice. I like your hair," Orchid replied, admiring her aunt's trim pants, slipper shoes, and puffy purple vest over a long-sleeved shirt.

Orchid took the handle of her aunt's bag and waved goodbye to Shifu. She led them into the apartment, seeing the space with her aunt's critical eye. The front door shut behind them with a creak as if the hinges needed WD-40. A scuff mark by their front door pedestal table seemed magnified. Orchid remembered she'd forgotten to dust the guest room molding. The pair doffed their shoes and changed into guest slippers lined up at the door.

The threesome that had been chatting came towards them. Orchid abandoned her aunt's luggage by the living room sofa. The guests paused near the credenza that doubled as a makeshift bar, stocked with bottles of wine, Chinese liquor, and myriad glasses.

Orchid facilitated introductions. She wondered how her aunt would judge Phoenix's residual limb clothed in loosely cuffed trousers, jutting out onto the chair's padded stump board. Stop, this line of thinking was treason.

Her aunt bent down towards Phoenix and offered her hand. Their shared smiles relaxed Orchid's abdomen. They were going to be fine. Why had she worried? "Nice to meet you," Phoenix offered. Orchid understood that his full lips widening in joy was for her. Because he cared about meeting her family. Because he loved her.

Next, Ayi introduced herself to Star. The two of them exchanged pleasantries in Chinese, Star cupping both of her hands around Ayi's, bowing lower than her elder, as was considered culturally appropriate.

Then Ayi turned to Billy whose boyish grin glowed white against his tanned skin. This time, she used both of her hands to take his and deepened her bend. "It's so good to meet you. Orchid told me about you. You're an entrepreneur?"

Billy rolled with the upgrade to his title. "Yeah, our work's entrepreneurial. Orchid told me about you too."

"What would you like to drink?" Phoenix asked, gesturing to the beverage choices lining the makeshift bar.

She pointed at the bottle of white wine and crossed her arms as he poured her a glass. "Orchid has always been smart. I'm proud that she won this assignment to Beijing," Aunt Lily said to Billy.

It struck Orchid that her whole upbringing had been characterized by this paradox: in public, her aunt would praise her, in private, she'd berate her. She wasn't alone. Her American Asian friends had shared similar stories.

"Yeah right," Billy said. "If only I had that luck. To have my company pay for me to come to China."

Aunt Lily accepted the wineglass from Phoenix and continued speaking with Billy.

A timer sounded in the kitchen. "Dinner's ready," Orchid said and hurried to the stove. She preferred being out of earshot while her aunt and Billy conversed as if she weren't there.

In the hum of voices, she could hear Star asking Phoenix about his brother.

With hot mitts on each hand, she brought a steaming tray of Chinese dim sum to the table. "Go ahead and sit, everyone," she instructed.

Phoenix circled the table, filling empty miniature shot glasses from their bottle of baijiu.

Ayi chose a spot between Billy and the open space where Phoenix wheeled his chair. Star took the chair next to Phoenix, continuing their conversation about twins. Orchid spooned dumplings, bamboo-wrapped zongzi, and fluffy baozi onto each person's plate, and then placed the still heaping serving tray onto the middle of the table. She sat in the last seat between Star and Billy, and smiled at Phoenix, pleased that the first party they were co-hosting was progressing smoothly.

"Let's say grace," Ayi suggested. She extended her reach to either side, indicating that the table should hold hands. Then she bowed her head to offer thanks to God.

While everyone else's eyes were closed, Orchid peeked at Star, wondering if her Chinese friend might feel offended at the religious practice in a country that didn't condone Christianity.

Star looked peaceful. Then Orchid caught sight of her aunt startle when she grasped Phoenix's rubber hand. Ayi glanced at the lifelike prosthesis, then refocused on the prayer. Orchid silently insisted that her aunt not judge the man she loved. Years of being critiqued for her hair, for her weight, for her friends, and for her grades came flooding back.

"Thank you, Lord, for the bounties of this table, and bless these young people," Ayi said.

"Amen," her friends intoned, then opened their eyes and tucked into the meal.

"This is all the food we talked about that day we met!" Billy exclaimed, as he unwrapped bamboo leaves to reveal the sticky rice zongzi.

"Exactly," Orchid said, his pleasure widening her cheeks.

Ayi swallowed her bite and turned to Billy. "Are your parents Chinese?"

"My dad's Chinese. I'm half Asian," he answered.

"Just like Orchid," Ayi nodded approvingly.

Phoenix lifted his shotglass and the guests followed suit. "To friends and family. Thanks for being here," he said.

"Ganbei," they chorused with him, and everyone emptied their glasses, Aunt Lily included.

Orchid had served herself two zongzi. Now that her guests were tucking into their meals, she untied the string on one of the dark green tetrahedrons, removed the fragrant leaves, and slipped it onto Phoenix's plate.

"Thank you. I'm excited to try your childhood favorites," he said and cut into the steaming rice with a fork.

"How was your trip?" Phoenix asked Ayi.

"A full day of travel and twelve hours' time difference. I'm too old for this," she said.

"Your room's ready whenever you want to go to bed," Orchid assured her.

"I'm packing it in right after dinner. When do you leave for the airport?"

"Crack of dawn. I'm glad we got to meet before I leave," Phoenix said.

Ayi blinked, absorbing something, or perhaps fatigue was setting in.

Star turned to Billy. "Where are you visiting in Beijing? Have you been to the Bird's Nest?" she asked, referring to the largest steel structure in the world, a stadium built for the 2008 Summer Olympics.

Talk turned to Tiananmen Square, the Temple of Heaven, the Forbidden Palace, and other cultural sights.

Before long, dinner finished, with only a few dumplings and a quarter bottle of wine left.

"Even though it's not autumn yet, I bought mooncakes for dessert," Orchid said.

"I'm going to bed," Ayi declared, and pushed back from the table.

"I'm going too. Everything was delicious," Star said, standing and taking several plates to the kitchen.

"I'll say goodnight and thank you," Billy said and apropos of nothing, saluted his tablemates.

Guests carried the dirty dishes to the sink. Phoenix blew out the candles. Orchid bade her guests farewell and wheeled her aunt's bag to the guest room while Phoenix accompanied Star and Billy to the door. She could hear their byes echoing down the hall.

Ayi looked towards the front door and then followed Orchid to her bedroom.

Orchid slung her aunt's bag onto the low dresser and waved towards the walk-in closet. "There are extra pillows and blankets in there. The guest bathroom has clean towels. You must be tired. Is there anything else you need?"

Ayi closed the bedroom door behind them and gestured towards the bed. "Have a seat," she said.

Orchid sank onto the soft coverlet patterned with red peonies.

"Are you happy?" she asked, unzipping her suitcase.

Orchid considered the options. She could list examples under each column: yes, no, maybe. "My life is good. There are challenges though, just like everyone."

Before she could question why Ayi was asking, her aunt weighed in. "At first, I thought Billy was your boyfriend," she said while placing underthings into the leftmost drawer.

Orchid wanted to laugh. "The retired surf teacher?"

"It'd be nice to have a Chinese boyfriend," she said while shoving folded garments into the righthand drawer.

Orchid blinked at the objection. "Why does that matter? Dad wasn't Asian. I'm half Asian."

Her aunt exited the closet to look at Orchid. "I'm not saying there's anything wrong with not being Asian. I'm just saying that you'd have an easier life without culture clashes. It doesn't have to be Billy, but wouldn't it be nice to be with someone who gets your background?"

"You should get to know Phoenix more. He gets my background just fine."

Ayi pulled out a toiletry bag from her suitcase and looked at her niece.

"As long as you're happy, your mom would be too. You deserve it."

Invoking the memory of her mom made Orchid's eyes sting. Mom would've loved Phoenix, right? They would've shared sophisticated conversations about novels and news headlines. The thud of a door closing made Orchid realize how late it was getting. "We can talk tomorrow, okay? I'm really glad you're here safely."

"Good night," her aunt replied, and pulled a toothbrush and toothpaste from her travel kit bag.

"Sleep well." Orchid slipped out of the guest room to find the dining area and kitchen cleaned up. A soft splashing sound rumbled inside the dishwasher.

Orchid turned off the overhead lights and pushed open the door to their bedroom suite. Phoenix had a dawn pickup time. Early bedtime was a good idea.

Phoenix's suitcase lay open on the bench at the foot of their bed, neatly folded clothes tucked beneath his arm prosthesis and skin balm. Together with her Lauder team, she'd been developing a new product line that was going to revolutionize the category. She couldn't wait to surprise Phoenix with her new products. She hoped he'd see how much the innovation was inspired by him.

Orchid changed into her summer nightgown and entered the en suite bathroom. Inside, she joined Phoenix at the double sink with a kiss to one cheek while he maneuvered a humming electric brush inside his mouth. He gave a crooked smile, distorted by the toothbrush.

"Thanks for doing the dishes," she said and began brushing her teeth.

He rinsed and his face brightened. "You're welcome. See you in bed."

Soon enough, she slipped under the covers, where Phoenix was already resting. He rolled onto his left side and opened his arms to her. This was the position that gave him the most mobility to hold her tight. She curled into her favorite spot and rested her cheek on his warm bicep. He smelled clean.

"Unfortunately, I can't suggest goodbye sex when my aunt's in the next room," she whispered.

He laughed, a low rumble that vibrated through her.

"Are you all set for your trip?" she asked.

"I'm packed," he said. "And I left you a birthday gift."

She leaned forward and pressed lips to his mouth.

He kissed her back and then pulled back to look at her. "Your aunt wants me to be Asian." He stated it as fact.

"Did you hear our conversation?"

"Enough of it. The walls are thin."

She traced the indentation of his sternum, feeling his fine hairs beneath her fingertips. "Being Asian doesn't matter to me," she said.

"Ha, that's good because that I can't change."

"Do you want me to go with you to the airport?"

"Nah it's too early. You sleep in."

She turned to curl her back into his torso and fell asleep to his lips pressed against her hair. The last words her conscious mind absorbed was his whisper, "Love you, hungry bird."

CHAPTER 25

ALONE TOGETHER

Orchid

O rchid buried herself beneath the mound of blankets. She hated goodbyes. Her logical mind supported Phoenix's trip. Of course, he should get the best medical care. There was no telling that to the hurt little girl inside who felt abandoned.

An idea had been sparked earlier during her outrage over Mrs. V. Come to think of it, it'd even implanted longer ago, when one kiss with Phoenix could dissolve Violet into a mumbling mess. That man could move some product as the face of a national ad campaign. He was still the model-ready entrepreneur who lit every room he entered. Maybe it was difficult for people, who'd not experienced this intimate before-after comparison, to imagine but the accident didn't lessen him, it made him stronger. Most of all, ads were one thing this man believed in. Her words hadn't been enough to heal his self-doubt. Instead, the power of visual storytelling might be the way to show Phoenix how Orchid perceived him.

Three packages stacked on her bedside table caught her attention. They rose from largest to smallest like the papa bear, mama bear, and baby bear from the Goldilocks children's story. They were wrapped in paper splashed with bright magenta peonies. He always remembered her favorite flowers. She fingered the smallest one. It felt like a jewelry box. Her mind pictured a solitaire diamond on an engagement band. No, even that flicker of imagination was toxic. Sure to lead to disappointment. She moved onto the middle box, a light thing. The largest, papa bear, held the proportions of a book, a slender volume. Her most tangible links to Phoenix.

Screw that. She didn't need to wallow.

She dressed and wandered to the kitchen to make Aunt Lily breakfast.

CHAPTER 26

ROBBER BARON

Roy

PRESENT DAY

Roy's one-year anniversary loomed large. The day he'd traded someone else's life for his clean slate blew guilt down his gullet, until its silent shriek haunted even his daytime hours.

Roy had stumbled into the shelter, incoherent, still drunk, full of suicidal thoughts, the roar of a train haunting his ears, the silk orchid deep in his pocket. Now, though his feet were shod in presentable hand-me-downs, they still easily recalled his harsh stride in cardboard-thin soles against the pavement on that fateful day. At night, alone in bed, the nightmarish whoosh of an impending train would wake him contorted in his sheets.

Guilt must be the devil's work. Penance had fueled the first runaway case he'd solved. Like a haunted man, he'd roamed shelters and questioned people on the street. The hunt kept his daytime mind occupied. The hard work had paid off. The teen's mom shouted her gratitude to local news outlets. Other families began to seek him out. He was humbled by the ones who insisted on gifting him rewards.

The shelter was grateful for the donations his work generated and allowed him to stay beyond the standard period. The pastor encouraged him to keep the rewards and save up for his own place. Roy trusted this gentleman, the Father who had listened to his stories that terrible day. As the anniversary approached, a desire flamed inside to tell the truth.

Roy found Father Lyndon in the quiet pews of the shelter's small sanctuary.

"How are you, my son?"

"I have something to confess."

"I'm all ears."

"Promise you won't hate me."

"God forgives all sins."

"We'll put that to the test," Roy muttered, then inhaled for courage. "That day I came in last July, I never told you what happened."

The cleric gestured for him to sit.

"I was going to jump in front of a train."

A breath escaped from the reverend in a gust of surprise.

"There's more. A guy was standing there. I guess he grabbed me. Pulled me back. Saved my life. But he fell."

The weight of what he owed Phoenix doubled as he told the story. Telling didn't lessen his guilt, it solidified the truth of what had happened. He could picture bright blue eyes under unruly dark hair, a generous mouth, unshaven scruff against pale skin.

"I saw him. On the tracks. By the time I got up, the train came so fast. And ... and he just ... he was gone. Under. I didn't mean to but *I killed the man who saved me.*"

Father Lyndon's ruddy complexion blanched. The man spoke carefully, "You've entrusted me with a great burden. It's life changing to see another man die."

Roy pinched the meat of his own thigh. The pain felt good. Self-inflicted retribution. He may as well get it all out. "I didn't exactly see him die. Under the train, on the tracks, was his ... hand. Just lying there. The wheels must've dismembered the guy. The nice guy with the smile, and the money for my cup. I didn't even help him. I just … ran."

"Dear boy." The pastor sat quietly for a long stretch. The twitch of his brows indicated some deep cogitation. The horror that haunted Roy was as bad as he thought, and worse.

Better for someone else to finally know the truth. He was reproachable, a reprobate, disgusting.

"I can sense your deep guilt. It's a terrible situation, of course. But do you know for certain he died?"

Roy blinked and leaned back. He had never considered an alternative. "I saw his … hand. He was hit by a train. I assume …"

"Of course. Either way, your contrition must be genuine."

"I've never been more sorry."

"The Lord forgives you, my son," he finally said.

Roy hissed a breath of relief. "Thank you." Pinch.

Alone in the din of that evening's dining hall, Roy's mind gravitated towards unanswerable questions. How did his life measure versus the dead man's? Could his ability to reunite fractured families absolve him for ending a life? Could the man have survived?

Nope, dumb ass.

He burned to know more about the man whose life he'd snuffed. The pain twisted hardest at night. How unbalanced was the trade, Phoenix's life for his. What happened afterwards?

Roy was a damned good detective now. He'd figure out who that charmed man was. Make good with his family. Or maybe he'd find out the guy was a wretch. He wanted to know what had actually happened.

He'd start with the reporters who wrote up the articles he'd seen in the paper.

Research.

At last, he had a plan.

CHAPTER 27

HOME SWEET NEW YORK

Phoenix

Each milestone during Phoenix's trip home echoed a reminder of Orchid. The thirteen-and-a-half-hour flight lacked the comfort of Orchid's presence laughing at in-flight rom-coms. Rolling through the airport, Phoenix missed the bounce of Orchid's step beside him.

Caleb met him at baggage claim. "Hey."

"Hey, thanks for coming."

His brother didn't mention Phoenix's seated stance. He simply hoisted the indicated suitcase from the belt and led the way to his pickup truck.

One night at Caleb's place and Phoenix was ready to flee to the city.

"You're supposed to outgrow being a slob," Phoenix told his brother.

"You're welcome for the ride from the airport," Caleb retorted.

"Wheelchairs aren't great over piles of dirty clothes and abandoned shoes."

"Ah, sorry about that," he said, kicking debris towards the wall. "How about I drive you to your place tomorrow?"

Phoenix texted Rina. "Hey, I'm coming in the morning. If you'll be out, please leave a key with the doorman for me."

The next day, morning turned to afternoon before Caleb was awake and able to function. Phoenix was dragging with jet lag and didn't mind having spare time for writing.

Most of Phoenix's stuff was still locked in the truck, so they piled in and drove north.

"Straight from one girl to another," Caleb observed, steering with one hand.

"I honestly don't know how my life got so complicated."

"Single is the simplest."

"But lonely." Phoenix wasn't technically single, yet their distance made their connection feel tenuous. His brother had described the spring day that Orchid arrived at Caleb's shop, making the case for his brother to help get them together. Caleb was the impetus for their Easter weekend down the shore.

"I don't know. You seemed okay after Tish."

"Because I was too busy being a workaholic to notice."

"Was?"

"Yeah, China changed me. Work doesn't seem important anymore."

"What, you Buddha or something now? Which by the way, I'd approve."

"I'm not, but it's interesting that you're a fan."

"The Buddhists I know are the most chill."

"The precepts all make sense to me, not that I can adhere to them."

"No killing, no stealing, no lyin', no adultery, no drugs." Caleb counted them off on his fingers.

"Yeah, except I haven't given up meat, so that's killing animals. And I can knock back booze with the best of them, and that's considered a drug."

"If you think *you'd* have a hard time, try being me." Caleb barked a sharp laugh.

Phoenix studied him closer. "What's up with you? How's Sascha?"

Caleb shrugged. "She's dating. She's happy. She comes in hummin' like a showgirl."

"Which you hate."

"That's one lucky guy, hope he knows it."

Humor played at the corners of Phoenix's lips. It bubbled from his diaphragm and erupted as guffaws.

"What the hell, I'm pourin' my guts out here." Caleb's downturned mouth looked hurt.

"I'm not laughing at you. I'm thinking, we come from a judge and a mom, who besides running her own design business, could probably be commander-in-chief. So, how come we're so messed up?"

"Well, you weren't messed up until the accident, you know."

"I was though. Why do you think I worked so hard? I was always trying to prove something. I still think I can never live up to Dad."

"You gotta be kidding me. He thought you walked on water."

"Not at all. He pushed me something fierce."

"I'm the one they gave up on."

"Mom and Dad would never give up on you, you know that. Plus, I was jealous of you in school."

Caleb's thick neck swiveled to stare at his brother.

"Eyes on the road," Phoenix directed.

"What the hell did you have to be jealous of?" Caleb asked with disbelief.

"Girls talked to me so they could find things out about you. If I could've monetized the line of Caleb fans at my locker, I would've pulled in a mint."

"Your memory's gone. Even before you left for that fancy college prep school, you were the one girls wanted."

Then they were both chuckling. It felt good.

The truck pulled in front of Phoenix's apartment building. The last time he'd been here, Orchid had stormed to the car after learning that Rina would be staying at his apartment. He'd spent that ride to the airport striving for honesty about their impending difficulties. In hindsight, his viewpoint seemed naïve, compared to the reality of today's travails.

Caleb swung out to grab Phoenix's things. He set up his brother's chair and watched him transfer into it. "You feeling okay?"

It was a complicated question. "Things aren't great," Phoenix said. Which summed up a lot. His physical, mental, *and* emotional states.

"Life sucks," Caleb agreed. He grabbed the rolling bag and pushed it over the rough sidewalk.

The brothers paused at the three stairs down to the lobby.

"How did I forget? I guess the Board was too busy to deal with accessibility," Phoenix said.

The doorman ran up with an apartment key for Phoenix. "There's a ramp down to the garage. You can take the elevator there," he said.

Phoenix glared at the lobby, mere strides away. "Never mind," Phoenix decided. He stood and held the right railing. One at a time, he hopped down the steps.

"Would you mind grabbing my chair?" he asked his brother.

They were rolling halfway through the lobby when Caleb grunted at the doorman. "How about getting a ramp here?" He sounded peeved.

"It's not his fault," Phoenix said as they awaited the elevator.

"ADA passed in 1990. Why the hell isn't every place accessible by now?"

"It's worse in China. Not just the accessibility, but the judgment, the staring."

"Think you'll get used to it?"

"I'm not sure I'm heading back," Phoenix replied. They boarded the lift and Caleb punched the button for Phoenix's floor.

Caleb peered down at his brother. "Not going back? What happened with Orchid?"

Last time he was in this elevator was with Orchid. It was four in the morning in Beijing. He hoped she was sleeping well.

"When I fell at the Great Wall, it was hard on her. All the medical stuff makes her nightmares return."

"We've been down this path. Just so I'm clear, is this you projecting or did she tell you to buzz off?"

Phoenix huffed air. "It's all fact, but she didn't tell me to buzz off."

The elevator doors parted.

"Ready to see your ex?" Caleb asked, mischief in his tone.

"Nope."

They wheeled down the corridor. Phoenix noticed the fresh coat of paint. While he was worse for the wear, his building had been getting a makeover.

"You probably don't want my advice, but I wouldn't write off Orchid so easy."

"It's like the universe has it out for us. The thing that's her kryptonite, her Achilles' heel, is the one thing I can't change about myself."

Caleb's forehead scrunched. "She was worried about you being depressed. You're not going to, you know, take yourself out or anything, are you?"

Phoenix puffed air without humor. "You know, with my prosthetic leg, I had gotten to a good place. Now, it feels like I'm back to square one. But no, I don't expect you'll be IDing me at the morgue anytime soon."

"That's not really resounding reassurance."

Phoenix fitted the key into the lock. The handle turned on its own and the door popped open.

"Phoenix!" Rina shouted. He checked her chubby fists for sharp objects. None. Must be the sound of joy.

"Rina, you remember Caleb?"

His brother grunted a greeting.

"I thought you guys would be here hours ago. I was getting worried," she said, following them into the interior. The door swung shut.

Caleb shoved Phoenix's bags through the apartment.

"Um, I'm actually not sure which room I'm taking," Phoenix said.

Caleb abandoned the suitcases in the living room and pivoted. "Cool. I'm heading out then. You good?"

"Nope but thanks for the ride," Phoenix said. His new policy was nothing but honesty.

"Call if you need anything. Bye, Rina," Caleb called over his shoulder on the way out the door.

The exes stood and looked at each other. Rina's hair had grown longer and blonder. They'd had good memories together, hockey, parties, intimacy.

"You take the bedroom. It's your place," Rina said.

"It doesn't seem fair to make you move. You're the guest."

"I've already moved all my stuff out. I'm looking for a new place anyway."

Phoenix paused. "You're just tired of the shower with the roll-in floor."

She played along. "I want easy access to the front door, so I can sneak out after curfew."

"Fine, done," he agreed, and pushed one bag at a time into his "wheel-in" closet. Frankly, he was relieved to have the accessibility features in his own bathroom.

Phoenix unpacked his essentials, then wheeled out to see Rina.

She was reading a book on the white settee, her legs tucked under her. Orchid was right. The sight was jolting, Rina resting on the place where he and Orchid had first kissed.

"Hey, we should catch up but my time's all screwed up, so I'm going to shower and go to bed. You need help with your apartment search?" Phoenix asked.

"Nah. How are you doing? You look good."

"Kinda crummy actually. I might have to undergo the knife again."

Her brown eyes studied his. "Sorry to hear that."

"Thanks for not trying to fix the unfixable," he said, relieved that his direct answer didn't release a barrage of worry and questions.

"Yup. Listen, this is short-term but should we discuss roomie rules? Like, is food shared? Do you want your driver back? What time is too late for loud music?" Rina asked.

"Eat all the food you want. Let's work out a schedule to share the car. And if you haven't already heard, loud anything after eleven is going to result in a call from the Board."

"They haven't called yet. And I used up your coffee pods. I'm going to buy more."

"My only ground rules are don't feel obligated to be social if you don't want to. If we're going to share this place for a little while, we both need to be comfortable, right?"

"Yup."

"I should've mentioned this sooner but, that sofa?"

"Yeah?" Rina looked askance at the velvet.

"I'm holding it for Orchid, so maybe best if neither of us uses it." He pictured a dark-haired beauty whom he missed.

Rina hopped up, book in hand. "Orchid. Tell me about her."

"She's pretty awesome, thoughtful, smart. You guys would get along."

She licked her lips and lobbed their old joke about her actuarial profession. "Fifty-fifty odds at best."

CHAPTER 28

GIFT OF TRUTH

Orchid

Orchid threw herself into her work at Lauder. Phoenix didn't know it, but he'd inspired a whole new direction for her skincare innovation. She hoped he'd be proud when she could show him.

The time difference made calls tough. So, their main means of communication was texts. *"Arrived safely,"* he'd let her know.

"Shifu says hi," she'd told him.

He mentioned he'd been writing.

One person who'd appreciate the new products she was developing was the person who helped shape her thinking on them. She returned Billy's texts and made plans to meet.

She and her aunt picked Billy up at his hotel. Shifu drove them to the Summer Palace, a sprawling square mile of Imperial Gardens and Qing Dynasty pavilions. The grounds spread over an area four times the size of the Forbidden Palace and were as big as New York City's Central Park. Shifu deposited them near the eastern Moon Gate, where Orchid paid their entrance fee.

"This place is gorgeous," Aunt Lily exclaimed as they followed crowds toward the famous Long Corridor. She craned her neck towards the ornate beams painted sea green, royal blue, bright red, gold, and purple.

"Let's take a picture," Billy offered, guiding them to an empty spot under the covered walkway. They stood beside Billy as he held out his camera and snapped a selfie. He pulled the phone towards his nose and clicked a few buttons. "It's posted!"

"Any luck with your visa?" Ayi asked Billy as they sauntered towards the UNESCO Heritage site.

He frowned. "It's like an endless loop. They want me to have a job to qualify for a visa, but the jobs I've found want me to have a visa first."

"You should try setting up a bank account here. My visa was delayed when I was coming, and I had corporate attorneys working on the case," Orchid said. They skirted around a group of schoolgirls taking photos.

He shook his head. "If nothing comes through by next week, I'm heading back."

"I'm flying to the US next week too," Ayi said. Her aunt's visit had filled her time, which lessened the impact of missing Phoenix.

Orchid recalled the personal significance of Billy's trip. "Even if you can't stay longer, just getting to China is a victory, right?"

Billy turned to Aunt Lily to explain. "My girlfriend and I were supposed to travel together until my accident. I'm here by myself because she left me because of my disability." He lifted his left pants leg to reveal the shiny metal of his prosthesis.

Her eyebrows knit. "She did? That's just wrong," she blurted.

Orchid's ribcage expanded, warming with newfound affection for her aunt.

"You don't understand how awesome it is for me to see you with Phoenix," Billy said to Orchid.

"You don't understand how awesome it is that it worked out. I was in love with him for the longest time and didn't want to admit it." Orchid couldn't dampen the smile that Phoenix's name evoked.

"How's Phoenix doing?" he asked.

"He's going for a consult soon. I feel like I should be there in case he needs surgery. But I had this breakthrough at work and don't want to lose momentum." They continued their path along the corridor's 728 meters, the longest covered walkway in the world.

"It's always like that for me too. Half my life is picking between hard choices. Like going to college or joining my buddy's surf school. Like my girlfriend getting too sloshed to drive home. I should've called her an Uber, but I went to pick her up myself. That's when a drunk driver T-boned me, and that ended up being the reason she couldn't stay."

"That's messed up. Your accident happened because you went to give her a ride, and then she leaves you?" Ayi's indignation stopped her in her tracks. Orchid paused and took in the blush traveling up her aunt's neck.

"Yup," he said.

"Give me her number. I'm not kidding." Orchid shook her head.

Billy's scrunched forehead relaxed as the two women came to his defense. He restarted their stroll through the open-air tunnel. "You said Phoenix tried to hide what happened to him from you. Tell me the truth. Is it ever hard?"

Aunt Lily tilted her chin to the right. "What?"

Seeing Phoenix's story from her aunt's viewpoint put it in fresh perspective. "His accident. He didn't want to tell me."

"Do you ever think about leaving?" Billy asked. She could tell that her answer mattered to him.

"If I understand what you're asking, no, what he's missing is never going to make me leave." She shook her head at the injustice that an injury like Billy's could trump love.

"Your conviction reminds me of the philosopher Confucius' poem. He said, 'The orchid grows where others cannot,'" Aunt Lily quoted, gifting Orchid acceptance she didn't know she'd craved. "It's why your parents named you Orchid. Because Confucius believes that an orchid's character shines through, no matter what hardships she endures."

"What? That's eerily prescient," she replied, thinking of her parents' accident, and Phoenix's.

Billy nodded. "That suits you."

Orchid felt her face grow warm with the compliment. "It almost makes me not mind getting orchids as gifts anymore."

"They're a sign of respect and admiration," Aunt Lily said.

Billy, his stride relaxed, changed the topic of discussion. "So, what's this work stuff you're doing?"

"It's amazing. You actually helped me, even if you didn't realize it. That night at Modernista, when you asked what I'd do if I could do anything, it made me think about what I could do at work that would make a difference."

They walked the remainder of the Long Corridor, talking about her ideas, then exited the western gate towards the setting sun.

They dropped off Billy and sped towards her Chaoyang neighborhood. Orchid's solar plexus relaxed, radiating love for all her good fortune. "Thinking of you," she texted Phoenix.

After her aunt retired following dinner that evening, Orchid allowed herself to open Phoenix's largest gift. Underneath the peony wrapping paper, he'd inscribed a blank notebook in his clear, dark handwriting.

> *Once upon a time, a girl and boy grew up in different places. She thought that missing family meant she was less than, but the boy knew she was more than. She was wild and beautiful and capable. She felt deeper, cared more. Her name was Orchid, the resilient plant that grows among thickets in the tropics. Perfect.*
>
> *As if a spell had been conjured, the boy fell madly in love.*

The boy, being the way boys are, cracked jokes and gave her gifts, just to see her happy. This is taboo, she'd told him. He tried to obey her rules. She'd become his kingdom. Each day together enhanced and heightened his life.

Orchid's burden was an old mirror. She'd had it with her since she was a whelp, so she held it dear. She didn't fully realize, because it happened little by little, but this looking glass had become warped over time, the shiny surface dulled to a patina, the edges chipped. It had become trapped in a long-ago moment, a freeze-frame, of a terrible accident. The reflection in the glass made her sad. It made her tear at her dress in horror. Worse, it distracted her from the truth.

Because now, she'd grown strong, and yet, when she palmed the handle of this beast, she couldn't see it. In secret, since the boy loved her, he built another reflector, not an exterior one that might age or grow worn but an interior one she could carry inside. Piece by piece, he erected the image of her kindness. Like a collage, he snapped their new moments and imprinted miniature triptychs on her heart. Each held his admiration, his love for her, and the love he so badly wanted her to have for herself.

Her remembering his double espresso, her teaching him to cook, and most of all, her teaching him to love. Truly, deeply, fully.

When, in a twisted parallel, a terrible accident shattered the boy, the girl became a queen. Her bravery,

*her empathy, her humanity forever inscribed not just
in her heart but his.*

Love, once blossomed, will always live.

Mirror no more.

The words were beautiful, and heartfelt. Yet, they left her sad.

Orchid flipped through the remaining pages. Nothing. She re-read the passages. She saw the truth in them, but they also made her frantic.

They read like a goodbye.

CHAPTER 29

RE-SEARCH

Roy

PRESENT DAY

Phoenix's case was like no other. When Roy researched teen runaways, he kept their mothers' pleading faces in mind. In contrast, when seeking the benevolent man who'd saved his life, Roy's own pathos motivated him.

Who did I kill?

Roy arrived at the transition center during a quiet hour. He chose a terminal facing the corner, where passersby couldn't easily see his monitor.

One click of the computer mouse, and the screen blinked to life.

Searching for "Phoenix train accident" gave him articles from the city in Arizona. He'd never forget the compassion of the man who'd introduced himself, offered to buy him a meal, and exchanged his life for Roy's.

He narrowed the results to New York headlines appearing the evening of July 29th. "Man falls onto subway tracks." The first article reminded the public to be careful along train tracks. "Victim's status unknown, name withheld," the piece concluded.

Roy knew his name. *Phoenix's must rise from ashes.*

The local papers sensationalized the incident with attention-grabbing headlines over the next few days. "Man on tracks may have been pushed." They noted that "... police are seeking someone who may have been involved. Please call with any information."

Roy shivered. Could the cops still be searching for him? What if his online activity piqued suspicions and led to him? He vowed to clear his search results from the cache.

Frustratingly, none of the articles revealed the man's full identity. Once the investigation turned into a manhunt, the focus was on the mysterious stranger whom officials sought for questioning. Then within a few days, reporting dropped off. News turned to stock market volatility and an insider swindling case.

Undaunted, Roy jotted down the reporters' names and contact info. A real private eye wouldn't impersonate someone. But his subterfuge felt justified because he was trying to take responsibility for his actions.

Roy created a new Gmail account and cold emailed the journalists on his list. One had even posted a phone number.

Next, he erased his digital trail, and scurried over to a quiet corner of the waiting room. He pulled out the phone that was nearly his most prized possession, second to the fabric flower that reminded him to avoid rock bottom at any cost.

He dialed the reporter's number.

"Hey, this is Roy Silver from *The Horn*," Roy lied. "I'm working on an anniversary piece for the subway accident you covered a year ago, you know, on July 29th, down at the 86th Street Station? I have some new info. Thought you might want to collaborate, trade notes."

The guy was feeling talkative. "Oh yeah, that was a gruesome one. I must've been the first one to hear it on the police scanner. I ran up there right away. Saw the guy being carried up on a stretcher. He was busted up real bad. What info do you have?"

"Looks like there was a jumper in the station with him," Roy said. The truth in the words made him tremble. It felt as if the stranger on the other end could pour out of the phone's receiver and jab a crooked finger of blame in his face. *Killer.*

"Well, yeah, how's that new news? The twin brother was hot on that track. You got this jumper's name?"

"The news is that it was a woman," he said, aiming to misdirect the newscaster. "And it was an accident. She didn't want him to fall."

"That sounds like bull. Did you talk to her? Because I spoke with both Dex and Caleb. They were damned sure it was a guy. With a beard. Unless she was wearing some disguise, which makes no sense. Anyway, I'm gonna go. Let me know if you get some real intel, and maybe call counterAgency. You know Dex kept all their names outta the news. But he'd want to know any new info." *Leads.*

"Yeah, yeah, maybe I will." Roy wiped the sweat from his forehead. The page before him was filled with scribbles. New names danced through his head. It wasn't just Roy's imagination. The reporter solidified the accident as real.

"Alright, well, I got your number here. Thanks for the idea. If it's a slow news day, anniversary articles are good fluff."

They hung up.

Dex. Caleb. *Twin* brothers! No last names. Roy leapt up to start the computer again. One of them must lead to the dead man. He'd figure out their relationships. He summoned a new search. "Counter agency NYC." He ignored the counter terrorism results and clicked on a link. The first website was a consultancy and didn't yield many clues. The next company, though, intensified Roy's stare.

counterAgency. The Chief Creative Officer and Acting CEO was named Dex, a burly fellow whose bio promised a tough wife and fun-loving agency-client relationships. Roy scrolled through some directors' photos, then searched for "Caleb." Nothing. Then the one he wanted to know most of all.

With shaking fingers, he typed "Phoenix." The cursor scrolled down to a photo he recognized.

Golden boy.

His full name was listed under the picture.

Chairman of the Board and Founder, Phoenix Walker.

Roy's vision blurred with recognition. A chill ran down his arms that wasn't triggered by the center's air conditioning. *Phoenix. This is Phoenix.*

The blue eyes and straight nose in the picture hunted Roy with a direct stare.

Phoenix's write-up read like a who's who of brands and advertising awards.

counterAgency must've preserved the info on their website in memoriam.

The columnist had mentioned twins. He knew the twin wouldn't be Dex. The company's CEO had a different last name.

Roy typed "Caleb Walker NYC." His sweaty palms nearly slipped on the rounded plastic mouse as he scrolled through the results. There were sports guys, photographers, and influencers. Not unique enough.

He tried the two names together: "Phoenix and Caleb Walker."

Scrolling down, Roy found a pair photographed and tagged at a triathlon in New Jersey. Earlier than that, the same tall twins were smiling together in a high school shot. Ding ding.

Now that he knew who he was seeking, the paths came quicker. Caleb owned tattoo shops in New Jersey.

Phoenix Walker had been interviewed in trade magazines. He attended awards shows. Photos from last year's Effies showed him laughing, between Dex and a striking woman with a blue tint to her hair. Roy skimmed the articles and names in the captions. The photos were taken before the fateful day that Phoenix had saved him. Of course, they were. Because there would be nothing afterwards.

Phoenix dedicated his work to Judge John Walker. According to the search results, this was Phoenix's father, an upstanding family court judge.

Unfortunately, Phoenix hadn't been a wretch that Roy could write off. He'd been an industry scion with a bright future. His kindly face haunted Roy. He held his breath, and then searched "Phoenix Walker obituary."

Roy pinched the flesh on his thigh. The pain refocused him. Lots of Walkers, but no Phoenix. In some ways, this was a relief. Not to have to read about the way he'd died.

An obituary for Judge John Walker caught his eye. The judge had died two years earlier, leaving behind his wife Veronica, sons Phoenix and Caleb, brother and sister-in-law George and Betsy, and nephews Harry and Stew. The date of his passing shot a shiver up Roy's spine: July 29th, the same as the day that Phoenix had saved his life.

Connections exploded in Roy's mind. Phoenix and his father had died on the same day, one year apart. Roy's guilt doubled.

What could he do? What could he do?

He searched for Phoenix and John's names together. He clicked on an article below the sponsored results.

> *"It's the greatest honor to be considered for a Cannes Lions Grand Prix for Good. We're proud of the work we do to support wounded veterans. I thank my dad, Judge John Walker, for inspiring me,"* the article quoted Phoenix Walker.

Roy reread the sentences. Could he do something to honor them both?

Mind spinning, Roy flipped over to a more personal approach than mainstream media. Phoenix Walker didn't seem to use social media. One of his cousins did. Roy sifted through photos of ski trips, beach vacations, coffee bars. The family appeared loaded.

He sighed. So, he'd found his savior. What could he do for the dead guy's family that would mean anything? If Roy showed up with an apology, who's to say they wouldn't toss him to the court system.

More photos passed by in a haze. Then his subconscious noticed a pattern that took a moment for his mind to register. Last year's Cannes awards show. Phoenix stood beside a woman who looked familiar. The same one from the Effies. He expanded the image's size. Her hair was no longer blue-tinted. Yet the slender figure and pretty features matched. Roy checked the names. Orchid Paige. Her name gave him pause. His mother's favorite flowers were orchids.

What a coincidence. The fabric flower in his pocket symbolized synchronicity.

In the photo, Orchid seemed to mean something special to Phoenix, the way the two of them huddled close and smiled with genuine joy.

Her unique name yielded easier searches. The congratulatory notes on her LinkedIn feed indicated she was working in China. *Dead end?*

Another name began to appear with increasing frequency. The name Mandy showed up in Orchid's social media feeds. Roy dug deeper. He located a photo of the two of them from their college magazine. The school paper had titled the write-up "Best Friends," and included both of their last names. Bingo! Roy viewed the date. Nearly ten years ago. An idea formed.

He searched for Mandy online. Several social media accounts popped up, some with a new married last name. He narrowed to those in Manhattan. Then he checked profile pictures. Bam! The third one looked similar to the smiling blonde in the college article.

He kept going. More good luck. A google search revealed a (646) area code number for a Mandy with an age that made sense for ten years after undergraduate studies. He'd call, but first he needed a solid cover. He pulled up a fresh screen and created a new email address: roysunreporter@gmail.com.

No one else was nearby in the quiet center. Roy picked up his phone and dialed.

"Hello?" a female voice asked.

"This is Roy from *The Sun*. Is this Mandy?"

"Um, yes," she sounded tentative.

"Don't hang up. This is your school. Congratulations on the ten-year anniversary of your Best Friends article." Roy stood to pace.

"My what?"

"The article with Orchid Paige that ran when you were freshmen."

"Oh, right. Okay, thanks. Do you need something?"

"We wanted to revisit the article, a decade later. See what you're up to, and maybe write another piece. We haven't been able to get in touch with Orchid since she's in China. Can you tell me what you've been doing since graduation?"

Roy waited.

"Well, the alumni magazine has the main info. I sent in my wedding announcement and haven't worked since Matty was born."

"I think the interesting angle is how you and Orchid are still friends. After all these years. What do you attribute that to? Our readers could really learn from you," he said.

The new angle worked. Mandy began to open up. "You know, it really is cool that we roomed together and are still besties. We both do our part, you know? Keep in touch, call each other. It's harder with the time difference but I just talked to her, I dunno, not too long ago."

"So, she's doing well in China? Tell me about her assignment."

"Maybe you should call her," she said.

Smart cookie, this one. Her trust needed to be earned. He improvised with a wild guess.

"She never updated her alumni profile. But I bet classmates would like to hear about how she's landed an international assignment."

"People would be amazed if they could see how far she's come. After her parents died, she had to do everything for herself.

She always worked through school, and now she got this plum international assignment. I'm proud of her." Admiration laced Mandy's voice.

"The school will love to hear that. Alum success stories. But things have been tough too, right?" Now he was going on scant info. Guesses really. "She was close with Phoenix Walker last year, before ..." Roy's voice trailed off. His throat closed on the words, unwilling to name the accidental death that was his fault.

"Oh my god you know about that too? Jesus, you're good. No one was happier than me when they finally got together. But now, I don't know what's going to happen. He's in New York for surgery. She's in Beijing."

In New York for surgery? What, he's ALIVE?

Roy's head was spinning. When she started talking about Phoenix in the present tense, Roy was convinced he'd found the wrong person. Not Phoenix at all. But then she said surgery ... *I mean, what are the chances?*

"Surgery. Was this related to a train accident on July 29th last year at 86th Street station?" he asked.

"I guess. Sounds about right. Because that's when Orchid left for China. Just some terrible luck. Saved a suicidal guy's life."

Roy paused his pacing. "Suicidal guy?" he echoed.

"Yeah, it's so sad, really."

"Yeah," Roy agreed.

"Anyway, do you have enough for the article now? I have to go. And we'd like to see the article before it's published."

"Okay, yeah. I'll call if I have more questions."

"Give me your contact info, and I can pass it along, okay?"

He recited his phone number and brand-new email address, then thanked Mandy.

"Bye." She hung up.

Roy rubbed his eyes in a daze. Everything had changed in that one call. His victim hadn't died. A weight lifted. *Am I off the hook?*

Yet Phoenix was undergoing surgery. An image filled his mind, Phoenix's disembodied hand protruding from a bloody sleeve, curled in a goodbye.

Roy gagged. His chair scraped backwards.

He hadn't killed the guy, he'd maimed him.

Forget about amends to his family. He needed to do right by Phoenix. Could he help with his medical issues? Doubtful. Roy's skills were military protocol, drinking, and now, sleuthing.

Sleuthing.

Roy returned to his keyboard and opened a new browser window.

He'd keep digging until he found something helpful.

CHAPTER 30

RE-UNIONS

Phoenix

Phoenix stepped off the elevator into counterAgency's lobby and absorbed the hum of the place he'd built. He blinked with affection at the sight of the white waiting area sofas punctuated by electric blue pillows, and his company's understated logo. One boon since arriving in New York was his physical therapist's genius. He'd visited Nadine, and she had him fitted for a custom crutch to prop his left side.

Miraculously, he was upright. His left elbow fit snug inside a sleeve that attached to a crutch that didn't require a wrist. The other side was supported by a forearm cane.

He swung on one foot towards the receptionist. Before he neared enough to say hello, her head snapped up and her jaw stopped working her gum. She ran around her desk tottering on five-inch heels. "Oh, my gawd, you should've called. We would've thrown you a party!" He wobbled for a moment with the force of her hug and kissed her cheek.

"Good to see you too," he said with a laugh.

"This is our founder," she said to a seated guest in a pencil skirt and blouse. The waiting visitor got up to introduce herself.

As they shook hands and exchanged pleasantries, the receptionist snatched up her phone. She delivered her side of the conversation like a rapper spitting bars to her personal beat. "You wouldn't believe who's here. In the lobby. Yeah, tell him. I'm not kidding. Right now."

Before they'd finished conversing, tapping heels echoed over the polished wood floors.

Liv rounded the corner and marched over to her longtime CEO. "We weren't expecting you until next month," she said, looking up through her cat-eyeglasses.

"I'm back early for medical stuff," he said.

His business partner, Dex, ambled over and hugged his friend. "Hey, I just saw your text," he said.

Creatives, planners, and account executives gathered into the open space, chattering with greetings and questions. Phoenix checked with each person. Staff members regaled him with stories about babies, college visits, winning campaigns, and industry gossip. His chest expanded with the feeling of belonging.

After several minutes, Dex emitted one sharp whistle. The crowd quieted.

"Boss guy's back!" he said and bowed towards his buddy.

Phoenix stepped into the center and nodded at his teams. "It's great to see you all. We've discussed your work at our Board meetings. Huge coup with REBBL," he said, naming one of their coveted accounts.

His fingers twitched with a desire to grab a Sharpie and scrawl creative ideas. "Now, you're probably missing meetings, so how about we talk more over drinks later this week? On me," he said.

People cheered.

Liv pulled open her ever-present notebook and scribbled in it.

As the crowd dispersed, Dex led Phoenix back towards his old office. "You know, we should get you in a few meetings while you're in town. Clients like hobnobbing with the agency founder."

"Yeah, I'd like that," he said. The energy of the place quickened his pulse.

"Oh, I almost forgot to mention. Some guy showed up asking about you. The receptionist said he was snooping around for info on your accident."

"Stupendous. Some reporter trying to sniff out a scoop?"

"Who knows. I'll give you the contact info he left."

"You guys did an exceptional job keeping my name out of the papers last year. Thanks."

"You're welcome. You didn't deserve a media circus."

"Instead, I get you clowns."

Dex guffawed, his beard bobbing with good cheer.

After meeting with Dex, Phoenix caught a ride share to a downtown restaurant to see his brother's ex-girlfriend, who had volunteered to be an early reader.

He tugged the restaurant door open and braced the portal with one tip of his crutch while he swung through on one foot. Entering the establishment unscathed felt like an accomplishment, since all three functioning limbs were engaged in moving him forward. He'd suggested the vegan eatery Orchid had loved.

Sascha rose from a brown square table, her latex shining a deep crimson.

"You sure know how to make an entrance." She reached up for a hug.

"You should see my juggling," he responded.

"I got you an espresso, if I remember correctly." She ignored his joke and waved at a miniature ceramic mug across from her steaming beverage.

"Coffee's okay, but vodka would be better."

"I concur," she said and chucked her cup against his.

They sank into chairs and started talking at the same time.

"I loved it," she declared, pointing to an inch-high stack of printed paper.

"How are you?" he asked and sipped the dark brew.

"I'm good. How about you?" she replied to his overlapped question, as Phoenix scanned familiar words stamped onto the first page. *"Shut up. I have abandonment issues, you know that."*

He missed Orchid. Writing allowed him to relive some of their history. Who knew the state of their futures. He imagined interviewing Orchid, and the swish of her hair as she relayed her side of the story.

"I'm good. So, you loved it. But I want to know what needs to be fixed. That's the point of you reading it, so I get it right."

"Oh, my gawd, it's perfect. You made me sound fab, luv."

"All wrapped in red latex, you are fab. I hope I did you justice."

"You gave me oodles of credit. Was I really the first one to make you laugh in the hospital?"

"You were, Sasch. I owe you. I really do. You kinda saved my life."

The hue of her face grew closer to the crimson of her outfit. "Anything for you, doll."

"Tell me about you. How are things?" he asked. He cared deeply, for her sake, and his brother's.

"Things aren't bad. I can't complain."

Phoenix studied her over the rim of his espresso. "That's not really resounding joy."

Sascha sighed and ran fingers through her bouncy locks. "It's nothing compared with what you've been through."

"People think they can't tell me stuff now that I'm all busted up. I'm stronger than you think. Maybe I can understand challenges even better now, after what I've been through."

"That's kinda deep, hun." Sascha touched a hand to his.

"So … what is it? Your mean boss at work?" Phoenix joked about his twin, picturing the ways she'd been together with Caleb as a happy couple, working side by side. Then, in a dark period, without speaking. Afterwards, they'd worked out a truce and like divorced parents, they shared custody of the shops they loved and found their personal rhythm.

"It's not work, though probably more to do with the mean boss," she admitted.

"Caleb still loves you, I think," he said, recalling the image of his brother's sadness whenever they spoke of Sascha.

Sascha startled, stared at him for an instant, then downcast her gaze, but not before he'd witnessed the rims of her eyes redden. He'd hit a tender spot. "Knife to the heart," she said.

"Sorry. Has he told you himself?"

"Hun, you know that man. Emotions aren't his strong suit."

"How about you? You still have feelings too. I can tell."

"Feelings aren't enough."

"Talk to him. One of you has to start, and like you said, that might not be his strong suit."

Sascha sighed, and he thought of all the ways she'd been there for him. "We're not here for me. I'm supposed to be your ... what'd you call it? Beta reader. Like those fighting fish."

Phoenix guffawed. It felt good. "Betta. Territorial Siamese fighting fish. Not quite the same but that's funny."

Sascha nodded. "Yeah, betta. That's like Caleb and me. Put us too close together and we fight for our territory to the death."

His experiences suddenly made him feel wise. "You'd be amazed what you can work through, if you keep lines of communication open." He'd been focused on what didn't work with Orchid. What about what *did* work? Her compassion, her kindness, their shared values. No one had ever been so suited for him. No one had ever been built to be more repelled by him.

Sascha pointed at the printed manuscript on their table. "What are you going to call it? Phoenix's autobiography?"

"Technically, it's a memoir, since it's only part of my life, and it's still a rough draft. In a lot of ways, it's not even about me, it's about what everyone did around me, which I didn't fully appreciate until I wrote this. And it doesn't even need a title since I don't think it'll ever see the light of day. In my mind though, I call it *Missing Pieces*." he said.

Sascha wrinkled her nose. "Kind of crass, no? Even you said, that's not the point of the story."

"What is the point?" he wondered aloud.

"Sappy me thinks the point is that love conquers all."

"I hope you're right."

Sascha stopped swirling her drink and studied him. "Did somethin' happen?"

"Orchid is great, she really is."

"Her parts were heartbreaking, absolutely wrenching. Will I get to meet her?"

"Only if you fancy a flight to China."

"Geography? You're going to let location be the issue?" Sascha was incredulous.

"It's not just that."

Sascha glared at him. "I read the ending. I loved the ending. *He was hers. She was his. Not a thing missing.* Don't make me throw this manuscript on the ground. I'll do it, ya know."

Phoenix threw his head back. "I've missed your directness, Sasch."

"Repeat after me: This woman is a saint for putting up with my BS."

"That's likely true. Unfortunately, there's more hassle coming."

"Caleb mentioned surgery?"

"Yeah, my leg. That's why I'm on crutches. I can't wear my prosthesis. There's this bony growth causing me pain."

"Sorry, luv."

"Orchid says she's okay with this. I think she means it, but a life with me is going to mean medical appointments, and I don't even know what else."

"Aw, hun, isn't that up to her?"

"Even so, odds are fifty-fifty at best."

"In that case, you could call the book *Maybe Orchid*."

"Yeah, I could." He paused over his cooling coffee. "I've got it. You've just read *Goodbye, Orchid*."

Sascha stared at him. "Phoenix, that's so sad."

He felt it. The weight of his pronouncement. He'd written from a place of honesty to Orchid. He wanted to picture them in their senior years together. The pre-accident him could've been that person.

Their waitstaff arrived, pad in hand. He could feel the devastation in his gut as he looked up into a familiar face. He hadn't wanted to admit it to himself, but he'd steeled himself that this could be the end of his relationship with Orchid.

"Hi. Can I get you anything?" Ana, the slender brunette, asked. He realized he'd unconsciously chosen this spot hoping to see her.

Sascha spoke first, explaining why Ana bore no expression of surprise. "Ana and I caught up. After we put two and two together as to why we looked familiar to each other."

"Rockwood Music Hall," Phoenix said, naming the place where the three of them had last been together.

"I'm kinda glad you're here. Your friend let me look at your book. I know some authors who are agents, if you want me to pass along your manuscript," Ana said.

"Really? I wasn't aiming for publication. Writing was therapy."

"Have you shown it to Orchid?" Sascha asked.

"Not yet. I want to but it's nerve-wracking too, to see what she thinks." He recalled the passages where she'd been repulsed by him in his nightmares.

"Would you like to order?" Ana touched the tip of her pen to her notepad.

"Do you like french toast? I'd recommend the french toast," Phoenix asked Sascha, invoking a dish from the fateful brunch with Orchid.

"I prefer spicy. Huevos rancheros for me," Sascha ordered.

"And you want french toast?" Ana asked.

"Yes. Cut up, please," he said remembering Orchid's thoughtfulness in dicing up their meal and all the ones that followed.

Ana jotted on her pad and tossed a note on their table before sashaying away. He glanced down to take in the name of a literary agent. One whom he didn't plan to call.

The doctor's office had rescheduled Phoenix's appointment. During the wait, he'd read research papers on revision surgery, their outcomes, their successes, their complications.

Today, he swung into the hospital building upright. His six-foot view of the world buoyed his mood. Even with his loss fully visible below board shorts.

The nurse accompanied him into an exam room. Though he was glad to be free of his wheels, he was also relieved to settle into a cushioned chair. He propped his crutches against the wall. Films of his injured leg were displayed on the lighted wall box.

The physician entered the room and shook his hand.

"Tell me what's going on," he said. He washed his hands and palpated the distal end of Phoenix's limb as he listened.

Phoenix unloaded all of it. The Great Wall fall. His twisted left knee. Prolonged physical therapy. His inability to use his prosthetic leg. The diagnosis of heterotopic ossification.

"Two options. We can wait and see, or we can discuss surgery. Unfortunately, this happens. Sometimes with traumatic amputation, bone fragments can try to reattach, and all that extra growth can be painful." The surgeon confirmed what Phoenix had feared.

"Would you need to take any length? What's recovery like?" Phoenix asked.

He was back in a medical world he wanted no part of. Loneliness threatened. If he'd asked, Mom would've come. Even Caleb. He missed the one person who shouldn't be here.

After the consultation, Phoenix crutched out of the facility, his future confirmed, his mind confined to one fate.

That night, Rina ordered take-out. Hand over her phone, she mouthed "Want Chinese?"

Phoenix shrugged. "Sure." He felt wistful for Chinese street food. Or more accurately, the woman who accompanied him along Beijing's alleyways to sample the unfamiliar fare.

After some time, Rina answered the door and returned with white cardboard containers. Phoenix chose Orchid's normal spot at the table, so that he didn't have to face Rina seated in that same position. He pushed her unneeded chair to one side. A space for the ghost of his girlfriend's presence.

"How was the food in China?" Rina asked. She slopped lo mein noodles onto her plate.

"There were all kinds, from the ordinary to the sublime. But I'll tell you, it's not the same as Americanized Chinese food."

"Well, I have no desire to go. I like Americanized Chinese food. It tastes like Canadianized Chinese food."

Phoenix laughed. Rina was still her no-nonsense self.

She speared a dumpling. "How'd your appointment go?"

Phoenix sighed. "It's what I thought. I scheduled surgery."

"Well, if it's when I'm still here, let me know if you need anything."

"Does this mean you've forgiven me?"

"Duh, I'm being nice for the free rent. My friends still call you The Jerk," Her teasing tone held no bitterness. Maybe time does heal.

Except limbs. Time doesn't regrow fingers and toes. Just bits of bone splinters that radiate excruciating pain.

After dinner, Phoenix rolled into his bedroom and closed the door. Having Rina at his place was nothing like having Orchid there. With Orchid, they'd want to be in the same room, subconsciously following each other from kitchen to sofa to each other's arms. Consciously, in that last case.

His phone on the bedside table was buzzing with a call.

"Hey there, I was going to call you," he said, pleased to see Orchid's name.

"Good. Tell me what the doctor said."

"Give me a sec, okay?" Phoenix pushed back the covers and transferred into bed. He didn't think about Rina resting here. He thought about Orchid wrapped around him, smelling of rose soap, her soft hair blanketing his bare chest.

"I'm back," he said, leaning against his propped pillows. "What are you doing?"

"I'm cleaning up after breakfast, then I'm heading to work. How about you?"

"Get this. I just finished Chinese food for dinner. Nothing was recognizable as actual Chinese. Nothing."

"Let me guess. The sauces were too sweet, the spices lack depth."

"What even are egg rolls? Do they have eggs in them?"

Orchid laughed. "I've recently learned that eggs are used in all kinds of Chinese curses."

"Did you sign up for the remedial Chinese class? You're supposed to learn curse words first."

"I'm going to curse you," she joked.

"There's no need. I'm cursed already. I scheduled surgery today."

Her tone sobered. "You did? When?"

"I took the first available. Next week."

"So soon. I'm sorry. Were you hoping for a different answer?"

"I kinda figured this was my future after reading more online. Which I wouldn't recommend for you, by the way."

"Don't worry. I'm hardly spending my days on WebMD."

Phoenix chuckled. "Good to hear. How are things going?"

"Work is amazing. I can't wait to show you my new project. I should come visit while you're recovering."

He pictured Orchid in his hospital room. Gawking at his shortened leg strapped in gauze. At his side for bandage changes that revealed black stitches like angry ants crawling over incision lines. Pitying him for umpteen weeks in his chair.

"No," His voice croaked as sharp as the pain he felt.

Her question lifted at the end in confusion. "No, don't come visit? Well, I just figured maybe you'd like company. Or a hand with stuff. I can work remote or take days off."

A hand with stuff? His ego couldn't handle her helping him into the shower. Company? If the pain would be like his first amputation recovery, he'd be in no shape for company.

"There's no space," he blurted.

She deflated. "Rina's still there," she guessed.

"Right. It's not that though. Even if she weren't here ..."

"You're not coming back to China, are you?"

"It's way early to predict any of that."

"So, it is a goodbye letter, your note to me."

"Goodbye, why do you say that? No, it's a love letter. To remind you how special you are. So, you always know that. No matter what." Of this, he was sure.

"It sounded wistful."

"Sorry. I'd hoped you'd like it."

"I do. I left something for you too."

"You did?"

"In your bag? Didn't you find it?"

"I haven't finished unpacking. I'll tell you when I do."

"Believe it or not, it's from my first trip to China. I'd bought you some things, and then we didn't talk for so long ..."

"Your first trip? I hope they're not thousand-year-old eggs. Because I'll be heading to the dry cleaner with seventy pounds of clothes."

"Cursing eggs again," she laughed.

"Love you," he said.

"Love you more," she said, and hung up.

A year ago, they'd kissed on her little settee. The next day, they set off in two directions. She'd lifted into the sky for Beijing. He'd fallen onto underground tracks. Three-hundred and sixty-four days later, no matter his deflection, they were entwined by adoration and admiration. They always would be, even if they never saw each other again.

CHAPTER 31

LESS IS LESS

Phoenix

JULY 29TH

This date held more grief than the other three-hundred and sixty-four. His dad had seemed too young to die. Phoenix had been on his way to comfort his mother when he'd exchanged his limbs for another man's life.

The elevator ride up to Phoenix's aunt and uncle's place was surreal. Rina was quiet by his side, her presence a last-minute plea on his part to stave off the enormity of his grief. Dad had been on his mind. Phoenix missed his dad's belly laugh, his sharpness when he was deducing a tough problem, the way he danced around the kitchen with their mom.

The duo arrived at the penthouse floor. Phoenix adjusted his stance, still not fully accustomed to being upright. He allowed Rina to alight first, then he swung his new gait. A forward motion in unison, his right hand on a cane, his left arm suctioned to a crutch, followed by the swing of one foot. His truncated leg followed with a swish of his pinned trousers.

Rina clutched her structured pocketbook and knocked on the heavy door.

Phoenix was less mobile than last time he'd been here with Rina, just four months after his accident. During Thanksgiving, he was upright on his prosthesis, with a cane.

He'd told Nadine during the visit to secure his new crutch configuration, "I'd thought things would get better. You taught me to always move forward." She'd tilted her head at him thoughtfully. "Sometimes things will get worse before they get better."

The difference this year was that Phoenix was prepared to fake it. He wouldn't allow his pain to burden anyone else. Today was about his dad. Not him.

Uncle George opened the door and pulled his nephew into a bear hug.

"I loved John like a brother, and you and Caleb like sons," George said.

"Love you too." He wobbled and managed an arm around his uncle.

"You remember Rina?" Phoenix asked.

Uncle George blinked. Then, recalibrating his manners, he clasped her hand. "Of course, please, come in."

Inside the carpeted hallway and upholstered sitting room, the plush rugs were harder to manage than Phoenix had recalled. Balancing on one foot and two sticks was as precarious as the delicate dance he and Orchid had managed.

His mom rose from the cushioned divan to embrace him. He managed to squeeze her with one arm while keeping one crutch floor bound. Safer this way.

"You doing okay, Mom?" he asked, pulling back.

"Two years, two long years. And one year for you, Phoenix."

"I can't believe it either. Sometimes, I feel like he's still here. I talk to him still, in my head," Phoenix said.

"Me too."

He didn't mention his own anniversary. He'd stuffed the idea of an Alive Day, the day he survived his accident, to an unreachable recess. He hoped his family wouldn't make a fuss.

Phoenix turned to the woman at his side. "Mom, you met Rina last year."

"I certainly recall," she said, and extended her grasp.

"Mrs. Walker, I'm so sorry about this anniversary," Rina said, and leaned into their handshake.

"Thank you."

Harry and Stew pulled themselves away from platters of cheese and bumbled over. His cousins raked their eyes over the whole asymmetry of him, his bandaged leg, and the elaborate getup propping his stance. "Aww, man, what the—what happened?"

Phoenix scanned the room, and the gloomy faces. Aunt Betsy was wringing her hands, vacillating between wanting to come over, and fighting tears. No one could make him feel better but maybe he could make them feel better. One evening with his family. He was fortunate to have them. His heart filled with love. Mischief spread over his cheeks.

"Before you freak, just know I left the crocodile in worse shape than he left me."

Rina boosted her alligator-skin bag into the air. "I'll vouch for that. Phoenix was a tiger."

"Pfft." Uncle George was the first to crack.

Lucy skedaddled over to join the fray. "Phoenix is a mythological god!"

Uncle George bounded towards a polished silver cart. "Let's drink to that!"

He filled lead crystal tumblers with rounds of ice and generous splashes of an amber liquid.

"You sit. I'll grab you one," Rina said to Phoenix.

Aunt Betsy approached, her face composed again. "How are you, dear?"

"I'm glad to see you, Aunt Betsy. How are you?"

She elbowed her sister in the arm. "Always better when your mom is here. I wish she'd move back East. And we have news to share. George?"

Phoenix recognized the beginning signs of a lecture and brought his scotch to his lips.

His uncle ambled over and addressed the room, Chivas in hand. "You know Betsy and I are active in philanthropy. Well, we're incorporating a new 501c3. Inspired by Phoenix. We want to give artificial limbs to those who can't afford them. We'd like to name it after you." He turned to face Phoenix.

Phoenix nearly sprayed his drink. His advertising brain stuttered. "You're going to donate prostheses from a nonprofit named Walker?"

Lucy tittered.

"The Walker Institute," Betsy clarified.

"TWI. Tweedledee, Tweedledum," Harry blurted out the acronym.

Stew attempted to stifle his humor.

Phoenix recovered his manners. "That's so generous of you."

"In honor of your living day," Betsy said.

"Alive Day," Uncle George reminded his wife.

Veronica hugged her sister. "Thanks to both of you."

They leaned their heads together. Lucy held up her phone. "Want a pic? You two are so cute."

Veronica swiped under one eye. "I'm a mess today. But being here with all of you does help. That's a nice idea, Lucy. Since we're all together, why don't we get a family photo?"

Rina placed her two glasses on a side table. "I can take it, so you'll all be in it."

"No, no, it's okay. Come here, dear," Aunt Betsy insisted.

Rina stood beside Phoenix and everyone leaned close as Lucy snapped several shots. "Insta okay?" she asked.

"Insta-pot? I have no idea what you mean but do as you wish," Betsy answered.

"Instagram. Lemme tag y'all so you can post it to your story," Lucy said to no one in particular. She was tapping on her phone. "Oh, look at Phoenix's tie, is that from China?"

"Yup." He glanced down at the dragon pattern, remembering the kohl-rimmed gaze of the beauty who'd hidden the gift-wrapped surprise in his suitcase.

Veronica looked Phoenix up and down. "Come sit with me," his mom requested.

Phoenix swung over to the sofa and glanced at Rina. "You're welcome to join us."

He sank into the seat and laid his crutches on the ground. Rina appeared to be mentally calculating his mom's intimidation factor.

Rina handed him a cool beverage and kept the water for herself. "I'm going to see what social media tricks I can learn from Lucy." She excused herself and joined the saucy redhead.

Veronica settled into the spot beside her son and swirled her wine glass.

"Caleb's not here yet?" he asked her.

"He said he was coming. It'll be good when we're all together. Where's Orchid?"

"Working in China. Before you get mad at her, she offered to come. I told her to stay."

"I'm not mad. What I want to know is how you're doing."

"Honestly, I've been thinking about Dad. I'd read that piece that says you'll spend 90 percent of the time you have with your parents by the time you're eighteen."

Veronica lifted an eyebrow. "Sounds like you'd best enjoy me while you can then."

He slung half an arm around her shoulders. "Ha. Sounds like it. What should we do tomorrow? Snookers? Skeet shooting?"

"And to think I was hoping for girls."

"Ha-ha. You and Aunt Betsy both lost out. Four boys between you."

Her neck swiveled. "Exactly why is Rina here?"

He sighed. "She's staying at my place while she's working in the city. Orchid's not thrilled."

"I don't blame her."

"I offered to ask Rina to leave. How did you and Dad do it? I hardly ever saw you fight."

"We did. In private. More like debated. It's hard to win against a judge. But bless John, he always listened. We both wanted the same thing, for ours to be a lifetime commitment. Mutual respect helps. You're both going to change. Being flexible is a good idea."

"Flexible," he ruminated. "I did go to dance class with Orchid."

"You went to China," she reminded him.

"You should see all the thoughtful stuff she does for me. We cook together, Mom. I'm practically vegetarian, and I don't even mind. She's been to doctor's appointments with me. She picked an accessible apartment."

"That's good. If it's important to you, it should be important to her, and vice versa."

"She did offer to come on this trip. I told her not to."

"Why not?"

"She's busy with work."

Caleb barreled into the room, waved in the general direction of his family, and sauntered over to their mother.

She got to her feet and hugged him. She looked diminutive next to his broad chest.

"You gave up cigarettes, but now you smell like marijuana," she said.

"Nice to see you too, Mom," he grunted.

"What'd the doc say?" he asked Phoenix.

"I'm having surgery next week."

Multiple faces turned towards him.

"The croc got me good," Phoenix said lightly.

"What specifically?" Veronica asked.

"It's called revision surgery. It's to remove extra bone growth. We don't need to get into details. People are eating." He waved with his truncated arm towards his shortened pants leg.

"I'm staying," his mom insisted.

"No need, really. How boring for you. I'll just binge Netflix," Phoenix shrugged, even though the doctor had run through a range of scenarios, none of which sounded like nothing.

Lucy stared at him, trying to decipher something. "You mean like they'll take more of your leg?"

A ripple of horror washed over each person, as understanding dawned at varying rates. Polite chatter quieted into open-mouthed "O's" and gestures frozen mid-air.

Phoenix needed someone to comfort him as much as they did, but he was the only one who could save them from sinking into pity.

"Think of it like Catholic tithing. You give another ten percent every year."

The image gutted them. His mom scrunched the throw pillow at her fingertips. Aunt Betsy raised a hand over her mouth.

"Too soon?" Phoenix checked.

Caleb chuckled darkly.

Rina turned towards Veronica. "I'll be around, Mrs. Walker, if Phoenix needs anything."

Caleb did a double take, registering Rina's presence as news.

"That's kind of you," Veronica responded.

Phoenix nodded a chin towards Caleb, seeking a change in topic away from his medical woes. "Hey, I saw Dex. He says some guy stopped by the agency sniffing out intel on my accident."

"Oh, I bet I know what it was. I wasn't going to say anything, but the rags wrote up something for the one-year anniversary of the accident."

"Great, my claim to fame."

"It didn't name you."

"Well, that's good. At least I don't have to be the poster child for not riding the subway."

Veronica squeezed his arm. Phoenix recalled that it wasn't just his tragedy. "Sorry for what I put you through," he told her. He wished for something to dilute the sadness in her frown.

George rose as emcee. "Now that we're all here, let's start this memorial with a prayer."

Phoenix shut out the room, lulled by the low hum of his uncle's voice, and accompanying amens. They shared stories commemorating his father's life. These kind faces played outsize roles in his life. Besides his father, another person was absent, like an empty form who should be at his side. His arm twitched with the desire to hold Orchid, to lean into her. She'd cocoon him with her rose-scented embrace. She'd lift his spirits. "Don't get maudlin on me, Walker," she'd say. But she wasn't here, and he might have to get used to that.

CHAPTER 32

THE GIFT OF BIRTH

Orchid

JULY 29TH

Today was a day for remembrances. The anniversary of Phoenix's accident, and the annual reminder of his dad's death. Knowing his stoicism, he might not shed tears.

She'd waited until this anniversary to open his other gifts, a way to feel closer to him. Aunt Lily and Billy had both returned to America. She perched alone on the sofa meant for two people.

Middle-sized mama bear revealed a new set of kitty playing cards. She tried the one-handed shuffling he'd shown her. Cards sprang from her grip and landed on their coffee table then spilled onto the floor. She laughed. Life had taught her that messiness was to be expected.

The smallest rectangle was a white jewelry box imprinted "DIOR."

She lifted the lid. He wouldn't give her an engagement ring without being present, would he?

Inside, a floral ring sparkled. This was no ordinary stone. He knew her so well.

Purple carved petals blossomed into an object of beauty.

Orchid lifted the stunning jewel. The rose gold band twisted like a vine, a diamond adorning the end of its solid stem.

The beautiful bauble slid down her ring finger. It came with a folded note. "Promise rings signify fidelity. This one holds my love. Whatever time we have, our days together will have made me complete. In life, we never know when goodbye might be around the corner. Whenever goodbye might be for us, next decade or next century, we will always be tethered by our shared memories, and now, this ring. You are more than I could've imagined. When you wear this, know you are cherished."

The poignancy of his sentiments squeezed her heart. All of his gifts and words were a cushion, to soften the blow of parting.

Orchid was studying his loose, confident scrawl when Mandy called on Orchid's cell phone.

"How are you, hon?" Mandy sang.

"I'm okay, it's late in New York. How are you?"

"Good. Um, have you looked at social media?"

"Kind of. Why, did you post something?"

"Not me. Your beau's family did," Mandy said.

"You're following Phoenix's family online?"

"I need something to break up my google searches on how to reduce stretch marks."

"I've heard olive oil," Orchid offered with a single eyebrow raised.

"You are the least likely source for that info. If you ever had a stretch mark, it'd be a dimple. If you ever have a baby, it'd be the size of a coffee bean."

"That's so unhealthy. I'd rather have a ten-pound butterball."

"You, okay? You don't sound like yourself."

"Get this, he left me a promise ring."

"That's so romantic!"

"It's beautiful, I'm sending you a photo. But what he wrote, it sounds like the swan song of a dying lover."

"What do you mean?"

"This is so sad. He says 'Whatever time we have, our days together will have made me complete. In life, we never know when goodbye might be around the corner. Whenever goodbye might be for us, next decade or next century, we will always be tethered by our shared memories.'"

"It's romantic. Like he's saying you'll always be together. He sounds like a poet to me," Mandy said.

Relief loosened inside of Orchid's chest. "He is a writer. He's writing a memoir."

"There you go. And I know what'll cheer you up. Look at his photo on Insta."

"I can't believe you found him online at all. He doesn't have a single account. He doesn't post anything unless Forbes is interviewing him."

"I just found it a second ago. I'll send you a screen shot."

Orchid clicked on the photo. She stared at Phoenix's wavy hair, and scruff shadowing his jawline. He carried himself like a warrior. But there was more. The flatness of his countenance, dark splotches beneath his lash line, the whisper of a downturn at either side of his mouth. He was in pain and trying to hide it.

She sucked a breath. "He looks so sad. You know it's the anniversary of his accident, and his dad's passing. I'm broken up that I'm not with him."

"Well, you're in a tough spot."

"True."

Orchid could make out crutches holding him up. That looked like progress.

"Who are those guys? Why do some families get all the good genes?" Mandy asked, making Orchid laugh.

"Cousins. Oh, that woman with the cardigan is their mom. She started out hating me, then she mellowed. I'm pretty sure she's pissed I dragged Phoenix to China."

"I don't remember any dragging. I think he made a damn good choice."

The penthouse apartment reminded Orchid of her home in New York. "You know, I miss the city. I miss my old team."

"That's easy. Come back. Please."

"Tempting."

"That place is real dolled up," Mandy said.

"I've been there. For our goodbye party before we left for China. It's posh but I couldn't wait to get outta there."

"Um, not to ring the five-alarm bell but I just zoomed in. Who's that woman hanging all over Phoenix?"

Orchid pinched her screen to make the photo bigger. She gasped.

"What?" Mandy asked.

"That bastard. He took his ex-girlfriend to this intimate family thing."

"No way. Which one, is that Tish?"

"Her name's Rina. He showed me her picture once. He told me he couldn't date anyone, and then he dated her."

"Oh crap, this is the one staying at his place? How's that going?"

"He said that he'd asked her to leave. But it looks like she's still around."

"Oh honey, she's got nothing on you."

Except she did. Orchid had been focused on Phoenix and hadn't noticed Rina's possessive pose. Rina leaned towards Phoenix, one hand on his forearm. Her smirk spoke of ownership, and a special link.

A thought struck Orchid. "If he's sentimental about the memories he and I have, and half of those are conflict, how do you think he feels about the angel who was 'just right' for him after his accident?"

"But they're not together, and you are. Who broke up with who anyway?"

"Oh, do you think Rina broke things off, and he might still have feelings?"

"I don't know about him. From the look of the picture, *she* might still have feelings."

"He promised me open communication. No secrets. He said he went back to New York early for medical reasons. But what if there's more? Why the hell did he give his apartment to Rina in the first place? She's using all the stuff in our place!"

"Maybe it's nothing," Mandy soothed.

Orchid noticed something else. "He's wearing the tie I gave him."

"Either he's thinking of you, or it was the first thing he grabbed."

"You know, I was thinking of coming to New York after his surgery."

"Do it. I miss you. Plus, I'm predicting a girl fight with Rina. Wait, surgery?"

"The whole thing with his leg. We thought it was from the fall at the Great Wall. But he's got some bone growth and they need to … operate." Orchid felt sympathy picturing what the words she was uttering actually meant. She'd seen the bone growth on x-rays. The doctors wanted to cut into his leg and shave down the excess.

"Well, if you come, you're welcome to stay here."

"You're the best. Now, tell me all about Matty!" Orchid said.

"He's way ahead on his growth charts and his milestones. You're going to be so proud when you see him. But wait, before I forget, how excited are you about our alumni article?"

"Alumni article? What alumni article?" Orchid searched her memory for a missed email.

"Didn't the guy contact you? He called me and said he wanted to do a piece to commemorate the ten-year anniversary of our 'best friends' article in the school paper."

"I have no idea what you're talking about."

"He asked me for your number but I told him he could get it from the alumni directory. Maybe he couldn't reach you in China."

"I'm glad you're excited. But do you think this makes sense? Our 'best friends' article was kind of a fluff piece. Why would they want a ten-year anniversary version of it?"

Her voice deflated. "I dunno. I liked it."

"Don't get me wrong, hon. I adored that piece. And look at us a decade later, still besties."

"Yeah, I thought that's what he'd like. Everything we've done since then. I mean, I've got Matty and all. You're the real success story. I laid it on thick, your big job, and assignment in China. He liked the human-interest angle with Phoenix. You know, the accident was really sad."

"You told him all that?!"

"Yeah, well, I don't think he'll use it. I just got to talking, you know me. He seemed real interested in how Phoenix needs surgery."

"Geez. Did you give him my social security number too?"

"Oh sorry, don't be mad. I think it'll be fun, seeing us in print!"

"I guess. Though both of our stories are still being written. Who knows how it'll end with Phoenix."

"Let me see if I can find the reporter's number. You can let him know what's off limits."

"Alright, thanks."

They hung up with plans to see each other in New York.

Orchid was filled with new resolve. Phoenix had been through so much. She knew where she needed to be. She pried open her laptop and bought plane tickets. Then she emailed her boss.

Absent-mindedly, she spun the promise ring around her finger on otherwise bare hands.

CHAPTER 33

UNDER THE KNIFE

Phoenix

The hospital's warnings before surgery were more dire than the pharmaceutical contraindications accompanying prescription medicines.

"Got it. I might die. I might lose my knee. And to be on the safe side, you won't guarantee I can have children after this," he exaggerated with sarcasm as he signed the waivers.

He didn't want any surgical risks to befall him. He didn't want to wake in pain. He didn't want to see his mother's worried expression. He thought he'd accepted his fate. Regret helped no one. Yet, for the first time in long months, he wished he hadn't descended into the subway station that Sunday a year ago. The best part of that day had been a brown-eyed beauty who had pressed him to talk about their relationship. "When you're back," he'd promised her, not knowing that by the time she'd returned, he'd have decided to let her go.

The anesthesiologist asked him to start counting backwards. Phoenix held onto images of Orchid as the numbers decremented. One hundred nights together, her silken skin sprawled on their satin sheets. Ninety watts for her bright smile when he made her laugh.

Eighty-eight, the lucky number she gravitated towards, despite claiming that she didn't buy Chinese superstitions. Fifty-fifty, for the chances they'd last.

Intuition flashed. He'd been wrong to turn down her offer to come to New York. Every day they'd been apart, he'd wanted to be together. For another forty years? Another thirty days?

Then, he was out.

Hours passed. Or minutes. More likely eons. Phoenix was now one with the granite of the earth. With no sense of time or place, Phoenix's consciousness fought through the thicket. Pain drummed his tender nerve endings. Fire shot through his missing toes, angry that their power had been diminished in the last year. The punishment was to double in fury.

"Help!" he couldn't even whisper. His mouth was desiccated. His eyelids were lead. His torturer threaded the barbs higher, wringing his ankle, shredding his calf, snapping every tendon of his knee, scrabbling up his thigh, into his groin to electrocute his whole torso.

"Die," the evil master hissed.

"Yes," he sobbed. "Let me go."

"Not even close. *I* decide when you're done." Spite cackled, and thrashed Phoenix's raw wounds until he was writhing and gasping, bleeding, and heaving.

The amplitude of Spite's glee grew and doubled, the whip end cracking a blow that hurled Phoenix against a cinder block Great Wall. Pain shattered him outwards into chunks, which exploded into shards, and then disintegrated. Phoenix imploded like a black hole.

He was nothing. No ego. No heart. Not a thing left.

At his father's funeral, the priest had intoned "Ashes to ashes. Dust to dust."

Ashes to ashes.

Dust to dust.

Nothing to nothing.

Goodbye.

The room spun into view. The angry green eye of a machine swayed. Overhead lights glared. Inside, pain pulsed. Nothing else was left.

"Hey, you, okay?" a sweet voice asked.

A delicate palm held his.

One eye rotated wildly, taking in dark hair and a wan smile.

His lids shut. *This must be a mirage, an impossible wish for Orchid.*

"Is it supposed to take this long? Let me talk to a doctor," a voice commanded.

He cracked an eyelid open. Stage left, his mother was wagging a finger at a nurse.

"Be nice, Ma," he managed to croak.

She strode over and held his arm. She avoided the one hand full of IV needles. "You're awake! You had me worried. How are you feeling?"

How was he feeling? He assessed himself. "Groggy. Drugged up. Terrible," he concluded.

She glared at the medical staff. "Terrible. See?"

The woman in scrubs left the room.

"Everyone's been by to see you," she informed him.

"No circus," he mumbled. His eyes closed.

CHAPTER 34

DELICIOUS DEMON

Orchid

Orchid had fled New York thinking China would give her a deeper connection to her mother's roots.

Yet, something released in her chest as she rolled her bag along the wide pathways of JFK's terminal. She sailed through passport control, relishing the feeling of freedom on the other side. Signs offered hot pizza and day drinking. No pictograms scrambled her brain.

Outside, a queue of people waited in line for taxis, giving each other appropriate distance, in contrast to the jostling, shouting, and occasional spitting she'd witnessed at Beijing's Capital Airport. Orchid relaxed into the crowd's hodgepodge of street styles, varied hair colors, and accents. She'd missed the diversity of New York City. When it was her turn, Orchid hefted her suitcase into the darkened trunk of a yellow cab, then slipped into the backseat.

"Hi, how are you? I'm going to the Marquis Hotel." Orchid told the driver where she'd be staying, without needing to practice the phrases in her mind before speaking. *What a relief.*

The highway led to the Queens Midtown tunnel, then transitioned into the congested streets of Manhattan. The narrow lanes felt cozier than the massive, paved avenues of Beijing. The City's honking cars, men in hardhats jackhammering pavement, and the stride of confident pedestrians warmed her with familiarity. There was no truer insight. Orchid was home.

Then, her thoughts turned to the reason she'd returned earlier than her original plans.

Phoenix, Phoenix, Phoenix.

Phoenix was in surgery so her best bet was his brooding brother. She called him from the back of the car.

"Hey, Caleb, I just landed into JFK. I'm coming by to see Phoenix, okay?"

"Whatevs. He's still on the operating table."

"On the operating table" generated images of Phoenix sprawled under a pool of light, in the middle of medical implements.

"Scalpel," the doctor would say to the staff, one latex-bound hand out. Like filleting a steak, he would deftly deglove the skin and tissue surrounding Phoenix's cleaved bone. Dispassionately wading through Phoenix's remaining muscle and nerves, he'd request, "Saw." He'd raise the serrated implement and decide how much of Phoenix to leave. The pale member would heave and beg. "Not again. I can't take anymore." Phoenix's sympathetic nervous system would gallop urgent signals to his brain. "Make it stop! He can't survive more loss." Later, the doctor's wife would ask "What'd you do today?" He'd toss back his beer and throw her a lackadaisical glance. "Nothing special."

Orchid wiped her eyes. Air. The sedan didn't house enough oxygen. She cracked her window, trying not to lose her sanity in front of the driver. She loved Phoenix. Yet anger simmered. In the past, this would be the recipe for raising walls around her vulnerability. This time, she'd stay present. They needed to talk.

"Wanna crash here?" Phoenix's brother Caleb asked.

Thoughtful. More than anything, though, she missed Phoenix's airy apartment with sofas for lounging, and oversized bed for luxuriating during weekends. Late morning sun would light Phoenix's handsome features and bathe his bare shoulders with warmth. She'd tuck close, in her favorite spot, encircled by his arms. "Love you, hungry bird," he'd murmur. Later, they'd pad into the kitchen and stir fry leftovers, laughing and dancing to Lady Gaga. None of this was remotely feasible. Phoenix was "under the knife." Orchid wasn't welcome in Rina's sublet.

"That's so nice. I've got reservations at a hotel already. You guys, okay? I've been thinking about you with the anniversary of your dad's death and how you're coping."

"Things kinda suck."

The car stopped in front of the hotel's gleaming glass, a reminder that she'd relinquished her apartment months ago and had no anchor to call home.

"Listen, can I ask you something?" she said.

"Shoot."

"I saw the photo. Of you guys and Rina at your aunt and uncle's. Tell me the truth, is there something between them?"

"I can tell you for a fact. Rina was there as a friend. There is zero chemistry between them. He was a totally different person to the guy he was when you came over."

She'd known the answer already. Their connection was forged through trust and care and love. He didn't deserve her doubt. "I believe you."

"Go see him. He needs you."

"Thanks, Caleb. Bye." She hung up.

A porter opened her door and fetched her valise. Orchid released a breath. No place like New York. *Home.*

At the reception desk, Orchid made a request. "If you have one, I'd prefer an accessible room."

It was subtle, the flick of eyes up and down Orchid's travel outfit.

"My boyfriend uses a wheelchair," she explained. This was a new sentence in her lexicon, one she'd first attempted in China when making lunch reservations. Such few words. Their new reality. This man had guarded her at the men's room, given her opportunities at work, mentored her, guided her through France, and moved with her to China.

The receptionist raised her eyebrows, then peered down at her computer screen. "Here you go. The room number is right here." She handed Orchid a plastic keycard inside its cardboard case. It was unlikely for Phoenix to visit, but if he did, she wanted him to be comfortable.

Orchid rode the lift to the high floor number on her keycard. Did it make any sense to put accessible rooms high up when stairs would have to be used in an emergency? He was an invisible form in the elevator beside her. She imagined him seated beside her. Wasn't this their fate? To be together.

Inside the mini-suite, the wheel-in shower and lowered sinks made her feel at home. The insight surprised her.

CHAPTER 35

INTO THE FIRE

Phoenix

When Phoenix woke, his body was burning. Its cells raw to every edge. He knew what was to come. The struggle of one-handed bandage changes. Checking for infection. Getting refitted for prostheses. Physical therapy. He'd been through this before, he'd survive it again.

He didn't want to be sad. His choice: buck up or give up. He'd work hard to get back to using his prosthesis. His goals used to be measured in revenues. Now they were measured one step at a time. Phoenix forced his eyes open. His vision fogged. Somewhere amidst the beeping machines, he'd find his resilience. The room swam beige, with industrial lighting glaring overhead. Before him, his left leg was elevated, grotesque in size. Bandages ballooned out below his knee. Pain pulsed beneath the gauze.

A movement to his left told him that he wasn't alone.

Dark hair framed knitted eyebrows above an onyx gaze. Orchid was grace incarnate. She'd risen from a guest chair to edge into his field of vision. His heart pulsed with hope.

"Hi, boo." *My honey.* Sweet voice. Kindness in her timbre. Wasn't her earlier visage a mirage? Resulting from psychotropic drugs and unspoken wishes?

He could feel her hand warm his forearm. "You're here." He heard wonder in the croak of his voice.

Don't look down the bed, he wanted to warn her. His tongue stuck to the roof of his mouth. He had trouble speaking through the dryness.

She leaned down to kiss his cheek. Roses. He lifted his hand to stroke her hair. So lifelike. Not his imagination?

"How are you feeling?" she asked.

"Super. Are you joining me for next week's triathlon?"

She laughed at his absurdity. The sound warmed him. "Not me. But I'll cheer you on."

"I can't believe you're here," he said.

"Ta da!" she said.

"Date night tonight?"

"Yes, I'm going to steal your hospital Jell-O," she threatened.

"After that, bed pan races."

"The doctor said surgery went well."

He hesitated. "That's good. Do you know if they took more of my leg?"

Orchid blinked in slow motion. "I don't know, Phoenix."

She stared down the bed as if she was imagining the details of the operation. He knew the images that haunted him. *The train slices. The surgeon chops.* He spoke up to derail this line of thinking, to save her. "Never mind. How are you doing?" he asked, really caring.

Orchid laid a hand on his arm. "So much better now that I'm here. You know how quiet Beijing is without you?"

"Am I that noisy?"

"After my aunt left, our apartment felt really empty. I almost got a goldfish."

"Replaced by a pair of fins. They don't hug as well, I have to warn you."

She encircled an arm around him and rested a cheek on his chest. "I did miss the hugs."

A wave of emotion threatened. She was soft and warm. Her dark hair fell and rose with each of his breaths.

"It's good you're here, so I can interview you in person," he said, injecting lightness into their mood.

She lifted her head and raised an eyebrow. "Are you interviewing candidates for the role of girlfriend because I thought I'd already won that job. And if you ask me to send Rina in next, I'll smack you. I saw your picture with her at your aunt and uncle's."

Phoenix's eyebrows raised. "I hope you know that means nothing."

"I believe you," she said.

"Here's something that does mean something though. I'm ready to show you our story."

"Any aha?"

Phoenix placed a hand on hers, his IV dragging along with the motion. "How hard it must've been on you to not know what happened. Maybe you blamed yourself, and that would've been really unfair. You probably thought I didn't care."

"You said goodbye when we'd barely gotten started, and then didn't answer my messages. I thought my feelings were one-sided. You put me through the wringer. You sure you want to go there?"

"Sorry. Writing this, it really hit me how unfair this whole situation was on you. I'm amazed you agreed to go to Tish's wedding with me."

Orchid tilted her face towards the foam ceiling tiles. "I thought it'd be good closure."

"Instead, it was an opening."

"The best kind," she agreed.

"I can guess some of what must've been going on for you, and it really makes me sorry. Maybe you can read it and tell me what you think. It was easier writing some of the tough stuff rather than saying it out loud."

"Like what?"

"Stuff I should've asked you earlier. Maybe I was afraid to hear the answers. Like is there anything I should do differently? It's better for me to know. I know you were having nightmares in Beijing. Did they stop after I left?"

She paused, then lifted her gaze to his. "Yes, they have. But you're not responsible for my nightmares, Phoenix. And there's nothing you need to do except to be honest. Like, how serious are we? Did you come back to New York just for surgery, or something more?"

Her childhood loss meant that she didn't trust easily. He was ready to reassure her for a lifetime. Purple jewelry adorned her hand. "My promise ring wasn't serious enough?"

She looked down at her ring finger and released a long breath. "I love it."

"I love you," he said.

In response, she cupped his chin and leaned in to kiss his cheek, then landed on his lips, erasing any conscious thought. Her mouth was tender. He'd missed her.

"When can I read your book?" she asked.

"Soon," he said, then winced. He'd put her through so much already. Now, she'd read the hard sentences that depicted his nightmares.

> *In the bright white of the light, I see what shocks her. The bandages covering my stumps are gone, discarded in the struggle. My wounds lie bare and ugly. Bloody lines wind around blunt, severed limbs like moss creeping up a tree. I scream. Orchid appears, grimacing.*

"What do you need, love?" She turns her back on my disfigurement. At least she called me "love." But then, what's wrong?

"Why are you crying, Orchid?"

"I'm about to be sick."

"Are you ill?"

"Only when I'm here." There'd be nothing hidden between them then. Every cold fact he'd shielded from her would be laid bare.

A nurse came into their room and glanced at the machine beside his bed. "I came to change your bandages. How are you feeling? Your blood pressure is rising."

Orchid blushed. "Sorry."

"It's not your fault," he said.

"It's usually the guy's fault," the nurse said.

Orchid stepped aside to allow the nurse to approach.

"You want to see how to do this, in case you're going to help with home care?" the nurse asked Orchid and began to unroll the tan gauze wrapped around his leg.

How would Orchid react to his puckered skin and angry stitches? Images of disgust skittered through his imagination. The pink creep up her cheeks. The rosebud 'O' of her mouth. Her eyes growing round as the rest of her shrank towards the door. He'd save her. He owed her this at least.

"You're still on China time. It's the middle of the night for you," he spat, waving her away before the nurse could expose his swollen limb. The first black stitch became visible like a gash against his ivory skin.

Orchid was already washing her hands at the stainless-steel sink. At the sound of his words, she came closer. "Nah, it's a good idea. I watched videos but it's good to see the process in-person."

"Videos?" In his shock, he barely registered the final tug before air cooled the skin around his sutures.

"This is tensor material, to shape the limb for wearing prostheses." The nurse handed Orchid the new roll of fabric to inspect.

She accepted the material then stretched a palm's width over his bare knee. "The technique I saw said to start on the diagonal."

The nurse nodded her approval. "That's right. Do you want to give it a try?"

He shifted in bed. This medical professional had no idea that Orchid's background might cause her to snap. An ochre liquid wept from the puckered scar.

Orchid surprised him, speaking with assurance as she worked. "The video said to crisscross the material into a figure-eight like this. And not put too much pressure near the bones."

"For now, lighter tension is good. As the wound heals, you'll be able to keep the compression tighter," the nurse instructed.

Orchid looked up at Phoenix. "Does that hurt, hon?"

Awed, he shook his head.

She tucked the end of the bandage into the final wrap above his knee.

"We should let the patient rest," the nurse said, and gathered the discarded bandages.

Orchid looped her grommet-studded purse over one arm and kissed his cheek. "I'm going to work tomorrow but text if you need anything."

She accompanied the nurse out of the room. He watched the door thud closed behind them and then leaned into his pillows.

Behind his closed lids, he could see Orchid wearing his promise ring. She'd flown half the circumference of the earth for him. He loved her, she loved him. Everything could work out. Of course, it could.

CHAPTER 36

WHO'S BETTER FOR WHOM?

Orchid

The next day, Orchid was greeted like a celebrity in the office. The receptionist hugged her. The conference room was laden with food. Suddenly, she realized how homesick she'd been. New York was the place that felt like home. Beijing was a distant memory, a place to visit.

Violet squealed upon spotting her friend.

"Aw, I missed you guys," Orchid said, and looked around at the dozens of colleagues who'd come by to see her. "Tell me about all of you. How was Pat's baby shower? You have to let me in on the office pool. And has anyone heard from Princeton?"

Violet brought over a plate while Orchid chatted with her co-workers.

"Your famous cinnamon streusel!" Orchid exclaimed and popped a bite into her mouth.

"You must have coffee cake in Beijing, right?"

"Not really. Chinese desserts are hard to get used to. They're sweet, but they're made with black beans. Or sesame. Or eggs."

"Ohh, I love egg custard," her flame-haired media analyst friend said.

Orchid remembered her conversation with Phoenix about the role of eggs in Mandarin profanities. *"Ben dan,"* she spoke one of the curses aloud.

"Show off," Violet said with a grin. Orchid didn't have time to explain this Chinese curse translated literally to stupid egg.

Joan clapped her ringed hands together. "Okay, let's hear about your experience, Orchid. Have a seat, everyone."

Orchid was the only one left standing. She moved towards the front of the space, much like Phoenix had the first time they'd met in the room adjacent to this one.

"First of all, thanks to so many of you for supporting this move. Joan, you gave me my first chance in China. A bunch of you, like Violet, handled double duty so I could go without worrying. It's really good to see everyone. My one lesson learned is that it's always worth going for the opportunities you want, even if it seems like a long shot."

She described her assignment. "China is an amazing place to live and work. The place has developed so fast. Their digital innovation would blow your mind. I have a new idea I'm just starting to formulate that could work here too."

Before she could unveil her project, Violet squealed from her front row seat.

"Do you have a question?" Orchid asked.

Violet stood and joined Orchid. She lifted Orchid's hand in hers. "Yes. Are you engaged, missy?"

Orchid looked down at the promise ring that had grown to be a part of her. "Nope, but it's pretty, isn't it?"

The redhead from media came over to peer around Violet. "Oh wow, did that come from Dior?"

Orchid thought of the understated white box. "Yeah, how'd you know?" she asked.

"My boyfriend and I were shopping. That one's really unique. It's carved amethyst, pink gold, and diamonds. It must be like tens of thousands of dollars."

"What?!"

"Top of the line."

Orchid's collection tended towards costume jewelry. *What did this mean?* Then she picked up on the first part of her friend's story. "Shopping? Are congrats in order for you?"

Her friend lifted her bare hand. "Not yet."

"You might consider getting that insured," Joan suggested.

"China's famous for fakes. Maybe it's a knockoff," a guy from finance noted.

"Actually, that might make me feel better," Orchid said, admiring the rose gold band and purple flower anew.

"I want to tell you about the new line we're working on." Orchid tapped her computer screen back to life. "Did you know one in five Americans has a disability? And one in three knows someone with one?" she began. Orchid pictured her beautiful entrepreneur as she spoke.

"Disability is under-represented," Joan nodded.

"Exactly. We're making great strides in gender and ethnic diversity. What we show in media matters. It reflects society. And disability can sometimes feel invisible."

She paged forward to a slide showcasing luxurious packages.

"The opportunity is bigger than just creative execution. I'm also excited about the potential in product. My R&D team has developed our new line to expand beyond cosmetic benefits. Skincare can solve real problems too. Think about the balms people use for burns, and rashes. They're packaged super functional. And yes, they need to be medicinal first. But here's the insight. For people who need to use them day in, day out, it just reminds them they have something that needs to be fixed. It's a constant reminder something's wrong. What about people who use stuff for the rest of their lives? Couldn't we brighten the experience by offering it under the luxury brands they go to for beauty? Normalize the experience as part of life?"

"I love it." Violet stood to view the screen closer.

"You're onto something," said the media analyst.

"Our new Asia line is going to offer night cream, eye cream, sunscreen, of course. But it's also going to have balm for people who wear prostheses. Aloe salve for burns. High-grade lotion to reduce scarring. We might not sell zillions of these specialized SKUs, but we send a message. This is part of everyday life and deserves to have a luxury brand just like all the beauty products," she concluded just as the meeting time ended.

"That's really differentiated. The message is powerful," Joan proclaimed, standing to head to their next meeting.

Orchid relished the buzz as her coworkers hugged her farewell. She thought she had no place to call home. Yet, she felt among family here.

When everyone else had left, her previous VP of marketing waved her into a chair. "I can be a few minutes late for my next meeting. Sit."

Orchid took the chair catty-corner to her previous boss.

"I know you're only months into the assignment, but the year will be up before you know it. Have you thought about whether you'd like to extend your time there?"

Orchid paused. She preferred being better prepared for career conversations. Her half-formed opinions swirled.

"I'm learning a lot. I'm also thinking about bigger opportunities."

"Good, because I wanted to talk with you about opportunities back on my team. Frankly, I'd consider expanding that idea you just presented globally."

Orchid stared at her, a possibility blossoming before her. "We're shooting ads in the US and China. I'd love for you to be on set for the New York spot."

"You've changed, Orchid. You've always been a go-getter, but there's something different about you."

"I feel like I'm growing up."

"I have to go, but if you decide not to extend your assignment, will you tell me?"

"I will," Orchid said, part of her wanted to accept her old boss's offer right there.

Orchid worked from the conference room, surrounded by half-eaten detritus. When Violet returned to the room, Orchid felt like no time had passed. She'd been engrossed in refining the pitch, fueled by Joan's enthusiasm.

Violet chirped. "You can have the coffee cake. Take the Tupperware I brought it in. I know you hate packaging waste."

"You should enjoy it."

"I made it for you," Violet coaxed.

"Okay, thank you. This way, we'll have to see each other again, so I can return the container."

"How long will you be staying?"

"I don't know. Probably a week or two, then I need to get back. I've been taking all my calls in the middle of the night."

"You seemed a little down when Phoenix came up. Are you okay?"

"He had surgery. I'm worried about him. It's why I came back to the city."

"Oh no! What happened?"

"It's follow-up surgery from his accident last year. It's complicated. You have time for cake?" Orchid said.

Violet tapped on her phone. "I have another meeting in five minutes. Joan's going to kill me if I'm late."

"Then, everything's okay, and you should go."

"You two are still the hottest couple ever," Violet whispered as they hugged. She flew out of the room.

Alone in the quiet, Orchid packed up the sweet bread. Her beautiful man was recovering from surgery she tried not to imagine.

She took her phone off airplane mode. The screen lit with missed messages.

Mandy texted. "You can't tell me you're in the city and then not get together."

Orchid missed her friend. She'd have to call and make plans soon.

Then she realized that during her workday, Phoenix had texted. "They're discharging me early. If you want to, come by and roll home with me."

Oh no. Was she too late? Already 2 pm. Orchid punched up his number. One ring, two rings.

"Hello?" a female voice answered. She recognized Rina's rounded vowels.

"It's Orchid. I'm looking for Phoenix."

"Phoenix? He's actually sleeping. Maybe you can try him later."

An image of Rina seated beside a sleeping Phoenix made her seethe. A dozen questions rouletted through her mind. She paused on one of the pressing ones. "Why are you answering his phone?"

"It was charging. I saw your name and thought it might be urgent."

"Shouldn't you be at work?"

"I wanted to be here in case Phoenix needed anything so I worked from home."

How surreal. Phoenix's apartment was his ex-girlfriend's "home."

"How's he doing?"

"Getting home was rough. I think he bumped his incision in the car."

Orchid rose above jealousy to feel gratitude that he hadn't been alone during his discharge from the hospital. "Rina, you can go to work. I can come over."

"It's too late. There's really no sense," Rina replied.

What was "too late?"

"Then maybe I'll see you later. Is there anything Phoenix needs?" Orchid asked.

"He's probably going to need more gauze pads and dressing. I can text you a shopping list."

"Thanks, Rina. Bye." Maybe his ex wasn't so bad.

An hour later, Orchid arrived at the Upper East Side building that had been her salvation just months earlier.

Phoenix's doorman recognized Orchid and high-fived her hello. She pulled him into a hug and asked about his family. Her true mission was eleven stories up. After a few minutes, she waved the fob that she still carried on her key ring and hurried up the elevator.

Orchid rotated her promise ring. It was loose on her slender digit, slipping like a half-hearted pledge.

At the door, she tapped the painted surface with one knuckle. No answer. She needed to drop off the medical supplies she'd bought, so she twisted the key in the lock until the deadbolt loosened. No one was in sight. Reflected in the mirror was her anxiety.

Inside the apartment, the familiarity of Phoenix's place filled her with nostalgia. His leather sofa sat adjacent to her swoop-armed settee. Business books lined his shelves. Yet, this wasn't the cocoon they'd enjoyed before China. The apartment smelled different. Musky. A black laptop rested on Phoenix's coffee table, clearly not his sleek MacBook.

Where could they be? Wouldn't Phoenix be resting? Orchid might as well take a peek in his bedroom. She'd be quiet in case he was sleeping. The foyer closet was ajar. The space that previously housed Orchid's edgy threads now showcased a woman's camel-colored trench coat and gray business suits. The sight was jarring.

She turned away from the view of Rina's things.

Voices rose from behind the hollow bedroom door.

"I made us some tea. I found Darjeeling in the cupboard," Rina said.

"Thanks. That's my girlfriend's. I used to hate the stuff."

"She called. She's on her way."

Orchid didn't want to eavesdrop. She called out "Hello, Phoenix? Rina?"

Her feet found the path through his apartment, past the kitchen where they'd cooked and danced to old-school punk songs, past the living room where they'd shared bubbly, right to the bedroom door where she'd coaxed Phoenix over the threshold one months-ago evening which hugged her with velvet memories.

She pushed the door open. The room where she'd first shared a bed with Phoenix smelled medicinal. Resting against his tufted headboard, Phoenix sat listening to the blond seated beside him.

Behind the woman in a gray tracksuit, two cups of tea steamed on Phoenix's nightstand. His twisted sheets painted a picture of intimacy.

"I'm Orchid," she introduced herself to Rina. Jealousy wouldn't help anyone. She walked over to Phoenix and deposited the gauze onto his nightstand.

"Hungry bird," he greeted her, his blue gaze crinkling. A white tee-shirt stretched against his broad chest.

"Thanks for bringing the stuff." Rina stood, color splashed across her round cheeks.

"How are you feeling?" Orchid asked Phoenix. She sat in the spot he patted beside him, the place still warm from Rina's haunches.

"Pretty awkward with both of you here."

"I'll look for a place," Rina said as she zipped her jacket.

"I think I have an idea," Orchid said.

"Oh yeah?" Phoenix tilted his head.

"If you'll have me, there's a hotel room looking for an occupant," she said.

As he absorbed her meaning, his mouth upturned.

"That's brilliant," he agreed.

Orchid pulled out a cardboard-sheathed card from her pocket and offered it to Phoenix's ex-girlfriend. "You okay with staying in Midtown?"

"Really? That'd be nice." Rina looked down at the address and room number on the key holder.

"I can use my spare key to get my stuff packed up and out of there tonight," Orchid offered.

"Thank you." Rina looked back and forth at the two of them and then departed.

"You know I asked her to leave, right?" Phoenix asked.

"I know, Phoenix, I trust you." Joy stretched her taller, as she realized the truth. His ex-girlfriend in his apartment, his wistful letter accompanying her promise ring, none of that could erase his care. She'd healed enough to trust him.

"That's good. How was your day?"

"So busy. Sorry I missed your message. How's your leg?" She looked down the bed and wondered when they should change his bandages again.

"It hurts but nothing I can't deal with."

Orchid kicked off her shoes and scooted around to what had been "her" side of the bed.

Phoenix threaded his embrace with hers.

"Best place in the world," he murmured. Their arms entwined, heads leaned close, breathing slowed to a matching pace. Orchid could detect the thump of his heart, and fainter yet, the ticking of the cycling clock in the kitchen.

"I should go pack," she mumbled, her eyelids heavy.

"Not yet," he suggested. "I've had a lot of time to think. When else will we have the opportunity to give into the magnetic pull of just resting? You know what we should call it? Bed-netism."

She chuckled. The soothing cadence of his words coaxed her eyes closed. Later, she'd tell him about the surprise she'd arranged for him. An idea that had been forming since Phoenix's neighbor Mrs. V had insulted his potential as a desirable mate. The world needed this. She'd tell him soon.

CHAPTER 37

CIRC DU STITCHES

Orchid

Heat shimmered off the Manhattan sidewalks. After she woke, Orchid had returned to the hotel for her belongings and packed. Now, she was back, pulling her suitcase through the cool lobby she'd once coveted as almost her own. Months ago, she'd wanted to believe she could belong. These next weeks, she could. She would immerse herself in time with Phoenix. She had one last gift to arrange for him before leaving New York.

Then, she'd return to Beijing. Her mom used to sing the Doris Day song, "Que Sera, Sera." *Whatever will be, will be.*

Mrs. V climbed into the elevator car with her. Here was the inconsiderate person who'd expressed doubt that a woman could want to be with an injured Phoenix. The same building board member who'd blabbed that Rina was moving in. That kerfuffle exposed Phoenix's flaw. Both memories surfaced ill feelings towards this nosy neighbor.

"Hello, Elton," Orchid greeted her dog. At least, the pooch hadn't wronged the person she most loved.

Mrs. V waved the pup's paw for him. "You're back," she said.

Orchid recalled the first accusation Mrs. V had launched towards her. "Yup. As an invited guest. Not through Airbnb."

"Of course."

The metal box pulled them upwards, numbers lighting as they ascended past each floor.

Inside the apartment, Orchid's banner draped over her settee in the living room.

"Welcome Home, Orchid."

She dropped her studded purse onto the pale wood floor and wandered towards the seat where they'd first kissed. One palm lifted to her mouth. She hadn't admitted how much she'd wanted a place to call home. Especially this one.

Inside their bedroom, she found Phoenix reading shirtless, propped against pillows, his residual limb freshly bandaged. She absorbed his muscular physique.

"Holy mother, you are gorgeous," she breathed.

"Jet lag is affecting your judgment," he countered.

She abandoned her suitcase at the bedroom threshold and closed the steps between them. He tossed his reading material onto the bedside table, where she noticed a familiar photo album. She leaned down to meet his lips, her hands steadied on his powerful biceps. Spice. And soap. *Home.* "My judgment is just fine. Right now, I'm objectifying you."

He returned her kiss. "Bad girl."

She stood, remembering the unpleasant elevator ride. "Bad girl is exactly Mrs. V's sentiments."

"Mrs. V? Uh-oh. What happened?"

"Let's just say I had company in the elevator."

"What now?"

"I simply reminded her that I'm an invited guest."

"You're more than a guest. This is your home too."

"Thank you." She waved towards the living room where his banner lay strewn across the one-armed sofa. "I never told you. I probably never told anyone. After my parents died, it was hard to call any place *home*. I had to be careful not to be a burden at my aunt's.

No one else has wanted to make a home with me. Until you. That's why your sign gets me every time."

Phoenix put a hand on her forearm. "Oh, Orchid."

She glanced at the furrow between his brows and couldn't take it. "I don't want your pity."

"This is part of why we get each other. I don't want your pity either." He encircled her waist with his embrace.

She bent towards him and returned his hug. "You have my admiration, not pity," she said.

"Don't get too full of admiration until you try dinner."

"You don't need to go to any trouble. I'll cook for you."

Phoenix scanned the storm behind her expression. "Hang on. Join me. I have something for you." His words filled her with curiosity.

She kicked off her shoes and climbed under the covers.

He plucked the sheaf of papers he'd been reading and held it aloft for her.

She accepted the bound pages and tucked close enough to feel his warmth. Before she opened it, she pointed towards his side table and blurted a confession.

"I should've told you sooner. I've seen that album and looked through it once. I wished I was in those photos. I should've been there with you," she said. A whole scene emerged in her mind, the two of them joking around in an exam room as a technician plastered his residual limb for his socket fitting.

Phoenix studied her. "I couldn't have imagined it then, but you're right. I wish you were there too."

A whoosh of forgiveness overcame her. Her conscience clear, she turned her attention to the spiralbound pages wrapped in a plastic cover. "Is this your book?" she guessed.

"My memoir. Our story. I want to know what you think and I'm also scared," he said.

"I only accept happy endings," she declared and snuggled against Phoenix's bare chest. Her lungs inhaled his clean scent. His strong pulse sounded against one eardrum. He cradled an arm around her and kissed the crown of her head.

"Is this not happy enough for you?" he laughed.

She was too warm and comforted to respond. Her eyelids wanted to seal shut. Her circadian rhythm still needed to adjust to New York time.

He answered for her, nodding his chin towards the paper packet heavy on her thighs.

"I've been afraid to show you what I've been writing. It has a happy ending. It's the in between that's raw. I don't know how else to make it up to you. This is the time we missed."

Orchid sat up to grab the spiralbound volume. She hesitated. Because really, what good could come of reliving the worst time of his life? Unless, discussing that time could deepen their relationship, and explain how he could've abandoned her last year.

"What's with the title?" Orchid asked, as she read the cover. "*Goodbye, Orchid* by Phoenix Walker?"

His chest pulsed with laughter. His arms around her kept her from leaping out of bed.

"Isn't that our story? From last year? It's the perfect working title."

"Walker, you have a death wish."

"Give it a chance. Read it as an apology, the pure unvarnished truth. I really want to know what you think."

Her fingers twisted the plastic cover as if the act could redo their history.

"Here. Let me show you," he said, and flipped open the manuscript to page one. "Dedicated to the most beautiful orchid on the most sparkling star in the sky. Chapter One. Phoenix never believed today was goodbye. Even though hellos come with goodbyes. Like black holes and Stephen Hawking. Like doughnuts and doughnut holes."

Swept up with curiosity, she picked up where he'd left off. "Today, she stood before him, in a leather-edged tunic layered over tights." Her mouth fell agape. "You remembered my outfit?"

"I remember everything, hungry bird. That's what love does."

She turned to the ending pages, as impatient as a child on Christmas morning, to see if she'd been gifted her wish. Her eyes skimmed the final paragraphs, then her lips uttered the lines. "He pulled her closer, his chest against hers. 'How I've wanted this.'

He bent and touched his lips to hers until every subatomic particle bloomed to its fullest glory. He tingled her skin with a kiss like no other, one that evoked thoughts of an expanding universe and the study of numbers beyond infinity.

"Me too," she said.

He tightened his hold on her. Time ticked forward to unearth each lost intersection, devotion, and affection."

Orchid looked into his placid blue gaze, storming below the surface.

"Happy enough ending?" he asked.

"Happy enough," she agreed, and leaned in to show him with a kiss. Then she leaned back. "Do you write a lot of science analogies?" she wondered aloud.

He swept a welcoming gesture over the pages. "A few. I didn't hold back on my love for physics. See for yourself."

She turned back to the beginning, while Phoenix settled beside her. "It was therapeutic to write but it can be tough to read. I don't want to keep anything from you. After all, it's our story," he murmured in his deep rumble. "And my family's. I hope it's okay, I asked Sascha and my mom for input."

As she read, the reality of his trauma saturated her memory. As if she had been there. As if she *were* him. The terror of falling onto the tracks gripped her. Her eyes watered as she read about him waking in the hospital. About his fear of her seeing his injuries. Hours passed. He'd leaned against his pillows and fallen asleep. His deep breathing accompanied the turning pages.

In the next chapter, he wrote about her return from China. She hadn't known he was in the hospital during her call from the airport.

He had let her go to protect her. Because she loved dancing and cobblestoned Paris, which he didn't want to prevent her from enjoying. His descent into depression after his self-sacrifice made her heart thump harder in her chest. The rage she'd felt towards him then dissipated into empathy.

Pretty soon, his passages tightened into a lump in her throat. In the story, he was naked in the shower, the full weight of his loss turning into rage. She could feel his desperation, and the conviction that there was nothing to live for. She sucked a breath as she guessed the impending plummet of the storyline. This was where it had almost happened.

The sound must've woken him. The mattress shifted under his weight, his movement jarring her into the present. He propped up, peering at the page that had sparked her pain.

"Hang on. I must've fallen asleep. There's something I should tell you." His eyebrows knitted together as he sat up beside her.

Her eyes swelled and pricked with unexpected tears. "Phoenix, honey, I think I know. It's just awful. Did you try to hurt yourself?" Her chin threatened to quake.

"Did Caleb tell you?" he asked.

"No, your therapist put a phone number in your album. I'm sorry I looked. I just wanted to know more about the time we were apart. I saw her number. Then I googled it. It was the National Suicide Hotline."

Somewhere down deep, he dug up a wavery smile for her. "It got bad. Believe me, you didn't want to be there." Except if she'd been there, wouldn't things have been better for him?

She enveloped him into her arms as if physical evidence of her care could protect him from the past. Her face buried into his shoulder. He smelled clean and sweet.

"I've lost enough people."

He pressed lips to her hair. "I know. I'm sorry. I was trying not to hurt you and did the opposite."

Orchid absorbed the feel of him, his bicep smooth against her cheek, his diaphragm expanding and contracting, his warmth soothing her until her eyelids wanted to close. She had an epiphany to share.

"So, you have two Alive Days," she said.

His chuckle rumbled through her. She thought of the antidote to his insecurity that she'd been preparing.

"I have something I want to run by you," she said.

"Oh yeah?"

"You know how I always said I could see you on a Times Square billboard?"

Though he hmphed a puff of air, she kept going. "I pitched Lauder to extend their line of skincare, to add luxury to stuff people might've considered medicinal. To elevate the experience beyond purely functional. We're going into production soon. I want you in the ads."

His gaze swept down past his lap.

"You'd be perfect," she said.

Before he could respond, a knock sounded at the front door.

"Promise me you'll think about it." Orchid's feet hit the floor. She slid out of bed.

Phoenix began transferring into his chair. He moved gingerly. Orchid reminded herself that he'd recently endured surgery.

"I'll get it." Orchid hurried out.

Rina had probably returned for some forgotten cosmetic item. She yanked open the entry door. "What is it—" she began to say.

A man cowered at the threshold, wisps of brown hair sprouting from his cheeks. A thick brown jacket over his t-shirt struck Orchid as out of place for a warm summer night. His paws were jammed into his pockets as if uncertain of himself. His bulbous nose quivered under the brim of a baseball cap.

She backed up. "Yes?"

"I'm here to see Phoenix," he said and stepped inside.

Phoenix's wheels squeaked against the wood floor behind her. "Who is it?" he called.

"I'm Roy," the man said. The door thudded closed.

CHAPTER 38

SO ALIVE

Roy

The man Roy had inadvertently harmed emerged from the back of the apartment. Orchid retreated towards the interior. In a protective gesture, Phoenix wheeled forward between them.

Emotions bucked through Roy stronger than he'd expected.

Phoenix emanated as much strength as he had remembered. Even seated, Roy was convinced this stallion could clock him in a millisecond.

Then, what was missing buckled Roy's kneecaps. Phoenix's elbow lay on the wheelchair armrest. He recalled Phoenix's grasp laying on the tracks, curled, abandoned. Guilt dropped Roy's view downwards. Lowered to his leg. There, his calf was a swollen mass wrapped in bandages. Here they were, a year later, and the guy was still dealing with Roy's impulsive leap. He would forever.

Roy couldn't say all that.

"God, it's good to see you alive," he choked out.

He could've absorbed this image for weeks. Seeing his pulse beating along his neck, his cheeks flushed with color, was a whole other joy.

Phoenix's worked-up mouth and angry lean meant he didn't feel the same way. He was pointing at the door and shoving his chair closer. He showed no fear. Just fury.

"You saved my life." Roy sidestepped deeper into the apartment, towards Orchid, before Phoenix could run him over.

His statement stopped Phoenix's wheels.

"Who *are* you?" he asked.

Roy cringed and tried honesty. "I'm the guy you saved from jumping onto the tracks. I was homeless at the time. My name is Roy."

Phoenix's face cycled through an entire movie's worth of emotions. Disbelief. Recognition. Fury.

Roy had waited so long for this moment. He fingered the fabric flower in his pocket to strengthen his resolve. "I came to say thank you. I'm sorry I didn't come sooner. I thought you'd died until Mandy ..." he babbled. "And clearly you haven't. Man, are you alive!"

"Mandy?" a higher voice interrupted, looking surprised he knew her best friend's name.

He'd forgotten about Orchid. She was tapping with both thumbs on a phone in her hands.

Who was she contacting? Hopefully not security. Security would be trouble. He closed their distance before she could react and grabbed at the device. It slipped from her grip and tumbled to a stop under a side table. He blocked her way from retrieving it.

"Hey!"

"Who are you texting?"

"Security is on their way," she said.

"You shouldn't have done that," he said.

"What do you want?" Phoenix demanded.

This wasn't going as he'd planned. Everything was happening so fast.

He backed towards the front door and spoke to the man in the chair. "I wanted to do something for you, to thank you. I'm a great investigator. I found out something you're going to want to know about your dad. He was in charge of Orchid's case."

Phoenix wheeled towards him, causing Roy's feet to cycle backwards faster. "We know that. I think you should leave now."

Somewhere below them, an elevator dinged to announce its ascent.

Roy's words tripped over each other as he aimed for the front door. He needed to be gone before security arrived. "Um …" He spat his trump card as he grabbed the door handle. He wanted to share the secret he'd unearthed. *Me, Roy.* "Your dad was supposed to recuse himself. Because your cousin Harry was at the party where Orchid's parents were. But he didn't. He had a reason—"

The elevator's tinny chime cut Roy's words short.

Orchid's mouth fell open.

He stumbled out the door. His feet pounded through the corridor and leapt down the fire stairs. He'd mapped out his escape just in case. His heart hammered. He'd be out of the building at street level in less than four minutes.

Things hadn't gone as planned. He hadn't been able to reveal his final insight.

CHAPTER 39

RECUSAL REFUSAL

Phoenix

"What?" Phoenix's brain was exploding, its neurons detangling into the expanding universe as his front door slammed shut behind Roy's escape.

"My aunt was always mad that we didn't get much from the court case," Orchid whispered, staring at him.

"Orchid, before you indict my dad, we haven't seen any solid evidence." Phoenix wheeled over to her, feeling horror tighten his brow.

Her eyes wide like a skittish wildcat, Orchid backed towards the bedroom. "I don't know what to make of all this."

A knock sounded at the door.

"Don't tell me the guy came back," he said and wheeled towards the peephole installed at wheelchair height.

"Security," called a high, nasal voice.

He opened the apartment door to a blue uniformed lady grasping a holstered firearm. He recognized her copper curls and short stature from trips through the building lobby.

"Phoenix Walker?" she asked, holding out her badge for him to examine.

"Yes, I'm Phoenix. My girlfriend texted." He heard Orchid close the bedroom door behind her.

"What happened?" she asked, and pocketed her ID. It could've been a toy store special, for all he'd know, so it was good he knew she worked in their building.

"Some guy showed up unexpectedly." He wheeled back to allow her to enter. His skin felt electrified from the interaction with the man whom he thought he'd never encounter again.

"Is he here?" she scanned the empty space behind him. The ghost of the intruder seemed to fill the air.

"He left a few minutes before you got here."

"Do you need me to go after him? Call law enforcement?"

He considered the bulbous nosed guy who had initially triggered a feeling of déjà vu before recognition had fully settled in his consciousness. "No, I don't think we need the police. Just make sure he doesn't come in here again. You must have him on the security cameras."

The guard nodded and strode to the front door, her marching order clear. "We'll review the footage, see how he got in, post his photo. We'll make sure the staff is on the lookout."

"Sounds good." He accompanied her to the foyer and opened his door for her.

"Do you need anything else?" she asked.

He shook his head. "Thanks for getting here so fast."

"That's what we're here for." She waved and left. He dead bolted the door.

Phoenix released a breath. His leg was throbbing, the stabbing sensation reminding him that he was supposed to rest. He wheeled towards the bedroom, sorting through layers of shock. The man he'd saved had been in his apartment. Roy knew where they lived. Phoenix didn't sense menace from the guy. His head pounded from the equation he had no way to weigh. His mobility in exchange for Roy's life. He believed he'd make the trade again.

A tingle began in his missing toes. The precursor to phantom pain. *Not now.*

None of that mattered. Only one person mattered. He'd suffered when she'd shared the pain of her parents' death. That paled compared to this gut twist. Were his father and cousin possibly implicated?

Phoenix wheeled towards their bedroom. He needed to talk with Orchid.

Except a new sight shocked him.

CHAPTER 40

WORLD-A-WHIRL

Orchid

What if. *What if.* Orchid had fled to the bedroom, her mind awhirl.

The concreteness of the security guard in their apartment had cemented the whole incident as real.

John Walker's refusal to recuse himself couldn't be heaped onto his son. Phoenix had only learned of this wrinkle tonight, at the same time as Orchid, from the sound of it. She could see the confusion in his scrunched eyebrows. She didn't blame him, but she needed space for herself.

She needed time to parse what had happened. She couldn't think straight here, in this apartment where she'd won the relationship lottery, where they'd cooked together, slept together, and found love, only to get a whiff that there might be rot beneath it all. For so long, she had tried not to dwell on the fact that the judge's final request had led Phoenix to her. But now, Roy's words fueled her insecurity. Was the Judge's true motivation guilt?

Out in the living room, the apartment had grown quiet.

Her suitcase's fuchsia hue shouted for attention like an alarm.

She used to wonder, what if she'd salted the driveway the night of the storm? What if she'd agreed to a babysitter so they didn't have to come home? Now, a new question haunted her. Had Judge Walker put some personal interest above a child's? Had he protected his family at her expense, and then asked Phoenix to right his wrong?

There was another mystery. She had swiped her phone from the floor on her way into the bedroom. She tapped it awake and called Mandy.

"Hey, hon!" her friend greeted her.

"Sweetie, this is going to sound random but have you talked to the guy that caused Phoenix's accident?"

"Um, that's out of the blue. No?"

"So, get this. Tonight, a guy shows up, says his name's Roy. Says he's the suicidal guy from the train station."

"Whoa, did you say his name was Roy?"

"Yeah."

"Roy's the name of the guy from our alma mater, who interviewed me."

"Bingo. In the middle of his rant, he said he realized Phoenix was alive because of you."

"Oh no. I didn't trust him at first, but he knew our backstory."

"What'd you tell him?"

Mandy paused. "Just that I was so proud of what you've accomplished. I did tell him you were with Phoenix. You guys are okay, right? I'll come right over if you want."

"We're okay but maybe I should come crash at your place."

"Do you want hubby to come get you?" Mandy asked.

A whir of rubber wheels against the wood floor interrupted her response. "It's okay. I'll text you later. Bye," Orchid said and ended the call.

She palmed her suitcase and swept out of the bedroom, just as Phoenix wheeled towards her. His expression tumbled from hope to despair. His nostrils quivered at the sight of her, luggage in hand, feet headed for the exit.

Orchid's heart went out to him. "Tonight was a lot to take in. You probably never thought you'd see the guy you saved again. Did Roy look the way you remembered?" she asked. His life would never be the same and now they'd met the man who was responsible.

"He changed. It was him though. His nose. The way he moved." Phoenix's voice emerged thick. "I'm such a prick, I wondered if he was worth what I went through."

His vulnerability broke her resolve. Her knees weakened. She was one of the few people to know how much saving Roy's life had cost him. It made her love him more. "It doesn't make you a prick. It makes you human. You told me once you'd regret it if you *hadn't* done anything."

Phoenix nodded. "Like tonight. I'd regret it if I didn't tell you how I feel. That you coming to New York to see me meant everything. That after I came home, I missed you so badly. We haven't had a chance to really talk about it but I can see us together forever. Maybe that's too much to think about right now. It looks like you're leaving." He gestured towards her suitcase.

"I'm going to Mandy's."

"Let me come with you. I'll finally get to meet Mandy. I've wanted to."

"Not tonight. I need time to think."

She continued through the living room. His wheels squeaked over the wood floor, his right arm pumping the rim of his chair, one limb making up for all that was missing. Apparently, more was missing between them than the pieces stolen by the train. Information about his father.

"Why don't we figure this out together? We don't know what Roy is basing any of this on. He's what novelists would call 'an unreliable narrator.'"

She laughed. It felt good. "I don't want to believe Roy. But it's suspicious, don't you think? Why would your dad leave you one request after his death?"

"Dad's not here to ask but I do know, his whole life, he preached morality."

"It sounds like he'd wronged me, and his morality made him feel guilty. His last request was to clear his conscience."

"I hope not."

She unbolted the front door and glanced over her shoulder. He closed the gap between them, his expression wrecked. She pushed her suitcase into the corridor.

He groaned. "You're killing me, Kai Lan. I missed you so much. Then you showed up like an angel. Like a dream. You're always running."

She studied his cobalt gaze, its electricity still able to spark love, lust, and longing. Orchid squeezed his hand. "I've been runnin' since I was twelve," she told him and exited the apartment. An insight struck her. She always pushed for hyper-independence as soon as someone grew too close. He followed her down the hallway.

She paused at the elevator bank to look at Phoenix. The sallow skin beneath his eyes appeared bruised. She observed his bandaged leg elevated onto the protruding board, his exertion slowed by the damned hallway carpet. She knew the feel of his callused palm since he'd been relying on his wheels.

Her assessment drew a light chuckle from Phoenix. "I'm looking that bad, huh?"

"It's not that. You just had surgery. There's no need for you to traipse across town."

Orchid jammed the button for the elevator, willing it to come faster. Before her aching emotions forced her stubborn feet back to the place she most wanted to be, in Phoenix's arms.

Her mistake was looking down into Phoenix's eyes. He'd paused beside her, searching her face, mouth opening to say something. His pink rims weren't shocked from meeting Roy or grieving because he'd just endured surgery. His emotions were for her.

The elevator sounded its cheery ding and opened.

Orchid let go of Phoenix and boarded with her luggage. One last look at him.

But he rolled over the lip of the lift and joined her.

The two of them in the little enclosed space, the doors slid shut. Phoenix took her hand. The rough pads of his fingers grasped hers. As the metal box descended, her heart begged her to reconsider. She might not be strong enough to say goodbye.

"Do you want me to call Caleb?" she asked.

He huffed. "You're worried about me while I'm worried about you."

She leaned down and pressed her lips to his cheek. She breathed in one more lungful. "That's love, boo."

"Orchid Kai Lan, I'm invoking every bit of goodwill for you to stay. From the very first ad assignment, every awards dinner, every drop of tequila between us. Every kiss, every fight. You remember the Wall of Love in Paris?"

She chuckled. "Followed by the catacombs."

"You made up that game for us to choose randomly." He tipped his head back.

"The thing is, with us, you didn't choose me randomly. Your dad made this whole thing happen, and we don't know his motivations."

He closed his eyes then looked up at her as if to ensure he had her attention. She was already memorizing every last detail.

"What if it's the other way around? Fate's way to bring us together. That we were meant to be?" he asked.

She gave in, leaned down and enveloped him with both arms. Her inhale took in his clean scent. He held her like he'd never let go.

"You okay, boo?" she asked. "We've both been through a lot."

"Honestly? I'm mad at my dad too. And my phantom pain's really bad right now," he said into her hair.

"Oh no. Please go rest."

He was so close. "It's just that I have this feeling...if you go now, you're not coming back," he said.

Orchid bent to press her lips to the scruff on his cheek. "I just need time to solve this," she said.

The elevator stopped on the ground floor and discharged them into the lobby. She looked around. No glimpses of a thick brown jacket.

Orchid pulled her bag over the smooth marble floors. She waved to the doorman.

The portly gentleman hurried to meet them. "I'm so sorry about that guy. He got away," he said, worry in his tone. His jacket buttons strained to maintain wardrobe decency. "Building security is putting up posters. We'll look out for him in case he comes here again."

Phoenix's motion paused, like the evening had weighted his casters with stone.

Orchid took advantage of their conversation to scamper up the few steps and drag her luggage out into the night air.

Phoenix reassured the doorman. "Thank you. I wouldn't worry about him too much. I don't think he's a bad person."

"Bye," Orchid called over her shoulder. Wait, there was no ramp. How would he exit his building in his chair?

Never mind. She needed to get away before she crumbled. As she hurried down the street, her habit to check for divots in the pavement was still intact. Even without Phoenix by her side, she wanted to point out the sidewalk's cracks, so his wheels could avoid them. She knew his chair was harder to navigate in between areas lit by streetlamps.

Within minutes, the subway sign loomed: 86th Street Station. Her subconscious had led her to the place where the train had taken his limbs. If he were here at the entrance to the station, his wheels would freeze, skirting the concrete lip.

His barriers were insurmountable. Physically.

Their barriers seemed insurmountable. Emotionally.

She was glad he wasn't here to witness her entering the place where the train had taken his limbs. Her knees felt weak.

She pulled her belongings down the steps, down to the last place he'd been on two feet. His presence followed her like a ghost. She imagined him pulling himself out of the chair, his hand on the stair railing, hopping to follow her. He loved her that much. She loved him too. To set them free from his father's wrong, whatever that might be, she'd impart tenderness in her words.

"Don't follow me. Don't get hurt. We'll talk later."

He'd halt, looking down at the body that couldn't get him down the stairs.

She fled his apparition, through the turnstile, past a man begging for money. The irony, he could've been in the same spot where Roy had been planning his demise in this same station a year ago. Her Keds finally came to a halt when her suitcase wheels bumped along the knobby yellow strip that marked the precipice before the tracks. Below the boundary of the platform, an empty chip bag trembled on the rusted rails.

She was free.

She was gutted.

A train flew into the station, squealing with the force of metal on metal. The foil bag swirled aloft and then was sucked under. The massive wheels sliced and screamed.

One of the passengers alighting the subway car bumped her motionless figure. Her free hand steadied herself against her suitcase handle. A stronger shove could've easily landed her onto the tracks.

She boarded and wiped away a tear that had started down one cheek.

Mandy had waited up for Orchid. She hugged her friend and ushered her into the living area. Her apartment had graduated from Baby Björn and bouncy seats to wooden blocks and safety gates.

"I made up the sofa bed for you. Can I get you a drink?"

"Aww, you're sweet." Orchid thanked her bestie with a hug. "I'm okay. How about you? It's late. Do you need to go to bed?"

"Not before I hear what's going on with you. Hubs and Matty are asleep. Catch me up. Why aren't you at your hotel?" Mandy asked.

"Rina's staying there." Orchid was struck by surprise again that Rina had turned out to be reasonable. At least Phoenix's ex-girlfriend was getting a good night's rest.

"What?" Mandy plopped onto one side of the foam mattress, her smirk awaited juicy gossip.

Orchid joined her. "Phoenix asked her to move out, and since I was in town, I figured she could use my hotel until she found a place."

Mandy attempted to prevent a burst of laughter with the back of her hand. "Smooth. You're better than a barrel of monkeys." Then her face fell as her mind caught up with the situation. "I can't believe you saw Roy."

"I can't begin to explain the roller coaster of emotions tonight was."

"Am I ever going to meet Phoenix?"

"Technically you've met him. That night at the club."

"Hotties are trouble."

Orchid laughed. She looked at the organized chaos around them. Piles of unfolded clothes draped across a laundry basket with a handle missing. Houseplants lined the windowsill, brown leaves reaching for the darkened sky. Baby bottles perched aside a half-empty fifth of bourbon along the kitchen counter.

"I love your place," Orchid said, apropos of nothing, changing the subject.

"Really? You can have it. Dust bunnies are taking over. We should charge the mice rent."

"Ha. You used to be such a neatnik."

"Yeah, in college, we did a decent job keeping our place nice. Speaking of school, this Roy guy is a creep. What was he like? Was the guy off his rocker?"

"He's excitable but he's more cleaned up than you'd think. He said he was thanking Phoenix by sharing what he found. Except, that makes no sense. I mean, we knew Phoenix's dad presided over my case. But he said the judge should've recused himself because his nephew was there. What's suspicious is Judge Walker asking Phoenix to do me a favor after his death."

"It certainly sounds sus."

"I know, I know. I'm still trying to wrap my head around it. None of us knows the whole story. Not Roy, not Phoenix."

"So why aren't you with Phoenix tonight?"

"I just need time to think."

Mandy stood and closed the distance to the kitchen. "I need a drink. You're having a nightcap with me. This whole night is unbelievable."

Orchid got up and joined her friend at the counter lined with three stools. Mandy slid a tumbler full of caramel-hued liquor towards her friend. They clinked glasses and sipped. The fire water burned her esophagus. Almost as serrated as Chinese baijiu.

"It's not like his late father is going to show up at Easter. Or Thanksgiving. So maybe it's not so bad? What can I do, hon?"

Orchid tossed back the rest of her drink. "You've done exactly what I need."

"You'd do the same for me," Mandy said.

"One hundred percent. Now, I should let you sleep."

"Hon, no matter what you find out," Mandy said, "I think your story's going to have a happy ending."

CHAPTER 41

SPRING TO ACTION

Phoenix

During the conversation with the night guard, Orchid had disappeared. Phoenix rode the elevator down to the garage level, cursing the lobby's steps, and flew up the ramp to the street. One day, he'd persuade the board to improve wheelchair access to his building.

Out in the warm night air, he swiveled, trying to deduce which way she could've gone.

She'd either call a ride share or catch the downtown train to Mandy's apartment. He pumped his chair rim towards the subway station, willing his wheels to close the blocks between them.

Soon enough, the stairway to the 86th Street stop yawned before him. The last time he'd been there, his brother had convinced him to go after being discharged from rehab. Now, his upper arms tingled as if warning him from the cursed place that had taken his limbs.

Commuters jogged past him down the stairs, their jaunty pace seeming unaware of the dangers that lay below. He shook his head to refocus. No sign of Orchid. The accessible elevator only deposited travelers on the uptown platform. If she was here, there was no way for him to get down to her. He'd left without even his phone to call her.

Phoenix sat, numb from the evening's turn of events.

Beneath him, the rumble of a speeding train vibrated through his torso. The rush of giant wheels squealed. As the decibels incremented, irrational as it was, so did his fear. He couldn't stay here. Orchid had rejected his pleas. A fool's errand. He wheeled away from the stairwell. Phoenix shoved his wheelchair rim towards his apartment. The motion set him free.

With Orchid's departure, his place would seem transformed from *home* to an empty shell. Despair ballooned into his bones, filled his flesh, whirred through his brain. It wasn't just Orchid leaving. It was questioning the motives of the people he loved. Could their dad have covered up something unethical and tried to use Phoenix to make amends for it?

Phoenix arrived at his building and entered. Fatigue pooled through his marrow.

Upstairs, Phoenix rolled through his bedroom, and into his bathroom. Orchid's forgotten fuchsia toothbrush angled in his marble holder, next to his own. The pair parted in opposite directions like divorcees. Forehead pressed against the cool counter, he palmed two pain pills and swallowed them without water.

On the bed, a pillow was indented on Orchid's side. Phoenix pulled himself onto the crinkled sheets and elevated his swollen knee. Once under the covers, he grabbed his phone. The home screen lit with missed messages.

First things first. With one thumb, Phoenix typed a text. "You get to Mandy's, okay?" he asked.

No three dots from Orchid. No immediate reply. Phoenix turned off the bedside light, and alone in the dark, Phoenix slid towards an uneasy sleep.

His whole life, he'd been seeking purpose. Now, a new mission was staring back at him. In China, he'd swayed Kit with an impassioned speech about changing people's perspectives on disability. He himself had seen that despite being triggered by medical reminders, Orchid never brought up his disability. Other issues might stand in their way, but she'd said that what he was missing was no barrier for her.

Come to think of it, the life he'd built didn't need to be defined by barriers either. He was fortunate to be starting physical therapy. Soon he'd be back on his prosthesis, back to morning runs and afternoon swims. He'd promised himself to begin biking and training for the next triathlon season.

God he'd been lucky. To save a life. To survive his fall. To be surrounded by unconditional acceptance.

What more could he do for others?

In the space before unconsciousness, an idea drifted into view.

He'd call his aunt and uncle in the morning.

CHAPTER 42

ALL IS LOST

Roy

Oh no.

Roy's thighs burned from galloping down the twelve flights of stairs in Phoenix's building. He emerged from the basement garage, hustled up the dark avenue, and pulled his baseball cap visor lower. He wouldn't draw attention to himself by running.

Stupid. Stupid.

He darted along his escape route, meandering extra blocks rather than taking the obvious route that law enforcement might search.

Roy had screwed up big time. Orchid answering the door had surprised him. Her presence vibrated through the silk flower in his pocket, as if his mother's spirit were trying to tell him something about the woman who had made Phoenix grin with joy in their online photos.

Signs for the 86th Street subway stop came into view. Revisiting the place where he'd almost killed Phoenix seemed like a deposit towards contrition.

He looked for any signs of police presence before approaching the station. He hadn't intended harm. Still, they could accuse him of breaking and entering. He planned to ride the train back to the shelter and seek Father Lyndon's advice.

No blue uniforms in sight. Roy hurried down the stairs. His secondhand sneakers cushioned each concrete step, in contrast to the thin-soled shoes he'd owned last year. Now, no blisters pained him. Even with his heart pounding and face sweating, others paid him no mind. No one gave him wide berth. Passersby didn't try to avoid eye contact.

The contrast between then and now struck him. A year ago, Phoenix had saved him, which triggered the changes that had turned around Roy's life.

At the bottom of the stairs, past the turnstiles, yellowed tiles lined the walls.

Out of habit, Roy turned towards the spot where he used to wait for handouts. On the ground, a man with a dirty face, clothed in army green layers, sat on an oil-spotted sheet of cardboard. He crouched over a paper cup, checking its contents.

When the man lifted his face towards Roy's approach, Roy feared seeing his own fleshy nose and overflowing beard, like a haunted mirror.

Instead, a bright blue gaze held his.

Roy screamed. "Phoenix?"

The mirage cleared, and the grubby man extended his empty cup. "Spare change?" he croaked, opening his mouth to reveal three blackened teeth.

Roy shoved his hands into his pockets and pulled out a fiver, a protein bar from Father Lyndon, and his mother's silk orchid. These items, along with Roy's rediscovered sense of purpose, represented wealth compared to his state a year ago.

"Hi I'm Roy. You hungry?" he asked. He emptied everything into the man's cup. The lavender-gray flower tumbled in last. Momma's orchid had kept him safe and maybe could help this man. Paying forward Phoenix's kindness made Roy's eyes prick with gratitude, remorse, and grief. He bade the soft petals goodbye and stumbled towards the tracks.

My god. Phoenix traded places with me.

Except Phoenix probably hated him. The couple had misunderstood his intentions. Roy's judgment in going there had been clouded by his desire to see Phoenix alive. He thought Phoenix would want to hear what he had to say, that the kind man might welcome him and offer him a glass of water.

Roy's research had exploded his mind. First, he'd discovered Judge Walker's connection to Orchid, then found a detective who'd worked the case. When Roy read the court papers, the judge's recusal seemed unsavory. So, he was relieved to find that the evidence was foolproof.

Finally, he had something to offer the man who'd saved his life. Roy had secured a curfew exception and hurried uptown right away. Phoenix would want to know this.

But the meeting had gone awry from the start. Roy's emotions had become unhinged by the fury in Phoenix's jawline and the fear in Orchid's. His lizard brain took over. He'd behaved badly. He hadn't even had a chance to share his most important finding, his conclusion that Judge Walker was upstanding.

Now what?

As Roy's feet hit the warning tactile tiles lining the edge of the subway platform, a clacking sound filled the station. A silver whoosh blew an empty snack bag off the tracks. Before his eyes, the ground appeared to be littered with scores of severed hands, their white shirt sleeves edged red. He choked out a gasp. The train's screeching stop drowned out the sound.

Roy's throat squeezed tight. He had hurt the same man twice. He needed to make it right. He blinked to clear his vision.

Just yards from him, a beautiful woman with the saddest face stood frozen, one hand clutching her suitcase handle. A traveler bumped her with his shoulder as he passed. Roy wanted to stop him and make him apologize. "That's Orchid, she's a good person," he'd say, his tone indignant.

The jostle woke her from her daze. She dragged her luggage onto the subway car. He saw her brush her wet cheek as the doors closed. The train clattered away.

His brain pieced together that things had just gotten worse. Orchid was crying. She had packed her belongings and was leaving Phoenix. No wonder. Roy had made it sound as if Phoenix's father had aggrieved her family.

I need to fix this. He could contact Phoenix, except the man despised him, especially with Orchid gone as a result of Roy's screw up. No, Roy would get in touch with Orchid and tell her the truth. His gift had been to share that John Walker had a good reason for refusing the recusal. But after tonight's fracas, chances were that she wouldn't believe him. The news had to come from a credible source.

CHAPTER 43

ORCHIDS IN THE WILD

Orchid

O rchid slept terribly which she couldn't blame on Mandy's lumpy sofa bed, emergency sirens at street level, or Matty's middle of the night feeding. Early in the morning, Orchid leaned against the sofa pillows and pulled out her phone. She was worried about Phoenix.

He had texted the night before. "You get to Mandy's okay?" he had asked. How thoughtful.

She typed a response. "Yes thanks. How are you? Is your phantom pain better?"

Then she opened a search bar. She read about Judge John Walker's legacy. There'd been a handful of disagreements over his judgements. By and large though, his staff and coworkers described him as an ethical, trustworthy person.

Orchid could ask Aunt Lily for information on Judge Walker's role, her aunt's perception of him, and any memory of a recusal. But then her mom's sister would want to know the reason for the request. Orchid hadn't even disclosed his relation to Phoenix and didn't want to share his possible culpability unless she had solid proof. Especially since her aunt already objected to Phoenix not being Asian. No sense adding more reasons for Aunt Lily to dislike him.

She'd try a different path. Phoenix spoke highly of Sascha. Orchid was able to easily find the number for the tattoo shop that Caleb's ex-girlfriend managed.

"Whadya know," Sascha replied to her greeting, "the famous Orchid." Her voice rang sweet. In his memoir, Phoenix wrote about Sascha's encouragement when she visited him in the hospital.

"I've heard about you, too. You did a lot for Phoenix."

"It's what any decent human would do. To what do I owe the pleasure?"

"You knew Phoenix's dad, right?"

"Yeah sure, I knew both his parents, why?"

"It's too complicated to explain everything but let me ask, can you imagine him doing something unethical?"

"Unethical, like what? Park without putting a quarter in the meter? Never."

"Like swing a court case to protect a family member?"

"No way. How did that come up?"

"As unbelievable as it sounds, the guy who Phoenix saved says his cousin was at the party where my parents were overserved before their car crash."

"The guy Phoenix saved?"

"Yeah, my head's still messed up over the whole thing."

"Caleb tried to find the guy and couldn't."

"He found us. And he raised a question whether Judge Walker had swung my parents' case to protect Harry."

"I can't believe that. You know who you should ask? His court clerk. Her name was Francine. I met her at the funeral. She was real broken up."

"Do you know how I can contact Francine?"

"Hmm, let me look."

Orchid typed a google search into her phone. "Oh, I see the courthouse number online. Thanks anyway."

"Well, let me know what she says," Sascha said.

"Thanks, bye."

The website provided a phone number for requesting court records. Orchid tapped the digits into her mobile device. As old-fashioned as a phone call felt, she introduced herself to the pleasant-sounding woman who answered.

"Hi. I'm looking for transcripts for a civil case, a personal injury case. From fifteen years ago."

"Hold on. I don't know the retention period off the top of my head."

While the woman tapped at her keyboard, Orchid perused Francine's LinkedIn profile. The stern-looking woman with hair pulled back into a gray bun had worked at the county courthouse for more than twenty years. This professional had probably seen hundreds of tragic cases like hers.

Her aunt had once explained that "social host" laws meant her dad's estate couldn't sue the party hosts for serving him alcohol that stormy night, but another person who was injured from her dad's driving could, so her mom's estate brought the lawsuit to court. As a kid, none of the nuances mattered. She'd only known the hard facts. She was alone.

"Sorry to keep you waiting. Our retention period is five years."

The mental calculation didn't take long. "You mean, you don't have the records?"

"Not that far back, no. We started keeping digital records after that."

"Do you have microfiche? Paper records?"

"Nope. Sorry."

Orchid thanked her and hung up. She'd really need Francine's help. Orchid dialed the number that appeared on the court's website and composed herself.

A perfunctory message greeted her. Orchid spoke with a friendly tone, aiming to convey trustworthiness. "Hello, this is Orchid Paige, Phoenix Walker's girlfriend. I'm hoping that we could speak briefly about Judge Walker." She left her contact information.

She'd extend her stay in New York until she had excavated some answers.

Meanwhile, being back in the city and living with Mandy would bring comfort like *home*, even with the inconvenience of working middle-of-the-night hours to collaborate with her Chinese colleagues.

Several days later, after back-and-forth rounds of phone tag, conveying what she was seeking, and completing the required administrative forms, Orchid had secured time to meet Francine. She arranged for a car service ride into New Jersey.

The following week, the car navigated through Jersey City streets to pull up to an imposing white building. Orchid smoothed her asymmetrical dress, whose bias-cut reflected the downward trajectory of the last week. Inside, Orchid showed her ID, stepped through a metal detector, and waited in the reception area. She admired the high ceilings and ornate stonework until a gray-haired woman approached her.

"You must be Orchid. I'm Francine," the woman introduced herself with a firm handshake and guided them to a small conference room.

"Nice to meet you. Thanks for making time." She appreciated the woman's direct manner.

"Can I offer you coffee?" she asked.

"No thanks." Orchid felt jittery enough. She took the indicated upholstered seat, and then her host joined her, leaning a briefcase against the leg of the table.

"I worked for Judge Walker for two ten-year terms," she said with a friendly drawl. "How are the Walkers?"

"They're doing fine."

"Such nice boys," she said. "So, you wanted to see the documents related to your parents' court case."

"Yes. I'm not a journalist. I'm not a lawyer. I just need to know what happened. For my peace of mind."

Francine's head cocked to one side, studying Orchid. "You know, you're lucky. Official records aren't kept that long, but I found your transcripts in the judge's stored files. I haven't had the heart to shred his old papers."

Orchid's chest lifted. Hope filled her lungs.

"Just sign here and let me borrow your ID."

Orchid scribbled her name next to the indicated spot and handed over her driver's license.

Francine stood. "I'll need to make a photocopy. Everything's here. Take a look and let me know if you have any questions." She pulled a thick brown folder from her briefcase and laid it on the table.

"It's here? The papers are here?"

Francine's chin dipped in one curt nod, and she left.

Orchid unsnapped the bungee-cord as the door swished closed behind Francine. Nerves tingled in her fingertips. Answers to her questions lay so close.

On page one, the black letters against the crisp white background swam before her eyes. Then, she shook her head and took in the official sounding language. The opening named the plaintiff and defendant. Clinical words described her parents' car accident. Her eyes watered at the word *deceased* after her parents' names.

As she became accustomed to the organization of the material, she was able to move more quickly, seeking what could be relevant. The transcript spelled out every question and response in the courtroom. She absorbed a sense for Judge Walker's no-nonsense manner of speaking. He asked direct questions. He made declarative statements. He quoted legal precedent with perfunctory confidence.

One sentence stopped her. "The plaintiff requests the judge recuse himself." There it was, printed forever. The court knew Judge Walker had a familial link and called him on it. Her brain reread the next sentence. "He declined, stating that the person in question was not a material witness." This corroborated Roy's declaration.

A later page catalogued attendees at the party. She scanned the unfamiliar names but couldn't find Harry's name. Multiple lines were redacted with thick black lines, probably marking out minors. She reread the names of people who could've seen her mom and dad on their final night. Maybe they'd toasted together, maybe they'd asked if the couple had children. "Our daughter, Orchid, is twelve and reading at a high school level," her dad would boast. "She's so creative," her mom would gush.

Francine tapped on the door and pushed it open. "I didn't want to startle you," she said. "Here's your ID." She placed the laminated card on the table beside the open folder.

"You were working for Judge Walker sixteen years ago, right? Do you remember this case?" Orchid asked.

"There are hundreds a year. Fairly impossible to remember them all. But seeing the file did jog my memory."

"The thing is the plaintiff's attorney asked Judge Walker to recuse himself. The judge's nephew was at the party where my parents were served before they drove home in an ice storm." Orchid stopped, not naming what had happened to them. Yet memories surfaced like daggers. *The slick driveway. The car's headlights waving wildly. Their broken bodies.* She drew a breath and held it for four counts.

"But he declined the recusal. I want to know why," Orchid said.

"He had the right to decline the recusal. His family member wasn't a material witness. It's in the public records." She tugged at one ear.

"I understand it's his prerogative. But why did he execute it?"

The court clerk tilted her head, and then bent over the file, her teeth working her lower lip. "I seem to remember something you might want to see. Hang on, let me see if I can find it."

In the lengthening silence punctuated by pages flipping, Orchid longed for an answer to her conundrum. She wanted an answer about Judge Walker's intentions. John Walker, father to the man she loved.

She yearned so hard that a solution popped into her mind. Clear as the blue sky overhead, the truth clam-shelled open, accompanied by church organs. *Because what did one man's action have to do with the care of the other?* The absolute truth was that the outcome wouldn't change her future. No matter what answer Francine produced, it changed nothing in her relationship with Phoenix. Of course, out of loyalty to her parents, she wanted to know whether Judge Walker had wronged them or not. But his father's judgment, poor or not, couldn't sheer them apart.

She loved Phoenix Walker. Like no other human ever.

Billy's girlfriend had unjustly left him over injuries he couldn't help. Orchid had fallen into the same trap, blaming Phoenix for an act over which he'd had no control.

She wanted to laugh with joy. "Never mind," nearly bubbled to her lips.

Before she could fully infer the implications of her insight, Francine spoke over the rustle of each page being turned. "You know, refusing a recusal might sound bad to a layman. What I recall is he didn't know about his nephew until a party guest list was later submitted. The prosecution asked for a recusal but Judge Walker wanted to stay on the case because he was invested in the outcome. He's not one to let something like that affect his judgment."

Then Francine jabbed at an image.

"Aha." She turned the folder towards Orchid. "Did you know that engineers came out and completed a study? Your parents' driveway grade would've never been approved today, especially on a curve and in the woods."

Orchid studied the printed survey that mapped the twisted road down to her parents' house. Phoenix had been the one to drive her to her childhood home. He'd walked that impossibly steep drop with her.

Francine continued. "As sad as it is, my dear, the crash was unavoidable. It was no one's fault."

"They weren't wearing seatbelts," Orchid remembered.

"That's right."

"Then why would Judge Walker want to grant me some goodwill deed as his final wish?"

"What do you mean?"

"He asked Phoenix to do something for me. That's how we met."

Suddenly, her smile blossomed like a sunflower on a summer day. Her hand went to her throat. "Oh, wow. That's so thoughtful. Judge Walker didn't let it show but cases could be hard on him. Now that I think about it, I recall that he donated to your parents' funeral, anonymously of course. Maybe he never forgot your case. For all of us, it can be hard because we don't know what happens to the people who come through here." She apprised Orchid's dress and corset-laced boots. "You look like you're doing well, my dear."

Orchid assessed herself, her body, her brain, her heart. "I am doing well. I really am. Thank you, Francine."

She left and slipped into her taxi. The time that the driver had waited would cost her a fortune. She didn't care.

As the sedan sped eastward, Orchid found her mood had loosened from self-righteous to a calm she hadn't felt since the night Roy blew up her peace. She believed Francine's kind voice. *Nothing could've been done.* She hadn't been wronged. Judge Walker's letter had felt like a lie between her and Phoenix but could be considered a benevolence. She had made him promise to never bring it up; now, seeing the place where he worked, hearing from his staff, her curiosity arose. She should ask Phoenix about his dad.

Oh, yes ... Phoenix. The whole reason she was here. The whole reason she'd been miserable since that last night together when Roy had robbed them of their peace.

He'd texted and called afterwards. "Did you arrive to Mandy's safely?" Then "Are you okay?" and "Want to talk?" Her agency had invited him to the advertising shoot. Shortly after, she'd heard that he'd returned the signed waivers. In his last missive, he sent her an endearment, "Ni hao, Kai-lan."

Still, she didn't respond beyond the first message because she had to learn the truth first. Until she realized today that she already had the only truth that mattered.

She had known it all along. Every day spent missing him, wondering how he was healing, was a sign that she loved him no matter what. Even if Francine had admitted Judge Walker's guilt, she would've gone back to Phoenix.

It wasn't his fault. He wasn't the same as his family. Love was love.

He had stopped texting. Could she still right things between them? If she couldn't, she didn't want to jeopardize the advertising shoot. That campaign was a gift to him, a tribute to their relationship. She'd let it play out, and then plan something grand.

CHAPTER 44

TURNING POINT

Phoenix

Aunt Betsy trilled with delight at Phoenix's call. "We were hoping you'd want an active role in The Walker Institute. Uncle George and I would love if you'd want to run with it, so to speak. Make it your own."

Phoenix sat on his sofa with his laptop. He opened a fresh document. He'd make his time count.

Hours passed as he brainstormed mission statements, debated criteria for Board members and drafted articles of organization. His aunt and uncle hadn't even formed the non-profit yet, so he studied legal terms for a 501(3)c.

In the coming week, he planned to tap his networks for an attorney and an accountant.

What he didn't expect was an email from a casting agent. He skimmed over the details. "You've been recommended for an ad campaign. Client: Estee Lauder." Orchid and Kit could imagine him in ads. Here was a way to help others see disability in a new light. Even though Orchid had only responded to one of his texts, he signed the contract and sent it back. Because this cause was bigger than either of them. He saw that now.

In the gap that was left by Orchid, Phoenix buried himself in productivity. He attacked his physical therapy routine with vigor, wrote at night, and established his charity's tax-free status. He could've contacted Mandy but what was the point? Orchid had responded that she'd arrived the night Roy had visited them, so he knew she was safe. She hadn't contacted him since then.

Today, Phoenix's physical therapist Nadine accompanied him to his prosthetist's appointment to check on his healing progress. More places were recommending this type of professional partnership to improve the socket and prosthesis fitting.

He sat on the exam table while the technician examined the stitches along the rounded bottom of his calf. The guy's braided hair bounced with his rhythmic nodding.

"Déjà vu?" Phoenix asked Nadine.

She tugged at the ruffled bottom of her blouse. "This won't be the last time, you know. People come back all the time. Residual limbs swell, shrink, change shape. You'll see."

The practitioner peered up from the plaster to flash a gold tooth at Phoenix. "Your charity's really gonna give away prostheses? How cool is that?"

Phoenix chuckled at the tanned gentleman's enthusiasm. "Yes, really, it is. There's such a huge need that we're a drop in the bucket."

Nadine plucked her shirt. "We have someone whose job it is to call insurance companies. They're strict about what they consider medically necessary."

Phoenix recalled the good fortune of his running leg. "As if all the stuff to get back to fully living is just a luxury."

"Mon, you could be the first recipient. Get that arm you want for biking!" Plaster guy nodded to some internal beat.

"Let's get him walking first," Nadine suggested.

"Unethical," Phoenix said. "I'm not donating prostheses to myself. There's plenty of deserving candidates. I'm going to set up the foundation to help survivors of trauma."

"Somethin' you can relate to." His bouncing chin gave approval.

The rounded end of his leg didn't look as foreign as it had a year ago. The new shape of him. "You know, Nadine, you were right. It's not so bad."

"You see? Did you celebrate your Alive Day?"

"That one's tough. It's the same date as my father's death, so no, it doesn't seem right. I was on my way to see my mom for the anniversary of his passing when ..." The scream of the train's wheels. The whoosh of air. Scrambling to get up only to stumble and fall.

"Ah. Sorry." Nadine crinkled the curly edges of her shirt then straightened with a new thought. "Maybe he was watching over you. His angel saved you on those train tracks."

Phoenix imagined a ghostly version of his father in judge's robes shoving his son aside to prevent mortal injuries. It helped to mollify the image of his dad leaving vague instructions for a client whose case he'd refused to recuse himself from.

He pulled fresh air into his lungs. "You're a softie, Nadine."

"That's not what you said when I used to make you do pushups."

Plaster guy chortled. "Y'all need to come back for the bikin' arm. I'm lovin' your entertainment value."

He and Nadine chatted about a 3D printed prosthesis with a fast-release hook for bicycling while Phoenix lost himself in another thought. It was debatable whether his dad's spirit could've changed the course of his accident. It wasn't debatable, though, whether he had a hand in finding the love of his son's life. Phoenix made a new vow. He was going to get back on his feet, launch this nonprofit, and be cleared for travel.

Soon, she'd be back in Beijing. Six thousand miles away.

He'd already purchased his plane ticket to go see her.

CHAPTER 45

ALWAYS ORCHID

Phoenix

The advertising set buzzed with production personnel. An enormous green screen covered the far side of the stage. Phoenix let the door close and leaned on his cane. The energy of the space rushed through him. *No place like being on set.*

He paused at the craft services table laden with platters of fruit, cheese, and other treats.

A woman with long lavender hair rushed towards him, a fast hare approaching his tortoise pace. Her beaming smile looked familiar.

"You're here!" she called.

She reached him and tiptoed up for a hug.

"Oh, hey," he said. His mind spun through options. New hire at counterAgency? A production assistant from another shoot? Little by little, another image emerged. Her doughy cheeks linked with memories of Orchid. This cheerful woman lived alongside vignettes of Orchid in sportswear at dance class, Orchid tucked beside him in the back of their car, Orchid showing him her phone and laughing with delight.

Before he could pinpoint their exact connection, she rat-ta-tatted more enthusiasm. "Everyone's going to be happy to see you. Let's do makeup first, okay?" Her lavender tresses bounced as she waved towards a woman at the far side of the stage in a smock.

Before they made it very far, Joan stood from a director's chair and bounded over. Her heavy earrings swung as she leaned to kiss Phoenix on the cheek. "Ah, here to spice things up," she said, her stiff suit matching her unmoving facial muscles.

"Always."

"Violet, this is one of the best ad guys in the business."

"He gave a hella presentation," she said.

Violet. Ah yes, Orchid's friend from Estee Lauder.

She'd been a hoot when she'd snapped the photo of him with Orchid at the gym. That picture captured the love and lust and tenderness of the deepest relationship he'd ever experienced. One that he was going to fight for. *I'm not giving up.*

Their hubbub attracted more people to join them.

A flame-haired woman in fatigues strode over. "Hey there."

The soldier's muscular figure rang a bell. "Tammy!"

"You talked me into making ads. Now, I can't seem to say no," she quipped.

He returned her hug.

"Oh my God, how the hell are you?"

"I'm awesome. My turn to pay you back for everything you've done for vets," she said.

Another figure ambled over. For a split-second, his barrel chest and tattooed biceps reminded Phoenix of Caleb. In the next millisecond, recognition dawned. Phoenix hobbled towards him, bursting with surprise.

"Aaron, my man!" He bumped elbows with the guy who'd given him perspective during one of the darkest times of his recovery. The left elbow to right elbow greeting matched them perfectly.

The redhead thumped an arm around Phoenix's back. "I told you to ditch the cane," he grunted.

"I wish. This is from revision surgery. At least I'm out of the chair."

"Amen."

"I'll be done with the cane before I know it. But enough about me. Damn, I can't believe you're here!" Phoenix studied his friend from his crew cut down to his prostheses.

"Last time was at Walter Reed."

"You're good? You look good," Phoenix said, feeling awed.

"I'm good. You too, from the looks of it." Aaron waved an arm around the set and stage.

"Yeah, shoots are always fun."

Violet beamed up at the soldier. "How long's it been since you've seen each other?" she asked.

"It must be what, eight months," Phoenix said.

"And now, we're the talent," he said, leaning in with swagger. "I learned that phrase today."

Phoenix looked down at himself, from cane to a slender prosthesis peeking out from beneath his joggers. "It's really something."

"The three of us are going to be fire," Tammy said.

"Don't say fire. Unless you want someone taken out," Aaron leaned towards Tammy, his grin spreading to her.

"Is Orchid here?" He spun to search the room. She must be behind this casting. She'd only responded to one of his texts.

"Nope." Violet shook her head.

Joan vouched for the idea. "Before you start thinking this is nepotism, you should know that Orchid pitched the management team, and we're all on board. The campaign we're shooting is completely consistent with our ad strategy."

Aaron swiped a slab of jerky from the craft services table. "I'm doing this because I want the world to see that we're strong, limbs or no limbs."

"You got my support," Tammy said.

A back door burst open and a burly fellow swaggered over to the group. "What? Did I miss the shoot?" Phoenix's business partner looked around, sporting a decidedly unfashionable plaid vest with a tweed bowtie.

"Dex, what are you doing here?" Phoenix asked.

"Ah, my main man. Liv sent me. Creative director on call."

"Chief Creative Officer on call," Phoenix reminded his friend.

"Don't tell me your rates just doubled," Joan chimed in.

"Tripled," Dex assured her. The burly fellow exuded good humor. He bestowed kisses on Joan's cheeks, and waved hellos.

"Makeup is ready for you when you are," Violet said and led Phoenix to a table with a lit mirror. A petite woman waved him into a swivel chair. "Have a seat." The cosmetologist talked as she worked. "Great cheekbones. You don't even need contouring. We'll just even out your skin tone for the camera."

She selected a brush and dipped it in powder. "Hold your breath." He did as he was told and closed his eyes. Circular feathering motions tickled his face.

He opened his eyes as she began to lift locks of his hair and spray them into an amplified version of his normal unruly style.

After a few minutes, the makeup artist stepped back.

"What do you think?" the beautician asked.

He saw echoes of his family in his reflection: his dad's blue eyes, waves through his hair like his mom's, and the dark eyebrows that he and Caleb shared. "You're good at what you do," he said.

"You're gorgeous," Violet answered for him. "Orchid would approve."

Dex came over to assess his buddy. "Wardrobe is perfect. Street cred."

"I'm not sure about your credentials for judging style choices." Phoenix said with a glance at his friend's bowtie.

His business partner chuckled and accompanied him to a marked spot under the lights.

Phoenix had perused the basic info provided to the talent. This wasn't a live action shoot. They were only taking still photos, so he had no lines to memorize. The three of them would converse as best friends in three different venues.

Dex pointed towards the stage. "Looks like they're ready for the first shot."

On the leftmost stage, beauty products and cocktails were laid out on a wooden bar inside a nightclub. The director instructed the trio to sit beside each other. The camera crew adjusted the lighting, the stylist fluffed their hair and then the director said, "Whenever you're ready."

Phoenix appreciated her understated way to ask them to start compared to an abrupt shout of 'Action!'

Tammy picked up a pale purple lipstick tube, etched with the word c-a-l-m, all in lower case. She unsheathed the cover, applied a nude smear to her bottom lip, and breathed deeply. The action relaxed her shoulders. Then she lifted her glass towards the two men. They leaned closer to clink tumblers. "Cheers!" Phoenix inhaled a whiff of lavender scent and glanced at the circle of information printed on the bottom of the tube.

The description read "Calming Potion for Crowds & More."

What a clever design. Lavender scent disguised as a lip gloss rather than an anti-anxiety treatment. It was elegantly packaged, elevating the functional treatment to an object of beauty. Orchid herself would've appreciated this product, for instance, at the hospital. His fingers twitched with the desire to text her a compliment.

The camera clicked, freeze framing images.

After some minutes, the director called "Next set!" and moved them to an area with a green screen. She seated the actors around a small table decorated with ceramic coffee demitasses, and described the outdoor Parisian café that would be the ad's backdrop.

When she directed them to start, Aaron pulled a fat rounded pen from his right shirt pocket. He bit on the wooden housing to toss aside the cap, revealing a pale felt tip. He leaned towards his buddies conspiratorially. "It's not ink. It's scar cream."

Aaron drew the soft tip along the spiderweb of angry purple marks encircling his right humerus. His grin telecast delight. "It looks like a damned Mont Blanc," he said. "I would use this everywhere, including the Eiffel Tower or wherever we're supposed to be."

"Good thing we're not recording audio." The director responded to Aaron's mild curse with a smile in her tone.

"The pens are swirled like petrified wood and refillable. Orchid told me that every design is different, just like every scar is unique," Tammy said, picking up the dropped cap.

Aaron, his face exuberant, stood to take Tammy in his arms. "Smarty pants," he said. They spun an adlibbed tango, and then he dipped her. The camera shutter whirred, capturing their ebullience.

"These products are pure brilliance," Phoenix said, gripping the pen that Aaron had left on the table. His chest puffed with pride for Orchid's accomplishment. Then he remembered the state of their relationship.

The wardrobe crew arrived with track jackets and asked the men to remove their jogger pants to reveal the shorts that they had been instructed to wear underneath. Phoenix stripped off his outer garments and wished he could whisper into Orchid's ear. "Clever way to get me out of my clothes."

"The next scene is a triathlon," the director said. "Phoenix, you'll use the product in your sports bag. Whenever you're ready."

Phoenix sat on the wooden bench next to Aaron. Inside the gym bag, he grasped a smooth cylinder, shaped like his shave gel.

He pulled out a tasteful tube with a matte finish. Its surface shimmered with blue ombre. In an understated sans serif font, the package promised "Natural Skin Protectant for Prosthetic Comfort." Underneath, the tagline read "Beauty Is More than Skin Deep."

What? Orchid had Lauder launching an amputee balm. Except it didn't look like the medicinal white packages that reminded him of a physical therapy room. It wasn't packed into a cheap plastic tub like carnauba wax for a car. This was a high-end, premium branded luxury item. One that made him feel cared for. Beauty *is* more than skin deep. A thought floated through his mind. *I'm loved.*

Phoenix laughed aloud and fist pumped the beautiful package into the air. He faintly heard the camera clicking. He didn't mind being photographed. His chest filled with pure joy. His stature rose until he felt that he'd grown twice as tall.

What had been the point of his insecurity around Orchid? She understood his sensitivities better than he did. Of course, she did. He'd once dubbed her the most empathetic person in the world. With this line of brilliant innovations, she'd earned the title all over again.

Then Phoenix paused, catching onto the pattern. The final pieces of the puzzle fell into place.

"Who wrote these vignettes?" he asked Dex.

"Miss O wrote the briefs herself," he said.

Of course, she did. These scenes replicated critical moments from their courtship. And yet were perfect for the ad campaign.

"Remember the beach?" Phoenix asked Tammy.

"Couldn't forget." She grinned back at him, their shared memory invoking Orchid's presence even though she was six thousand miles away.

"Great job. We got the shots we needed," the director called.

"Magic," Dex confirmed, and leaned back with satisfaction. "Come, let's go see."

Dex waved him along a snaked path between electric cables to reach the director. The woman was engrossed in the pictures on her camera screen and making notes on a lined yellow pad.

"What'd you think?" Dex boomed as they approached.

The director peered up through round spectacles. "Magnifique, come look. This is one of my best shoots yet. Even the outtakes are spectacular."

The short-haired woman stepped to one side so they had full view of the still images of Lauder's new line of beauty products set against each of the scenes: one at a beach, one at a bar. The elegantly packaged balm and burn crème were at home in all these everyday settings. The director paused onto a long shot of Aaron and Tammy together.

"The casting was perfect," she said.

In the photo, Aaron flexed his biceps for the lens. His chemistry with Tammy lit her face with some shared humor as he dipped her towards his plastic feet.

"There's more," the director said. She swiped through more scenes. The film shifted to images of Phoenix.

In one black and white frame, his teeth shone bright, his head thrown back with confidence, full of life. One hand pumped the air. The lens clicked to freeze frame his intensity.

"Buddy, you're a rock star."

"The camera loves you. You should send your headshots to some modeling agencies," the director suggested to Phoenix.

"Sure, once my time frees up, after I solve income inequality," he said.

"Seriously. Check this out," the director instructed, paging through more photos.

She paused on a closeup shot. Phoenix's dark locks offset Aaron's copper shine to create a study of contrasts. These photos extended beyond advertising. This was art.

"Wow," Violet said. The image projected more than their physical presence. The camera had preserved the millisecond between thought and action and exploded into camaraderie. The lens immortalized the purity of friendship.

"Yeah. That's your money shot right there," the director declared.

"I took a screenshot of that one. I'll text it to you," Dex said.

Then Dex tipped his head back, cupped his hands around his beard, and directed his voice towards the gathering crowd. "Wrap party!" Dex shouted. The Lauder and agency teams flowed like lemmings behind Dex's victorious fist pump. They tumbled through the steel door which led upstairs to the open-air penthouse bar.

Phoenix let the others speed ahead. His emotions cantered like wild stallions. He turned, almost expecting to see a dark-haired beauty. "Surprise!" this imaginary Orchid would say, holding her arms wide for him. She'd arranged this reunion of some of the most important people in his life. She'd demonstrated the strength that she saw in him, through the camera's lens. Joan said Orchid had been working on this for months. It wasn't surprising that she'd started before their split. What was surprising was that she continued the work even after she'd broken off communication between them.

The shoot was an hours-long ode to their relationship.

In the most heartfelt way, she'd shouted to the world and whispered in his ear that she'd forgiven everything.

Her campaign was an intricate love letter, an homage to their relationship.

"Hang on one sec," Violet called and trotted towards Phoenix, her bag bouncing over one shoulder.

"You don't have to run. I'm not that hard to catch," he said. He paused by the craft services table that appeared to have been half-cleared by a horde of locusts.

With most of the cast gone, the place was quiet, punctuated by the rumble of stage crew breaking down the set, wheeling carts, snapping off lights.

"Orchid always said you were funny." She rummaged in her purse.

"She's a good judge of character," he quipped.

"Good taste too."

The insights from the day bubbled to his lips. "She always brought out the best in me. And today? I could feel her thumbprint. Those scenes were layered with meaning for us." The shoot was simultaneously public and intensely personal. A place from which powerful art emerges.

Violet stilled, her reach frozen inside her bag. "She told me how much you meant to her."

"I'm going to see her. As soon as I'm cleared to travel."

"I wanted to show you something," she said and pulled out her phone.

She swiped through images and handed him her device. "Today reminded me of this picture," she said. Inside the phone's frame, a photo showed him and Orchid kissing, the whirl of a gym behind them.

"That was when we were still in New York."

She watched him absorbing the image and squared the edges of uneaten saltines on a tray. Orchid had swiped butterfly crackers before their flight to Paris. Her face lit with excitement the first time they'd traveled internationally, when he'd gifted her his business class seat. "Can I ask something, and just tell me if it's too personal. It's clear you two still have feelings and she told me you hadn't done anything wrong but she still went back to China. So, my question is... do you forgive her?"

Phoenix returned the phone and ran a hand through his hair. It was stiff with the spray the cosmetologist had applied. *Forgiveness.* At Tish's wedding, he'd been filled with gratitude that Orchid didn't hold a grudge for the pain he'd caused and had vowed to never hurt her again. In these last months, he'd learned of his father's flaws and still loved him. He'd come face-to-face with the man who'd cost him limbs and would save the guy all over again.

"There's nothing to forgive," he said. It was true, even though Violet couldn't have known a fraction of what had transpired between them.

Violet slid the phone back into her bag and took a long look at him. "She told me she'd never loved anyone as much as you. I can see why." Then she scampered up the stairs, leaving the door ajar for him to follow.

Alone, Phoenix inhaled a cleansing breath. He relived their moment of happiness, immortalized in the photo. They'd shared the car to work that day, they'd met at the gym. Then sometime after that, the strands of their lives had disentangled, through no fault of either of theirs.

An insight struck him.

More powerful than even the others.

The clarity punched him in the gut.

He didn't just forgive his dad, and Roy, he extended that compassion to himself.

From his pocket, he retrieved a thin wallet. Inside, a laminated scrap of napkin was inscribed with Orchid's looped handwriting. It read, "You're a prince." At the time, when he'd read it on the plane to Paris, he understood the note to mean he'd done everything right, on that trip to France, and gifting Orchid the assignment. What a one-dimensional interpretation. Because even princes in fairy tales make mistakes. They fail to slay the dragon, or save the kingdom, or rescue the princess.

Self-judgments fell away like scales, for hiding his injuries from Orchid, for his pridefulness, for standards he could never meet.

It startled him, the freedom of forgiving himself. Peace flowed through his veins, relaxing his stance down to his toes.

He was human, as flawed and foolhardy and fallible as anyone. Like everyone on this spinning rock through space, he was doing the best he could for the moment at hand.

It was enough. It had always been enough.

Revelatory sounds echoed down the stairwell.

He replaced the laminated memento in its safe spot next to his organ donation card and retrieved his phone. One more text to send, one without expectations for a response. A new message from Dex included a closeup picture from the shoot. He chose to forward the snapshot and added a note. "Orchid, thank you for today...and all our other days."

He stared at the words. Simple. True. Thousands of snippets of time in each letter, each word representing the scores of memories at Le Mur de Je t'Aimes, at the underground market in Paris, Orchid visiting his office, his apartment, the little conference room at Lauder's offices, their time in Beijing, supporting and listening to each other, and where it all started, in a dark club with tacky floors. *In the men's room, Orchid Kai Lan.* The memories didn't exclude their imperfections, disagreements, altercations, or ways they'd hurt and cared for each other.

With one thumb, Phoenix added another truth. "I'll always love you." He hit send, slipped the device back into his pocket and caned towards the elevator.

His pained, whole, human heart was bruised yet more open than ever.

She'd always live within. *Always Orchid.*

He was ready to join their friends.

He'd forgiven her.

As he caned over to the elevator to join the others, a figure emerged from the shadows beside the stage.

Before he fully registered her slender form, his lungs filled with hope.

He watched Orchid approach, her eyes rounded.

Her steps slowed and then stopped several paces out of his reach.

He absorbed the image of her in flowy tulle and platform heels. "You're here?"

"I came to see you." She tipped her chin towards him.

"Really? I bought tickets to China to come see you."

"Oh, wow." She stepped closer.

Here was the test he needed to know more than anything. He leaned his weight on his cane. "Have you forgiven my dad? Or is that still between us?"

She surprised him by smiling. "You're never going to believe this. He did nothing wrong."

He felt his forehead raise.

"I got the transcripts from his clerk. Francine."

"Ah, dad's clerk Francine."

"Yeah, and here's the clincher. An engineer backtracked every-thing that night. The weather, the roads, the news reports."

"And?"

"Mathematically, there's nothing my parents could've done. The steepness of the driveway, the ice storm. The fact that my parents weren't wearing seat belts. It was a disaster waiting to happen."

His mind was whirling. "Really?"

"Get this, driveways nowadays wouldn't even be allowed to be that steep. Ours was grandfathered in."

"It's still a complete tragedy. But you're not mad at my dad anymore?"

"There's nothing to be mad at. Not even Roy. I just found a message from him buried in my LinkedIn notifications."

"What'd he say?"

"He offered to send me the file. His gift to you was supposed to be clearing your dad's name, but he didn't get to tell us the full story. He's dedicated himself to helping runaway teens. He's sorry the way our last interaction ended. He'd do anything you wanted, including leaving you alone."

Phoenix nodded. "I'm glad he's okay."

"Weirdly enough, me too."

"So, Harry didn't have anything to do with your parents' accident. Is that why you're talking to me again?"

Orchid rotated so that he felt the full force of her intensity. "No, and this is super important. Doing the research made me realize that it didn't matter what I'd learned. Even before I saw the report, I'd already decided to come back. And if you turned me away, then the shoot would be my last gift to you."

The elevator's arrival sounded.

"No lasts. If there's any hope for us, come upstairs with me," he said, gripping his cane with so many wishes that the polished handle felt as if it could splinter.

She accepted his elbow and stepped into the elevator with him.

He leaned his cane against the wall to skim his thumb along her cheek. "These past few weeks, I realize you're all that mattered."

Orchid pressed her cheek into his palm and encircled arms around his waist.

"Matters, present tense," she reminded him with a laugh.

"And always will matter, future tense." He returned her embrace.

"Nothing can scare me away, Phoenix. I'm here for all of it. For all of you."

"So why didn't you come to the shoot? Why didn't you tell me all this sooner?" he asked, wondering if she'd evaporate like a mirage.

"By the time I figured out all this stuff, it was so close to the shoot. I didn't know if you'd forgive me for leaving. In case you were mad, I didn't want to mess it up. Because besides the ads being brilliant for business, the shoot was a way to show you that no matter what, you are amazing. Everything about you." She recited the words he'd uttered to her, the night before his accident, after their first kiss.

All of him, holding all of her vibrated through him like *acceptance.*

"I fell in love with you the day we met. Kismet, they call it," he said.

"Fate, again."

His unconditional love had helped heal her missing pieces, and now her unequivocal acceptance had done the same for him. The two of them together summed to more than either of them apart. He felt their connection in his bones. Like sunshine, the feeling extended to every friend on the rooftop lounge, then spilled to every citizen in the city and beyond, until their love expanded infinitely to encompass billions of souls on earth.

"One time we discussed parallel universes. Remember you wanted to go back and change stuff?" she asked.

"Not anymore. No regrets. Our history makes us stronger."

They could spend the rest of their days doing more of the good they'd started today.

They deserved this. Everyone does.

As they ascended, he could hear revelers chattering in the open-air rooftop above them. Soon, they'd be clinking celebratory toasts with their friends. In the space of final moments before the elevator doors slid open, his lungs expanded, replacing what was with what was about to be.

He was hers. She was his. Not a thing missing.

ACKNOWLEDGEMENTS

The pages of *Always Orchid* are fiction, yet Orchid and Phoenix's challenges and joys are real.

Therefore, I'll start by honoring those with disabilities who inspired this series.

Thank you to my sensitivity readers who were critical to ensuring that the story delivered authenticity and respect. Purple Heart decorated Sgt Bryan Anderson spent hours with me on the earliest iterations of *Always Orchid*. He suggested Phoenix's medical issues with heterotopic ossification and subsequent revision surgery. Bronze Star with Valor decorated Navy Corpsman Doc Jacobs read *Always Orchid* during finals week and brought tears to my eyes when he said, "You have done an excellent job on every small detail down to why Phoenix wears pants or tucks his arm out of sight, and how comforting Orchid's protectiveness of Phoenix is."

Dr. Linda Olson, whose memoir details the train accident that took her legs and arm, generously returned *Always Orchid* with notes in the margins like "you've done a very good job showing uncertainty, insecurity, and anxiety; and how the able-bodied and disabled persons worry about themselves but even more about their loved one." As a radiologist, she also ensured that the medical descriptions were accurate.

For more on their real-life stories, check out *No Turning Back, There and Back Again,* and *Gone.* I'm eternally grateful for their input. Any errors are mine.

Much gratitude to the myriad people who helped birth *Always Orchid.* Caroline Leavitt's developmental edit shaped not just the story but also the wisdom imparted on the pages of *Always Orchid* and *Orchid Blooming.* My collaboration with Ellie Maas-Davis on copy and line edits was magic. Credit to Ellie for knowing that Confucius admired orchids for "enduring hardship yet still gracing the world with beauty." Sarah Flood-Baumann built on Kellie Emery's award-winning designs to create a line of covers that capture the emotional and physical vitality of the characters.

Thank you to the early readers who provided input. Rachel Mack ensured the characters' humanity was front and center. Laura Rogers named this novel. My Women Who Write novelists, Mary, Pat, Michele and Michelle, provided perspective, and met my intense deadlines. Christine Tsai built depth into the fall at the Great Wall. Melody Morris and Colleen Tucciarone's observations were invaluable. Corrie Viola gave me the gift of loving the story. Thank you to my proofreading team Barb, Arminda, Phyllis, Claudia, and Amy, for taking the final step to identify errors before the book went to print.

Original book mama Nadine Vogel continues to generously give this series as gifts, after giving me the greatest gift of all: the honor of being named Disability Hero of the Year. I'm sending much respect for Nadine's work in disability advocacy through Springboard Consulting.

Judge Walker's storyline required legal expertise. I'm grateful for the social host laws and other legal details from Murray A. Klayman, Esquire and retention period information from Judiciary Clerk Maya Walker-Smith.

The *Goodbye, Orchid* series seeks to deepen hope and empathy, so thanks to the bookstores, libraries and book clubs who've hosted me for events and book signings. Thank you to all the book lovers who've read this series, posted ratings and reviews, gifted these books and told your friends about the optimism in these novels. Special gratitude to the book clubs who've invited me time and again, including the Bridgewater Book Club, Rehoboth Book Club, Lake Forest IL Book Club, Literary Libationists, and Summit Book Club (who hosted my first in-person event and asked me to expand *Goodbye, Orchid* into a trilogy). Others who've helped to spread the word and engage with readers include Book Sparks' PR team, Crystal Patriarche and Tabitha, and Novel Network's Susan and Debbie. Thanks to Bambi Rathman, Robin Batterson and Michele Anderson for helping to administer the *Goodbye, Orchid* Facebook group and street team.

To my friends, colleagues, and family, your care and asking about my work means the world to me. To my humorous hubby and twins, you truly do prove that love can conquer all.

DISCUSSION QUESTIONS

1. In *Always Orchid*, Phoenix Walker must move from New York to Beijing to be with Orchid. What did he give up and gain in doing so? What are examples of compromises you've seen in real-life relationships?

2. Although Phoenix and Orchid have known each other for a year, they must adjust to his life-changing accident together. Which parts of his adaptations and their discovery surprised you?

3. In Beijing, the characters experience bias from Chinese superstitions that disability is a sign of sins from a prior life. What do you think are effective ways to shift long-held biases?

4. In book one, *Orchid Blooming*, images of combat-wounded veterans trigger Orchid's Post Traumatic Stress Disorder from witnessing her parents' car accident. How has she healed by the time she and Phoenix reunite in *Always Orchid*? What strategies does she use to help ameliorate her PTSD?

5. When Phoenix arrives in China, he reconnects with his agency friend, Kit. In what ways did Kit's appreciation for disability inclusion grow?

6. Readers meet Billy at the Great Wall. He's drawn to Phoenix when he realizes that they're both amputees. How did the fact that his girlfriend's parents didn't want her to be with someone with a disability make you feel? How did this rally Phoenix and Orchid towards inspiring more inclusivity?

7. In *Always Orchid*, we get to know Roy, the man that Phoenix saved in the subway station. When did you feel empathy for Roy? Anger? How did his character change your perceptions of people who are temporarily unhoused?

8. Roy botches his attempt at reparations. Have you seen real-life examples of good intentions gone awry? Please share.

9. This novel delves into themes of forgiveness, unconditional acceptance, and self-compassion. Which moments in the story illuminated insights in these areas for you?

10. Throughout the book, what are ways that each character discovers their purpose in life—Roy, Phoenix, and Orchid?

11. The book's final scene takes place at an advertising shoot for products that elevate medicinal care to luxury levels. How does using the medium of ads coupled with products for amputees help Phoenix grow and feel loved? How did the ending make you feel?

12. Taking a page from favorite literary works, *Always Orchid* ends at an emotionally-satisfying yet real-life juncture for Phoenix and Orchid. Some readers, though, have requested books about other characters from this series. Would you purchase a novel about Caleb & Sascha or others? Message me at https://carolvandenhende.com/contact to let me know.

If your book club would like to meet with me, schedule a virtual author visit through Novel Network: https://novelnetwork.com/vendor/carol-van-den-hende/

Excerpt from the prequel, *Orchid Blooming*

C H A P T E R 1

WILD ORCHIDS

Orchid

SPRING, NEW YORK CITY

Fifteen years ago, Orchid Paige could've never imagined a world without her mother.

Today, April rain swept away the thought, blurring her view of Manhattan skyscrapers outside of the conference room windows.

She straightened in her seat, surrounded by her Estee Lauder co-workers. Her cobalt-highlighted hair shone in the window's reflection. If the black strands of her Asian heritage could transform, what else could change?

Her boss, Joan, commanded the front of the room. She wore a structured suit and heavy earrings. Her mouth barely creased as she shared company news. "International experience is essential for the next level up. Here's a rare opportunity..."

The atmosphere became electrified.

Princeton, an Ivy League-educated coworker, leaned closer. His nostrils widened, like a racehorse chomping at the starting gate.

He was named after the university that his parents believed he was destined to attend.

"Lauder China wants someone for six-weeks in Beijing. It'll be a high visibility assignment," Joan said.

Orchid's pulse quickened. Her imagination tipped halfway around the world, to a place where terra cotta soldiers guarded a long-dead emperor, where the age of dynasties was measured in millennia, and the scale of The Great Wall made it visible from the skies. *Visible from my mother's vantage point in heaven,* she thought, as an image danced in her imagination.

Beautiful, dark-haired Mom was the artist in the family, the woman who amused young Orchid with drawings of dogs in tutus, and cat soirees. When she was little, Orchid thought her Chinese half was connected to her creative side. Her analytical brain was from her dad's side, his long English ancestry stamped with stories of tradesmen and entrepreneurs.

Memories of her mother were faded. She pictured her, still young, unmarred by the accident that took her life, gliding carefree through the grounds of an Oriental palace. "You should visit China someday," her mom had said.

She realized that Joan was still speaking.

"If you're interested, let me know by—"

"*Song wo,*" Princeton trilled in Mandarin. *Send him? His grin telegraphed his assumption that privileged schooling and language skills would assure him the coveted assignment.*

Chinese warriors from her mother's ancestry beckoned...*your opportunity! Not his!*

She stifled an urge to nudge Princeton, to cuff him the way he'd snubbed her non-Ivy schooling. With his proud pedigree, his fat nostrils would likely drip blue blood, marring the silk of his pocket handkerchief. "Where did you attend uni?" he'd asked her by way of introduction, then sniffed at the response.

Princeton's smugness sparked her competitiveness. She'd earned everything in her life: every scholarship, every opportunity. This would be no different. The challenges from childhood had strengthened her for this battle. She would test her savvy against her colleague's arrogance. To give herself a chance.

After the meeting, she closed her notebook and walked out of the room with her boss. "I could add value to the team," she said. "Can we set up some time to discuss the assignment?"

Joan tilted her head at Orchid's blue locks; her expression was unreadable. "I'm free tomorrow. Schedule some time on my calendar." Her Christian Louboutin heels clicked down the hall.

Orchid hurried to her desk, opened her computer, and sent an invitation to Joan to meet her in the morning. Then she tapped open a new window to search for information about expatriate assignments. She lost herself in photos. Pictures of smog and crowded highways competed with images of cherry blossoms and temples. She knew that her mother's nostalgia was for China's ancient history rather than its present-day complications. Still, she nearly forgot to breathe as she sought her mother's features in the faces of pedestrians.

At the end of the workday, she exited her office building. The rain had stopped, leaving the evening air humid. Her phone buzzed with a baby picture from her best friend Mandy. The infant's halo of hair glowed in the sunshine.

Orchid was eager to share this China goal with Mandy. As she crossed the street towards her subway station, she decided to call, rather than send a text.

"Hey, hon," Mandy greeted her.

"Miss you, honey. How's my favorite godson?"

"There's a study that shows smarter babies sleep less. So, your godson must be a genius."

"Ha. Sleep-deprived parents everywhere will be wishing for less intellect."

She paused at the top of the steps leading down to her subway stop. Phone reception was always a problem two flights down.

"Speaking of intellect, how's the glamorous life of a beauty executive?"

"I'm going to burst your bubble. Glamorous and executive aren't part of my everyday vocabulary. There is news, though."

"Tell me! I need something more than eco-friendly diapers to spice up my week."

"Sustainable diapers are exciting," she said. "But let me fill you in in-person. Are you free tonight? To get a drink?"

"Did you forget that I'm breastfeeding? No alcohol for me, but I'm up for a night out."

"Cool, 'cause I figured out what I want... but chances are not looking good."

"I'm dying to know. Text me a time and place."

"Will do. Can't wait!"

That evening, Orchid hurried along the avenue. With few commuters, she made good time to the Pyramid nightclub. Sitting at the curb was an idling cab, its windows reflecting her slender figure in a post-punk black minidress with silver-toothed zippers.

She paid the bouncer and pushed through the doors into the black-painted dance club. Ever since the childhood trauma of witnessing her parents' accident, she needed to calm her nerves in busy places. It was a quiet night in this dive. She stilled her trembling hands, and checked for the exit, her escape route. This was an automatic response she had adopted as a teen.

One red sign shone at the hallway leading to the bathrooms. EXIT. *Good.*

Orchid spotted Mandy, who had secured a spot at the edge of the room and loped across the sticky floor to join her. Mandy wasn't only her best friend; she was her confidante.

"Sorry, I got lost in research," Orchid apologized, and hugged her friend.

Mandy raised her voice over the percussion notes. "As long as you made it. Now spill the beans. Your call has me on the edge of my seat!"

Even though Orchid's ebony-lined eyes and edgy attire telegraphed an effortless cool, she knew that Mandy could see through that.

"You told me you figured out something. Tell!"

"Chances are, like, nil that I'll get it," Orchid said.

Mandy pushed a ruby-shaded cocktail towards her. Orchid clinked her tumbler against her friend's glass of Perrier. "Thank you," she said, and sipped the cool drink.

Mandy straightened on her bar stool, ready to dig into what Orchid recognized as her favorite problem-solving mode. "Let's see. What do you want more than anything? I know. Tickets to Fashion Week. Or that thrifted Dolce & Gabbana peony-print dress."

"Better peonies than orchids." Orchid said. It wasn't just her pet peeve over orchid everything; it was the memory of her mother's dress, the one decorated with peonies. "Good guess, but no."

"Girls' night with your bestie?" Mandy stirred her sparkling water with a paper straw.

Nothing like Mandy's optimism to buoy spirits. "Love you. Okay, second best."

"A tattooed god who eats calculus for breakfast and gets into every club in the city?" Mandy gave her an impish grin, swinging her blonde bob.

"That sounds awesome, except you know I can't trust anyone. Dating's not in my future."

"Aww c'mon," said Mandy. "I need to live vicariously through my single friends." She tilted her head towards the end of the bar.

She glanced in the direction of Mandy's gaze. She saw a burly fellow with snake tattoos that ran along his thick neck. He seemed to be glowering at the ground. Counter-culture level: a near-perfect six. Not high enough to trigger cultish fears, and not low enough to scream *wannabe*.

The two friends became immersed in their conversation. The increased hum in the place made it harder to hear each other speak.

Hang on. Next to tatt-guy, a young David Beckham lookalike curved long fingers around a bottle of beer. Eyes thick with lashes met her gaze, and her chest thumped with something akin to recognition. Impossible. They'd never met. Yet his eyebrows lifted, as if she had sparked something in him, too.

Orchid tossed the split-second connection into her brain's dustbin, along with today's forgotten dry cleaning.

She downed her drink and refocused on Mandy. "Get your mind off guys. What I want more than anything has to do with work."

"Work?"

"My boss said we need international experience for any shot at a promotion. And, oh, by the way, they're recruiting a Lauder marketer for an assignment to China."

"China? You know you can't leave me!"

"It's a temporary assignment, six weeks. And there's no way they're going to pick me."

"Who better than you?"

"Someone with more experience. The Princeton pedigree in my office, for one. He started speaking Mandarin during the meeting, for crying out loud."

Mandy nearly spit the mouthful she'd just taken. "Mandarin? But you can too, right?"

"I have the vocabulary of a two-year old." She inhaled, the truth spilling out. "The weird thing is, with this Princeton wretch vying for the spot, it makes me want it even more. If I get this, leave baby Matty with hubby and come with me!"

Mandy faced her phone screen towards Orchid. "I cannot leave this munchkin."

Cherub cheeks, ruddy with sleep, topped with a bunny-soft tuft of blond hair.

"Aww, he's the cutest."

Without prompting, Mandy swiped and paused on another photo of her son, his fists pumping in excitement over a spoon headed for his round mouth. "His favorite is barley."

"Neigh," Orchid whinnied.

Mandy snorted. "Back to you. Do you have family there?"

"None that I know of. But this is a fast track to promotion." Thinking in terms of her future with the company made more sense than talking about the growing urge she had to visit her mother's home country. She figured that her features were mirrored somewhere in the faces of those billion people. Just like her mom's.

"So, what's the plan?" Mandy asked, getting the bartender's attention and pointing to her glass.

"I've set up time with my boss, and I'm going to let her know I'll do anything. Study, learn the language, whatever it takes."

Mandy gave her a broad smile. "You go, girl! There's research about guys going for an opportunity even if they have only half the qualifications, but women feel they need a hundred percent to even apply."

"Don't worry, I'm going for it. It's perfect for me. It's the only way to a promotion, and I can't stand the thought of Princeton winning."

"I'd pick you," said Mandy.

Orchid gave Mandy's arm a gentle squeeze. "You're the sweetest. I'd pick you too. Now, I need the bathroom." She slid off the seat and straightened her minidress. In Hell's Kitchen, rocking an attitude was essential.

David Beckham was gone. Snake-tatt guy was still slumped on the bar stool. His slouch emanated an angst that Orchid could relate to.

The DJ seated on the far side of the bar transitioned to a driving bass line that urged Orchid towards the dance floor. The restrooms were situated down a corridor, somewhere on the other side of the writhing bodies.

The tacky floor tugged at the soles of her platform boots as she bopped along to the beat. A hiss accompanied a familiar scent. Faux smoke shrouded the space. Like she needed additional obstacles to finding the loo. That is, besides her buzz.

Orchid's bladder moved her toward the hallway and then the bathroom. The little symbol with the arrow was the women's room, right? How quaint that this throwback place didn't have gender neutral washrooms.

The handle turned easily, so she pushed through the door, flimsy like the card house of her life.

"Aiya!" came a deep voice. A tall figure jumped back from the sink. The door barely missed his athletic form. Orchid almost tumbled into him.

"What are you doing in here?" she cried out.

His azure eyes reflected kindness, and his full lips widening in a field of stubble caused her breath to hitch. The David Beckham doppelganger! His baritone rumbled with good humor. "I don't know about you...but I'M in the men's room."

She felt her cheeks warm. *Oops.* Before she walked out, she commented on his Chinese expression. "I speak English, you know, even if I look Chinese."

His eyes widened. Did cobalt blaze that bright? "Of course, you do. It's not you. *Aiya* just spills out. I keep forgetting. I'm just back from Beijing."

"Beijing!" she exclaimed. "That's where I want to go. How was it?" The connection of a faraway land made this stranger feel familiar.

Long fingers swung the spigot closed, then swiped a paper towel. He dried between each digit. "Hai keyi."

She couldn't help herself, air expelled at his use of the phrase that roughly translated to *pretty good*. "You sound like a native," she said.

"Hardly. Do you speak Mandarin?"

Her vision adjusted to the brightness. Light surfed his wavy hair. His blue eyes crinkled. "Bu hui." She shook her head *no*.

Humor erupted from him. "You could've fooled me, since you answered in Chinese."

Despite her bladder's protests, he'd made her chuckle again. "I need to learn more, if I want a shot at this overseas assignment. I'm too old for the kids' TV series *Ni Hao, Kai Lan*, and I don't have enough time for a semester at NYU." *Why am I babbling to this stranger?*

He chuckled again, balled up his paper towel, and lobbed it towards the garbage can. It sailed like a swan dive, as if refusing to mess with this guy's perfection. "The key is getting the accent right. In Beijing, they add an 'r' sound at the end of certain words."

"Then I'm completely screwed."

"If you're smart enough for an overseas assignment, I'm sure you could learn Chinese. Do you need the bathroom?" he asked. "I think the lock's broken. I'll stand guard for you, like this is Mao's tomb."

She guffawed. This guy was a riot.

He left the bathroom and stood just outside the door.

She finished using the bathroom and regarded her reflection as she washed her hands. Blue-streaked locks were swept to one side. She had figured that the drama of kohl-rimmed eyes for an evening out would deter most ordinary men. The darker she could amplify her appearance, perhaps the safer she could keep herself. Self-protection came first.

She refocused on what really mattered. *Now that I've told Mandy, I really need to make this assignment happen.* Internally armored, she stepped out. There was Beckham, protecting the broken door. Someone who kept promises.

"Mao's safe," she shouted over the deafening beat.

His lips widened over ultra-white teeth, brightened by the club's blacklight. His easy charm could belong on a men's fashion shoot.

"That was embarrassing," she admitted.

"Not really. It's dark in here."

The bar's partygoers grooved across the dance floor. Orchid paused, and saw that he had noticed her hesitation at the crowd.

One deft move, and he parted a clearing through the dancers. He beckoned for her to follow. Looking after her again.

Away from the density of bodies, Beckham looked back to check on her. Seeing her a few steps behind, he grinned and busted a move.

She couldn't help her mirth. How had she left for a simple trip to the loo and returned with a bilingual Adonis?

As they neared Mandy and her pace slowed. Her friend looked back and forth between them.

"You were gone forever. I almost called the National Guard," Mandy yelled over the music.

"Speaking of guard, this is..." Orchid ogled her kind protector.

He saved her. "Phoenix. Nice to meet you," he raised a hand in greeting. Mandy's mouth parted and nothing came out. He really was drop-dead gorgeous. *Stop.*

"Thanks again." Orchid waved and turned to speak with her friend.

"Bye...um," he paused, waiting for Orchid to fill in the blank.

"Kai Lan," she deadpanned.

He threw his head back in appreciation and then made his way through the crowd to the burly fellow. The tattooed guy's dour mood had faded. He said something, and Phoenix's glance alighted on her.

"I need to skedaddle," said Mandy. But before we go, do you have something you want to tell me?"

"Not a thing. I ended up in the wrong bathroom."

"That's an interesting approach. I thought the tattooed one was more your type."

"I have no type, because I'm staying single."

Orchid refocused on her goal. Tomorrow, she'd meet with her boss. *Goodbye, New York.*

To continue reading award-winning *Orchid Blooming*, purchase your copy through this link and remember to leave a rating or review: https://linktr.ee/cvdh

Printed in the USA
CPSIA information can be obtained
at www.ICGtesting.com
JSHW021803300723
45171JS00005B/12/J